Siege Perilous
A Novel of Foreworld

SIEGE PERILOUS

A NOVEL OF FOREWORLD

—— BY ——

E. D. deBIRMINGHAM

This is a work of fiction. Names, characters, organizations, places, events, and incidents are either products of the author's imagination or are used fictitiously.

Text copyright © 2014 by FOREWORLD LLC
All rights reserved.

No part of this book may be reproduced, or stored in a retrieval system, or transmitted in any form or by any means, electronic, mechanical, photocopying, recording, or otherwise, without express written permission of the publisher.

Published by 47North, Seattle
www.apub.com

Amazon, the Amazon logo, and 47North are trademarks of Amazon.com, Inc., or its affiliates.

ISBN-13: 9781477817599
ISBN-10: 147781759X

Cover design by: Kerrie Robertson
Illustrated by : Nekro

Library of Congress Control Number: 2013949128

Printed in the United States of America

To the spirits of Chrétien de Troyes and Wolfram von Eschenbach.

CAST OF CHARACTERS

Ocyrhoe: an orphan of Rome
Ferenc: a young Magyar hunter
Percival: a Shield-Brethren knight initiate
Raphael: a Shield-Brethren knight initiate
Vera: a Shield-Maiden, once of Kiev
Frederick II: the Holy Roman Emperor
Léna: a Binder

Innocent IV: Pope of the Roman Catholic Church, born Sinibaldo Fieschi
Romano Bonaventura: a Cardinal of the Roman Catholic Church
Dietrich von Grüningen: the *Heermeister* of the Livonian Order

Ferrer: a scout of Montségur
Artal: a scout of Montségur
Peire-Roger: the ruling lord of Montségur
Raimon de Perelha: the titular lord of Montségur
Bishop Bertran en Marti: a Cathar priest
Rixenda: a candlemaker, elder of Montségur
Milos: a captain of the night watch
Otz: a soldier of Montségur
Savis: a soldier of Montségur

Hugue de Arcis: the lord of Carcassonne
Pierre Amelii: the Archbishop of Narbonne
Vidal: a soldier of Toulouse

1241
VETURNÆTUR

CHAPTER 1:
CAPTURE

Ocyrhoe was startled awake to the cold morning air by something very sharp poking her face. She sucked her cheeks in and glanced up, scowling.

"If you move, you die," said the young man at the other end of the spear. He looked strappy. Probably a well-fed serf by the quality of his boots, which were close to her face. His vaporous breath was backlit by the rising sun. His arms were trembling; either he was unaccountably frightened of her, or his muscles were fatigued from the weight of the weapon.

"How long have you been standing there?" she asked, without uncurling. "Been passing the time, have you, waiting for me to wake up?"

"Do you hear her, Ferrer?" he said to an older fellow behind him, similarly dressed. If the fellow had been holding a knife, or threatening with his fist, she'd know how to land him on his arse despite her small size. But she was not used to threats by spear, so she decided to wait the moment out. He clearly had no idea how to use the weapon.

"Yes, Artal," said Ferrer as he moved closer, almost absently pushed the spear aside before turning his direction to Ocyrhoe.

"You speak in the dialect of *Rome*. I've heard that before." It was a condemnation.

"I'm a native of that city," she answered, still curled around her satchel, glancing up. "I never left its walls until a few months past. Is it a fatal offense in these parts to be from Rome?"

"You're a spy," said Artal. "We're taking you to Toulouse, where the Count will pay a great sum for your capture."

"Sit up," said Ferrer. He seemed civil. The younger Artal, she thought, was rather beastly. She uncurled carefully and sat up, pulling the wool blanket around her narrow shoulders for warmth. Her tunic and leggings were too thin for this weather; her breath, too, was vaporous. This was the coldest morning she had waked to yet.

"For whom am I spying?" she asked, genuinely curious.

"The Pope," said Artal. Ferrer, to his credit, winced at that.

Ocyrhoe laughed bitterly. "I am most assuredly not spying for the Pope. The Pope is dead. May I stand?"

They both took a cautious step back in unison, and Artal rested the makeshift spear over his shoulder. Ocyrhoe was stiff from sleeping on the ground; the cold earth had chilled her from below despite the wool cloak, so she moved slowly, working her fingers and shoulders to warm her joints.

She glanced around the cypress copse where she had slept, wondering what had given her away. She'd suffocated the ashes from the fire with dirt. She was shielded from the nearest road by trees. The mare, despite the tether, must have grazed out into the broad field. In these huge open tracts of wheat fields, you could see a horse from half a mile away. She should have stuck to the roads that bisected the vineyards.

"You are spying for the College of Cardinals," said Ferrer decisively. "There is no sensible reason for a Roman citizen to be in the mountains of Toulouse, alone, this time of year."

"That's true, no sensible reason," Ocyrhoe said. "But it is not because I am a spy. The Cardinals are a nest of vipers, and the most powerful man among them would like to see me dead."

Stop talking, she thought. The abrupt awakening had thrown her. And she was not used to human company. Best not to speak at all.

"That is a horse only a well-positioned spy could possibly afford," Artal pointed out.

"Is it? If you look at the saddle-blanket," she said, "you will notice it bears the insignia of His Majesty Frederick Hohenstaufen. Do you think the College of Cardinals outfits its spies with horses from the stables of the Holy Roman Emperor? Although," she added, mostly to herself, "that *would* be an excellent cover."

Artal handed Ferrer the spear—so clumsily and casually, Ocryhoe could have grabbed it from them if she'd had the confidence to use it. The younger man walked irritably to the log on which Ocyrhoe had set the saddle and blanket the night before. The mare, tethered, raised her head and moved away from him, ears set back and eyes disapproving. Ocyrhoe sent the horse the message to stay calm. It snorted, relaxed, looked away.

"There is something very strange about all this," Artal declared.

You have no idea, thought the girl, but this time kept her tongue in check.

"We are apprehending you," Ferrer informed her, in a tone more courteous than Artal's.

"Are you?" Ocyrhoe replied, sardonically.

She considered her situation strategically.

She had avoided populated areas most of the time, learning slowly and ineptly how to survive outside the walls of Rome. She had spent her first week as a fugitive in a state of panic, even though the imperial grooms had filled her saddlebags with food and water-skins and coins. When the food ran out, she'd invented a routine: she would tether the mare someplace outside a large town—of which there were very few, and certainly no cities—dart into the market with a few coins to buy provisions, and then dart back out again. She could never have explained how a filthy urchin could honestly come by a mount of that magnificence.

When she'd seen the walls of Toulouse rising up from a distance, she was comforted by the sight: it was enormous, almost as large as Rome. A raggedy youngster leading a fine horse through the streets was less of an oddity within a city than in a mere town; she easily convinced the proprietor of a large stable in Toulouse that she and the horse were the only survivors of an Imperial riding party heading this way; she'd given him most of the rest of her coins as an advance against the reward he was sure to receive once His Imperial Majesty learned how kind he had been to the little imperial page girl.

That had worked for several weeks, and she had surprised herself with her quick grasp of Occitan. But she had abandoned Toulouse because she found herself increasingly terrified that someone should find out about the cup.

She'd heard rumors the Emperor was moving his court to a place called Cremona, and she determined to find it, to beg relief from her burden. Growing unaccountably disoriented, she'd left the city walls behind her and headed not back east as she'd intended, but almost due south, into this mountainous terrain. Winter was now upon her, and she knew she could not survive on her own in the wilderness.

Maybe it was better these clumsy men were taking her captive...at least they would take her somewhere sheltered. She could easily prove she wasn't a spy once she got there.

She hoped.

"All right, then," said Ocyrhoe. "I'm yours. Where are we going?"

"The Count's—" began Artal.

"The Count has enough to contend with, and he's too far away," said Ferrer. "We shall take her directly up to Montségur."

"What's that?" asked Ocyrhoe.

"The horse can't make that trek," Artal protested.

Ferrer shrugged. "We'll keep the horse," he said. "That will be our reward for warning the Good Ones about this Catholic spy."

CHAPTER 2:

ARRIVAL

They walked for hours without conversation, as the beautiful broad fields began to roll and swell into foothills. There were vineyards, and then fields, and then groves of trees she thought she recognized as olive, and then more fields, some with windmills. Occasionally plumes of smoke nestling together above a rise revealed a village nearby, but they never headed toward one. It was cold, but the sky was an incredible blue and she knew that she eventually would be indoors.

Ocyrhoe had attempted to be civil at first, partly out of boredom and partly as a tactical maneuver. She wanted her captors to hand her over to their superiors with good report of her. But her first bland attempt—"So where are we going?"—received a stony, silent glare from Artal. Her next foray into interlocution—"Are the two of you kinsmen?"—was simply ignored. She resigned herself to silence and walked.

They were headed toward a mountain range that had been in sight all the way from Toulouse. By midday, she feared their destination might be on the other side—a concern neither man would quell, for neither would answer any of her questions. But finally there was a smell of woodsmoke, and they turned off the broad, beaten road onto an oxcart-path to a small but bustling village with a windmill. The village, situated at the foot of a steep mountain, had a shallow moat and low earthen berm as additional protection; colorful blankets and banners with images sewn onto them had been flung over the berm to welcome travelers coming from the main road, an invitation to the hamlet's merchant attractions. She saw banners for a blacksmith, a tailor, a brewer, a baker—the smell of warm bread, late in the day though it was for baking, wafted by—and her stomach growled. The air was loud with tradesmen haggling and children calling to each other playfully. Oh, how badly she wanted to be back in society.

The peak towering above the village rose steeply out of the cluster of foothills, extravagantly toward Heaven; it did not seem climbable, yet there was a stone building at the top, almost too small to see. Surely they could not be headed up there.

They stopped outside the village.

"Is this our destination, then?" she asked. The question evaporated into the dry bright air, unanswered.

Ferrer led her horse through the gate in the low berm to an outlying stable where he haggled briefly with the stable owner, then left the horse and came out again. Ocyrhoe glared at him.

"That was *my* horse," she said.

"'Twas Emperor Frederick's, you said. He's not likely to come after it. Let's go." It was the only thing either of them had said to her for hours.

They continued on past the village, right toward the gorse-covered slope as if they would encounter a hidden door where soil met limestone. After staring at the mountain a moment, Ocyrhoe realized that there was actually a path steeply zigzagging up it through the brush. Small figures were walking both to and from the speck of a building at the top.

But she and her captors did not take this path; instead they veered hard to the right, as if they would scale the steeper and undomesticated southern slope. She was alarmed at the prospect.

"Are we climbing up there? What's up there?" She felt mildly ridiculous for continuing to talk, as she had over the past months when trying to make conversation with the horse. No response, except a brief gesture from Ferrer toward their destination.

As insubstantial as a cobweb, a smaller trail worked its way through bushes and grass and rocks almost invisibly across the mountainside. For some reason they were taking this indirect and steeper route. She guessed her captors wanted her to marvel at how remote and challenging a destination they were headed for. It was probably supposed to fill her with dread. She defied them. "Oh, good, we'll have the sun on us for the trek," she said.

Silence.

"Are you afraid I'll bewitch you if we have a conversation?" she asked.

"We've got nothing to say to Roman spies," Artal huffed. "We'll not pollute our ears with your lies."

"I didn't realize 'Where are we going?' was a lie," said Ocyrhoe.

"Shut up and climb," said Artal.

With twigs tugging at their woebegone wool wraps—they were all three equally ill-kempt—they began a frightful ascent up the narrow footpath. Ocyrhoe kept her eyes on the path, occasionally glancing up at Ferrer's back. She was aware that to their right, the view must be growing magnificent and broad, but she was too afraid of a misstep to look. Their way was treacherously steep, terrifying in its sheer cliff-drops, the path doubling back on hairpin turns over and again for what seemed like hours. Limestone pebbles, roots, and slick dead leaves colluded against sure footing. As they trudged closer and upward to the eastern extreme, their going grew so steep that they were grasping on to branches and limestone bulges with their hands, tugging themselves up as much as climbing. In a final effort that was almost vertical, they crested the eastern end of the narrow mountaintop, collapsing onto their knees, gulping for breath, skin chilled from the wind yet lungs burning from exertion. Finally Ocyrhoe dared to look around.

She had to clutch Ferrer's arm. They were as high up as a pair of griffon vultures on the prowl, and the wind was not only cold but felt thin. It did not nourish her lungs as it should have. The view around them described almost a full circle, all of it breathtaking: farm-filled valleys and wooded mountains, many with higher peaks than this. It felt as if they were in the center of an orb filled with frigid air, its walls suffused with the grey-greens and browns of late autumn. Only to the west was the vista blocked, by the remainder of the mountain rise. Ocyrhoe was too dizzy and disoriented to appreciate the view. She was no longer sure this was better than being left to her own in the lowland wilderness for the winter.

"What are we to do up here?" she asked, her cockiness evaporated.

"You'll see in a moment," said Ferrer.

A squat, stone watch-tower rose up from a crag here, and Ferrer called out a password to a disinterested sentry within. The sentry—about Artal's age—stuck his head out the door. He looked at Ocyrhoe, then at the men. "Why'd you come up this way?" he asked. "Much easier to take the path from the village."

"We wanted to give this one some time to prepare herself," said Artal.

"For what?" asked Ocyrhoe.

"You'll see," said Artal.

She wanted to argue with his obstinancy, but reserved her energy for standing upright.

The sentry went back inside. At Ferrer's nudging, they walked past the tower westward.

Ocyrhoe made a dismayed noise before she could stop herself. A long bowshot, perhaps two, away up a final incline, at the very highest point of the mountain, was the building she had seen from below. It was a fortress, with a small barbican jutting out toward them as a separate building. The banner of Toulouse—red with a yellow cross—flew atop the donjon, something she could not see from below. To get to the barbican, they would have to walk about five hundred strides up an ascending mountain crest no wider than a large Roman market green, perhaps treble the breadth her favorite childhood slingshot could have hurled a pebble; beyond the crest on either side, the mountain lumbered downward steeply. She kept her hand clenched to Ferrer's sleeve as they moved, and her trembling muscles shook her entire small frame.

"Who is in there?" she demanded.

"The Good Ones," Ferrer said, reverentially. He gave her a knowing look, but her brief returning stare was blank.

When they reached the barbican—an unoccupied building similar to the watchtower—there was a final distance to be crossed to the fortress itself. This final trek was far more harrowing than anything so far: the limestone crest between barbican and fortress thinned here to a very narrow passway. It looked as if giants had clawed away at either side of the mountain ridge, so that for the length of two dozen strides, the ridge itself was perhaps three strides across. The peak broadened out again beyond this limestone bridge, and there loomed the fortress. Everything inside Ocyrhoe trembled, and it was hard to breathe. She grabbed Ferrer's arm again desperately to keep her balance.

"One gets used to it," he said, not unkindly, as an icy breeze nudged them from the east. "Look straight ahead at the walls; looking down will make you dizzy."

Ocyrhoe nodded, her breath ragged and shallow. She willed her mind to stop telling her they were about to tumble to their deaths. Without looking down, she could not guess how far she would fall before some projecting jut of limestone snapped her spine or dashed in her skull. She tried not to think about that. Instead she looked at the building looming before her.

The stone walls, gleaming roughly in the winter sun, were nowhere near as impressive as Rome's defenses, but their presence up here was almost inconceivable. If one of her street-rascal friends had described this to her, she would have laughed it off as exaggeration.

The ridge widened out just before the fortress's iron-covered gate. When they reached this islet of land in a sea of mountain air, she sighed, and her muscles relaxed a little, although she could not convince her hand to let go of Ferrer's sleeve. To their right, a narrow beaten path sloped down alongside the fortress, to a lower stone wall that continued all the way to the northern extreme of the mountain. Over this lower wall she glimpsed dozens of small stone buildings snuggled on a rocky terrace, a higher wall beyond them. Past that last wall was nothing but air. Those must be storage sheds, she decided. But what a peculiar place to store anything.

Ferrer pounded on the gate, and a porter within opened it almost immediately on whining hinges. The three of them entered a small, stony courtyard, partly in shadow from the southern battlement. It was broadest in the middle, narrowing to either end. Bulges of limestone blended almost seamlessly into manmade stone walls, as if the fortress were growing organically out of the peak. Sturdy wooden buildings filled the yard in rows along each wall; from the hut to her immediate right came the sound of hens clucking. Across the yard, a little to the right and half hidden by the largest wooden building, was a much bigger gate than the one they'd entered; this was the gate used by the people she'd seen going up and down the western slope. At the extreme right of the courtyard, two stone's throws at most, the limestone bulged up out of the ground and extended upward, in man-made form, to the stone donjon, a keep at least two floors high.

Within the yard, several armed soldiers scurried between the wooden buildings in the cold, with quick, suspicious glances at the newcomers. Recognizing her captors, they lost interest and returned their attention to their destination. There were soldiers up along the battlement, watching them incuriously.

A handful of women in simple black habits emerged from one of the smaller buildings and began crossing toward them, as if to exit. Ocyrhoe's confusion was tinged with alarm: a religious order, up here? To whom were they allied? Ferrer pushed Ocyrhoe's grip away, and then, together with Artal, immediately knelt on the rocky courtyard ground and bowed three times in the direction of the approaching robed figures. "Bless me, Lord, pray for me," the two men said in unison, and in unison, the robed women paused to respond: "Lead us to our rightful end. God bless you and lead you to your rightful end." They continued on out the gate.

Ferrer and Artal got to their feet as the robed ones passed, with no further attention paid to them. "This way," said Ferrer gruffly, and took Ocyrhoe by the arm. He pulled her toward the donjon, past smaller buildings, including—from their scents—a bakery and a drying shed for herbs. In the other direction she noticed a smithy with storage sheds beside it, probably for charcoal and wood. An immense amount of industry was squeezed into this little space.

Wooden steps up to the donjon had been built over a bulge of natural limestone; they walked up these to a wooden door that led them to the first floor. Artal opened the door and nudged Ocyrhoe sharply.

As the door opened, she heard conversation and noise aplenty within, but by the time it was fully ajar so that she stood backlit and vulnerable, squinting sunblinded into the room, all talk had stopped.

Inside was another world: dim, warmer, crowded with human figures, pungent. Ocyrhoe was disoriented, to go from such bright cold spaciousness to this claustrophobic setting.

Her eyes blinked in the dim candlelight—for this spare room was, impossibly, lit by dozens and dozens of candles, an extravagance she could not fathom even in the richest Roman palace. When she could make out more than mere forms, the motley collection of people gathered around trestle tables confused her. There were hundreds of them, in a hall that could comfortably hold only scores. There were women dressed as the nuns outside, of different ages; and bearded men dressed likewise, also of all ages; there were more soldiers; there were a number of lords; most confusingly there were scores of well-dressed ladies and several children, none of whom she'd expect to find inside a mountaintop fortress.

What was this?

"Found a spy, milord," said Artal importantly. She did not give him the satisfaction of arguing.

From the score of well-dressed men, two of them—each at the head of one table—stood up. They were both dressed in black wool with bright silken decorations embroidered on their hems and cuffs. They were a generation apart in age. The handsome, stormy-looking younger one, with dramatic dark eyes and a bared head of thick black hair, reached out his hand as if summoning them.

"Bring him to me."

"It's a girl, milord," said Ferrer, almost as if he were embarrassed for Ocyrhoe's sake.

"Bring her to me and I will take her up for questioning."

Ocyrhoe felt her gut clench at that, but she did not show any outward resistance. There was no place to which she could flee, and a show of compliance might relax their guard.

And so Ocyrhoe was paraded between two trestle tables, hundreds of eyes upon her, her satchel clutched tightly under her arm. She tried not to stare, but she felt her eyes linger now and then on unexpected figures: a sickly young woman in pale silks and furs; solemn-faced toddlers holding hands; several serving women, dressed in black, who ate at the table alongside well-dressed matrons three times their age of obviously higher pedigree. Even in a city like Rome, where patricians and urchins walked the same streets sometimes cheek by jowl, she could never imagine such a disparate lot breaking bread together.

When they reached the far end of the table, the dark-haired lord gestured imperiously toward a very old, black-robed man near him, and a black-robed woman with a pensive, weathered face. With a jerk of his head he indicated a set of stairs behind him; these two in robes headed toward the stairs, with candles taken from the table. So did three or four young men whom Ocyrhoe assumed must be the lord's bodyguard, although why he needed a bodyguard against her was beyond imagining. She weighed about as much as his cloak.

Upstairs was an open room the same size as the one below, empty but for them, with stacks of sleeping rolls and blankets against the walls. The narrow windows—wider than arrow-slits, but not by much—were covered with parchment against the winter chill. The room was dim beyond the candles they brought with them.

"Stand there," the lord ordered, pointing to a spot near the door. Ocyrhoe walked there, the satchel clutched to her side. The lord and his party gathered in a semi-circle, staring at her. Again she wondered if she'd made the right decision by not running from the men.

"Go," said the lord gruffly to Ferrer and Artal, with a wave of his hand. "Or eat if you like, and then go."

Artal and Ferrer lingered a moment, clearly hoping for a reward without wanting to be so rude as to request one.

"They've already taken my horse," Ocyrhoe informed the lord. "They require no further compensation for their efforts."

"Milord Peire-Roger, hers is the accent of Rome," warned Ferrer, as he headed down the stairs.

For a moment, the concert of secular and religious faces stared at her in the candlelight, and she stared back at them, pretending not to feel alarm. She had no idea what religious order this was, but all orders traced their chain of command back to the Vatican. Which meant—since the death of the Pope—to the College of Cardinals. Which meant, in effect, to Cardinal Sinibaldo di Fieschi. Who wanted the cup. And wanted her dead.

"Well?" demanded Peire-Roger. "Who are you and what are you doing here?"

Ocryhoe shrugged. "Those fellows grabbed me. I was minding my own business."

"You were minding your own business alone in the foothills of the Pyrenees?"

"I was seeking lost family members," she finally said. That was, in a way, not untrue.

"And what would compel your Roman family members to migrate to these heretical lands?"

Ocyhroe blinked. "Heretical?" A terrible dread filled her. "Are you implying I am a heretic? Are you Dominicans?" she asked the elderly man in black robes. "Is this the Inquisition?"

Everyone in the room exchanged glances.

"Are you mocking us?" asked the lord. "This is Montségur."

"That name means nothing to me, I apologize for my ignorance."

A shifting of weight and attention among all assembled. More exchanged looks.

"This is the land of the so-called Cathars," announced Peire-Roger. Ocyrhoe had heard that word before, but could not remember where, or what it meant. "The Cathars are called heretics," the lord was saying. "The Catholic Church wants to destroy all Cathars and all their supporters. What do you think of that?" he demanded, studying her.

"Are...are you, you in robes, sir, lady, are you Cathars, then?" Ocyrhoe said.

"This is Montségur," said the bearded, black-habited elder, a hint of impatience in his sharp tenor voice. "Of course we are Cathars. I am Bishop Bertran En Marti."

Ocryhoe gasped with the realization: "Then you're heretics yourselves! So you are *not* in allegiance with Rome?" A brief laugh escaped her. "That is the best news I have heard in weeks. I thought I was doomed." *Shut up*, she told herself, but the relief was too visceral for her to entirely suppress it.

Now even more bemusement from the assembly. "Why doomed?" Marti demanded.

"I'm on the run from Church officers," she risked offering. "That's why I left Rome." She held her right hand up and pressed it to her heart. "I give you my oath, by all that's holy."

The old man frowned. "Do you believe in the need to perform an oath?" he interrupted. "Is your word not intrinsically honest?"

That stumped Ocyrhoe, oath-breaker that she was. "I do not know how to answer that," she admitted.

"Gently, Your Eminence," the robed women advised. She had a calm voice, and her wide-set eyes, peering out of her wimple on her round face, were the kindest in the room. "She need not know our precepts to prove that she is not an enemy."

"You are too trusting, Rixenda," said His Eminence. Then back to Ocyrhoe: "Who are you?"

She pursed her lips. "My name is Ocyrhoe. I am really nobody. My family were destroyed by Senator Orsini of Rome—"

"For their beliefs?"

"For their identity. We are an unusual race. Tribe. I'm the only one left. Orsini and the cardinals want me dead—it's true I am not a good Catholic—and so I fled as well." That was true enough; she was simply leaving out the cup, with its attendant farce and tragedy.

"But why here?" asked Rixenda.

Ocyrhoe made a helpless gesture. "Random chance. I swear to you."

"Again, your oath is meaningless," insisted the bishop. Having no response to that, Ocryhoe pressed on: "I am from a city, I have no idea how to negotiate the countryside. I just wanted to be safe. I was in Toulouse until a few days ago."

The bishop looked thoughtful. "You left Rome for Toulouse? Because you knew an outcast might find safety in the land of heretics?"

"I had no idea where I was going, and no idea where I'd arrived. But I confess I am very glad to be among you. I have not felt safe for months."

"Why did you leave Toulouse?" Marti demanded.

She opened her mouth, then closed it again. "I wanted to find someone," she said carefully. "I became very lost. As I said, I am inept outside a city." She thought of the chasm of cold empty space outside the fortress. Four hundred feet down lay the vibrant little village, surrounded by barely inhabited foothills, and below that, sparsely inhabited plains, and beyond those, the city of Toulouse, where she dare not return because of the cup's unpredictable power. Winter was coming.

"May I stay?" she said. She was surprised by how pleading her own voice sounded. "Through the winter? I'm not good for much, but I'd make myself useful somehow."

Peire-Roger and Bishop Marti exchanged looks. After a moment, the bishop muttered to the lord, "She is hounded by the Catholics much as we are; she is closer to being one of us than one of them."

Peire-Roger huffed with annoyance. "Show us your possessions, that we may know you," he said, and gestured to the satchel.

At this, her stomach sank. They would see the cup—worse, they would sense the cup's power, she was certain. She did not quite manage to keep the flicker of worry from her face, and they all noticed it. Peire-Roger took two steps forward crossly, grabbed the bag from her with a warning look, pulled open the drawstrings, and dumped the contents onto the floor before Ocyrhoe. The silver cup clanged out on top of the meager other items—some coins, jerky, a few strips of leather, a carrot for the horse, some rags. The cup rolled briefly and was still. *Please don't glow*, she begged. On rare occasions it emitted heat and light, usually when she was thinking hard about it. She tried not to think about it now.

That, of course, made her think about it.

And it was glowing. She saw the rosy luster in the dish reflect off the wooden floor of the room, and add warmth to the cold, dim-lit space. Alarmed, she looked up at all of them, frantically trying to think of some excuse for possessing such an item.

It had been merely a chalice from a wealthy table, but events in Rome—events that even now she did not understand—had transformed it, as if by alchemy, into an object of occasional but mesmerizing power. Once it had been wrenched from the madman who wielded it, Emperor Frederick had charged Ocyrhoe to keep it safe from mischief, and safe from those who would do mischief with it—especially his nemesis and hers alike, Cardinal Sinibaldo di Fieschi.

Peire-Roger gestured to one of his guards, who knelt and held his candle closer to the pile. He picked up the cup and handed it to his lord. Peire-Roger considered it a moment, then shrugged and handed it off to Rixenda. "That's a fine cup for such a scrap of a thing as you are," said Rixenda, pleasantly.

"Stolen, no doubt," muttered Peire-Roger.

"It was given to me," Ocyrhoe said nervously. "I was told to keep it for somebody. I must hold on to it."

"We are not going to take it from you," the bishop said condescendingly. "We do not prize such trifles. Material objects are a necessary evil, but we do not covet the possession of any of them."

Peire-Roger picked up each other item in turn—there were few things enough—and exchanged a look each time with the bishop. Then he dropped each back to the floor. Everyone nodded their head in passive dismissal: they saw nothing suspicious in her bag.

She tried to mask her confusion at their indifference to the cup. Did they not see the glow?

"For whom are you holding the cup?" asked Bishop Marti.

Oh, damn, thought Ocyrhoe. "For..." She tried to think tactically. Church and Emperor were at loggerheads, and these people were not on the side of the Church. Hopefully that put them in collusion with the Emperor.

"Out with it, daughter," Marti demanded. "If we are to house you in our midst there must be absolute candor between us. Hide nothing."

That was impossible, she knew. But she did not want to raise their suspicions. "It was given to me by Fredrick Hohenstaufen. The Holy Roman Emperor," she said, almost apologetically.

Their sober faces grew more sober. None of them seemed surprised or curious that a girl in rags would possess a gift from the most powerful man in Europe.

"Frederick is as bad as the cardinals," declared the bishop.

"That's all for show," said Lord Peire-Roger. "He has never sent troops against us."

"He told Pope Gregory that we are the greatest danger to Christendom."

"That's only because Pope Gregory first accused Frederick himself of that distinction, and Frederick was trying to deflect it," the lord explained.

"That does sound like him," Ocyrhoe volunteered without thinking. All eyes turned to her. "The little that I know of him," she added hurriedly. "I was only in his presence for a day or so. When I was fleeing Rome, Frederick was camped outside the walls, and I found myself in his camp. Briefly."

"And he gave you the cup."

She did not like the direction this was going. She could not possibly explain everything to them.

"I am stewarding it until I receive further instructions."

"From Frederick?" asked the bishop suspiciously.

"From *anyone*," said Ocyrhoe.

"And how will Frederick—or anyone—find you?"

Ocyrhoe gave him a helpless expression. "I have no idea. I'm stuck with it for the foreseeable future."

"Do you think Frederick is seeking you out?" Peire-Roger demanded.

"Oh, no," said Ocyrhoe with a pained laugh. "He doesn't want it either." She glanced nervously at the cup in Rixenda's hands. It was glowing. They either didn't see it or they didn't care.

"It's just a cup," said Rixenda. She crossed toward Ocyrhoe, and held it out to her. The inside beamed its faint rosy glow, enough to light Rixenda's gentle, wrinkled face from below. "You do understand that, don't you, child? It's just a cup. It has no intrinsic value or power of any kind."

Ocyrhoe looked in amazement from the bowl of the cup to the face that was illuminated by it. "Just a cup," she said tentatively.

"Yes," said Rixenda with emphatic reassurance. "No material object is worthy of reverence. If someone has told you otherwise, it is just another hoax of the Church. Do not be burdened with it. You do not seem pleased to carry it. We have no interest in it, but if you wish to sell it, we can find you a buyer. Money is always useful to fugitives."

Ocyrhoe again looked from the cup to the face that it was unaccountably illuminating. "All right," she said uncertainly. "But I do not wish to let go of it now. I am…fond of it."

Now Rixenda's expression was one of sympathy. "It is certainly a lovely cup, but I hope you do not suffer for having that attachment," she said. She placed the cup in Ocyrhoe's hand and looked over her shoulder at the bishop and the lord. "Well?" she said.

The bishop grimaced thoughtfully. "We call this place a refuge, and a sanctuary."

"Yes, we do," said Rixenda.

Peire-Roger also grimaced. "Rixenda, if she stays, you will take responsibility for her. Find some way for her to earn her food."

Rixenda smiled at her in a way that made Ocyrhoe feel she was about to be wrapped in a warm blanket. "I will," Rixenda said.

"If I stay, must I become a believer?" the girl asked. "Is it acceptable simply that I do not cross you? Is there a bed for me? Shall I be a servant?"

Lord Peire-Roger gestured impatiently about at the room. "If we give you a blanket, you may make shift to find a spot on the floor to sleep at night. My own bed is hardly more than that these days."

She felt a wave of alarm. To be this close with so many strangers, who believed uncommon things…what mischief might the cup engender?

"You are welcome to stay in my hut with me. What are your skills, child?" asked Rixenda gently.

Ocyhroe felt her face pink. "Precious few for this environment, lady. Mine has been a strange life and my skills are equally peculiar. I am…" she considered it. "I am mostly a messenger. Rome is my element, and I am not good for much outside its walls. But I am willing to learn whatever needs doing to earn the right to shelter through the winter. I will not stay beyond my welcome."

1243
HAVERFEST

CHAPTER 3:

THE WONDER OF THE WORLD

"Well," said Frederick Hohenstaufen, Holy Roman Emperor, Wonder of the World. He squinted one final time at the scroll in the ambient sunlight, then crumpled the vellum in his hand and tossed it, with calm annoyance, to the marble floor of the porch. "The College of Cardinals has finally selected its *papa*. It took them long enough. A new day breaks. Let us pray it doesn't break civilization along with it."

Léna, standing tall and serene to the right of his chair, raised one eyebrow.

"You already knew," he said, glaring up at her with grudging affection.

"My messengers are swifter than yours," she said, with a reassuring smile. "It's Sinibaldo di Fieschi."

"Of course it is," he said.

"Now to be known as Pope Innocent IV."

Frederick squinted into the sunlight. "I wonder how quickly he will excommunicate me," he said philosophically.

"Are you not already excommunicated?"

"Oh. Perhaps. I don't keep track anymore." He gestured to a servant standing at attention by a column on the near side of the porch. "We are waiting on some viands," he said. "Wine and cheese at the very least. Go to the kitchens and see what is keeping them."

"I hear the vote was unanimous, and that he accepted only grudgingly," Léna mused.

"I believe both of those things," said Frederick. "It's exasperating, trying to control the world when you are formally in power. I'd be much more efficient if somebody else were on my throne and I could machinate behind curtains."

"You tried that with Germany, and as I recall it did not work out well for you," Léna said demurely.

Frederick grimaced. "Still I wonder if for all his ambition, was Fieschi unhappy to give up hiding in the shadows."

"You can't control the person on the throne if there *is* no person on the throne."

"Yes," said Frederick, with a sigh. "I learned *that* in Germany, too. So now Sinibaldo and I are to deal with each other directly." He considered this. "That should make for an interesting epoch. I must make sure the chroniclers give me all the best quips."

"Send for Raphael of Acre."

Frederick squinted up at her in confusion. "Raphael? I would hardly call his scribbles a *chronicle*."

"If Fieschi is the Pope, you should send Raphael to Toulouse."

For a moment he stared at her, dumbfounded. "Toulouse? Why Raphael? And why *Toulouse?* Because of the Cathar heretics? Of course I have to keep an eye on the ground wherever Fieschi—Pope Innocent—has an interest, but I have plenty of spies much closer to Toulouse. I shall send some of them."

"Raphael of Acre," she said with simple conviction.

A pause.

"Will you condescend to tell me why?" he asked sardonically.

"A friend of Raphael—one of those who traveled east with him—is said to be in the region. Raphael would be very grateful, I am sure, to receive news of his friend, and will no doubt speed toward Montségur. Why send your own man when you can use someone else who is already going there?"

Frederick rubbed his ruddy face, his squinting eyes, his thinning, tousled red hair. Brilliant and capable as he was, he never looked much like an emperor, and at the moment he did not feel like one.

"There is, of course, some other reason for sending Raphael there, which you are choosing not to tell me."

"If you insist, Your Majesty."

It was, frankly, a relief to know that somebody in spitting distance knew more than he did, and had a strong opinion about what to do. Were it anyone but Léna, he would not take them seriously. Not even his most valued advisors had half his brains. But Léna matched him thought for thought, and it was relaxing, sometimes, to be bossed about by her.

"I'll send for Raphael," he said. "To hell with waiting for the wine. Let's take a nap."

CHAPTER 4:

THE SYNAGOGUE OF SATAN

For two years, in the strange little world atop the mountain, Ocyrhoe gazed into the cup with frustrated wistfulness, wanting to understand it. By the time she realized everyone here was indifferent to it, she had become accustomed to its presence when she slept. Through the winter nights it was inexplicably warming, and in the summer heat it remained, also inexplicably, cool.

It was a cup. A simple, silver table-chalice. She knew that. But the mad priest, Father Rodrigo, had changed it somehow when he pinched it from Frederick's camp table. Suddenly Rodrigo had half of Frederick's personal guard ready to march with him against the Mongol invaders. The alarmed Emperor immediately sent the priest out into the hills to hide him from the Roman cardinals, with only young Ferenc—and the cup— for company.

But almost immediately afterward, he ordered Ocyrhoe after them, with instructions to separate the man from the cup and undo the inexplicable alchemy. Tragedy came of it. Yes, she had gotten the cup, but the price had been Rodrigo's life. She had no choice but to vanish into the hills because Cardinal Fieschi and Senator Orsini wanted her dead in Rome.

Hardest of all was her sundering from Ferenc—he taking Roderigo's body back to Frederick's camp, she taking the cup into the wilderness per Frederick's orders. The cup should have returned to normal when Rodrigo died. It did not. It frightened and confused her, the shimmer the cup still possessed. She wished she had more complete training as a Binder, for she was certain any real Binder—Léna, for example—would understand what to make of its alarming mystery. Often she reached out to Léna in her mind, craving assistance, begging permission to either return to Rome or head to the Emperor's court. She felt Léna's presence, so she knew the older woman was aware of her, but the messages she received were not the maternal reassurance she had hoped for. Always she received the impression that she must move onward, outward, away.

I am a Binder, Ocryhoe had argued. *I am not bound to wander aimless, I am bound to deliver messages. If this accursed cup is a message, to whom should I deliver it?*

Léna never replied.

And so Ocryhoe had spent her free moments in the fortress of Montségur staring into the bowl of the chalice, trying to understand the message.

The first year she lived here, she was given menial tasks under Rixenda's supervision, usually to do with Rixenda's trade of candle-making. When she was free, she often went down into the village at the foot of the mountain. She liked the energy of traders and craftsmen and merchants. It was a far cry from Rome or even Toulouse; still, the hubbub of town life consoled her. But there was nothing for her to do there. She was an outsider, with no useful skills to contribute. Over time she had retreated to the rugged mountaintop and applied herself to becoming accepted in Peire-Roger's dominion.

It was a strange little world. The regular denizens of the fortress itself were its two lords; their families and servants; a garrison of a dozen knights and a hundred men at arms; *their* families and servants; and a handful of *faidit*—minor lords who had been stripped of their estates by the ever-encroaching French. And of course, their families and servants too.

But all of them, rulers and ruled alike, were there to support and protect the elite of the so-called Cathar heresy. These were the men and women dressed in the black robes of friars and nuns, who had renounced their attachment to the world. "Good Ones," they were referred to by those who cherished them, and Bishop Marti was their leader. The Good Ones contributed to the well-being of the mountain settlement that protected them: many of the men were weavers, and some were smiths; many of the women were candle-makers. Good Ones of both sexes were herbalists and healers; farmers and peasants from all over the countryside would bring their ailing kin to them for help. The southwest slope of Montségur saw regular daily traffic up and down to the village.

The oddest thing about the Good Ones, to Ocyrhoe, was where and how they lived. While they spent much of their daylight hours in the village or fortress—some of their workshops being among the wooden buildings of the courtyard—they actually resided in the small stone shacks Ocyrhoe had seen when she first arrived, shacks she had assumed were storage sheds. These cramped, unadorned huts were clustered on two walled terraces that faced almost directly into the northern wind. The men were on the lower terrace and the women on the upper, nearly a hundred of each sex. Some shared small huts with other Good Ones; some lived alone. Some lived in cave-like recesses bored by nature into the mountainside. When she first arrived, Ocyrhoe had gratefully accepted Rixenda's offer to stay with her in her hut, because that meant she had a private place to stow the cup.

She had allowed herself to become civilized; her hair, once untangled, was plaited behind her, and she was given a more feminine tunic that went below her knees. By the second year, she was fully an apprentice in the candle-making enterprise that filled one corner of the tight courtyard; she'd also grudgingly learned to spin wool, as all the women in the fortress did for hours every day. Her small fingers were already both calloused and nimble, and despite her disinterest in it, she'd quickly earned a reputation as the most efficient spinner on the mountain.

To avoid such tedious women's work, she had convinced Peire-Roger to use her as a messenger. She demonstrated to him her remarkable ability to recite long passages verbatim days after she had heard them; she clambered up and down the courtyard walls to prove her agility. Unsure at first, he had made her an assistant to their only female messenger, an older Perfect who was going deaf. They usually traveled with at least two soldiers. Within two months, she had overcome her fear of alpine trekking and was racing up and down the secret paths and limestone tunnels, much faster than her mentor or the soldiers.

Soon she was spending many hours of a week carrying news from Bishop Marti down the mountain to outlying villages, where she would meet with agents from Toulouse or Usson or the Sabarthes mountains. In this way she learned a little of the reason for the Good Ones to be up here, shielded by their supporters, who called themselves Credents, or Believers. Months passed. And seasons.

She tried not to think about the world beyond the Pyrenees. There were people and places she missed terribly, but she did not know how to reach them. And she still hoped the cup would make its message plain to her.

One breezy spring evening after a full winter of Ocyrhoe trying to pretend she was not waiting for anything, Peire-Roger left the fortress with three of his knights. He almost never left. They returned two days later with dried blood on their clothes. For days they remained behind the bolted door of the chapel with Bishop Marti and other lords. A chill dread settled over Montségur. The names Count Raimundo and Guillem Arnaud—and the word, "Inquisition"—were whispered fearfully about the keep.

A full year passed before she fully understood what had happened. By then, she had become the ablest mountain-climber of Montségur, the most deft at moving undetected through the underbrush, for hiding in plain sight, and Peire-Roger now trusted her entirely. He sent her out, with messages or scouting missions, not only unsupervised but unguarded, so to make best use of her speed and stealth. Those few rare hours that she was not shepherding supplies up and down the mountain, or running messages to other Perfecti or Credents, she maintained her secret meditative vigil over the cup.

That meditation was interrupted one afternoon by a growing rumble in the courtyard. She left Rixenda's hut, scrambled up the path and through the gate into the courtyard.

The entire population of Montségur was clustered here, crowded together along with most of the villagers from below. The villagers' faces were red from tears or anger. The wall-walks were full of soldiers staring down toward the village with bows strung and arrows ready; everyone else was looking up expectantly at the men-in-arms, anxious and quiet.

Peire-Roger hollered down from the northern tower. "The troops are led by that French whoreson Hugue de Arcis who has taken over Carcassonne. Also there are pennants from Gascony and the Aquitaine. And the Archbishop of Narbonne." He spat.

"Toulouse?" his wife Philippa called up from the yard. "Is the Count of Toulouse with them?"

"No, thank God for that at least," said Peire-Roger. "They'll expect him, but I hope he can stay away."

"Foix?" somebody else asked plaintively. "Sure the Count of Foix is not besieging his own kin?"

"He has in the past," said a bitter voice from within the courtyard.

"I don't see his pennant," Peire-Roger announced, "but there are troops still arriving."

Ocyrhoe examined the crowd. Children were crying in confusion, clinging to their mothers' skirts; the mothers were turning to husbands or friends for support; everyone was regarding the overstuffed courtyard with the same unspoken thought: *there is not enough room for all of us to stay here for long.*

"Don't worry," Rixenda said, seeing Ocyrhoe's face pucker. "We are unassailable here. Most of the men down there are conscripted from local estates. They owe military service to the King of France, but they have no desire to be here; they do not want to see the Good Ones persecuted nor do they want to see France's power become more entrenched. When their forty days of duty are up, they will go home, and their leaders will be left alone in their army tents."

Forty days came and went; soldiers left, but more soldiers came to take their place. The crusaders, as they called themselves, tried to storm the mountainside; the knights and men-at-arms of Montségur showered arrows and stones and debris down on their heads. There was a constant garrison vigil. But the Good Ones continued to weave and spin and make candles and pray. Ocyrhoe helped spirit the villagers down the mountain to other towns for shelter; she helped spirit food and supplies from sympathizers up the mountainside after dark. She even forced herself to memorize the labyrinthine cave and tunnel system within the mountain, although she dreaded tunnels, and many of these were treacherous, requiring rope ladders to move between levels. To the relief of all, the French never found these passages—indeed, for months, they did not seem to consider the possibility of them, keeping their attention trained only on the slopes.

The well of Montségur was deep and the water cool. The days grew long until the summer solstice, and the earth baked there beneath the thin air on the mountain face. But the water held, and Credents from the valleys, with Ocyrhoe's aid, snuck food through the supply lines under cover of night. The Good Ones prayed and meditated, and the endless sorties up the western face of the mountain were always stopped by the garrison. The days were uncomfortable, but never truly frightening.

Another forty days had come and gone, and still more soldiers came, and more, and more, with no success at all in getting a foothold on the mountainside. The days grew shorter but the army continued to grow in size, if not enthusiasm.

Even Rixenda frowned a little now, tutted, shook her head in confusion. "Four *months*," she said. "No siege by the Catholics ever lasted so long." They were in the candle-shed melting the beeswax into a vat.

"You do not know your history," said Alis, who made candles with them. "The French besieged Toulouse for eight months back in '17, and finally lost. Long sieges bode ill for them. They are probably more perturbed by the length of the siege than we are."

"In that case, let us hope they leave soon," said Rixenda.

CHAPTER 5:

THE KNIGHT'S ARRIVAL

Percival had recognized the shape of the stark mountain peak from his confusing visions; it called out to him although there were other higher peaks near it. It was not one peak within a range, but a *pog*, standing out on its own high above all the surrounding plains. At the top—a detail missing from his visions—was a stone building so small it might have been a chapel. It was too small to be a church or a castle, and it was a nonsensical place for a fortress.

Riding slowly up into the foothills, he saw the disturbance of an army a day before he saw the army itself. His horse grew wary; so did he. Small clusters of houses and farms were deserted, had been ransacked; no livestock remained, barns were emptied of grain and hay, and there was careless destruction everywhere, not only to homesteads but to oak groves, vineyards, and mountain fields. Early snow was ground into mud in places where it should have lain unmolested until thawing. Small roads and footpaths had been trampled into broad avenues, but whoever had first come through here in large numbers had done it months ago. Yet, the scarring on young trees where branches had been ripped away was not new: The area was being patrolled.

For all the warning signs, when he first saw the army, the size of it surprised him. They were camped on the foothills out of which the limestone peak erupted like a fat stalagmite from the landscape. They were also camped in the fields lying farther out, as if trying to spread their number around the entire perimeter of the pog. Judging by a cluster of smoke plumes, they must have taken over a village at the foot of the mountain.

As he rode closer, he saw that the masses of men were grouped under a rainbow of insignia—the King of France and at least five banners Percival did not know. There were thousands of men. How ironic, that so many men were bent on destroying a place to small to hold their number; and how ironic again that no matter their number, they could not reach it. But they were entrenched; they were dedicated.

As he rode closer, Percival saw that most of the troops wore the cross of crusading pilgrims on the shoulders of their tunics. Had the followers of Mohammed taken over the mountain? Confused, he glanced around for papal banners—the crossed keys to the kingdom of St. Peter. He saw none.

Halting before he attracted attention, Percival considered his choices. The troops of men around the base of the mountain were obviously there to prevent traffic in either direction. If they were completely successful, the little bastion above would have given in by now, for nothing so small could keep stores enough for months, and this army camp had—even in winter—the stench of a place that had been lived in for a while. So there were ways up and down to the fortress, ways the army could not find. But somebody could. There was local support for whoever was up in the eyrie of stone.

If he could find those supporters, and convince them he was not a soldier of this army, perhaps they would take him up with them. He knew he was meant to be up there, only he did not know why—or how. But fully armed, with a decent horse, he was clearly a soldier; in a region whose language he was not even sure of, he could not possibly talk his way into a stranger's trust.

On the other hand, if he presented himself to the leader of the besieging army, he would be expected to join in its efforts. That felt dishonorable, given the size of the attack against whoever had been reduced to cowering in a stone barricade hundreds of feet above the rest of the world.

His need for information pushed him toward the outskirts of the army camp. Without hesitation now, he rode straight toward a set of guards on the long-trampled footpath. They looked bored until they noticed him. Then they stood up straighter and moved shoulder to shoulder, muttering to each other excitedly. They hoped that he was bringing news.

❖ ❖ ❖

Percival was delivered, dismounted, to a sergeant in a large tent. The sergeant crossed his arms over his puffed-up chest and eyed Percival's ragged, rose-emblazoned tunic with suspicion. "I do not know your blazon," he said. "Who is your lord?"

"I am a knight initiate of the *Ordo Militum Vindicis Intactae*," said Percival. When he saw those words meant nothing to the sergeant, he clarified for the man. "I serve the Holy Virgin." As an afterthought, he crossed himself.

"Where do you come from?"

I recently saved Christendom from the Mongol hordes, he thought of saying, but did not, as that would sound immodest. Aloud, only, "I received a message to come here."

"Why were you summoned?"

"I cannot tell you that," Percival said with absolute candor. "But it is of pressing importance."

"How many are you?"

"Just myself. My mission does not rely on force of arms."

The sergeant scrunched closed one eye, to demonstrate what a thoughtful man he was. "Were you summoned by Hugue de Arcis?"

"I have no knowledge of this man," Percival said. "Nor does he have the authority to summon me. It is a much higher authority that has sent me here."

The man's eyes widened. He turned to one of the bevy of pages clustered around him. "You," he said, picking one at random, "Tell his lordship that King Louis has sent a special messenger."

Percival smiled and did not correct him.

◆ ◆ ◆

The army leadership—both secular and religious, judging by their pennants—were in residence in what had been a village. As Percival followed the sergeant through the well-trodden avenues of the tent-city and across the earthen berm that had failed to protect the town, he noted the outlying areas of now-empty livestock pens. The workshops that had probably been for weavers, tanners, and smiths were now overrun with troops from Carcassonne, the sergeant importantly bragged to him, pointing out the pennant of Hugue de Arcis. The windmill, on a rise just west of the village, was still operating although, Percival guessed, not by its actual owner.

Moving closer to the source of chimney smoke, he saw what had been huts and shops, now all overtaken as offices and sleeping barracks. These were for the King of France's own corps who had come all the way from the Isle de France.

Finally they reached what had been the market green, and around it, snug cottages that had belonged to the burghers of the village. The green was covered over by one enormous pavilion, empty now; it was from the cottages that the smoke, and promise of warmth, arose. Beyond these houses were stables, and then the northern road out of the village, which—Percival made a mental note—led into a dense but low forest that hemmed the northern side of the mountain.

They approached the largest cottage. The Carcassonne pennant hung limp and damp from a rod protruding above the door. A guard saluted and stood away from the door to let them enter.

Percival could not remember the last time he had been inside a normal domicile. The relative coziness of it was almost poignant. The main room contained a table and some stools, and the central firepit dug out of the pounded-earth floor. Four young soldiers squatted about this with hands carefully outstretched.

Beyond the firepit, at the back wall, was a cushioned stool with a back on it, and on this sat the leader of this army. A burly man with a broad face and stout arms, he was wearing leather that was almost the same texture as his skin. Across his lap was a board, and on the board was a platter of what Percival supposed was meat. It was most likely jerky soaked in water and then heated, but the smell of it permeated the room and everyone else was glancing at it with hunger. Percival supposed they would not be given dinner until His Lordship had finished his repast.

The sergeant crossed to Hugue de Arcis and muttered something quietly at his ear. Hugue raised his eyebrows and nodded. The sergeant bowed, and left the room without another look at Percival.

Hugue looked expectantly at Percival. "You have brought a message from His Majesty?" asked the husky voice of the Lord of Carcassonne.

"No," said Percival pleasantly. "I am here on an errand."

"Well, it's a fool's errand," said Hugue lugubriously. "There is no way to get up there. If we cannot freeze them out over the winter—before we freeze ourselves—I don't see how we can do it. It is impossible to get to the summit."

"It is impossible for an army to get to the summit," agreed Percival. "But individuals are, by stealth, already leaving and approaching the fortress all the time, without difficulty."

Hugue bristled. "Is His Majesty's messenger implying we are incompetent at our work?" he demanded.

"What *is* your work?" asked Percival, wondering how quickly he could get an answer, and then how quickly after that he could end this conversation and set about the more interesting task of getting to the summit.

Hugue looked at him critically. "Show me your seal. How do I know you are who you say you are?"

"I haven't said who I am," Percival replied.

"You told my men you were from the king."

"I did not exactly say that. And I didn't give them my name. My name is Percival, and I am a knight initiate of the *Ordo Militum Vindicis Intactae.*"

As with the sergeant, there was no flicker of recognition on the man's face at the mention of the name of the Shield-Brethren. Rather than mocking the man for not knowing his order, Percival smiled politely.

"And did King Louis send you? What exactly are you trying to accomplish here?" Hugue demanded.

"I'm on an errand."

"What is the errand?"

"I can't tell you that," said Percival. "But I need to get up the mountain right away."

Another frown from Hugue. "How do I know you're not one of *them*, and you're trying to sneak in as reinforcement?"

Percival shook his head. "That would be dishonorable conduct for a knight," he said. "And if that were the case, offering myself up to your men would make me extremely stupid. I give you my oath, I will swear upon the Holy Mother's trust in me."

"That's nothing. The Cathars don't believe in oaths, so if you're one of them you could be lying to me right now without violating your beliefs."

The Cathars. He knew *of* the Cathars, but not much *about* them. Only that they were heretics who refused to acknowledge the authority of the Pope. He remembered no other details, but that was enough for him to suspect he would find more common ground with them than with their besiegers.

"Put me to a test," offered Percival. "Let me prove my virtue to you."

Hugue considered him a moment. Then he stabbed his table-knife into the small slab of meat on his tray, and handed the knife toward Percival. "Here," he said. "Eat this."

Percival blinked in confusion. "To prove my virtue, I should take food out of your mouth?"

"Are you refusing to eat it?" Hugue said, and met the eyes of his sergeant by the door. Percival heard the young men around the firepit murmur and nudge each other.

"I will happily eat your dinner," said Percival, "but I don't see how that proves my virtue."

"Eat it," said Hugue, brandishing the knife at him.

Percival took it from him and dug his teeth into the meat. It was overcooked, but compared to his diet for several years now, it was sumptuous. He made an appreciative noise as he chewed it, and the smile on his face was broad and sincere. "That's delicious," he said with his mouth full. "Would you like me to eat all of it?"

"Swallow it," said Hugue.

"I was planning to," said Percival, and did so. The smile broadened. "I'll drink your wine as well, if you require it."

"Enough," said Hugue. "Give me back the knife."

With a disappointed grin, Percival returned it to him.

Hugue said grudgingly, after a pause, "Cathars do not eat flesh."

"Ah," said Percival. "I'll remember that if I find myself among them. There are many kind of folk in the world, and I would not offend anybody's sensibilities."

Hugue stared at him. "They are heretics," he said. "Damn their sensibilities!"

"Excuse my manners," said Percival with a disarming smile. "Have I reassured you I am not a Cathar?"

"I won't permit you to go up there unless you tell me what your mission is."

"And I can't tell you my mission, so I suppose that puts us in stalemate," said Percival, standing. "In which case, thank you for the mouthful of sustenance. I'll be on my way."

Hugue looked nearly flummoxed. "You claim you are here on a mission and you are simply going to walk away from it?"

"Oh, no, I am going to walk *to* it," Percival replied. "But apparently not with your help."

"You can't do that," said Hugue, incredulous. "I am the commander."

"I'm not a member of your army," Percival reminded him pleasantly. "That's not why I was sent here."

"Where the hell are you going?"

Percival peaceably pointed out the door and upwards. "There," he said. "You are not in command of that place so you cannot forbid me to go to it."

"How do you intend to get there?" Hugue demanded.

"By the use of my hands and feet, and the Grace of God," said Percival, and strode out of the cottage.

CHAPTER 6:

ENTER THE OTHER KNIGHT

Dietrich von Grüningen and a few of Dietrich's fellow Livonian knights had come to the siege of Montségur on behalf of His Holiness Innocent IV, né Sinibaldo di Fieschi. The Pope himself sent no official troops, needing to reserve his manpower to face down Emperor Frederick. But this was a religious war, so Dietrich was here to keep an eye on things for His Holiness. He and his men shared a tent and ate mess with Hugue's men, but they were neither French nor local and had found companionship with no-one.

Dietrich would, of course, do whatever His Holiness requested of him. But freezing his arse off in Occitania, staring up at an impregnable fortress containing a few hundred heretical hermits, was not a satisfying tour of duty for a knight. Day after day, troops would try to force their way up the steep southwestern slopes of the mountain, the only apparent means of ascent. With little effort, the Montségur garrison—no more than a hundred men, the space being too small to hold half that number comfortably—repelled them all with stones and arrows. They had a suspicious amount of artillery for having been isolated for half a year; they slung down arrows, even crossbow arrows, with abandon.

Obviously they had a hidden arsenal up there, and very likely were getting reinforcements.

Dietrich had argued repeatedly in favor of a small band of skilled warriors—his own men, of course—sneaking up the paths under cover of night, finding their way into the fortress however the locals managed to do it, and reducing the garrison in direct combat. It would be a suicidal mission for most corps, and Hugue always refused him.

As evening fell, Dietrich felt the cold settle onto his clothes and work its way through layers to his skin. It was hard to find seasoned wood for fires for such a host—there were thousands of men nestled up against the western flank of the pog. When he first arrived, he had tried to impress upon both the Seneschal of Carcassonne and the Archbishop of Narbonne that, as knights in service to His Holiness, Dietrich and his men deserved some consideration above the rest of the soldiers. At the very least, housing in a village hut. Neither Hugue nor the Archbishop of Narbonne, Pierre Amelii, agreed with him.

At that point—not because he wanted housing but because he wanted respect for his office, at least from the archbishop—Dietrich decided to his disgust that this siege was not really a religious purge, and these two men burned not with spiritual zeal, but only with ambition.

Crown and church needed each other but they were not, in fact, unified. Dietrich was in awe of the machinations of both sides, but disgusted by the shortsighted, petty bickering that had killed tens of thousands of innocent Catholics over the years, just to root out a few hundred heretics. The crusading army of Simon de Montfort had killed every person in the city then—twenty thousand men, women and children, most of them devout Catholics—and then razed it to the ground.

That, to Dietrich, *Heermeister* of the Livonian Order, was sloppy and undisciplined, and brought shame to those who would honorably protect the Holy Church. He could hardly blame the local heathens for their stubborn failure to submit. There was almost something admirable to them.

Now he approached the largest cottage, where he knew Hugue and the archbishop would be having their weekly discussion. There was never anything new to say. When he'd first arrived, he'd had to argue to be allowed to attend these strategy meetings. Within three weeks he realized they were just an excuse for the two men to get drunk together, as there was absolutely nothing to talk about. Winter was setting in; supplies were running low. These very pressing problems were attended to at other meetings.

Tonight, however, as he nodded to the guard and crossed the threshold, he heard lively conversation. He hoped there was some news that would break the soporific impasse of the siege. As his eyes adjusted to the smoky light, he saw the archbishop's tall form pacing in stiff agitation.

"What do you mean he *disappeared?*" His Eminence demanded.

Hugue shrugged his broad, rumpled shoulders. "I was questioning him. He refused to give me a satisfactory answer, but he was quiet and well-mannered. And then he simply walked out of the building." He spoke in a tone that suggested he was repeating the story for at least the third time.

"And you sent nobody after him?"

Hugue took a husky breath. "As I told you, I sent three scouts after him. They couldn't find him. I do not think he's a threat. He's only one man, and we have his horse. He would have to be quite desperate to abandon his horse."

"Can I help you?" asked Dietrich, bowing his head to the archbishop and making no sign of respect at all to the Seneschal.

"There was a spy in the camp, and this fool let him get away," said the archbishop gruffly.

"He was not a spy," the impatient Hugue said as patiently as he could. "Why would a spy deliver himself to the leader of the army? He learned nothing from me or anyone else he spoke to, so if he was a spy, he was a lousy one." His voice changed pitch; he was running through a list he had already recited. Dietrich wondered how long this meeting had been going on for, and how often they had repeated themselves. "He claimed he was here on orders of the king. He satisfied me that he was not a Cathar, and he was certainly a knight, although I didn't recognize the insignia. He voluntarily left his horse with our grooms and was gracious to every individual who spoke to him."

"Did he identify himself?" asked Dietrich.

"He called himself Percival," said the Seneschal. "His order had some long name in Latin referring to the Holy Virgin."

Dietrich took a breath and then clenched his mouth shut. *In the name of the Father*, he thought, *they are here, too. What do they want?*

"Was it *Ordo Militum Vindicis Intactae?*" he asked, as calmly as he could manage. "Was there a flower on his surcoat?"

Hugue blinked. "Yes," he said. "Do you know him?"

"I know his brotherhood," Dietrich said, in a tight voice. God was rewarding him for his loyalty. *The Lord has brought us together that I may have my vengeance*, he thought hungrily. Whoever this knight was, Dietrich would shame and kill him, just as the knight's brethren had tried—*but failed*—to shame and kill Dietrich and his brothers in Hünern. Aloud he said only, "They are not Cathars, but they are most definitely heretics. I assure you, he was not sent by the King of France."

"Fool," growled the archbishop, and reached out in a swiping gesture toward Hugue, who ignored him. "We had one of Satan's own in our midst and you let him escape!"

"If I may suggest calm, Your Grace," said Dietrich, trying to mask a strange, pleasurable thrill. "My men and I are very familiar with his order. If you would give us the run of the camp to find him, I am confident we can extract from him a satisfactory answer regarding his presence here."

The two leaders exchanged looks. "It'll give him something to *do*," Hugue said briskly. Dietrich ignored the insult inherent in the comment.

"You'd better hope he succeeds," the archbishop retorted.

❖ ❖ ❖

Dietrich, at his tent, settled onto his camp-stool and called for a quill and vellum. "Greetings to His Holiness Innocent IV from your humble servant Dietrich of the Livonian Order," he began. "Your Holiness, I write merely to alert you to an interesting and unexpected development in the army camp below Montségur."

❖ ❖ ❖

It was easy to walk out of a camp at dusk when nobody suspected you, or was truly on guard for mischief, or really even wanted to be there.

On approaching the general's cottage earlier, Percival had noted the direction where the forest was the densest. That would be where sympathizers slipped up steep, overgrown paths and somehow made their way up to the little building in the sky.

And so, after exiting the hut with composure, Percival strode into the darkness as if he knew exactly where he was going. It was the kind of casual confidence that rendered him unremarkable in the chilly, grumpy hum of a camp settling down to sleep. Within twenty paces he was invisible.

He had left his horse behind. That troubled him, although he was sure the groom would recognize its worth and treat it well. He had pulled the saddlebag off when he'd dismounted and so had some basic supplies with him, although he doubted he would ever see the saddle again. But it did not matter, really. He sensed he was very near to what called him.

He continued to walk as if he knew exactly where he was going. Every hundred steps or so, a soldier's voice would call out in French, asking him to identify himself. With an accent that was clearly not local, he would reply that he was here on a special mission. Nobody challenged him. Nobody was interested.

Raphael, now—Raphael would have made sure to get as much information as possible before casually destroying any future relationship with the leader of the army. The only thing Percival knew for sure was that he did not know very much. Somehow he sensed it did not matter; whatever he needed would present itself to him. Without hesitation he strode on into the darkness.

CHAPTER 7:

A RETURN TO COURT

"How much of this shit must I ingest?" Frederick demanded, his voice echoing in the vastness of the stone hall. Tapestries hung from the walls, and also on large wooden upright frames, to create the illusion of separate chambers within the large expanse. "There is little enough natural sunlight for reading this time of year; must I waste good beeswax candles on such literary flatulence?"

"You are the leader of the Holy Roman Empire," said Léna dryly. "You need not do anything at my request. I offer you these as *divertissements* only."

Frederick squinted in annoyance at the scroll he had been reading. "French dog-shit," he said. He rolled the scroll up tightly and tossed it to the pale-haired youth standing guard at the door. The young man caught it one-handed, unrolled it slightly, and stared at the first few lines. "All yours, my little polyglot," Frederick said indulgently. "Improve your French."

"Yes, the original *trouvere* was French," Léna said, immediately offering the emperor a much thicker scroll from off a small table. "This variant is German. If it strains your eyes to read, a minnesinger will perform it for you during supper. He is tuning his instrument across the avenue, even as we speak."

Frederick's brows rose with dismay at the weight of the scroll. He cracked open the seal and unrolled the vellum a palm's width. "Wolfram von Eschenbach," he read aloud. "*Parzifal.*" He blinked. "I knew this fellow!" He sat up a little taller. "This Wolfram fellow. He was a Bavarian—in my court in Germany when I was first crowned. He must be dead by now. He had an appalling obsession with puns. The crudest form of humor." He frowned, almost resentfully, at the scroll. "This must be ten times as long as the Chretien de Troyes poem."

"Not quite," she said sympathetically. "And at least this one is complete, which de Troyes' is not."

"I trust you, Léna, and I do like to indulge you when I can, but I do not have the time to read one hundred thousand lines of bad verse—"

"It's twenty-four thousand, eight hundred and ten lines," she corrected placidly.

He tossed the scroll to the marble floor, where it landed with a dull thud. "I have an empire to keep intact, Mongols to fight off, and a pope to bring to heel. And I want to go hawking with my young friend there. Tell me the point of this exercise. I read the first one. It's all invented nonsense."

"Of course it is," Léna said. "Deliberately so. A specious distraction. But it's important that you recognize the invented nonsense, so that you do not mistake it for the real thing, should you encounter the real thing."

"*Why* such fuss about a supposedly ancient, so-called sacred chalice that nobody had even fucking heard of half a century ago?"

"It was spoken of for centuries before it was written of. You are not so naïve as to think Chretien de Troyes was inventing the Grail. He was merely inventing a *story* about it. A misleading one, of course, but that's how these things are done. As you know."

"It was a cup *from my own table*," Frederick protested. "It was nothing but a gleam in my silversmith's eyes when De Troyes wrote that dreck."

The blonde youth standing watch startled at this, broke from his position and turned to them. "Your Majesty?" he began. "Do you…"

But Léna gave him a warning head-shake. And a pageboy came running from the broad entrance on the far side of the cavernous room, sailing past all the tapestry-partitions as a cacophony of animal noises, especially the screeching of birds, rose up to the plastered ceiling. The boy, inured to this, kept running until he reached the stately and well-appointed farthest partition. "Raphael of Acre presents him to Your Imperial Majesty," he said, and bowed.

The Emperor smiled broadly. "Send him back to us. He may remain armed."

The pageboy's face registered some surprise at this. "He has a woman with him, Your Majesty."

Frederick grinned indulgently. "Does he, now? She may remain armed, too, then."

The boy bowed and darted back, this time raising a smaller uproar from the menagerie. The young guard at the door pursed his lips together and returned to his position of attention.

Frederick stood up from his chair, stretched and yawned. "They don't like to be bothered after their feeding time," he said of the menagerie, "nor do I, just before my own. But for Raphael"—and here he raised his voice deliberately to be heard over the partitions—"for *Raphael*, my home is always welcoming."

The several footsteps on the marble floor grew slightly swifter. The young guard stood aside; the pageboy and two other figures entered into the space: a dark-haired man with a somberly intelligent, Levantine face, and a broad-shouldered, fair-haired woman who looked as if she could easily beat him in a brawl. The man wore a tunic emblazoned with a rose and was armed with sword, dagger, and knife at his belt. The woman, in a tunic too long for a man but not long enough to be a woman's gown, had not only sword, dagger, and knife, but also two different kind of bows slung over her shoulder.

"Good Lord," said Frederick, upon seeing her.

"Your Majesty," said Raphael warmly, and sank immediately onto one knee, reaching toward the royal person to kiss his hand. Frederick almost didn't offer it, then grinned and reached toward Raphael—but only to smack him gently on the cheek.

"Get up, my friend," he said. "Embrace me."

Raphael looked up, then stood and clapped his arms around Frederick. Frederick grunted happily. "You are a sight for sore eyes," he said, almost accusingly. "Next time, show yourself before my eyes are quite *this* sore."

"You do appear to be squinting more than I recall, Your Majesty, but perhaps that is due to the dimness of the room," said Raphael of Acre with a diplomatic smile.

"I'm squinting because the glare of all that silver at your temples is blinding me. You did not have that before. Nor did you have such a lovely bodyguard." He looked at Vera for one heartbeat.

"This is Vera of Kiev," said Raphael, gesturing her toward the emperor. "She is of the order of Shield-Maidens, and my comrade in arms."

Frederick leered happily. "In arms, eh?"

"In combat," Raphael said, abruptly humorless.

Frederick and Vera sized each other up a moment. He held out his hand, waist-level, ring up, for her to kiss. She studied it a moment. Then without kneeling or bending over, she reached out for it, brusquely pulled it up to her mouth, kissed it, and released it.

"You have many animals," she said.

Frederick decided to like her. "I do," he said. "This is my traveling menagerie. I keep them with me whenever possible, and since I am settled here in Cremona for a while, and they add a lot of body heat, I have decided they will share this ridiculous so-called palace with me over the winter. That tall one in the middle is called a giraffe. Do you enjoy hawking?"

The expression on her face suggested she did not.

"Never mind," said Frederick. "I'll take Raphael and Ferenc, and you may stay here with Léna and hopefully find something to gossip about. This is Léna." He gestured to her with a small smile but no further introduction.

Léna and Raphael nodded with careful politeness to each other across the lantern-lit space. Vera took several steps closer to Léna, staring at her long, uncovered hair. "You are a Binder," she announced.

Léna smiled, unruffled. "That is generally not a comment one makes in public," she said graciously.

"We are not in public," Vera observed. "I recognize the knotted strands in your hair. I have known another Binder, younger and smaller than you."

Before the young man at the entrance could react, Léna held out a hand toward him and said quietly, "She doesn't mean your Binder, Ferenc."

"Well," said Frederick, clapping his hands together. "It's damn lovely to see you. Shall we go across to supper? There is a smaller hall in the building beside this one. My steward and butler have taken it over so that we don't have to move the animals every mealtime. I believe Léna has arranged some very boring entertainment for you, a dreadful poem in German. I apologize. I shall have the steward arrange bedding across the way. One bed?"

"Two," said Vera.

"My sympathies," said Frederick to Raphael.

Neither of the new arrivals looked at each other. Raphael glanced at the ground.

"Take them across," Frederick ordered Léna casually. "I want to check on the gyrfalcon's wing and then I will join you. If you were serious about the minnesinger, have him start as soon as possible so I miss most of the recitation."

Léna acquiesced with her expression only.

"Normally I wouldn't ask her to perform a steward's job," said Frederick in a conspiring voice. "It's only because you're here, Raphael. I'm showing off that I can make beautiful women do my bidding."

"I never thought otherwise, Your Majesty," said Raphael, with an apologetic and amused glance toward Léna. Léna looked bored.

"Oh for the love of Mary, stop Your-Majestying me. That's an order. Go on, freshen up and get yourselves some nourishment. I'll join you soon."

The trio headed toward the partition, and again the young guard stood aside. "Raphael," said Frederick suddenly, in a very different tone. The trio paused before disappearing behind the tapestry. "Have you heard there is a new pope?"

"Yes. He's taken the name Innocent," said Raphael. "News reached us on our way here."

"Do you know it's my old chess-partner Sinibaldo?"

"Fieschi?" said Raphael, barely hiding alarm.

Frederick nodded.

"Good luck to you," said Raphael.

"And to you," said Frederick. "My spies tell me he has a close relationship with the Livonian order. As I recall, your order is not cordial with them. I thought you might want to know."

"Is that why you've summoned me here?" asked Raphael. "You might have simply sent a message to Petraathen."

"No," said Frederick, "there's more. We'll talk about it at dinner. Regardless, I wanted to see your ugly mug again. Thank you for bringing it."

Raphael smiled tiredly. "It's always a pleasure to see Your Majest...ic head of red hair, Frederick."

❖ ❖ ❖

"Before I sign this, let me be sure I understand it correctly," said His Holiness Innocent IV, reviewing several haphazard piles of vellum stacked before him on the marble table. "The Count of Toulouse was excommunicated for refusing to adequately persecute the Cathars. And now, *because* he is excommunicate, he cannot join the army that *is* persecuting the Cathars, because it will not receive into its company an excommunicated leader."

Cardinal Bonaventura, standing to the left side of the table, nodded thoughtfully. "Yes, Your Holiness."

"Which means he can't persecute the Cathars."

"It is ironic, Your Holiness."

"It's worse than ironic, it's counterproductive," said His Holiness impatiently. "He's the overlord there. His family have been Cathar sympathizers for generations. I'm sure he's supporting them covertly, but none of the faithful can call him to account because none of the faithful can talk to him, because he's an excommunicate!" Nearly snarling, he muttered, "There's only one way to hold the little snake accountable."

He dipped the quill into a pot of ink, blotted it once on a scrap of vellum by the pot, and signed his name to the one pristine parchment that lay before him. He gestured, and the cardinal heated some sealing wax over the candle. As it melted to a resinous glow, he moved it over the bottom of the parchment and let it drip onto the surface. Innocent immediately pressed his signet ring into the warm wax. "There," he said, in the resonant tone of an indulgent, loving father. "We have forgiven our son Raimondo of Toulouse, and we bring him back into the fold." He crossed himself, kissed his fingers, and pressed them briefly onto the seal. Then he pushed the parchment over the pile toward Bonaventura. "See that this is sent to Toulouse as fast as possible so the Count can help to persecute heretics with the rest of those tiresome souls."

As Cardinal Bonaventura turned to pass these orders on to a deacon, the Pope snapped his fingers and added, "We must tell Pierre Amelii, the Archbishop of Narbonne, to follow suit. I believe he excommunicated the Count independently of us. That should not be allowed, it leads to abuses of power among the higher churchmen. The Pope should be the only one with the power to excommunicate." Turning to Cardinal da Capua on his right, he said tiredly, "Make a note of that. We'll need to call a council soon to address such issues."

"Yes, Your Holiness," said da Capua.

"I also want to allow the Inquisitors to use torture to extract confessions, but it might take a few years to get all the bishops' spines stiff enough for that."

Sinibaldo di Fieschi, Pope Innocent for less than two seasons of a year, was a man who seldom yawned or expressed the slightest bit of tiredness. But now he was exhausted. He rubbed his elegant fingers across his hawk-like, chiseled face. "That is enough for tonight." Around him, the exhausted servants of the throne of St. Peter almost sagged with relief. He kept them working far into the darkness after supper. After a year and a half without a leader, the Church of Rome had much housekeeping to catch up on.

"Your Holiness," said an ostiarius from the entrance behind the throne. "You have evening visitors." This was the unsubtle code-phrase for announcing the arrival of a spy with news.

"I will receive them. Everyone else is dismissed."

Sighs of relief were barely muted as most of the men and youths in the hall bowed toward Innocent's chair and shuffled as quickly as they could away to the far entrance, toward their beds.

The papal spymaster, Rufus, entered from the small postern door. Innocent admired this man although he did not know him well. He had the bearing and costume of minor nobility, and a pallor to him that should have attracted shocked attention and yet allowed him to disappear into a crowd of any size or temperament. He had been a spy, when young, for the earlier Pope Innocent, then for Honorius, then for Gregory. He was now the groom in a stable full of young men, and a few women, who served as agents for the Church.

"Rufus, please tell me you have news that I will want to hear."

"Very little this evening, Your Holiness. Arnault has arrived with news that a knight he identifies as belonging to the order of the Shield-Brethren is traveling south in what might be the direction of Rome, but could just as easily be…"

"Cremona," Innocent finished for him. "Perhaps going to speak with Frederick. Send somebody to Cremona to be our eyes and ears there. Fredrick and I are pretending to work out a truce but if it falls apart, I do not want him to have the help of the Shield-Brethren. What else? Please tell me there is something else."

The tall, gaunt man clasped his hands together and shook his head with a regretful smile. "There is nothing else tonight, Your Holiness, I am sorry to inform you. I will report to you again after mass tomorrow."

"Dammit," His Holiness muttered to himself. "Where is she?"

CHAPTER 8:

PARZIVAL

The dinner was not a feast, but merely dinner, with no more than one hundred of Frederick's retainers on benches along either side of the trestle tables. The white tiles everywhere gave brightness, but there was no firepit in this hall, which was in a smaller stone building, like the adolescent offspring of the main palace.

Feast or no, dining at the emperor's table was nothing Raphael was recently accustomed to, and he knew it must be even stranger for Vera. They had been told to leave their weapons with Frederick's squire—except of course their knives, for eating—and that felt alien enough. Besides the sumptuous and hearty portions of several kinds of meat and bread, there were vegetables that Vera eyed and poked at suspiciously. "We do not eat these things in Rus," she said to Léna, who was to her right. It sounded, Raphael feared, almost like a condemnation.

"It is a Sicilian cuisine His Majesty was raised on, and he maintains that diet whenever possible in all his palaces," Léna replied indulgently. "If it does not agree with you, I will ask the kitchens to prepare something else."

Vera looked taken aback. "I would not put anyone out," she said, and picked up a small handful of wilted greens with her fingers.

Raphael was not sure what to make of Léna. He'd heard of her over the years; he knew exactly who she was. Tall, graceful, in an undecorated blue gown and with uncovered head, she had been standoffish when they first arrived, but grew increasingly relaxed as she settled in, toward Vera in particular. To be honest, Vera had been the more standoffish.

As well as the rich food, and the rich texture, hue, and warmth of the hanging tapestries, the visitors were also distracted by the entertainment. That there was entertainment at all was unusual, although Raphael had fond memories of Sicilian and Ladino singers, from his days by Frederick's side. Unfortunately, this performer sat in the corner nearest to them and droned on in maudlin and uninteresting tones in German; it was all Raphael could do to mentally drown it out.

Following Frederick's example, Raphael focused on very little but eating through the several courses. As dishes were taken away and the pages were bringing out warm water for handwashing (another long-forgotten marvel), Raphael finally asked, "Why you have sent for me? Truly? It cannot be a casual visit you are after."

"We'll discuss it in a bit," said Frederick, his pink complexion even pinker and his smile made jovial by the wine. "Tell me first, what do you think of this entertainment?"

Raphael leaned back on the bench so that he could see both Frederick to his left and Vera to his right. He exchanged glances with Vera. He knew the poem, could even pluck out the melody of it on a gittern. She gave him a look of undisguised bemusement at the music.

"It is not my usual entertainment," Raphael said diplomatically.

"Mine neither," Frederick said. "It's awful. Do you know what it's called?"

Raphael smiled wryly. "I do, actually. *Parzival*. I had a friend whose parents named him for this poem, and he seemed to have inherited the protagonist's personality. Sometimes it was a dreadful burden."

"Not for him, but for the rest of us," Vera contributed.

Frederick grinned at her and raised his cup approvingly. "Ha! I like your sentiment." Léna rose from her spot beside Vera and moved around to the other side of the table, facing them, to be a part of the conversation. Watching her as she moved, Frederick told Raphael, "The lovely Léna has some interesting thoughts about this friend of yours. She thinks this song was written in prophecy of him."

"I most certainly do not," said Léna, as she settled onto the stool. "I wish you would pay attention when I explain things to you, Your Majesty." Her elbow on the tablecloth, she rested her chin on her elegant hand and looked meaningfully at Raphael. "It is true, however, that I am interested in your friend. Some of my Binder sisters have been following him over the past years."

"You know where he is?" Raphael demanded, one palm landing hard on the table, leaning forward with a jerk toward her before he caught himself.

"I believe I do," Léna calmly, and gestured to him to relax. Embarrassed, he leaned back and slowly slid his hand from the table to a small leather bag he wore on a chain around his neck. Léna continued. "I am sure it is coincidence, that he is named after this particular romantic hero. However, I think he shares more than a few traits with Parzival. Perhaps he believes himself to be in search of something? And yet he may lack the sense to survive on his own?"

"Absolutely," Vera said heartily.

"How do you know that?" Raphael demanded. "How can you know something so personal about a man you've never met?"

"If there was ever a Binder who knew your friend, it is almost as if all of us knew him."

Raphael grimaced. "Is he alone, then?" he asked Léna with some concern. "He left us in the company of two traveling companions, an alchemist and a...I'm not quite sure how to describe Bruno, but two burly fellows I hoped would look out for him."

"They parted company a while back," Léna informed him. "As I have heard from my sisters. The others are fine, but *your* Parzival is now someplace he should not be."

"And where is that?"

"He is near Provence, in the county of Toulouse."

"The land where they speak Occitan," said Raphael. To Vera he added, almost sheepishly, "That is the language of the troubadours."

"What, this?" Vera said dismissively, with a gesture to the singer in the corner. "This is German."

"Something like this, but prettier."

"Spare me," muttered Vera, and reached with her knife for another chunk of roasted goat.

"He is headed toward the siege of Montségur," Léna cut in sharply. "We thought you should know." She softened. "So you can go and get him. If you wish."

There was a pause as, in the background, the minnesinger moaned about the Fisher King.

Raphael thought about this a moment, grimacing. "If he is on his vision quest, he won't heed me. He believes he answers to a higher calling."

"You've the best hope of getting through to him," Léna said. She took Raphael's goblet, brought it to her side of the table, and began to refill it with wine from a clay jar. "You are a brother in arms," she said, her attention focused on pouring. "Consider it a battle between the obsessive madness of his vision quest and your influence on him as a man of reason."

"Vision quests are dangerous," Raphael said. "Especially Percival's." Again his fingers strayed to the object around his neck.

"Then you'd best put an end to it," said Léna. The goblet full, she offered it to him with a friendly expression. He accepted it, and nodded his head curtly in thanks. Léna reached for Vera's cup as well, but the Shield-Maiden put her hand over the top: no more.

"And while you're there," added Frederick, with patently false off-handedness, "just look around and take the pulse of the place, would you? As my Saracen physicians would say."

Raphael nodded, understanding. "You want me to spy for you. I am a knight of a holy order, and you are asking me to spy."

"*Scout* is a nicer term, isn't it?" Frederick smiled, as Léna began to fill his cup. "His Holiness, I am sure, has a few fellows there himself. It would be such an embarrassment if there was something worth knowing, and he knew it before I did."

"Anything in particular you wish me to *scout* for?" asked Raphael, sounding resigned.

Frederick shook his head and received his cup from Léna. "No. Truly. But the situation is a smoldering volcano that could erupt at any moment. Do not let it erupt into my empire."

Raphael heaved a sigh, leaned farther back from the table, and glanced at Vera. She gave him a knowing look. She would go with him, of course, wherever he was bound.

"Very well," said Raphael. "Toulouse. The Occitan. Let's see if I am up to date." He tapped his chin. "That's been a turbulent region for decades. Why would Percival be drawn there? Last I heard, the fortress of Montségur had been designated the official refuge of the Cathar faith."

"The Cathar heresy, you mean," Frederick snorted. "That fucking Cathar heresy."

Raphael frowned. "I am surprised to hear you say that, Frederick."

The emperor laughed. "Are you? Why?"

The knight shrugged. "You have hardly been an ardent supporter for the catholicity of the Catholic Church. You and Gregory nearly killed each other over it. Can a man so often and so blithely excommunicated as you truly be so orthodox as to condemn heresies? After what we saw in the Levant? Given your friendship with the Hebrews and Moslems of Sicily and elsewhere? You give Jews all manner of powers and rights the Pope says you shouldn't give them. How can you take issue with fellow Christians who also disregard the Pope's authority?"

Frederick harrumphed. "You are looking at it through the wrong lens, Raphael. The Jews don't cause me any grief, and the Patriarch of the east is weak and keeps to himself. But between the Pope and the Caliph I have my hands full. I don't care one way or the other about anyone's fucking beliefs, I just want to minimize the number of different religious leaders I have to contend with."

Raphael looked into his lap a moment, thoughtfully, and tried to hide a smile. "You actually share some beliefs with the Cathars, Frederick, from what I remember of them."

Frederick harrumphed again. "Not the *important* beliefs. They don't like fornication, or roasted goat, or hawking. At this point, the tensions there are more political than spiritual. Simon de Montfort."

"He led the Albigensian crusade against the Cathars at the beginning of the century," Raphael explained to Vera, holding up a hand to signal Frederick to pause. "The Pope empowered him to root out not only the actual Cathars, but their sympathizers, and that meant nearly everyone in the Occitan. Simon drove most of the local lords out of their lands, in the name of the Church, and as reward, the Pope let him keep all those lands for himself. He ended up ruling an area far larger than the kingdom of France. Of course all of his subjects loathed him."

"And that's why," Léna continued, "in the end, his family handed it all over to the King of France, who is still the suzerain. The most powerful lords there now are the king's own men, from Isle de France. But many of the minor barons are natives, who have been given back their family estates on the condition that they accept King Louis as their feudal lord."

"They're pretty grumpy about that," said Frederick, with the long-suffering insight of a ruler who knew about these things. "They'd love to throw off the French yoke, so Louis needs an excuse to bully them into submission."

"Still?" said Raphael. "I thought that all settled down years ago."

Frederick gave him a knowing look. "No conquered people is ever content with staying conquered, Raphael; that should not be news to your ears. Louis is working now with the Archbishop of Narbonne to unite everyone in the Occitan under—*quelle surprise*—the crusading banner against the heretical Cathars. Montségur has become the symbol of the Cathars, so even though the place is inarguably un-take-able, they're trying to take it."

Raphael winced. "My God, what that land has been through."

"The local lords are obliged to send men as their feudal duty, but they're not happy about it, and neither are the men they send. All of them, soldiers and lords alike, have loved ones who are part of the Cathar cause. It's so clearly just a means for King Louis to display his power, but if the lords do not send troops, they risk excommunication by the Archbishop of Narbonne. They're being forced to attack their own people and in many cases their own beliefs. So it's a messy little army camp they have at the foot of that mountain."

"And even if they are successful at taking Montségur," contributed Léna, "it's not as if they've defeated Catharism itself. It's prospering in other places. In fact, the Cathar Bishop right here in Cremona."

"Oh, Christ, that's right," said Frederick, with a comically pained expression. "He wrote to Marti, the Bishop up in Montségur, to say 'We're doing *so well*, with *so many* converts right under Frederick's fucking nose, that we could really use another Perfecti or two, if you can spare one from your flock.'"

"A perfect what?" asked Vera.

"It's a term for the Cathar spiritual leaders," said Raphael.

"Luckily," Frederick continued, "one of my spies intercepted the message and informed His Heretical Eminence that the folks up on Montségur are not going *anywhere*. Now do you see what I mean about the annoyance of heresies? You corral one leader into a corner and another one pops up hundreds of miles away. It's exhausting just to keep track. At least the Pope and I are one on one when *we* grapple."

"I assume you mean that figuratively," said Vera, unimpressed. "But if you meant it literally, I would be interested to watch."

Frederick grinned at Raphael. "This one," he said. "Hold on to her."

Raphael reddened slightly and said purposefully, "So you are sending us into a siege."

"Of a sort," said Frederick expansively. The wine was beginning to take its toll on His Majesty's majesty. "It's doomed to fail. They've been there at least half a year without gaining an inch. I think the winter will freeze them out and they'll go home by solstice. But I've had no reports for weeks, and I want to know what's going on. So there is a slight chance you will have to do battle with about ten thousand men who mostly don't want to be there, before you actually are able to get up the mountain to find Percival."

"And then do battle with *his* demons," said Raphael softly, fingering the chain around his neck again. He took a deep breath and looked up at Frederick. "Well, that's much more interesting than my original impression. I will gladly take it on."

"I go with him," Vera said, a statement of fact delivered to nobody in particular, as there was nobody in particular she needed to convince or to grant her permission.

"Well that's a deal done, then," said Frederick, grabbing Raphael's hand and shaking it heartily. "Thank you for that."

He stretched expansively, and yawned. "I'm ready to fall asleep now, but tomorrow please come hawking with young Ferenc and myself. Did you meet Ferenc?"

"I don't believe so..."

"I love that lad," gushed Frederick. "He's a Magyar. Hungarian. I took him in when he was nothing but a wild thing, and after we cut his hair and gave him a bath and some decent clothes, he turned out to be a better investment than the whole city of Foggia. He has a gift with horses the way I do with birds. I've taught him four languages, and algebra, and impeccable manners, and swordsmanship. I like him more than I do my actual children. You can meet him tomorrow. You'll need a few days to rest and resupply after this journey and, as I said, I can show you my menagerie. You can watch Ferenc wrestle with the tiger." He lowered his voice conspiratorially. "They're not really wrestling, of course. They're just playing."

CHAPTER 9:

THE KNIGHT ON THE MOUNTAIN

Percival could vaguely make out, from the low glister of campfires, a footpath leading out of the village to the north. He followed it into the darkness, striding with casual purpose, as if he knew exactly where he was going. Once the camp noises faded behind him, he paused a long moment, waiting for his eyes to adjust to the dark. Then he turned to his right and walked purposefully straight into the undergrowth, intending to muscle his way in the direction most likely to lead to a covert path.

This worked for all of one stride. The bushes came to his waist and were far denser than he had anticipated, as interwoven as a tapestry. He could have pushed his way forward by sheer force—could even have used his knife to hack through some of it—but having taken the first impetuous step, he realized how foolish it was to go on. The moon was new and he could barely see the hump of the pog against the stars, let alone discern any way to move up its slopes. He backed out onto the path. He would have to bushwhack by daylight.

Behind him, from the camp, he heard voices, then saw a glimmer of torchlight. He jerked his head away from the direction of the light so as not to ruin his night vision, but even that brief gleam meant that now the darkness around him was darker than before.

The footpath was broad enough that he could run, although he was sure there would be outlying sentries further along down the path. He had to get as far away as possible tonight, and then determine how to get around to the far side of the mountain by daylight—surely the army did not entirely surround the mountain.

He ran two hundred paces or so, his eyes re-adjusting to the darkness. He heard the voices behind him gaining—but here suddenly before him, just visible in the starlight, was a fork. One path continued straight north, while the other veered to the west. He paused a moment, to hear how many were after him. *Three,* he thought, *all on foot and all armed,* for he heard their weapons rattle. He turned toward the westward trail.

From out of the darkness behind him, a small, strong hand grabbed his wrist and pulled him backwards into the underbrush onto his ass. "Come with me!" a voice hissed in his ear. "Keep your mouth shut, get your feet under you, and move toward my voice the length of two strides. And then *stop.* Don't even breathe."

He did take a breath, to reply, but was warned, "If you argue with me I'll disappear and they'll find you. Your choice."

Percival pushed himself up far enough off the ground that he could collect his legs under him. Twigs and dead leaves poked and teased him from every angle; he inhaled dead leaves into his mouth. He clasped his sword to his side to avoid a tug-of-war with the undergrowth, and on his knees he moved as quickly as he could through the stubborn brush, up an incline he hadn't realized was there. Perhaps four knee-strides along, he suddenly felt the brush give way a little.

"Stop," the voice whispered. "Stay here until they've gone."

The incline allowed a view down the slope, obstructed by the brush. Three soldiers with knives, ropes, and torches had come running, and stopped at the fork. They bootlessly held their torches out and craned their necks to look down the two directions, then back at each other with frustration. The one with the biggest knife pointed up to the hillside. They held the torches high above their heads, and all three sets of eyes scanned the brush. Their night vision was already ruined from running with the torches, and even with the light over their heads their sight was poor here. One man shook his head in disgust: They would find nothing. After some muttering together, they foolishly split up the search party, one man going down either road alone, the third returning to the camp.

When the two scouts were safely out of hearing, the voice hissed in Percival's ear again. "Can you feel the path we're on? They don't know about it. Stay at my heel. Don't make any noise."

"Who..."

"Shh!" The nimble figure turned and headed up the path.

For the time it takes to amble a mile, the two of them moved with exasperating slowness through the underbrush. Straight above, the stars were sensational. But Percival could only tell they were on a path because the boy ahead of him kept moving forward; the brush closed in on him regardless, twigs prying into his ears and catching in his hair, small branches tugging at his belt. The smell of dry-rotting leaves filled his nostrils, and much of his attention was spent on squelching sneezes. Cold rose up out of the root-ropey ground, and his knees, taking so much of his weight, grew numb in the cold.

They climbed up, then across, then up, then down, then seemed to turn back on their tracks. The tension of such careful movement generated some little heat, not enough to fight off the chill. He had no way to chart their progress. They did not seem to be getting any closer, and his guide was leading him up an ever-increasing slope that appeared, in the starlight, about to turn into a vertical cliff. Down to their right were the dotted campfires and baritone murmurs of the occupied village.

Very abruptly, the boy stopped. He hissed irritably. "You're making as much noise as an ox. This is the most important place not to be overheard. So."

Suddenly the boy had reversed his position, and was facing Percival directly—and had a knife to his chin. "What are you doing here?" the whispered voice demanded.

Percival almost laughed aloud. "Don't you think you should have asked me that at the bottom of the hill?" he answered calmly. "Rather than bring me halfway to your secret hideout? I would hate to kill a youth but I can snap your neck faster than you can use that knife on me."

"If you do that, you'll be stuck on the middle of a mountainside under a new moon with enemies in all directions."

"Why did you bring me this far?" Percival asked. "Put the knife down, my lad. It is unnecessary and irritating."

The knife did not move. "Don't call me your lad. I realize you're not on *their* side, given they were chasing you with weapons. As a rule we protect those in need of refuge. But you've the stink of meat on your breath, so I know you are not one of us."

"So you are a Cathar," Percival said.

"What are you after? Why should I take you any farther up?"

"I am curious to see what is in the chapel."

A short, breathy laugh. "It's not a chapel," he said condescendingly. "Although it is a sanctuary. If you are a pilgrim, then you are welcome."

"I am not a pilgrim, but I am a monk," said Percival.

"With a sword?" asked the boy accusingly.

"I belong to an order of warrior-monks. We devote ourselves to the Virgin Mother." It felt ridiculous to be having this conversation, in a pitched whisper, in this setting.

"How can any follower of the Virgin be violent? That is against everything the Lady stands for. Besides, if you belong to an order of monks then you're with the Roman church, and so I will not be bringing you any further upwards."

"If you feel this is the appropriate place for a theological debate," said Percival calmly, "then I will answer you. I think, however, that perhaps it isn't. My word is impeccable and I tell you, I am not from Rome. Will you take me up there? I have been seeking this place a long time now and have a deep longing to arrive."

He waited while the boy considered this. He heard the boy's breathing patterns change as, presumably, his thoughts did. Finally he said, deliberately: "You cannot get up there on your own, so if you want me to lead you there, you'll have to do what I tell you."

"Gladly, young sir."

"*Young sir* is even worse than *my lad*. My first demand is that you turn over all of your weapons to me. I see you have a sword and a dagger, and my guess is there's probably another dagger hidden in your boot." He held out his hand. "Right now. Give them to me."

"I will not," Percival said. "I could *use* them on you. You do realize that, yes? To force you to show me the way up."

"Wouldn't work," the boy informed him. "I'd kick up a fuss and it would attract the attention of the guards below and we'd be taken in to the army camp, where nobody knows me but you're wanted for questioning. Did you think I didn't think this through? Give me your sword."

"No," Percival said, resting his left hand on the hilt.

"God be with you, then," the boy said briskly, and scampered into the bush as neatly as a rabbit.

Percival was alone in the darkness.

He waited a long moment, but there was no sound at all. The scout had left him alone on the bare mountainside. Even without moonlight, to go up or down was impossible without attracting unwanted attention. But he had to go one way or the other, or the cold would stiffen him within an hour.

He had to go up. He felt drawn to something up there, something holy, something somehow connected to his visions. Surely the Lady would show him the way. He prayed for a moment, and then tried, in the shadow of the mountain, to find the path the boy had disappeared along.

There was nothing. In all directions—even directly behind him where he knew he had just trampled—the brush was impossibly thick, appearing never to have been approached by a bird, let alone human traffic. In some places he could just barely make out the traces of snow still resting on the tops of the bushes—absolute proof nobody had come along to disturb the area. With a heavy sigh he groped around directly in front of him and a little to the left, the direction the boy had disappeared. Nothing in the brush gave way. He decided to force himself in that direction nonetheless. Moving slowly was better than not moving at all, and surely there were numerous subtle paths crossing the slope; he would eventually find *something*, even if it led him back down to the foot. He knew he could be quiet enough not to be detected. It just meant moving very, very slowly.

And very, very slowly he moved. The cold of the mountain kneaded into his knees and feet and hands. His breath felt labored and his muscles tensed, although he was doing almost nothing; it was not the kind of exercise he was accustomed to.

He heard church bells toll and figured he had moved a stone's throw since the boy had left him, but he had not noticed church bells earlier and so had no idea how to gauge his rate of progress. He did not blame his guide for the decision to depart; the boy was very protective of whoever or whatever was up there, which only clarified for him that this must be a destination worthy of his visions. That knowledge, that certainty, thrilled him so much the sleepy sensation of cold fell away.

After an eternity, he heard the church bell toll again, and estimated he had not moved more than another stone's throw. That disheartened him, true believer though he was. He allowed himself a sigh of frustration.

"Ready to negotiate?" said the whispered voice at his temple, and at the same moment he felt the knife press against his cheek again. He controlled the impulse to backhand the lad. "I've been watching you the whole time," the boy announced, in a cheeky whisper. "Do you think I'm stupid enough to let an armed man roam around Montségur? What if the French discovered you just as you were discovering one of our footpaths? We can't have that. Disarm yourself and come with me."

"Absolutely not," said Percival. "A knight does not give up his sword."

"A knight does not find himself in the absurd predicament you're in, either," said the boy. "You'll get your weapons back, provided the bishop and Peire-Roger are satisfied with your answers to their questions."

"No," Percival said patiently, as if gently informing a toddler he may not have a tidbit to eat.

"As you prefer," he said, "God ye goodnight. I won't come back this time." And again, like a rabbit, he was gone into the underbrush somewhere above Percival's head.

"All right!" Percival said in a loud whisper. "I relent. I agree to your terms."

"About time, I was getting chilled," the boy whispered, beside him again. "Sword." He began to unsheathe it but the boy corrected quickly: "The whole thing, belt and all. I don't want to be crawling around in the dark with a naked blade." Percival grunted acknowledgement and unbuckled the sword, elbowing the clawing scrub-branches out of the way. He held it out, and the scout's skinny arms sagged briefly under the weight of it.

"Dagger," the boy added. This was tucked into Percival's tunic-belt; he pulled it out and offered it hilt first.

"Knife. I'm sure you have a knife."

Percival pulled the knife from his belt and offered it, too, hilt first.

"Anything else?"

"No," Percival said, feeling almost naked.

The lad set the weight of the sword belt down in the space before him, lay the dagger and knife on top of it, and announced, "I choose to believe you." He reached for his own narrow belt, and unstrapped a wine skin and a small bag. "Here," he said. "To keep you fortified. Wine, and there is some bread in the bag. You have a wait ahead of you yet." He picked up the weapons again. "Stay here. I will be back as soon as possible. But you might have an hour to wait." Before Percival could answer, the stranger disappeared. Even weighted down with the unfamiliar ballast of weapons, he was silent in the dark.

Percival considered the wine and the bread. But not for very long; he was ravenous and thirsty, the cold had crept in despite his rapturous delight that he was near the end of his quest, and he had nothing else to do.

Again the church bells tolled the hours, waking him from a chilled dreamscape full of whirling light. Without warning, the boy was suddenly beside him in the dark again. "I've taken your weapons up to the fortress for safekeeping, and now I'll take you up yourself. You'll be interrogated and if his lordship has no quarrel with you, you'll get your armaments back."

"I am a stranger here. Who is his lordship?"

"Ask questions once you're up there. Let's go. Try not to sound like an ox."

The lad moved forward, now slowly enough for him to follow. It was as if the brush miraculously moved aside to create a path for them that closed up behind Percival.

Less than another stone's throw, the air grew even colder. The brush abruptly fell sparse, and then altogether away. Ahead of them, barely discernible in the dark, rose a cliff face of limestone. He had brought them to a dead end. Frustrated, Percival stood up.

"Well," the boy said, "It's all uphill from here."

"How can we possibly climb that?"

"We don't," said the boy. He reached toward the cliff face, and, as if by an act of magic, proffered a piece of rope from the rock that rose straight up into the dark heights of the cliff. "Take this. I'll show you how to tie it around yourself to keep your balance."

Speechless, Percival received the rope. The boy reached into the darkness and magically produced a second one. "Like this," he said, and showed Percival how to tie it: a length of it around his waist with a long tail, which became a figure-eight loop around his upper thighs.

"We rappel ourselves *up* the mountain," the boy whispered. "There are men at the top who will pull us but we have to help them by going hand over hand and shortening the distance as they lift. Yank on the rope to tell them you are ready. Like this," he said, with a yank, and effortlessly leapt in the air to the height of the knight's head. He turned away from Percival toward the cliff-face and began to pull himself up the rope. Because the rope was being lifted from above, it created the impression that he was scampering up the side like a squirrel up a tree. He disappeared into the darkness almost instantly.

CHAPTER 10:

A SEEKER REACHES SANCTUARY

Percival's eyes hurt from the candlelight by the time he was inside, he had grown so used to the dark of the mountain.

He was in a corner of the small main hall of the fortress. Eccentrically, several hundred people from all walks of life were gathered here for warmth. He had expected a quiet sanctuary, the sort of place Raphael had described as Francis of Assisi's meditation hut. Here was rude noise and bustle, more soldiers than worshippers—and most bizarrely, hundreds of ordinary people of all ranks and ages, sleeping alongside each other on the floor of the keep.

The lord of the fortress was questioning him. Peire-Roger did not strike Percival as a spiritual warrior of any sort. The expression on his handsome face gave him a look of perpetual anger, although there was nothing, at this moment, to be angry about: The Lord had just provided him with a fully armed knight, something he was surely in need of.

"You have been sent by neither Bertran d'Alion nor Arnaud d'Usson? Then who has sent you?" Eyes widening: "You are not come from Corbario, are you? Or from the Count?"

"But I have told you, I came here on a spiritual pilgrimage," Percival repeated. He spoke softly, aware of all the interested eyes upon him, the scores of people pretending to be sleeping.

"The only people with the determination to make it to Montségur on a spiritual pilgrimage are Cathars, and you freely admit you are not a Cathar, so I fail to make sense of your claim."

Percival considered this almost dreamily, his fingers tapping the cup of heated wine. "Perhaps I am a Cathar and do not realize it with my waking mind," he proposed. "I was drawn here by dreams and visions that have plagued me for years. Perhaps the spirits of the Cathars have been drawing me here. Is that possible? According to your philosophy?"

Peire-Roger made a noise. "Ask Bishop Marti about that," he said. "But do not use the word *Cathar*. It's an insult. I used it only to see if you recognized the name. I did not realize you were a seeker or I'd have had him here to start with. Can you tell me anything else about this fellow, Ocyrhoe?"

His mountain-guide stepped forward into the candlelight, and for the first time he could see him—no, *her*—clearly. "You're a girl," Percival said in surprise.

She gave him a strange look, not irritated so much as examining. She ran her upper teeth over her lower lip, brows furrowed, considering him. She ignored his comment.

"No, milord," she said at last to Peire-Roger. "But I know he isn't one of them. He was fleeing from their soldiers and he cooperated with me, as you know, giving up his weapons."

"If you cannot tell me more about yourself, sir, or prove the purpose of your coming here, I'll be holding onto your weapons for a while," Peire-Roger informed him.

Percival grimaced regretfully. "I've told you everything I can," he said honestly. "If you must keep my weapons hostage, I cannot lend you my strength in arms, which you clearly need. In the meantime, however, I would be very grateful to be told more about your faith. I believe I have been drawn here for a reason, and I hope the answer to that mystery can be revealed to me quickly."

"Send for Bishop Marti," the lord said to the girl. She nodded and scampered off.

"Where is that young lady from? She looks familiar."

Peire-Roger laughed harshly. Even his laughter seemed angry. "She's not a lady. She's a beggar girl from Rome. I don't remember what brought her here but she's been a Credent for the past two years. She is unrivaled at getting up and down the mountain invisibly. You're very lucky she was on patrol tonight—nobody else could have gotten you out of the French camp and up here without your getting caught or freezing to death. Speaking of which, we have more hot wine if you would like it."

"No thank you," said Percival. "I wish to keep my head clear for the conversation I believe I am about to have." He gestured with anticipation toward the approaching figure. "But I thank you for the gesture."

Gaunt, upright, Bertrand Marti approached them, wearing a simple black robe tied at the waist—the same garment worn by about a third of the population in the hall. Behind him, Ocyrhoe hovered uncomfortably, as if she were not sure she was supposed to be here.

The bishop sat beside Percival and looked at him a moment as if waiting for something. Percival supposed there was some coded greeting he was now supposed to utter, but having no idea what it was, he simply smiled benignly at the old man.

After a few heartbeats, the bishop pursed his lips in disappointment. "Lead us to our rightful end," he muttered to himself. Then, to Percival: "God bless you and lead you to your rightful end."

"Thank you," said the knight.

"Are you a Catholic?"

"I am a Christian, Father," Percival said carefully.

"What brings you here to us?"

Percival was not sure how to respond. "I believe I am here for two different reasons, although only one of them accounts for my actual arrival."

Marti frowned. "Explain yourself, my son."

"I was brought here by a vision," Percival said softly. It was very strange, after years of struggling in near-silence, to speak so bluntly about this to a stranger. And yet this dignified, old man seemed like the right, the best, the first person to confess to fully. "A series of visions. I have seen great whorls of light and they drew me in this direction. I have been having these visions for years, but my circumstances did not allow me to come here any sooner."

Marti's rheumy hazel eyes widened with sudden approving interest. "Light? Was it shining against the darkness?"

That seemed a peculiar question to Percival, who could not imagine light without dark. He said simply, "There was darkness and light, but the light was in spirals and that is what attracted me."

"And were there images in the darkness or the whirls of light? Devils or angels or saints or crucifixes or..."

Percival shook his head. "No, nothing as symbolic or literal as that. Just light."

Marti nodded. "This vision expresses the true nature of the universe," he began, as if there were nothing particularly remarkable about having such a vision. "All of creation is either of the light or of the dark. Our desire, as Goodmen, is to return to the light. That is why we come here to Montségur, Goodmen and Goodwomen alike."

Percival nearly gasped. Could it really be that straightforward? "You keep the light here in this fortress?" he asked excitedly.

Marti scowled as the girl, Ocyrhoe, covered her mouth with both hands to stifle a sneering laugh. "The light cannot be kept," Marti said. "It is the light of the spirit of God. It does not exist on this plane, which is why it can only be seen in visions. You are touched by a gift, that you can see the light while you yourself are trapped in darkness."

Percival frowned. "What darkness? I do not feel trapped in any darkness. I live a very pure life. I am decent."

"That you are in this life at all, in a human body, traps you in darkness," Marti informed him soberly. "As it traps all of us. This world, this plane, all of this is the making of Satan. Our material life, everything, the food we eat, the clothes we wear—it is all necessary evils brought about by being trapped in this world."

"Oh," said Percival, who could not think of anything else to say. This information did not fill him with the satisfaction he'd expected he would feel, when he finally reached the source of his vision. He tried, tentatively. "But I am pure. I treat my body as a temple to the Virgin, and I...everything I do is in service to what you call the light. How then can any part of me belong to Satan?"

Marti gave him a tired, knowing smile, as if bored from spending decades answering this specific question. "It is wonderful that you strive in that way, my son, to approach the light through your actions, but you are misguided. We all crave a return to the light. But the only way to achieve that is to forswear everything—*everything*—that keeps us bound to this life. Then, when our bodies die, our spirits are free to return to God."

"And if we don't forswear," Percival said carefully, "if we don't forswear those things, then we go to hell instead?"

"*This* is hell," Marti corrected emphatically.

Percival looked around in alarm. The girl Ocyrhoe made a derisive sound.

"This existence," Marti clarified. "This life. If we do not purify ourselves so that we can be released into the light of God's spirit, then we are condemned to return to this world, in another body. This continues until we learn the truth and do whatever is necessary to free ourselves from the repeating cycle of birth and death, and be released into the bliss of formless light." A pause. He gently smiled, as if just remembering that a reassuring smile was called for when delivering such heavy news. "I do not normally explain things so directly to somebody I have just met, but you have made a remarkable effort to arrive here, and perhaps you are touched with a special gift. It is a great thing that you have seen the light, and that it has brought you here to us."

"Yes," said Percival, rubbing one cheek. "Truly remarkable." He pursed his lips. "But I am not sure why I would need to come *here*. If the light is everywhere and nowhere, then why would my visions have led me here specifically?"

Marti's hazel eyes grew placid. "I believe you know already," he said. "I think it is the second reason you referred to."

Percival nodded. "I am a knight," he said, far more confidently than he had said anything so far. "I see a small group of innocents—you certainly strike me as innocent—beset by foreign invaders. It is my duty to lend my sword to your cause."

"That is it exactly," said Bishop Marti. "You are a special child of the light in this lifetime, but you are also of this world, as a soldier. Your visions have brought you here that you might use your soldier's ethos to protect those of us who may not fight. We are grateful for your arrival."

"Yes, we are," Peire-Roger said immediately, now that the conversation was on familiar terrain for him. "We have only ninety-eight men-at-arms against an army of ten thousand."

"Why are they here?" asked Percival. "What is the cause?"

"Twofold," said Peire-Roger. Percival was not certain if he was frowning or if his face was naturally shaped that way. "The king of France claims dominion over Toulouse and Provence and other areas, and the Bishop of Narbonne wishes to stamp out the Good Ones and their adherents, who do not follow the Pope or the dictates of the Roman Church."

"It is fear," Marti said in his clear, tenor voice. "It is always fear that drives violence. The Church wants to control all Christians, and they are frightened by our lack of compliance. So they are trying to destroy us. The King of France is frightened of the rightful rulers of this area reclaiming their estates. Their two fears dovetail neatly, and so they have joined together to destroy us."

"That's appalling," said Percival. "On both accounts. I will be honored to lend my sword to fight your cause—as soon as his lordship sees fit to return it to me."

Peire-Roger gestured brusquely toward Ocyrhoe. "Get the man his weapons." She ran toward the far side of the hall. Peire-Roger returned his attention to Percival. "May the God of Light and the Light of God guide your hand to kill a cartload of those whoresons."

CHAPTER 11:

DEPARTURE

The next morning, Frederick failed in his attempt to keep Raphael on for a day of hawking. They spent a leisurely morning on his favorite open porch, wrapped in silk blankets against the winter chill, playing chess and talking with Vera and Léna, but Raphael was eager to get on the road and find Percival. It was a conflicted eagerness, but it kept him from accepting any of the distractions Frederick offered to tempt him with—riding, hunting, a feast, a tour of the menagerie, a display by a famous troupe of acrobats. Vera, of course, was stoically indifferent to all temptations. Raphael admired, and envied, her unrelenting purposefulness. Having received their assignment, she saw no reason to do anything but begin to follow it.

"But you are no fun at all," Frederick complained, when Raphael politely declined to watch a performance by Frederick's famed collection of dancing girls. "And here I had told Ferenc to expect someone from my sinful youth. Ferenc!" he called to the young blonde man, who had been some dozen paces from the Emperor every moment they had been here. "Come finally and meet my friends."

The young man left his position by one of the columns, walked to them smartly, and snapped to attention. He gave Raphael an extremely formal salute in greeting, an almost angry expression on his face, so focused was he on proper behavior.

"Drop that, Ferenc," Frederick said with an affectionate chuckle. "They're friends. We may be free of all court frippery in their company."

The young man visibly relaxed, and a brightness slid across his face that Raphael had not expected. He went down on one knee and clasped Raphael's hand between his own. "I am honored to meet you, sir," he said, in a voice of simple sincerity. Releasing Raphael's hand, he took Vera's. "And you as well, lady. I hope to be worthy of your regard."

Vera, uncharacteristically, grinned. "You," she informed him in a friendly tone, "are very nearly what one might call dashing."

"That's my influence, of course," said Frederick.

Frederick sent Ferenc to the stables with orders to saddle up fast horses and see them equipped with light saddlebags, food, and gold. Then he called for his steward and chamberlain, who brought out to the porch a waxen stamp that Frederick presented to Raphael. This would allow them to change horses at the imperial post stables as far as the sea, and assured them passage westward to Narbonne.

When Ferenc returned to announce that the horses were ready, the Emperor and Léna went with them through the gardens and past the armory to the stables. As they approached the open-sided end of the wooden building, a half-dozen grooms scurried into the mounting area and stood at attention, forming a loose semicircle. Ferenc brought the horses out to two mounting blocks and, after a tap on their brow-bands, gave them their heads. They did not move. He joined the arc of grooms.

"So," said Frederick, holding his arms out for a farewell embrace. "This has been too brief a visit but I trust that when you return, you may linger."

Raphael nodded his head slightly, his expression noncommittal. "As my comrade requests," he said. He turned toward the mounting block where the horse awaited, then paused and turned back to face Frederick. "All that you require of us is to bring back intelligence of the situation at Montségur?"

Frederick nodded.

"And there is nothing else to be said between us before we depart?"

The emperor made a strange face, as if squelching amusement. "Actually, Léna has a minor item to take up with you."

Léna grimaced, in a way that appeared to Raphael to be almost apologetic. He felt the hair on the back of his neck shiver. She stepped toward him and said, in a low voice, "The sprig must stay here."

Raphael felt a wave of panic. "What?" he demanded, and on reflex reached toward the little bag on the chain around his neck. He stopped himself and forced his hand to stay at his side.

"The little sprig of wood that my kin-sisters inform me you have been traveling with. It won't be safe in Montségur."

"I don't know what you're talking about," said Raphael, fighting off a sudden cold sweat.

"It needs to stay here, to guarantee that you will actually return."

It felt as if his stomach had flipped over. Willing himself to stay calm, he glanced at his friend. "What is she talking about, Frederick?" he asked, his voice a quarter-octave higher than normal. Out of the corner of his eye he saw Vera frown at Léna.

Frederick huffed expansively, held his arms out, and glanced heavenward. "The little piece of wood? I have no idea, I assure you. However, I do want to ensure you will return here, and I approve of her strategy of holding something of yours hostage to guarantee your return."

"I've given you my word that I'll return," Raphael protested. "Do you not trust me, my lord? Frederick? You require a ransom of a friend?"

"To indulge a woman's fancy," said Frederick. "Even wise women sometimes have fancies."

"This is not a request," Léna said gently. "I am informing you that it is staying here."

"I don't know what you're talking about and you can't have it," Raphael said, in a desperate tone.

"Oh, well done," Vera muttered sardonically.

Raphael took a breath to steady himself. He kept both hands gripping his sword-belt to keep from reaching on reflex for the chain around his neck. His color high, his eyes focused slightly away from Léna, he said sternly, "I do not know or understand your kind as well as I would like to. I do not condemn you as witches, but I do not understand how you can know anything about what you speak of. Certainly you cannot know more about it than I do—which is almost nothing."

"All I need to know is that it's important to you, so I want it, here, as insurance that you will come back to give His Majesty your intelligence report," she said reasonably.

"You can't have it," Raphael said decisively.

"Too late for that," said Léna. "We've already got it."

Raphael felt his face pale. His left hand flew to his chest; there was something in the little bag, but in his sudden anxiety he could not tell if it had the right weight and shape.

Suddenly Frederick's face broke into a grin. "We got it from you overnight," he said, sounding like a boy delighted with himself for getting away with a prank. "Ferenc took it right off you while you slept. He has *tremendous* promise, that boy."

Raphael was speechless.

"He replaced it with a little wooden button that was the nose on one of my dolls when I was a child. You can keep that," Frederick said indulgently. "Someday it will be worth a fortune. Go on, open the bag, take a look at it!" Frederick, who had come of age in a street gang in the alleys of Sicily, had a hearty demeanor that made Raphael feel stodgier than a scholar.

Trying to collect himself, Raphael pointedly turned away from the Emperor and called to Ferenc, "Lad, you said you wanted to be worthy of my regard. I'll tell you how—return my property to me at once, and beg pardon for having robbed me."

"He performed at his emperor's command," Frederick said, abruptly sobering. "You will not seek satisfaction from him. And he no longer has the thing."

"May I have my property back, please, Your Majesty?" said Raphael through gritted teeth. "It was entrusted to me by an elder of my order, and I promised him I would not part with it."

"You will get it back when you return," said Frederick, in a voice that brooked no argument.

"I am offended," said Raphael.

"I am *impressed*," said Vera unexpectedly. "In fact, I'd like to bring the fellow with us. We can surely use somebody of such dexterity."

Léna folded her hands together. "I was so hoping you would see it that way. His saddlebag is packed, and there is a horse geared up for him waiting in the barn." She glanced behind Frederick to the grooms and men-at-arms standing silently at attention. "Come, Ferenc. You are going with these warriors to Montségur."

CHAPTER 12:

THE ANGEL IN THE WINDOW

Before retiring, Peire-Roger called for a volunteer to take a message to the Count of Toulouse before dawn. Ocyrhoe instantly put herself forward. Something about the new arrival unnerved her, and she wanted to get away from him.

As usual, she took the cup with her. Privately she believed the ineffable strangeness of it protected her from being caught—although she had not had it with her on patrol the night before, and nothing ill had come of it. Rixenda, who like all Cathars did not believe in talismans, found it a strange and cumbersome talisman indeed but had ceased to comment on it many months ago.

By the time the sun rose the next morning to singe the frost, Ocyrhoe was down the mountain and miles north of the army camp. Her errand took her not into Toulouse itself, but to an outlying village halfway between Montségur and the walls of the city. Here she would meet with a Credent, to exchange information between the Count of Toulouse and Peire-Roger.

Peire-Roger was waiting for the Count to send men to Montségur (although where they would sleep, Ocyrhoe could not imagine; it was tight enough quarters already). The Count could not openly send men to defend the fortress, as he had been forced to swear to the King of France that he would send men to *attack* the fortress. He had made this oath both in order to keep his title and to have the curse of excommunication lifted from his soul. He retained his title, but until he actually showed up with troops to destroy the heretics, he was going to remain an excommunicate.

There was virtually no need for subterfuge in this meeting. Almost everyone in the village was sympathetic to the Cathar cause, and the few who weren't had left to fight with the King of France, hoping they would eventually be rewarded with their heretical neighbors' farms and properties.

Her contact was the nondescript wife of a toothless, grinning ironsmith. He was a very savvy man who came across as witless, a quality Ocyrhoe admired greatly and even enjoyed. The visit was brief, with no real news on either side. The Count had heard a rumor that Pope Innocent was going to reprieve his excommunication; Peire-Roger would appreciate as much charcoal as could be spirited up the mountain, and he recommended the tunnels as the best means of transport.

There were natural tunnels curving and meandering all through the limestone mountain range. Several of these led from the eastern edge of Montségur up to the fortress. The smallest—so small only Ocyrhoe could navigate it—led up from the south side of the mountain. Any tunnel trek was a long, damp, unpleasant trip, and required lots of candles; any other light source caused so much smoke it choked whoever was trying to ascend. Ocyrhoe, having a very bad association with tunnels from her days in Rome, avoided these when possible, even when the gods sent sleet.

She was fed a lunch of bread and stewed mutton, the mutton being an extraordinary indulgence and a strong incentive to offer to run this errand. She accepted a new, woolen wrap from the wife, intending to wear it for the trip home but then give it to Rixenda for warmth. The days were very short now and there was no moon, but Ocyrhoe planned her trip so that she would arrive at the foot of Montségur just as the sun was setting.

On the way she passed by several villages and farmsteads. Most people either took no notice of her or knew who she was—she had been in the area two years now and been a regular messenger for his lordship since before the siege began in May. So, generally, she traveled with a simple indifference to whomever she met, at least this far from the camp.

Today, however, something felt different. She was thirsty and near a farmstead she knew, so decided she would stop in to pay her respects, fill her waterskin, and see if there was any useful gossip to bring back to the fortress.

As she approached the simple hut that was the central farmhouse, she heard voices and saw figures moving in agitation through the open door. She paused. Perhaps it would be better to listen for a moment before making her presence known. She slipped over to the right side of the building, where a small window was covered with vellum, and listened.

"We know there is a secret path," said a voice with a local accent. The speaker sounded reasonable, but forceful. "This standoff will last forever if something does not change."

"It won't last forever. Winter's coming and eventually the damned French will have to pack up and go home," said a voice. Ocyrhoe grinned despite herself—it was Ferrer, the older of the two men who had nabbed her as a supposed spy two years ago and had brought her to Montségur. "We are happy to replenish the fortress, while the army has no easy way to replenish itself."

"That's my very point," said the stranger. "We all have loved ones up in Montségur. All of us. Every local man in the army here knows somebody up there. None of us want to be here, and none of us want the French whoresons to win."

"Then desert!" said another voice—Ferrer's young friend Artal.

"And be hanged?" said the stranger. "And leave my children fatherless? What does that accomplish? It is much easier to give those bastards my forty days of service, sitting around scratching my arse in the camp, and then pack up and go home. But there were others here before me, and others will come to take my place. The army is not going to give up and go home. The French king has too much riding on this siege."

"It's one fucking mountain fortress," said another voice, irritably. "There's about a hundred men-at-arms in there. How could it possibly be worth the amount of energy and manpower he is wasting on it?"

"It *stands for* far more than that," said Ferrer. "I do understand that. But because it does, I cannot believe you are exhorting us, Vidal, to betray our people."

"It would end the siege. There would be a short battle, and then surrender, and this nightmare would be over."

"And our loved ones destroyed," said Ferrer.

"Far more than that will be destroyed if you don't give them up," Vidal warned sharply. "Do you think the King of France is going to provide for his troops by sending food all the way from Isle de France? When his troops are surrounded by fruitful farmland? If this siege does not end by Christmas, I warn you: The army, even conscripted men like me, will be raiding storage barns and taking livestock for many days' ride in all directions. There has already been pillaging."

At this, a loud chorus of annoyed agreement; the room was full of men.

"And so," Vidal continued, "I am begging you, as your countryman, for the collective good: Help us to get up there. Reveal the path, or the tunnel. Guide us. Betray the few to save the many. Your children's children will still be suffering if this is not resolved soon."

"It is dishonorable to betray their trust," said Ferrer.

"It's more dishonorable to starve the families who are not hiding up there, living off our largesse," said another voice. "Before the siege, I gave Peire-Roger my forty days of service, but since May there has not been one single day where some of my efforts have not gone to helping a few hundred heretics up on that hill. I've given far more than forty days to him. I am suffering here on my own farm more than he is in that fortress."

Hearty agreement on that. Ocyrhoe felt her heart thudding. Her fingers, resting against the mud wall of the building, trembled briefly from more than mere cold. She recognized the voices of many within. All of them knew the hidden ways up the mountain. Even if she fled home now and warned Peire-Roger of the danger— even if every possible entrance was shored up against invasion— how would they ever get new supplies in? How would they ever know if the reliable farmer was still the reliable farmer, or the latest informant? *Please*, she prayed, *please let these men choose wisely.*

For a few moments, everyone inside seemed to be talking at once. There was loud disagreement, which gradually turned to a grudging consensus. The one holdout was Ferrer, who insisted they were disgraceful.

"I promise you," Vidal said, above the hubbub, which quieted to hear him. "I promise you that if help us to get into the fortress, we will keep violence to a minimum, and only among the men-at-arms. All women and children will be spared, and all Good Ones will be allowed to leave the area unharmed and to practice elsewhere."

"Why should we believe you, when for decades…"

"This is different," Vidal insisted. "We are you. We are your kinsmen. We will do this without the French king or the archbishop even knowing. It is a local militia I come to represent, not Hugue de Arcis or Pierre Amelii. You all know me. You know my father and my brothers and my sons. And I know yours. We will go into the fortress. We will get everyone out of there. And then—only then—will we alert the army that there is victory. If it happens in any other manner, you may tear me limb from limb with your own hands."

There was a rumble of supportive grunts; Ocyrhoe's fingers were so tense they started cramping. These men were about to march out of this building straight along her path of travel and show Vidal how to get into the fortress. She had no idea if Vidal was an honorable man or not, but the tribal loyalty she'd developed over the last two years made it impossible for her to stay mute.

An impulse overwhelmed her, born of fear. Without thinking about what she was doing, she reached into her satchel and grabbed the cup. It was glowing, more brightly than usual, as if it fed off of her desperation. With an agility that surprised her, she hefted herself up onto the narrow external sill, and then hurled herself against the vellum that was nailed over the window.

The men in the room yelled in shock as suddenly the window-covering imploded inward, bringing light, cold, and a small ferocious figure brandishing a mysterious light source. They instinctively herded together at one end of the room. Ocyrhoe knew the power of a mob, however small: she had no more than a heartbeat to convince them not to attack her.

"Men of Toulouse!" she shouted, shaking her left fist high in the air at them. Immediately the room silenced and all eyes in the room went to her fist. They were staring at the cup. She wondered what they saw as they were looking at it. She thought of Father Rodrigo, wielding the cup outside the ruin of the Coliseum in Rome, and prayed she was not about to succumb to his madness. "You must not betray the Good Ones. They are the symbol of who you are as a people! Already this land has survived decades of rape and pillage, of crops being destroyed and livestock slaughtered, or vineyards torn up and orchards despoiled. Your father and your grandfathers survived all of that and never thought of giving in—that is why you are here today, proud strong men that you are! And will you, now, at the moment that the Good Ones need you most, will you throw that heritage away to avoid one measly winter's worth of inconvenience? What would the rightful lords of Carcassonne say if they knew you were doing anything to help the French imposter in power there now? Do! Not! Betray! Your! People!"

By now her eyes had adjusted to the dimness of the room; the window vellum was ripped open behind her and low-slanting, afternoon sunlight was spilling onto the faces of the half-score men she was scolding. They could not see her face, as she was backlit by the sun-filled window, so she could examine them as she spoke. Their faces were uniformly astounded. All of them were familiar to her except one fair-haired man dressed as a soldier. This must be Vidal.

"And you!" she said fiercely, pointing the cup accusingly at him. "You are the greatest sinner in here! How dare you exhort your countrymen to turn on their own! You do not deserve to be considered a citizen by any of these men! They should foreswear you as a kinsman and a neighbor. If you truly believe you are helping anyone but the French with this plan, then the French have made an ass of you. Is your kinswoman not among the Credents up there?" That was a wild guess but his alarmed face revealed she had hit the mark. "You say that they will all be released to safety, but what do you really think will happen to them? What future is there for the young women other than to be married off to one of those brutish French soldiers as a war prize? You are a disgrace to this land. You should desert the army and offer up your limp sword, for whatever good it's worth, to the service of the Good Ones of Montségur!"

She had started with no plan, and she did not know what to do next. She shook the cup again, and then with a prayer to the gods of acrobatics, she turned around, jumped up into the small open space of the window, fell to the ground, and quickly rolled around to the back of the small building. She knew this property well enough. From here it was a quick dash to the chicken coop—no, that would not work; the hens would raise a fuss. Same with the horses in the stables, although horses sometimes listened to her. She darted past the chicken coop and threw herself face forward onto the ground, sliding under the lower rail of the gate.

The stable was empty; the men's horses were all ground-tied outside on the other side of the building. They snorted when the dust kicked up from her unnecessarily dramatic move, but otherwise, they ignored her.

She caught her breath and looked at the cup. It was not glowing. It was just a tarnished silver cup. "That was interesting," she muttered, and put it back into the satchel at her waist.

Nobody came near the stable. If there was argument in the house, or even discussion, she could not hear it over the pounding of her pulse in her ears. Finally, after a wait long enough to count to 500, she stood up and looked over the upper rails of the stable. The men were outside of the house, walking stupidly about looking up into the sky and sometimes toward the horizon. Not one of them was glancing toward the stable. Not one of them seemed to think the strange interloper might be on the premises.

How annoying. She might have been able to leave on foot and never be noticed.

After a few moments, Ferrer called them all together, and they went back inside to confer. Once they were safely out of sight, she climbed over the stable-railing. She briefly considered taking one of the horses, but if they thought she was angelic, it was best not to ruin the impression. She took off at a jog back toward Montségur.

Because of her own role in what had just happened—no, because of the cup's role—she could not tell anyone about it.

She trusted that Ferrer, who was an alarmist, would alert Peire-Roger if he felt there was any lurking danger.

❖ ❖ ❖

Ocyrhoe avoided the new knight. She was glad he was there—indeed she felt some pride for having found him and brought him home. But the earnest glow of his handsome face alarmed her. The light in his eyes reminded her of Father Rodrigo when his madness was upon him. Not that there was anything about Percival that implied a lack of reason. He was more civilized in his demeanor than almost anyone else in the fortress, lords and ladies included.

But even that was strange, given the vague references to his past. He had traveled all the way to the land of the Mongols' leader and come back to speak of it. He had traveled through the ruins of the worst of the Mongols' atrocities closer to home. He lived in the wild and killed without conscience, for he believed with a gentle simplicity that the world was made of Good and Bad, and since he was Good, whoever he brought down was Bad.

Or something like that. Because she kept a distance from him, she was not sure of the details. Once or twice she eavesdropped on his conversation at dinner—he was usually surrounded by the more properly raised female denizens, who all were moonishly attracted to him. They did not have the common sense to be wary of that gleam in his eye.

Two days after the farmhouse adventure, Ocyrhoe and Rixenda were helping the Goodmen tidy the smithy in the eastern end of the courtyard; the smiths were eagerly awaiting the large delivery of charcoal they had been promised from the Count of Toulouse. Scouts on the tower had seen a transport coming from the north, disappearing into a nearby valley which had entry to one of the tunnels. It would be close to an hour before whatever was in the transport made it up to the fortress. Ocryhoe made a mental note of that and then forgot about it.

Until she heard Rixenda shouting.

On impulse she ducked around the corner of the smithy, and stared nervously toward the northern gate. There was a group of men, red-faced and breathing hard from exertion, all holding bundles of charcoal in their arms; there also was Rixenda, her arms clasped around Vidal.

Civilians came to the door of the keep and then began pouring into the yard to great the charcoal-bearers. Percival, just relieved from garrison duty on the wall, came down into the increasingly crowded courtyard. He was tall enough to see the newcomers over the crowd, and he remained apart, watching. Behind the wave of women and children, Peire-Roger rushed out of the donjon, his face as angry and suspicious as ever.

Rixenda's face glistened with tears. "This is my nephew!" she called out to Peire-Roger as he approached. "He has deserted the French army to join us!"

Peire-Roger cleared his throat, which he had the ability to do very loudly and unattractively in a manner that commanded the immediate attention of the entire courtyard.

"Fellow," he said.

Vidal bowed briefly. Then he went down on one knee and bowed his head. He still wore his soldier's uniform, and his left hand moved to his empty sword-belt, unaccustomed to being unarmed. "My lord," he said.

"What am I to make of this change of heart? It seems a suspiciously convenient way to…"

"My nephew would not do that!" Rixenda interrupted.

"My lord, I asked to be blindfolded to come up here," Vidal said peaceably, head still bowed. "I cannot get in or out of this place on my own. I do not wish to. There was an angel came to the valley and showed me the error of my ways."

Good Heavens, thought Ocyrhoe, and took a few cautious steps into the courtyard. She felt exposed, although she knew he could not possibly have seen the features of her face with the light in the window behind her.

"What angel?" Peire-Roger said scornfully.

"A beautiful young woman appeared suddenly in a farmhouse where I was trying to compel the locals to give away your secret paths," said Vidal.

Ocyrhoe grinned despite herself. She very nearly giggled.

"She held in her hand a chalice of pure gold," continued Vidal emotionally. "It shone like the sun glinting on diamonds. She held it out to me, and a ray of light careened off the chalice and pierced me through the heart and awakened me to the light, and I repented the wickedness of my ways."

Ocyrhoe turned away and ran back into the smithy, shoving her knuckles into her mouth to keep from squealing. This was both hilarious and terrifying.

"And then she vanished!" she heard Vidal continue. "We all saw it, all of us! Once we had calmed ourselves from our amazement, we compared stories and indeed we all saw exactly the same thing. One moment she was there and suddenly she was not. It was a miracle. She was an angel. And she did me the great honor of appearing to prevent my evil. At her request, I am devoting my life to the fierce defense of Montségur."

From the smithy, she could see Percival, a look of rapt astonishment on his face. He peered around the courtyard, and Ocyrhoe was irrationally certain that he was seeking her. She ducked back into the smithy. "Damn all visions," she muttered to herself.

CHAPTER 13:

THE BIRTH OF A RUMOR

An hour later, Ocyrhoe was sitting on her bedroll, shivering, staring in distress at the dull silver cup on her lap.

Rixenda entered the tiny hut. She took a single step and was beside Ocyrhoe. She knelt. Gently she placed one hand on Ocyrhoe's shoulder, and the other she rested on the bowl of the cup.

"It was you," she said.

Ocyrhoe nodded, still shaken. "But it wasn't like that, it wasn't how he described it. I jumped in the window and I jumped back out the window. The sunlight caught the rim of the cup, that's all."

"Imagination is a very powerful tool," said Rixenda. "It is usually used for nefarious purposes—like the invention of heaven and hell, the hoax of holy rituals, the farce of marriage vows. But sometimes, happily, accidentally, it can be useful."

"I'm glad he's here," said Ocyrhoe. "And I'm very glad the others did not reveal the paths or the tunnels. But I don't want that kind of power. I don't understand it."

"And you think it is in the cup?" Rixenda's tone made it clear she herself did not believe this.

"The cup is a part of it," Ocyrhoe said. "But I did not create the power in the cup. Somebody else did. I don't think I should destroy it. I just don't want it anymore."

Rixenda chuckled. "There are greedy fools enough in this world ready to take whatever you would cast away."

Ocyrhoe looked at her. "But something so powerful?"

"Things are powerful only if you believe in their power."

Ocyrhoe laughed bitterly. "Sometimes things are powerful whether you want them so or not."

"Mmm," Rixenda said. "Thunderstorms, for instance. I am glad the season for them is over."

A pause.

"I will not tell anyone about it," said Rixenda. "I am sure Peire-Roger and the others do not even recall what you had with you when you first came. I'd forgotten myself until I saw you just now. I believe the cup has no power. Whenever you would like to start believing that with me, you will be very welcome. In the meantime, let it sit idly in here."

◆ ◆ ◆

The rumors became so rampant and exaggerated that Archbishop Pierre Amelii put on all of his ecclesial finery and appeared in the pavilion that was used for morning mass among the locals. There was no danger the French would be moved by the outrageous stories, although the Gascony men might fall prey, and certainly the overimaginative and romantic Provencals.

Dietrich, who had been the first knight to hear the story directly, had marveled at its rapid growth, and was heartily interested to hear how the uninspiring, upright archbishop would tamp down the sense of the marvelous.

"There has been a story circulating among the local population, especially among those of you who are here serving your feudal duties," the archbishop intoned, without any greeting. "A story that is clearly a product of the heretics' wiles. Do you know what story I speak of?"

A pause while about a third of the congregants sheepishly muttered among themselves.

In a louder voice, the tall, stern figure lectured, "I speak of the heretical lie that an angel came down among you and spoke to a weak-willed local soldier, who abandoned his vows to his feudal lord and turned himself over to the heretical cause. I am not saying the soldier did not commit such an objectionable act. But only the devil in disguise would exhort a good Catholic to violate his holy obligations to his feudal lord, which are as sacrosanct in the eyes of God as those of the clergy to the church. Any angel, any *true angel*, coming down from heaven to mix among us, would, by *definition*, speak only *angelic* words, and such words would intrinsically lead the hearer toward the kingdom of heaven. And the kingdom of heaven can only be achieved by uprightness and steadfastness and loyalty. I challenge any good Christian in this room to explain how a soldier can abjure his responsibility to his lord and yet remain upright and steadfast and loyal? How can such a thing be? Can you give me an example?"

Nobody spoke.

"Then I thank you all for acknowledging the obvious truth of what I am saying. One of your comrades has been deceived by an agent of Satan. Do you understand what that means?" He took a luxuriant pause. "It means this cause is so important to Lucifer that he himself is showing up to defend his believers! This is the most lackluster army I have ever heard of. You act as if this cause were a farce, as if your presence here was nothing but a tiresome obligation you cannot wait to be done with. Do not deny it. I know your thoughts as I know the thoughts of all sinners. But this, this *event*, surely proves to you what an immensely significant danger we are up against! We are fighting the agents of Lucifer!

This may be the most important holy war in the history of mankind!" His eyes were wide and the wrinkles in the back of his neck compressed as his chin and neck jutted out with tension.

Dietrich looked away; the histrionics embarrassed him. He believed in the Devil, but he did not believe the story that was circulating through this part of the camp had any connection to the Devil at all.

However, it intrigued him that such an upset would happen immediately after the arrival of a member of the Shield-Brethren—who were, inarguably, heathen. It was coincidence, perhaps; but perhaps not.

And the story in itself, dripping with religious significance, might be of interest to His Holiness. So when His Eminence Pierre Amelii had finished his exhortation, Dietrich went back to his tent, back to his desk, and wrote a new dispatch for Pope Innocent.

CHAPTER 14:

MARE NOSTRUM

Ferenc sat wrapped in his sleeping blanket in the middle of the boat, starting straight up at the cold blue of heaven. Reverentially, he fingered the slender, braided bracelet around his left wrist. He had almost come to consider it a talisman, the only thing that eased his physical wretchedness.

He had survived the battle of Mohi, one of the worst atrocities committed by the Mongols upon their conquered. He had been nearly crushed beneath the gruesome corpse of an enemy who'd almost killed him. Being stuck on a boat for a week was nowhere near as horrific, but it was easily worse than anything else in living memory.

His stomach was constantly moving in the wrong direction, and so was everything else. His innards were tied into knots, and he had almost no control over his own limbs when he tried to walk. For nearly a week he'd felt possessed by a malevolent spirit who used him as a toy. He knew that Vera suffered from the same symptoms he did, but she was astonishingly stoic about it—standing silent and grim, until suddenly she would turn and retch over the side of the boat, then turn back expressionless, as if nothing had happened. He could not follow her example; he felt misery oozing out of his pores. Raphael made a brew for them both, of mint and pennyroyal and other herbs. It helped a little, but only immediately after they had eaten.

At night they slept in cramped quarters below, sailors and passengers together. This created some heat, which was helpful, but the whole placed reeked of disinfectant vinegar. In contrast, dawn till dusk was freezing raw, the wind unrelenting and sticky, every surface damp, and the sailors the most sour-faced, superstitious lot Ferenc had ever encountered. Even though the ship was in Frederick's pay, it cost them extra coin because the sailors did not want to sail with a woman on board. When Ferenc first walked onto the boat, he had unthinkingly stepped with his left foot. This had distressed the crew so much that the pilot had ordered him to go back to the dock. His gear was brought up from below and given back to him, and he was instructed to pray forgiveness to Our Lady, Star of the Sea, as well as Saint Nicholas, before carrying his baggage on board, right foot first.

"Is that human hair?" asked Vera. Ferenc startled, returned his gaze to the deck, and clumsily covered his wrist with his other hand; he forgot she had been sitting next to him. For a moment, he had forgotten he was even in the boat.

"It is human hair," he said carefully, without moving his hand.

Vera calmly but forcefully moved his hand out of the way and brought his wrist closer to her face so she could examine the bracelet in the sunlight. "Those are knots," she said.

"Yes," he said, feeling strangely defensive.

"A gift? Or a prize?"

He bit his lip. "Definitely not a prize."

"From Léna?" she asked in a meaningful tone of voice. "Or some other Binder?"

"Not from Léna," he said. He snatched his arm back as his stomach lurched in the opposite direction of the ocean—which should have been impossible, since the ocean was lurching in all directions at once.

Raphael moved about the ship as comfortably as the sailors did, lightly grasping lines and bulwarks; he seemed, perversely, to enjoy the bounding of the ship into the waves. The two of them watched him approach from the stern, contentment on his wind-slapped face.

"There is an unnatural elasticity to the umbilical cord between Raphael and Mother Earth," said Ferenc. To his surprise, Vera chortled beside him.

"You're more eloquent than me," she said. "I tell him he looks like somebody waiting to get pitched over the side."

He had reached them. Rubbing his salt-sticky, cold-chafed hands together as if he were about to announce a festival, Raphael settled himself onto the boards beside Vera. "You two look bored beyond tears," he said.

"Not at all," said Vera. "At least dry heaves give us some exercise. You have nothing to distract you at all."

Raphael smiled slightly. "I'm glad you can keep this in perspective, Vera. I'm glad for your sake it isn't raining. What do you two talk about to pass the time as you stare up into the heavens here amidships?"

"We have been discussing the Apollonian versus Dionysian qualities of certain individuals," said Ferenc, on impulse.

Vera gave him a strange look, but Raphael's reaction was the one that interested him.

Raphael smiled and nodded. "You are Frederick's creature, indeed," he said. "How do I rate? Apollo or Dionysus?"

"Apollo. Almost everyone Frederick surrounds himself with is Apollonian, so that he can indulge in being Dionysian," said Ferenc.

"What is that?" Vera demanded. In a rare show of emotion, she looked irked at being excluded from the conversation.

"The Emperor is enamored of a dead culture," said Ferenc. "The Greeks. He likes their thinkers, their gods, their stories. In some of those stories there are two gods, Apollo and Dionysus."

"They are not dead," said Raphael. "They've just been lying quietly for a while. They embody two elements of man's behavior. Apollo represents righteousness, justice, and abiding by the law. He is self-awareness and containment. Dionysus is just the opposite. He is about emotion, impulse, humor, and irrational impulses."

Vera frowned. "The Emperor has to be Apollo or his rule is faulty."

Raphael and Ferenc both shook their heads. "Frederick grew up in the streets of Palermo," Raphael said. "He was virtually an orphan. He belonged to a street gang. Many of his qualities are born of impulse and intuition as much as strategy and reason."

"Also," Ferenc volunteered, "Dionysus is tricky, and so is Frederick."

"Ah," said Vera.

"Apollo isn't tricky," Ferenc went on. "It's not in his nature. And he isn't always kind. He's too strong to understand the need to be kind. All of us have a little of both—that's what the Greeks say, and Frederick likes to categorize people by how Apollonian or Dionysian they are. The useful ones, his favorites, lean toward Apollo."

"Including Léna?" asked Raphael.

Ferenc nodded, stroking the bracelet at his wrist. "Léna is *very* much Apollo. I know she is a good person. And so I trust her. I know she will always do the *right* thing, but often that does not mean the *best* thing."

"That makes absolutely no sense," said Vera.

"I think he means in comparison to the Emperor," Raphael said. "Frederick will *not* always do the right thing."

"Yes, exactly," said Ferenc. "But at least I understand *why* Frederick does what he does. Léna is mysterious. She sees more than Frederick, but she does not always tell him everything she sees."

"And how would you know that?" Raphael asked slyly. "Who are you to be in a position to judge these things?"

Ferenc pursed his lips. His mother was a Binder, but he did not want to tell them that; it was personal and they had not earned the right to know. Certainly there were times he knew in his gut that he understood Léna more clearly than even His Majesty did, although His Majesty was surely a hundred times more intelligent than Ferenc himself.

"I am nobody," he said. "But I will tell you what I think, if you're interested. If Léna says your friend is in Montségur, then he is probably in Montségur. Whether she knows that from her Binder sisters, or from second sight, or some other source, I can't say, but if she says it with confidence it is probably true. And if she says you should go there and take him away, that is also probably true. However, that doesn't mean she isn't using you as pawns for something else."

Raphael took this in without surprise. "You are saying she doesn't lie by commission but she might lie by omission."

"Yes," said Ferenc. "She does that not uncommonly. She always does it for a good reason—certainly what she believes to be a good reason—but I still don't like it. To me it feels as if she is breaking rules of human conduct I never thought of as rules until I realized I did not like to watch her break them."

Then he felt sick and empty from speaking too much. He clapped his hand protectively over the bracelet, and rested his forehead on his arm, wishing he could sleep until they reached Narbonne.

CHAPTER 15:

THE WEARY SHEPHERD

"You may tell the Wonder of the World," said His Holiness Innocent IV, "that if he would only start building churches instead of governmental buildings, I might consider his plea for pardon." He pretended to examine his nails a moment, then glanced up coldly at Pero della Vigna and Taddeo da Suessa, Imperial legates. They stood before him, well-dressed, exhausted, dusty noblemen, in the smallest receiving chamber in the Lateran Palace. The room was cold and not well lit; no libations had been offered them, and they had been kept waiting several hours since their arrival.

Innocent, in the full regalia of his office, had eaten a leisurely meal, relieved himself, warmed his hands by the fire, and then entered unannounced, settling on the room's only chair. He was well rested and resplendent in white, gold, and red silk, the papal tiara glinting over his mitre, the papal ring on one ring finger, Gregory IX's more personal ring on the other. "Frederick was not excommunicated without reason," he continued. "He already knows exactly the terms for the censure to be lifted. He must build a few churches, to at least create the appearance of devoutness."

"I assure you His Majesty is very devout," said della Vigna fervently, from his knees. "Else why would he have sworn to call a new crusade?"

"It is not enough for him to call it; he must actually enact it," said Innocent impatiently. "If you are scribing the next draft of a proposed treaty between his court and mine, let it reflect that. I will not negotiate on that end. He has treasure enough. He might put his resources to glorifying Our Lord, rather than to caretaking the unorthodox collection of wild beasts he insists on lugging around with him for sport."

"What else may we report?" asked da Suessa, the dispassionate one. He held a stub of lead and vellum scroll. "Your Holiness requires churches built, and a crusade. Other demands? I am sure His Majesty will want to know your position on the Lombard lands."

Innocent hissed slightly. "We will address that when we meet face to face next year. For now let it rest that he must show in earnest that he would build a church and summon pilgrims to the holy land. Do not bother me again until there is evidence of these achievements. Remind him that his subjects in the east blame him for the Mongolian invasion, or at least, for their not being protected from it. You are dismissed. You may stay in the guest dormitories for the night. My steward is just outside the door. He will see to the arrangements."

He held out his right hand for them to kiss the ring, but already his attention was distracted. He did not even notice them leave; his eyes were boring into the dark corner of the receiving room. From the hidden door, his spymaster Rufus was waiting quietly for a private audience. Innocent shook his head once—there were other messengers to be received openly. The man sank deeper into the shadows made behind a hanging silk tapestry depicting Our Lord in His Passion.

There were no messages from the east, from the lands where the Mongols still claimed control. Despite his cutting comment to Frederick's men, Innocent was painfully aware that the flamboyant upheaval between Church and Emperor had distracted both from protecting the eastern flank of the Catholic world, and too many true believers had lost their lives to the heathen marauders. He had not been pope during the worst of that, but he had been the most powerful man in the College of Cardinals, and in retrospect he recognized a missed opportunity: The feud over Lombardy could have been played out hundreds of miles to the east and north, with both Frederick's troops and those of the Vatican defending the undefended of Catholicism. It had not occurred to either man to turn his attention there. And now thousands of Catholic souls were lost to purgatory, the unrest in Lombardy remained completely unresolved, and both Church and Crown were condemned by much of Christendom as indifferent patriarchs to their suffering children.

All in all, he was glad there were no messages from the east. That front was exhausting.

Toward the other end of the Catholic world were different heathens to attend to. He was waiting to hear how things went in Toulouse. The King of France was using the Archbishop of Narbonne as an excuse to take over Occitania, symbolized by the tiny mountain fortress, Montségur. Dietrich of the Livonian Order was Innocent's agent there, but had reported little beyond what a waste of human energy and resources the whole thing seemed to him. Privately, Innocent agreed with that assessment. But it was not convenient to upset the King of France by demanding he call off his attack, and so Innocent remained silent on it.

When all the messengers had left, he nodded again toward the darkness behind the curtain. The spymaster stepped forward into the room. He paused, and a strained look passed between the two men.

The spymaster shook his head once, grim. Innocent cursed under his breath. He resented receiving Rufus when Rufus had no news.

The week he was enthroned, Innocent had taken three men out of the general circulation of intrigue and given them the full-time assignment of finding the girl with the cup. One shadowed the emperor's court in Cremona; one moved south toward Sicily; one was working his way northward in the unlikely case Frederick had sent her to his German dominions. He had carefully separated them from the spies who were watching Frederick for other reasons. Now, months later, they had all sent first reports that happened to arrive in a single week. None of them had any leads at all. She was a better Binder than he'd given her credit for. She had completely vanished.

❖ ❖ ❖

After a miserable week on board, they landed at last in a seaport near Narbonne, and had the almost-as-miserable experience of learning to walk again.

Ferenc wobbled about the wooden docks of the port like a newborn foal, as the ship's freight was transferred to canal-barges to move up the Aude River. Vera and Raphael wobbled as well, although Raphael collected himself within moments and Vera, having survived the gangplank, simply chose not to walk while anyone could see her. Ferenc, however, lurched gamely about in front of everyone, ignoring the sneers and smirks of the sailors, who had been looking forward to this moment—a landlubber's first return to land was always good for a laugh.

Raphael still had Frederick's seal, which was not as powerful a tool here in Toulouse as it was within the Empire. But he also had Frederick's gold, and that worked everywhere. While Ferenc was still recovering his land-legs, Raphael had found local agents of His Majesty's and gotten three fresh horses and a day's supplies. He decided, due to the shortness of the day and to the nearness of sunset, that they would ride into the city, take a room in Narbonne, and then depart first thing in the morning. A day's brisk ride along the Aude would get them to Carcassonne. His Majesty had no agents there, but the Narbonne agent had reliable contacts for them, where they could rest safely and exchange horses for the final leg of the trip, a direct track to the southwest.

The days were very short now. The solstice was almost upon them; Ferenc could feel it in his blood without knowing the exact date. It was a relief to be back on solid ground.

❖ ❖ ❖

Still there was nothing from Rufus's sources, but today at least brought a first message from Dietrich in Montségur. It was written in Dietrich's own hand and sealed with his personal signet, not the papal signet of his clerk. That made it mildly intriguing.

"Greetings to His Holiness Innocent IV from your humble servant, Dietrich of the Livonian Order," it began. "Your Holiness, I write merely to alert you of an interesting and unexpected development in the army camp below Montségur. It has been brought to my attention that at least one member of the order of the Shield-Brethren has appeared in camp recently. He announced himself, spoke to the leader, Hugue de Arcis, and then immediately vanished. Nobody has been able to find him since. Given the heretical leanings of his entire order, I consider it possible that the *Ordo Militum Vindicis Intactae* have sent men here to protect the heretics on the mountain. I am familiar with their tactics and will, at your demand, readily take on the burden of uncovering them, if they are hidden among us, or leading a charge against them if God grants us a way up the mountain."

Dietrich, thought His Holiness with grim appreciation, had a tendency to look for trouble. His Holiness did not require any more trouble than was already brewing in other corners of Christendom.

His response was terse and simple:

"Thank you, my son, for alerting us to the possible presence of such insidious heretics within the ranks of our otherwise devout and Catholic troops. We are grateful for the presence of such wise and rational counsel as yours is, that will keep us informed of any suspicious developments. There is of course no need to alarm His Eminence Pierre Amelii, nor any of the secular leaders of the army of this danger. Keep eyes alert and lips closed, but keep ink and parchment at hand to write to us if the need arises."

◆ ◆ ◆

They knew Montségur would be surrounded by an army. As they drew nearer, they chose an oxcart path and trotted along as if they were travelers bound elsewhere. Because they were approaching the area from the northeast and the village was to the southwest of the mountain, they first encountered only the outlying dregs, in a sense, of the army: clusters of shabbily dressed local farmers and hunters using weapons loaned to them by the French stewards and bailiffs who acted as lieutenants. They were probably intended to form a loose ring all the way around the mountain, but from a distance they looked like a large gypsy caravan. If the point was to barricade the fortress from the world, that wasn't happening.

As the sun settled between higher peaks beyond Montségur, they reined in, contemplating the mountain and the men loitering around the foot of it. It would be dark soon, but the moon was nearly full. On the other hand, it would damn cold. "Let's head north toward Toulouse," Raphael said. "We'll need to camp tonight, but tomorrow we will find a village, and I am certain, sympathizers. They can smuggle us up to the top whenever they next bring supplies."

"I doubt there are many villages between here and Toulouse," said Ferenc. "And it's too cold to camp."

"It is not," said Vera. "You do not know what cold is."

"I think we should go up to the fortress, ourselves, tonight," Ferenc insisted.

"We cannot do that without assistance," said Raphael, patient and a little patronizing.

Ferenc offered his hand out over his horse's withers. "I wager you that I can find a way up there on my own."

"Ferenc, it is a wondrous thing to see how much Frederick has imprinted himself onto you. It is unfortunate that one of those qualities is his desire to bet on things. It is unbecoming in him and frankly ludicrous in you, as you have no wealth to wager with."

"I'll wager my dagger." Ferenc draped the reins over his horse's neck and clapped his left hand to his belt, reaching for the hilt.

"I don't need your dagger, and you do. Nothing is accomplished if I end up with your dagger because you fail to get us up the mountain before nightfall."

"I didn't say before nightfall," Ferenc retorted. "But if it offends your sensibilities, no need to wager." He lowered his extended hand. "I'll still do it."

"I do not think so," Vera added to the conversation. Her tone was almost apologetic.

Ferenc gave her a look of mock dismay. "After all we suffered through together on the boat, how can you lose your faith in me now, good lady?"

"Sentimentality will get you nowhere with the good lady," said Raphael.

"And Raphael would know," Vera said, not unsympathetically.

"Consider," said Ferenc. "Look around." They did so. They were still on the oxcart path, with the mountain's northern face exploding out of the hills a couple of bow-shots ahead to the left.

Ferenc pointed to a particular point on the steep slope. "There are ropes hanging down from the side of the mountain," he said. "Do you see where the shadow catches in a diagonal line? It's all scree below and sheer limestone above. That is where the ropes are lowered *to*. They are lowered *from*..." his middle finger gently traced an imaginary, subtle path in the dimming air, "...lowered from a point just below those terraces, where those little sheds are. I think there must be a natural well or trench or tunnel up on the mountainside. The ropes must be stored in there. And the men who lift the ropes up when they are freighted leverage themselves there somehow."

"You can see that?" demanded Vera, staring at the mountain. "Even with the sun in your eyes? Or you are guessing?"

"I can see enough to know my guess is correct," said Ferenc. He turned to Raphael. "What do you say I approach?"

Raphael shook his head. "You may be right, but they won't lower the ropes for you just because you've found the rope-lowering site. We need to demonstrate that we come in peace, that we are not with the French army. In any case, getting from here to there undetected after sunset will be difficult when we are on the outskirts of an army camp."

"I can do it," said Ferenc. "About a quarter-mile back we passed the opening to a cave—"

"We did?" both of his elders said in identical voices of bemusement.

Ferenc nodded, but was too discreet to preen. "I assumed you'd noticed. Let's ride back there and you both wait with the horses while I go up to the fortress. The cave is obvious enough that the soldiers have surely already tried to use it as an entrance up the mountain and they've failed, so chances are it does not go directly up. But it will keep you sheltered if you need to be out here all night."

Vera turned to Raphael, who shook his head in resignation. "I trust his young eyes," he said. "Let's go back to the cave."

CHAPTER 16:

REUNION

"I am not what you expected," Peire-Roger declared, almost smugly. "You expected some sort of holy man would be in charge."

Raphael looked up at him, still speechless. He could not quite believe Ferenc had accomplished it: here they were, within the fortress, and it was nowhere near dawn.

He considered the scowling, inebriated nobleman seated across from him in the small, wooden hut. This was a workshop; a large, shallow vat took up most of the center of the room, supported from the roofbeams over still-warm coals. The humans were hunched on low stools between this and the door, their backsides as near to the warmth of the fire as they could manage. The room smelled of honey, and their gathering was lit by a single beeswax candle—an unexpected extravagance in such an austere place.

Peire-Roger's features were handsome but unfriendly. He had demanded Raphael and Vera yield up their weapons before they were allowed through the gate. Raphael understood the caution, but wished Peire-Roger did not get such enjoyment out of flouting his own metal now: His sword lay unsheathed across his lap. *I could grab that from you and lop your head off*, Raphael thought irritably.

Especially with you half in your cups. He was also irked about the appropriation of their horses.

"My name is Raphael of Acre," he said. "I am of the order of the Shield-Brethren. This is Vera, of the Shield-Maidens, and this is Ferenc." He considered saying Ferenc was from Frederick's court, but thought better of it. "My squire. We have come in search of a knight, a friend."

"His name is Percival," said Vera. Raphael frowned at her. "Well, it is," she said gruffly. "There is no reason to keep that a secret." She turned back to the lord, her eyes looking as bleary as Raphael's felt—a combination of cold, travel exhaustion, and being plucked so rudely from sleep. "His name is Percival. He is a member of Raphael's order. He should not be here and so we have come to take him home."

"What do you mean, he shouldn't be here?" Peire-Roger asked, with a strange expression that resembled a derisive smirk.

"Percival is gifted and, in some ways, perhaps touched," Raphael said urgently. He had spent hours today considering the best way to explain Percival to someone in Peire-Roger's position—although the lord was right: Raphael had assumed he would be explaining himself to a holy sage, not a drunk. "He has a sickness of the soul that sometimes tricks his reason. When he comes to himself, he always regrets having gone away from us."

"And has he gone away from you, Raphael of the Shield-Brethren?" asked Peire-Roger, with a knowing look. "Run away, I mean?"

Raphael grimaced, glad the candlelight kept much of his face shadowed. "I would prefer to say..."

"Because if he ran off, and if he is here, then he has come seeking refuge, and we do not yield up our refugees. If he is here, he will remain here as long as he likes. I will not let you take him away. If he is here."

A pause.

"So he is here?" Raphael ventured.

"I did not say that," said Peire-Roger quickly. "I only said that *if* he is here you cannot remove him against his will."

"Oh, for the love of heaven, of course he's here," said Vera irritably. "The fellow wouldn't be holding forth like this if Percival weren't here. He'd tell us we had the wrong mountain and send us packing."

Peire-Roger scowled at her. "You are not ladylike of tongue."

"I am not ladylike at all," Vera corrected. "Especially when I've been wakened from a deep sleep and dragged through the dark by strangers to the top of a mountain."

"Your young friend told us where to find you and said you wished immediate entrance," Peire-Roger cut her off. "It was an imposition upon us, not upon you, for us to bring you to the safety of this sanctuary in the middle of the longest night of the year. That's five men-at-arms who will be groggy tomorrow."

"We will put in time on watch to make up for it," Raphael said. "Of course. As long as we are here, we are *with you*, and *as* you. But you must tell me if Percival is here."

"Must I?" said Peire-Roger, examining his cup. "I am not clear what part of this conversation has led you to think that I must."

"The man is drunk," said Vera with disgust.

"We are not quite alert ourselves," said Raphael. "I suggest we all sleep and have this conversation when the sun rises."

"You're going up to the tower on guard-duty before the sun rises," Peire-Roger said, and then gestured with a flapping hand in Vera's direction. "She'll be on breakfast duty."

Ferenc, despite himself, giggled. "That's not a good idea, milord," he said. "Not unless you want your bread burnt."

Peire-Roger looked at Vera with even greater contempt. "You're ill-kempt, ill-spoken, and you can't even cook?"

Raphael very quickly put a hand on Vera's arm without looking at her, and sat upright to catch Peire-Roger's attention. "My understanding of your religious doctrine," he said, "is that it is equitable regarding the sexes. Women are of equal worth to men."

"Certainly. Does that mean nobody cooks breakfast? I highly value whoever cooks my breakfast. In fact, lady, to demonstrate how highly I value you, I will have my breakfast made by nobody but you as long as you are here." He grinned at her.

"I am sure there is somebody running the kitchens who can sort that out in the morning," Raphael said, urgently willing Vera not to rise to the bait. "We will all benefit from sleep tonight, surely. Only please be so good as to tell us if Percival is here safely."

"Nobody is here *safely*. We're under siege, did you miss that somehow? We've been under siege for nearly as long as Toulouse under Raimundo the Sixth was besieged, God bless his glorious defiant name. If only his son were as committed to justice. That man—that glorious, blessed man, the old count—openly defied the Church and King and went to his very grave an excommunicate because he refused to persecute his own subjects at their whim. May his twelve-pointed gold cross shine down from Heaven and kick a little backbone into his son. The young count, the present count, now," he clicked his tongue disapprovingly and shook his head, "he is feisty enough in his own defense, but he hedges his bets when it comes to the rest of us."

"So Percival is here," said Raphael.

"Although," Peire-Roger continued, disregarding him, "he has handled the Inquisition masterfully. For years, the Inquisition tried to set up shop in Toulouse, but as soon as they tortured anyone, Raimundo would run them out of town, so in revenge they'd put the town under Interdict. Raimundo would petition the Pope, saying, 'Here's an idea: I'll fight against Emperor Frederick on your behalf if you'll just lift this damn Interdict.' So the Pope would lift it, but then he'd send the Inquisitors back into town, and they'd torture someone, so Raimundo would run them out, and so it went on. Clever fellow. He protected the Good Ones and he never had to fight against Frederick."

"So Percival is here," Raphael said with frustration. "Please allow enough goodwill between us to allow that he is here."

A pause.

"He is here," said Peire-Roger. "And well."

A long-held tension within Raphael relaxed a little; he heard himself sigh with relief. "Thank you," he said. "May I see him?"

"I am suspicious of your motives, Raphael of the Shield-Brethren," said Peire-Roger, without malice, almost casually. He took another swig from his wineskin. Then he turned to the young man, about Ferenc's age, who had shadowed him from the moment this audience began. He made a hand-gesture. The youth nodded, rose, and ran out of the room into the frigid, moonlit courtyard.

"Percival is a brother-in-arms," said Raphael. "My only motive is to make sure he is, and remains, well. He has been tormented by irrational visions for years, and sometimes he does irrational things."

"If I may for a moment presume to speak on behalf of our beloved Bishop Marti," said Peire-Roger, almost singsong. "Let me say that God is the best physician of all, and provides the best remedy. Percival is aware of this. Far from being out of his wits—well, any more out of his wits than any of us who are choosing to spend the winter up here when it would be just as easy to sneak out through a tunnel—where was I?"

"God is the best physician," said Raphael tersely.

"Yes," said Peire-Roger. "And Percival knows this. He has found his calling here. Those visions you speak of—which I warrant I can describe in greater detail than even you can—they have led him here. He is in prayer and meditation all the day now, when he's not on garrison duty, preparing to take the consolamentum of the Good Ones."

"That is preposterous," said Raphael.

"What is the consola...?" Ferenc asked quietly.

"Consolamentum. It's the oath they take right before they die," Raphael said to him. "It's a sort of last rite to make sure they don't..."

"No it's not," spat Peire-Roger in a mocking slur. "Dilettante. Don't speak of what you do not know. The consolamentum, young man, is the oath taken by a Credent when they are prepared to become Perfect."

"Perfect?" Ferenc echoed in bemusement.

"A perfect heretic," Peire-Roger said heartily. "In the eyes of the Catholic Church. A Good One. Like a monk or a priest. All of us up here, we're all Credents. We believe in what they believe, but we are, for this lifetime, obliged to partake in the sorrows of the world. And the joys."

"Like too much wine," Raphael muttered.

"The Good Ones have moved beyond that," the lord continued expansively. "They are in the world, but not of it. They're involved in trades—they support themselves, and their community, but they do nothing to cause harm to anyone. Ever. We protect them so that they can stay safe, in their meditation and prayer, and then, when we die, we come back in another body and if we're lucky, we get to be the Good Ones and everyone else takes care of us." He chortled a little and took another sip of wine.

"That is not a very evolved expression of Cathar philosophy," Raphael said, *sotto voce,* to Ferenc. "I will explain it to you more clearly tomorrow. He's right, though, that the consolamentum is also used as a vow to lead a perfectly pure life."

"From what you've told me about Percival, his life sounded very pure already," said Ferenc, trying to be helpful.

"No, he's a soldier and a warrior," said Peire-Roger, now beginning to overenunciate to make up for his tipsiness. "He kills people. That's not pure. When he takes the vow, he will stop killing people. Personally," he went on, in a more intimate tone, to Raphael, "I find that a pity, as he looks like he's probably very good at killing people, and I would like to maximize that ability given our circumstances. But he says he's taking the vows, and it's not my place to stop him. Nor," he added, sitting up and speaking as soberly as possible, "is it yours. There are customs we abide by here."

Raphael stood with impatient agitation. "My friend is already a monk. A warrior-monk. I know his very soul in this regard. There are no further vows the man needs to take to dedicate his life to good. He is, however maddeningly, the purest person I have ever known."

The sound of footsteps outside stopped him; he turned to look through the open doorway. In stepped the youth whom Peire-Roger had sent on an errand. Beside him stood a tall, broad-shouldered, handsome man, devoid of all weapons or decoration, dressed in a simple black gown tied at the waist with rope.

"My dear brother Raphael!" said Percival, and held his arms out for embrace.

CHAPTER 17:

THE PERFECT KNIGHT

Raphael stared at Percival's priestly garb in astonishment for the length of one heartbeat. "Have you taken leave of your senses?" he demanded loudly. He shoved the Percival out of the way and stormed out of the hut into the darkened courtyard.

Even from inside the workshop, Ferenc noticed several things happening at once. Most dramatically, the whole armed garrison up on the limestone walls swung their attention down into the courtyard, and a dozen bows were pulled taut, their arrows tracking Raphael in his torch-lit agitation. A heartbeat later, Peire-Roger pulled himself together enough to rush out past the bemused Percival, and shouted to the garrison to stand down. Then Ferenc heard him yell something similar, but slurred, toward the far end of the courtyard; presumably people in the donjon had awakened and come outside to see the source of the midnight uproar.

As all this was happening, the handsome man in the monk's robe turned and quietly followed Peire-Roger into the courtyard.

In the candlelight, Ferenc exchanged a look with Vera and they both followed quickly at his heels.

Silhouetted by a torch, their breath all intermingling to form a cloud, Percival, Raphael, and Peire-Roger were apparently entangled. As Ferenc watched, Percival tried to calm Raphael, who was violently throwing off Percival's embraces and dodging Peire-Roger's drunken attempts to calm him down by patting him on the back.

"Please, brother," said Percival gently. "There are many people living in this very small space. You are disturbing the respite of hundreds. Come back with me into the chandlery and let us speak in lower voices."

Raphael threw his arms up, hands clenched, and spun away, stalking several strides into the darkness. Ferenc had never seen him this upset; even Vera seemed surprised.

But he contained it within a few heartbeats. After a deep breath, which billowed vaporously up into the cold night, he turned back, walked past Percival, and gestured almost defiantly back toward the shed. Ferenc and Vera ducked inside and waited for them. Ferenc was grateful for the relative warmth.

Raphael sat where he had before. Percival remained standing. Peire-Roger began to sit, but Raphael shook his head. "If you please, milord, this is a private conversation."

Peire-Roger scowled, looking back and forth between the two knights. "Do you require protection from these people?" he asked Percival, with the studied, intense seriousness of inebriation.

"Oh, for the love of the Virgin," Raphael said in a disgusted voice. "This man could kill all of us with his bare hands before we even had a chance to notice. And you have taken all our weapons. He is perfectly safe."

"The guard at the gate will not allow you to remove him unless he is alert and willing to go," Peire-Roger said. "This is a sanctuary."

"A sanctuary," Raphael interrupted, speaking over him. "Yes, we will respect that. Please let us be."

He crossed his arms and said nothing more until Peire-Roger and his squire had left.

Then he stared daggers at Percival. There was a long pause.

"I have been having visions, Raphael," Percival began, with an almost helpless gesture.

"What good has ever come from those visions?" Raphael demanded.

Percival looked down into his hands and considered his words. "I have erred in the past."

"And in the present," said Raphael.

"Let him speak at least," said Vera, slapping at Raphael's sleeve. "Let him get it out."

"Thank you," Percival said with a brief nod toward her. Then his attention went back to Raphael. "I have been following these visions for years. You know that."

"I do," said Raphael tersely.

"And they have brought me here."

"It's not the first place they've brought you," said Raphael pointedly.

"Please, let the past go," Percival said, looking into his hands again. "I cannot undo what has been done. I can only try to correct my future course, and I believe I have done so, by coming here. I do not know why I have been brought here, or what is supposed to come of it. But given where I am, and who I am surrounded by, it seems clear that I must reconcile myself to God."

Raphael stared at him for a moment in disbelief. "What does that even *mean*?" he demanded impatiently. "This rude drunkard who was just interrogating us and claiming to protect you—has he 'reconciled himself to God'? He's in charge of this place, but he's not wearing a monk's robe; he's not living a pure life. Why on earth should you—who have already taken sacred vows elsewhere and are a stranger here—be called upon to do more than that fellow?"

"Perhaps you were just called here by your visions to help defend the fortress, if you are a warrior," Ferenc offered, timidly.

Percival looked over at him and smiled. He was even more handsome when he smiled. "Hello," he said. "We weren't introduced. I'm Percival."

"He knows who you are. We've been talking about you for the past ten days," Raphael muttered.

"My name is Ferenc," said the youth. He brought his fist to his heart and bowed his head.

"Oh, that's wonderful," said Raphael. "Greet him as if he were your emperor. Please, everyone, let's worship Percival and indulge his dangerous visions—"

"I do not believe in the wisdom of visions," Ferenc reassured Raphael quickly. "You and I are alike that way. But I do believe in the *power* of them. Percival has been drawn here for some reason, and as he is a knight, then probably the reason is to defend those who need defending. That seems very reasonable to me."

"Not if he's taken vows not to harm another human being," Raphael protested impatiently. "There are thousands of armed men down the slopes who want to destroy everyone up here. Percival, how can you possibly defend them without being willing to harm those who would cause harm? Can you *pray* them away?"

"I agree that he should remove the monk's robe and arm himself," said Ferenc.

"Why don't you both shut up and listen to him," said Vera. "After the headache he has caused us, I would like to hear what he has to say for himself."

Raphael barreled on. "There are only a few dozen men up here."

"I believe the number is about one hundred," Percival said. "And there are close to ten thousand in the camp below."

"Well, then," said Raphael, standing, still agitated. He had quieted his voice but his tone could have felled trees. "It seems to me that either you gear up and we prepare to take on far more than we possibly can survive, or we get the hell out of here and let this history unfold as it must. As Frederick's Greeks would say, we either play *deus ex machina*, or we get off the stage."

"What?" Percival asked, confused.

"We do not wallow in somebody else's story if there is no part for us to play. We *cannot* save them. I am not saying they're doomed," he said, as Percival seemed about to disagree. "This is a siege. They are in an exceptional defensive position here. At the moment, they are probably defending themselves entirely by dumping buckets of debris over the fortress walls onto the heads of anyone trying to climb the mountain."

Percival nodded. "Yes, in fact—"

"They do not need us to do that. We should leave." He took a final breath, and then sat again, as if his sitting made that the last word on the matter.

"I'm not the only one to have a vision of this place," said Percival. "An angel appeared at a nearby farm—"

"Of course he did," said Raphael wearily.

"A female angel," Percival corrected.

Raphael gave him a strange look. "There are no female Christian angels. In fact, as far as the Cathars are concerned, there are no angels at *all.*"

"She prevented a terrible betrayal. A French soldier defected to our cause."

"*Your* cause?" Vera echoed, witheringly.

Percival nodded. "And while you are here, my brothers and sister, it should be your cause as well. These people need your swords and arrows. Just last week they received word here that the Count of Toulouse is sending troops. Many troops. You should at least stay until those troops have arrived. You can help with garrison patrol, even if that just means throwing buckets of debris on the enemy's head, and generally making sure they are doing everything they can to defend themselves. Only until the troops come. Then, when you know we are all in good hands, you can leave us."

Ferenc, although not a knight, appreciated the sentiment. He studied Raphael's face and saw that he did, too. The dark-haired man grimaced. "If we're here as knights, I expect no less from you, *brother*. Take off that night-robe you're wearing and dress like a soldier."

Percival looked down at his robe, deflated. "You are right, of course," he said after a moment. "I should return to arms as long as they need me to. But I go back to my robe once we have vanquished the enemy."

Raphael looked impatient, but Ferenc held out a hand toward him and shook his head.

"Do not argue with men who have visions, sir," he whispered. "Surely you know that." He heard Vera make a sound on the stool behind him.

Raphael heaved a sigh, leaned forward on his elbows, and rubbed his face with the heels of his hands. "Very well. We stay until the reinforcements arrive. And then we leave."

"If you wish to," said Percival, firmly excluding himself. "And while you are here, we will all make ourselves useful."

"We'll make ourselves useful at sun-up," said Vera. "We have bedrolls and it's warmer in here than the courtyard, I say we sleep in here."

"*You*," said Ferenc, risking a grin, "have to make Peire-Roger his breakfast."

Vera smacked him on the shoulder. Hard.

CHAPTER 18:

FAMILIAR FACES

Ocyrhoe returned from her overnight trek a few hours before dawn. She had been to a village to the east, and so approached the pog in the bright moonlight by clambering up the treacherous cliff-like ascent by the watchtower on the lower end of the crest. Since the siege began last May, this tower—Roc de la Tour, the army below called it—had been garrisoned heavily, as it overlooked the second-likeliest path up the mountain. (The first likeliest was up the gentler southwest slope, but that was overlooked by the fortress and easily defended.)

It was a very cold although strangely still night, and she had not brought the cup with her, which usually protected her from the worst of the chill. By the time she arrived at the top, her feet were numb, her fingers pulsing painfully with cold, and her whole body shivering. The guards in the watchtower recognized her coded whistle. They invited her in and gave her a warm woolen blanket. She curled up under the table, to sleep until morning.

❖ ❖ ❖

Near dawn, a groggy but sober Lord Peire-Roger came to the hut to greet the newcomers. With the light slanting in through small windows, Ferenc saw they had slept under and around the equipment for a small but ambitious candle-making workshop. The large, raised vat was for melting wax; below it was a brazier, and above it several paned frames hung from the ceiling by ropes with pulleys.

Peire-Roger gruffly ushered them outside to the bright courtyard. It was very breezy. Now that he could really see the space they were in, Ferenc was astonished. He could not have guessed the night before how populated this place was. The lozenge-shaped courtyard was a rugged mish-mash of wooden buildings and uncut limestone swells. It was full of people bundled up against the cold—many of them dressed as Percival had been the night before, but many others dressed in finery that rivaled the Emperor's courtiers. There were servants, children, merchants, and soldiers, all working and living tightly together in a buzz of activity. There was a smithy next to the chandlery, and already charcoal was being fired up there. From the pervasive scent of lanolin, Ferenc judged there was also plenty of spinning and weaving happening in these workshops. He caught the smell of chickens, but saw no farmyard scat.

Percival was waiting for them just outside the chandlery. He was now dressed similarly to Raphael, including the rose-emblazoned surcoat. He introduced them to stern old Bishop Marti, whom Ferenc distrusted on sight mostly because he was a bishop, even if heretical. The young Hungarian felt better-disposed toward Percival's other elderly companion, Raimon de Perelha. He was Peire-Roger's father-in-law, and the actual lord of Montségur, although his son-in-law was ruling in his name.

Raphael volunteered for and was immediately put on garrison duty. Vera was assigned, once again, to the kitchen by Peire-Roger, but Raphael requested her presence with him, and Raimon indulgently granted that. Ferenc watched an entire, tense conversation pass between Vera and Raphael without either saying a word out loud.

"And you, lad?" said Raimon. "We can put you on garrison as well, but I hear you were pretty clever getting up the mountain without our lookouts hearing you. Perhaps you have some skills we can make use of."

"I am best at hunting and trapping," Ferenc said.

The ancient Bishop Marti shook his head. "Our diet contains no animal flesh. We do not require those services."

"If he can get up and down the mountain so invisibly, he should help with messages and transport," said Raimon.

"I would be happy to help in any way I can," Ferenc said, adding to himself, *as long as we have to stay here.* There was something surreal and unsettling about this place. He did not want to be here any longer than required. Percival was a little strange, but so were all the rest of them.

"I should orient you all to the fortress before anyone does anything," said Peire-Roger, stepping in over his father-in-law's conversation. "And then I'll send the lad to Matheus. Matheus is headed off the pog today but he can introduce him to some of the other fellows in scouting and supply."

✦ ✦ ✦

The sky was bright, dazzling blue as Ocyrhoe made her way from the watchtower up the crest to the barbican and the northern entrance. She grinned, remembering how terrified she'd been of these heights a little more than two years ago. Now she felt as much at home as a bird would, even in this whipping breeze. She loved the panoramic view; she loved her own agility scrambling up and down the mountain, her ability to disappear and reappear almost at will. She suspected she was redirecting some of her Binder abilities into non-Binderlike activities. But did that matter? She lived in a world where nobody knew or cared about the Binders—certainly nobody had called her out as one, and she openly wore the knots in her hair as a reminder of her lost sisters in Rome.

She was beginning to feel truly at home here. The younger children were fond of her and wanted to learn to climb the mountain like she did. She was used to the meatless diet and the strictness of the Good Ones. They did not forbid the troubadour *faidits* from performing in the evening, and they did not prevent her from studying the stars, which were impossibly brilliant and clear. She wished she knew more about the stars. She wished she knew more about a lot of things.

She hardly noticed the thrill of danger as she crossed past the barbican and took those several dozen strides along the thinnest strip of mountain crest—three paces across, and the pog's north and south limestone faces fell sheer away to either side. And then, the sanctuary of the fortress itself. She signaled up to the wall guards; one of them called out to the porter below, and she was immediately admitted. She wanted only to see if there was any breakfast left, and to stop by the chandlery to greet Rixenda; the rest of the day was hers to rest and recover from her travel, and despite her hearty enjoyment of the morning's briskness, her entire body sagged with exhaustion. She could hardly wait to slip between the covers of her hard, little bed in Rixenda's hut, and sleep.

The courtyard looked like it did most chilly mornings: emptier than in the warmer months, people wrapped in mantles or blankets hurrying from one needful place to another. Artal and Ferrer, who had joined the fortress company shortly after Vidal had, nodded to Ocyrhoe. Artal's hat blew off in the wind. A wan young noblewoman en route to the spinning shed caught it and handed it back as their paths crossed. Artal nodded thanks as if they were peers; she took no offense at his lack of deference. Ocyrhoe loved that about these people.

She was about to take herself to the kitchens below the keep when she noticed Peire-Roger leading several strangers around the courtyard as if giving them a tour. The knight named Percival was with them—Percival, whom she had continued to avoid, for no reason she could really name.

He had donned the black robe of a Goodman the day after Vidal had shown up to convert to Catharism, and so he had been easy to avoid; he'd spent most of his time in prayer and fasting, as he had absolutely no practical nonviolent skills like the other Good Ones did. This morning, however, he was back in his regular clothes. The newcomers must have arrived while she was away to the east these past few days, and perhaps they knew Percival—why else would he be tagging along with them? One of them, a dark-haired man who looked like a Saracen, was dressed like Percival.

The shortest of the newcomers reminded her a little of her friend, Ferenc, whom she had not seen since the day she and the cup took possession of each other. Ferenc, with whom she had spent less than a week and shared no language, but who had become one of the dearest, closest people in her life. Ferenc, who had sacrificed someone he loved to save Ocyrhoe's life.

Ferenc, who was standing right there in the courtyard, not twenty paces from her, staring at her open-mouthed.

No, it could not be Ferenc. This fellow was taller, broader, well-dressed, and well-groomed. Ferenc had been practically feral. This was not Ferenc.

But he was staring at her as if he thought he knew her. Then he must have decided—mistakenly, of course—that he did know her, for he suddenly grinned widely and held out his arms in greeting. Ignoring whatever Peire-Roger was telling them about the armory, he shouted out "*Ocyrhoe!*"

He shouted so loudly that even in the brisk breeze, his voice filled the courtyard enough to echo. For a moment, everyone paused in their speech and their action to see who had shouted. He was running toward her now, the sky making his eyes bright.

"Ocyrhoe!" he repeated, slightly quieter. "You are here! There is nobody in the world I could be happier to see at this moment. What are you doing here?"

Ocyrhoe froze by the gate, overwhelmed with confusion. She sensed the general courtyard hush. Then she sensed things return to normal, but still she was rooted to the spot. How could that possibly be Ferenc? That man was speaking to her using words she understood—he had a strong accent, but it was not Ferenc's gibberish.

He was directly in front of her now. If it was Ferenc, he had grown by a head. He had a beard. His voice was low.

"Ferenc?" she said, guardedly.

He smiled. "You know me!"

"How...how can you speak to me?"

He grinned. "The emperor taught me new languages. And other things. I know a lot of things I want to tell you." He was beaming. She could hardly think. Here was Ferenc.

Abruptly she threw her arms around him and squeezed herself against him as hard as she could. He made a surprised sound and then hugged her too. For a long moment, Ocyrhoe was happier than she had ever been in her life. Even the scent of his skin—which she did not realize she remembered or had ever noticed—was familiar.

Ferenc released her and took her forearm. He began to tap it, and then caught himself, and laughed. "Ha, just like that, I forgot that I can speak to you, all my memories are of the difficulties! Look!" He patted his wrist, to show her the bracelet of her own hair. "You are in my thoughts all the time."

"Oh..." she breathed, and ran her fingers over the bracelet. A wash of emotion left her breathless, and she felt her eyes well up.

She glanced up at Ferenc. He pursed his lips—such a mature, almost fatherly expression—and nodded with understanding. Protectively, he wrapped his arms around her again, and held her against himself. "You are never forgotten, not for one moment," he whispered in her ear.

"Or blamed? Or hated?" She was embarrassed by how fragile, how girlish, she sounded.

Now one large hand pressed the back of her head closer in to his shoulder. "Of course not," he whispered. "I thought you must hate me for not going with you into the world."

"You had to take Father Rodrigo to be buried!" And then suddenly she was sobbing.

Ferenc squeezed her tighter, rocking slightly side to side in a comforting gesture. She was appalled at her show of emotion, especially in the middle of the courtyard, but it took a moment to control herself.

"All is well," Ferenc whispered to her. "All is well."

"What is this?" Peire-Roger demanded sharply. Startled, Ocyrhoe pulled away from Ferenc, and fiercely began to wipe her face dry on her sleeve. Ferenc was blinking rapidly. Peire-Roger's face, fashioned by nature to always look somewhat suspicious, looked very suspicious now. She knew him well enough to understand his pique: This disruption, any disruption, interfered with the efficiency of the day. "Explain this. Whatever it is."

Ocyrhoe, being the resident offender, took a breath to collect herself, but Ferenc spoke first. "Excuse me, milord. Ocyhroe is a very dear friend. When we were last together, a friend of ours died horribly and then, moments later, we were severed. Seeing each other is very joyful but also reminds us of our fallen friend and the horror of that day."

Peire-Roger looked searchingly at Ocyrhoe. She lowered her eyes. "That is true, milord," she said.

He softened slightly. "Is this related to why you fled Rome?"

She nodded, not trusting herself to speak. She wanted desperately to be alone with Ferenc so they could talk freely, but there was no privacy in Montségur, nowhere at all. And even if they could find a way to talk, the first thing he would ask about would be the cup. She was suddenly relieved she had not brought it with her on this last trip; the queerness of keeping it about her would disquiet him if he realized.

Peire-Roger looked back and forth between them. "May I presume, young man, that you are also not in the good graces of the Church of Rome?"

Ferenc's barely checked emotions spilled over into bitter humor. "Yes, milord," he said, with a tenor laugh. "That is a very safe presumption." He sobered. "The friend I spoke of was a priest, and he died because I killed him." Ocyrhoe could see how close he was to tears himself. It was disorienting to hear him speak a language she could actually understand. Disorienting and yet enthralling.

Peire-Roger blinked in surprise. He took a step back and Ocyrhoe saw that Percival and the other two newcomers—a man and a woman—were clustered nearby. They looked equally taken aback by Ferenc's declaration.

"Why did you kill a priest?" asked Percival into the growing silence around them.

"Because the priest was about to kill my friend Ocyrhoe," said Ferenc, looking at her.

"That is a forgivable reason," decided Percival comfortingly. "Even a noble reason."

"Why was he about to kill her?" asked the Saracen.

Ferenc paused, then looked up meaningfully at the man, nodding, and said, "Because a vision had driven him mad and he had lost his reason."

The dark-haired man made a gesture toward Percival that was noncommittal and yet immediately told Ocyrhoe volumes. She already knew Percival had visions; now she knew what this man thought about them.

"I do not know you, sir," she said to the dark-complexioned man, "But if you it is who brought Ferenc here, I thank you. I am very glad to see him."

The man offered his hand to her as if they were peers. "My name is Raphael of Acre," he said. "And I thank you in turn. I did not know what this young man was made of until he saw you." He gestured for the other figure to come closer. It was a woman, who held herself like a man and dressed almost like a man—in a more martial version of how she herself often dressed, especially when she was on a mission. "This is Vera of Kiev," he said. "We are comrades in arms."

"A friend of Ferenc's is a friend of mine," said Vera. Ferenc looked surprised by the declaration. So did Raphael.

"There will be time enough for talk later," said Peire-Roger roughly. "The morning has started and you all promised to contribute to our labors, so begin. Ocyrhoe, take your friend to Matheus. He will be on scouting and transport."

Ocyhroe cheered. "With me," she said to him. "I'll show you all the secret ways up and down the mountain. It will be like running around Rome, only with no Rome."

"And no evil cardinals," added Ferenc.

CHAPTER 19:

HAPPY DAY

Matheus, like so many men in this region, was tall and thin, with a grave, intelligent face. He was perhaps five and twenty. By costume and physical demeanor, Ferenc could not determine what his rank was in this strange little world-away-from-the-world. He was most likely the younger son of some lord, but he could as easily have been a cocky tradesman in hand-me-down woolens. He displayed not the slightest interest in Ferenc's identity. This suggested to Ferenc that he was close enough to Peire-Roger to trust his judgment. Not everyone in this compound, he suspected, would share that trust.

They met with Matheus inside the great hall of the donjon, in a quiet corner away from the door. On a small stone shelf were several codices, quills, parchment scraps, and a jar of ink. "These are where we keep track of what is coming and going, and who is coming and going," he said, brushing his fingers over the books without offering to show them. "I don't know if you read or write, but these aren't for you. You talk directly to me or my brother, Peire. We'll tell you where you are going, or who you are finding, or what you are bringing. Do you know the area?"

"I'll be showing him around," said Ocyrhoe cheerfully.

Matheus looked at her critically a moment, chewing on his inner cheek. "I suppose you are the person to train him," he said, almost grudgingly. "You are the only one with no assignment today." He turned his attention to Ferenc. "We move people, messages, and supplies up and down the mountain daily. There is a team working all the time. She'll introduce you to the men you need to know and show you what to do. But you look pretty strong, and if you can use a bow, you'll be called to garrison duty as well. So do not get too attached to scouting and transport."

Ferenc shrugged. "I will go wherever I am most useful."

"That's right, you will," Matheus said. Again, his brown eyes strayed to Ocyrhoe and then back to Ferenc. "And once she has trained you, you will only be working with the men. Women and men should not be working with each other. It is distracting and causes impure thoughts."

"It does?" Ferenc said, startled. He felt himself blush, for no good reason, as if he'd been accused of something. He was glad the light was dim.

"This is not the place for that," Matheus said, as much to Ocyrhoe as to Ferenc.

Ocyrhoe appeared genuinely not to have heard him. Ferenc found her obliviousness reassuring. She grinned at him. "Let's go," she said, and walked briskly through the din and dim of the donjon back to the door.

Outside, Ferenc squinted into the bright sun and wrapped his mantle tighter around himself against the breeze. Ocyrhoe trotted down the steps that led into the courtyard; he followed. Up on the western parapets, archers were on duty, arrows nocked, occasionally shooting down the western slope. Around them in the courtyard, other soldiers in pairs were lugging large pails filled with something heavy—fist-sized stones, he saw when they passed by a pair. These were being trundled to the ladders leading up the wall-walks. All of this was done with watchfulness, but just the slightest air of urgency.

"After six months, it's become routine," Ocyrhoe said, noticing his gaze. "For our work, there is only so much we can do by daylight outside the walls, but you can meet everyone and I can explain things. And so can you—like how came you to be here?"

They were at the northern gate. A man Ocyrhoe called by name released the bolt to let them out. Ferenc stopped abruptly on the outside of the wall, staring into the air. "*Boldogasszony,*" he whispered without thinking, reverting to his native tongue. He put his hand over his heart.

"Magnificent, yes?" said Ocyrhoe. "It used to terrify me."

Slowly Ferenc gazed north to south. His eyes widened at the path directly ahead of them—three or four strides wide, if that, and dozens of paces long—that went to the outer defensive tower. Beyond that, a long bowshot down a gentle incline, was a watchtower that overlooked the entire eastern half of the pog. The slope between barbican and watchtower was mottled with pairs of men, some with pails, collecting rocks to throw down from the battlement, others harvesting scraggly branches from the wind-stunted vegetation to use for firewood.

Ocyrhoe tugged his sleeve, and pointed down the slope to their left, where a path led to a stoned-in enclosure. "That is where the Good Ones live," said Ocyrhoe. She had to raise her voice to carry on a conversation, the wind was so brisk. "Me, too. I stay in Rixenda's hut."

"That is also where the ropes are hoisted from," said Ferenc. "I saw that from the ground."

Ocyrhoe gaped. "You did?" She frowned. "That means others can see it too!"

He shook his head reassuringly. "I do not think so." He smiled and pointed to his face. "Very sharp eyes."

"We go there first. I'll show you how we arrange it," said Ocyrhoe. "And you must tell me why you're here!" As back in Rome, she grabbed his hand unselfconsciously, and began to lead him down the path to the Good Ones' settlement.

His hand had grown over the past two years; hers hardly had, and it felt so pleasantly familiar to him. She squeezed tighter a moment, then relaxed her grip. After a moment, she glanced over her shoulder as they went, her brows raised questioningly: *Why didn't you squeeze back?* Ferenc smiled awkwardly and pointed beyond her with his free hand. They were entering the settlement.

They were on the upper of two rocky, terraced shelves in the face of the northern slope. Each terrace was filled with very small buildings, shacks really, made of limestone with some kind of mud-plaster over them. They had no windows, but a rude opening in the top of each released woodsmoke; their doors were wood. They faced directly out over a huge gulf of empty air, from which they were protected only by a stone wall. It was hard to imagine a bleaker place, despite the soaring view: being below the north side of the peak, this natural shelf received little direct winter sunlight, while wide open to the icy, northern winds.

"This is where the Goodwomen live," explained Ocyrhoe. Still gripping his hand, she pointed to one building that was indistinguishable from any of the others. "That is Rixenda's, where I have lived the past two years. I'd invite you to visit but only females are allowed inside." She grinned at him, to reassure him she did not abide too fervently by the rules of conduct here. Ferenc nodded, dazed.

"You live *here?* All the time?" he finally asked.

She nodded. "During the day we are up in the courtyard working, although the Goodwomen often return here for prayer or meditation. They spend many hours every day praying. Rixenda must have knees of stone; she is on them all day long and never once complains. Down on the lower terrace are the Goodmen's homes. Here's the path." She led him over to the steep, short stairway hewn into the stone.

There were about the same number of men's huts as women's. The difference on the men's terrace—as he had guessed, when examining it from a distance—was that, by the outer wall, there was a natural depression in the limestone, almost like a cellar for a house that had never been built. It was waist-deep, with a wooden cover that was currently pulled off. It was filled with coils of rope.

"I know where these go," he said.

"Of course you do," said Ocyrhoe, sounding proud of him. "After dark, I'll take you down and show you the hidden paths that lead through the brush to the two main roads. But there are other ways straight down the mountain, especially down the southeast slope. I'll show you that as well, but again, only at night—the French army can see us otherwise. They probably could not get to us with their weapons, because the guards in the barbican and the eastern watchtower can fend them off, but they would see where we are on the mountain, and that would give them a clue as to where to look for purchase. So all that has to wait till after dark." She said this all rapidly, efficiently, then paused. Ferenc stared out over the valley and the foothills, and up at the larger mountain peaks. He shivered in the wind.

"We are close to the gods here, surely," he said.

"We are supposed to be heretics, not heathens," Ocyrhoe said pertly. "*God,* if you please, not *gods*. Let me show you the tunnels now. We can use them in daylight hours."

Ferenc gave her a look of mock pain. "Ocyrhoe," he said. "You, and me, and tunnels? Again?"

She put her hands over her mouth and giggled like a child. "I hate the tunnels," she confessed. "Because of Rome. But we can take lights with us into these tunnels, so that helps."

They returned to the courtyard and entered the small building where Peire-Roger had interrogated the newcomers the night before. Here it was warm and smelled vaguely of honey. Several Goodwomen were testing the consistency of something in a large vat.

"Rixenda!" Ocyrhoe said merrily. The oldest woman looked up. Ferenc liked her round face immediately: she reminded him of his own grandmother, but with greyer hair and bluer eyes. "This is my friend Ferenc. He arrived last night with the new knight. Is not God kind?"

Rixenda's eyes widened in surprise. "My goodness," she said, and then smiled at Ferenc. "Welcome to Montségur," she said. The other women glanced at him briefly, nodded, and turned their attention back to the vat.

"We need light for the tunnels," Ocyrhoe said, and went to a shelf above a bin on the left-hand wall, reaching for a covered lantern. Ferenc glanced into the bin, and his mouth fell open: it was filled with hundreds and hundreds of candles. He could hardly have been more amazed if he'd found himself staring at solid gold bricks.

"Are those all beeswax?" he marveled.

"Of course," said Rixenda, reaching for the rectangular frame suspended above the vat. "We do not use tallow. That requires the killing of animals."

"I don't think the Emperor has that many candles stored in one place," he said.

"The local farmers bring up the comb. We make the candles here and sell them in Toulouse," said Rixenda, her attention focused on the frame. Ocyrhoe was lighting the lantern from one of several candles in wall sconces. "We used to make them down in the village. From Toulouse they are sold all over the Occitan and the Pyrenees. They earn us a lot of money."

"You've probably burned some of these at Frederick's court," Ocyrhoe said. She carefully closed the casing around the lantern, then wrapped a rag around the whole thing, leaving a gap at the top for air. "You must tell me about Frederick's court. See you later," she said over her shoulder to Rixenda.

"What are you doing?" Rixenda asked.

"I am training him on scouting and transport. Matheus said so."

Rixenda frowned at her in a mothering sort of way that made Ferenc feel sheepish.

"The lantern will go out in such a wind," Rixenda cautioned.

"No, I've wrapped it well. I learned from the best lantern-wrapper on the pog," Ocyrhoe said, grinning affectionately. Rixenda clucked her tongue with mock annoyance.

Ocyrhoe stepped outside, carrying the lantern, and Ferenc followed her. She took him by the hand with a blithe lack of self-consciousness, hurried through the courtyard and out of the gate, and this time led him across the narrow crest to the barbican, where stood a lone sentinel. Ocyrhoe let go of Ferenc's hand and waved to the guard. "New scout, Artal," she called up, nodding toward Ferenc. "I'll introduce you when we come up from the tunnels." The fellow nodded solemnly to acknowledge Ferenc; Ferenc nodded back.

Ocyrhoe led him a few steps further along the path. "Pay attention. This is hidden," she said. "Do you see from here, down the slope to the watchtower?"

Ferenc nodded.

"The entrance to the tunnel is one third of the way down this slope, three paces to the north of the path. I know what to look for. Let's see if you can find it." She grinned adoringly. "I know you're going to find it."

"I have no idea what it looks like, Ocyrhoe," he said, indulgently. "I can't find something if I don't know what I'm looking for."

She waved her hand. "Go on, find it," she said. "I want to watch you in action."

"You have a strange sense of gaiety for the middle of a siege."

"I'm very happy to see you, Ferenc. I've seen nobody from my past life since I last saw you. You connect me to my past. Please tell me what has happened since I last saw you."

"In a moment," said Ferenc, glad to have a task to focus on. He examined the sloping path. A third of the way was easy to mark, and he walked briskly, pushing against the wind, until he had reckoned he was there. Ocyrhoe moved behind him, almost on tip-toe, shielding the covered lantern with her arms.

When he stopped, he looked to his left, which was the north flank of the mountain. The sides did not fall away so steeply here as they did in that brief dash between the barbican and the courtyard—but still, he would not want to lose his footing. Carefully, he took three paces, and looked around on the ground. On the windswept mountain-crest even the scrub woods could barely survive, especially in winter; the fuel-gatherers were not having an easy time of it. The limestone was pockmarked with little dishes of ice, some shallow and wide as a table, others small as a fist, but deep. Nothing looked like the entrance to a tunnel.

And then he realized. He had walked out onto a small spur of rock. He turned, and knelt, and reached down to touch the northern side of the spur. His hands found nothing there. He lay on his stomach and pulled his head over to look.

He had actually walked onto a ledge, a lip, which covered the entrance to a very narrow tunnel.

"I knew you'd find it," said Ocyrhoe approvingly, behind him. "Let's go in."

They walked around the overhang of rock, and huddled together under it, somewhat out of the wind. Ocyrhoe carefully unwrapped the rag from around the lantern and held it down into the tunnel so the wind was less likely to douse the flame. She gave him the same adoring grin. It made him feel funny, although he wanted to smile at her the same way.

"I'm a mountain girl now. No more little city rat," she said.

"While you look like you're being groomed to be a troubadour."

"I've been in Frederick's court. He made me a squire. I had to cut my hair and wear fancy clothes. It was awful."

A pause, and then they both laughed slightly.

"It hasn't ruined you," said Ocryhoe heartily. "Let's go in."

"What has your lot been, here, these past two years?" he asked.

"I'll tell you my story when we're back from below," she said, ducking her hand deeper into the limestone crack. "We must pay absolute attention to what we're doing now or we'll get lost."

◆ ◆ ◆

Within the mountain, it was quiet, still...and warm. After slithering and climbing down for the length of time it would take to walk a quarter mile, they took off their wraps and left them at an intersection of tunnels. In places the tunnels were barely wide enough for Ferenc to move abreast in them. No wonder Ocyrhoe was valuable here—she was tiny enough to slip through very narrow passages. These were nothing like the tunnels of Rome, which had been broad, level, and manmade. They had a pattern to them; here was utter randomness. Get lost in here and you'd be lost forever. Ocyrhoe's insouciance amazed him.

As they moved slowly through the tight spaces, the lantern casting playfully monstrous shadows, he coaxed from her a cursory depiction of her life here. She said nothing about the accursed cup, and he did not want to ruin the mood by mentioning something so loathed. She must have rid herself of it so long ago that now she did not even think about it. A good thing.

Ocyrhoe showed Ferenc the clever, subtle glyphs that were carved into the tunnel walls in such a way that they could be seen only by a light held at a certain angle. He would never remember the actual trail from the endless branches, but at least he could follow the signs.

She held his hand much of the way, whenever they did not need hands free to balance. Occasionally, he thought he sensed her trying to speak to him without speaking, as if she were testing either her own Binder abilities or the possibility that he might have them. He did not hear words; he only sensed a kind of pressure behind his eyes. It might have been his imagination. He liked the pressure of her hand in his. He really did not remember her hand being so small before.

By the time they had made their way down through the labyrinth deep within the mountain—once having to feel their way down a slender, long, rope ladder—touched ground at the bottom, and come back up again, the shadows of the day had shifted, the wind had died a bit, and Ferenc's stomach was rumbling. He didn't like the cold, but he was mightily glad to come back out into the winter air. "We've survived the tunnels again!" she grinned at him.

There had been few enough occasions to smile in Rome, and he was not used to the expression on her face. Not that there were reasons to smile now either, of course, but that made her smiles flattering, for she was smiling simply at his presence. *I wonder what Léna would make of that*, he thought.

And then he realized that Léna, of course, had sent him here. She had known—she *must* have known—that Ocyrhoe was here. Hadn't she anticipated Vera would want to bring him?

"We are being set up," he said suddenly, when they were halfway across the incline back toward the fortress.

"What?" she asked, amused. Her fingers were wrapped around the lantern's top ring—the candle had burned to a stub, and she had blown it out at the entrance. He saw the ash-marks on her knuckle from the blackened wick.

"Léna wanted me to go with Raphael and Vera. She did not give a reason. I think she knew that you were here."

Ocyrhoe pursed her lips. "I think you might be right." She smiled. "It was kind of her to reunite us."

"Was it?" said Ferenc darkly.

Ocyrhoe stopped walking and stared at him. "I do not remember you being suspicious," she said.

"You forget I've spent two years in Frederick's court. And Léna was frequently there. She is..." he grimaced. "She sent me here for some purpose."

Ocyrhoe shrugged. "Well, until we know, I'm just going to enjoy your company. I'm very glad to see you. To listen to you *speak*. It's as if I am meeting you all over again. This time around you are eloquent and well-dressed and rather courtly. Like a troubadour."

"The second time you've said that," Ferenc said. "Do you like troubadours?"

"Their music? Pah, not at all," said Ocyrhoe. In a confiding tone, she added, "But they are quite dashing when they're strumming their instruments. Although Rixenda doesn't like me to say so."

An alien, unpleasant sensation rushed through Ferenc, almost a flutter of panic mixed with anger. It lingered only long enough for him to be aware of it and then it was gone before he could even set his inner eye on it.

They were back at the gate. "Come, let's go to dinner. I think they'll seat us now," said Ocyrhoe, pulling at the bell for the gate. "I want to hear you speak some more. You must tell me about life at the court. It is surely more exciting than what happens here. Ferrer! Open please! It's chilling out here!"

After they returned the lantern to the chandlery, they crossed to the donjon for a very dull meal devoid of any animal products, not even butter or cheese. After they finished, Ocyrhoe cheerfully led Ferenc about the fortress, while up on the battlements archers continued their intermittent warning shots and younger soldiers hurled occasional rocks. There was something almost placid to their watchfulness. Ocyrhoe introduced him to the men and women who were part of the scouting and transport missions.

These included half a dozen garrison guards who helped to lower the ropes; a *faidit* who kept track of the immigration to and emigration from the fortress; Matheus's brother, Peire, who was updating the codices; the assistant at the smithy who kept track of charcoal; two women in the kitchens who managed food supplies; and several Goodmen and a Goodwoman whose positions were never specified.

With each introduction, Ferenc noticed how the men and women looked not at him, but at Ocyrhoe. Then—each time—they gave Ferenc the kind of smile that looked as if a wink might accompany it. Except for the Good Ones, who gave him a warning look similar to the look that Rixenda had given Ocyrhoe.

They returned to Rixenda, red-cheeked from cold and exertion, at the end of the afternoon. The old woman was finishing the workday; she sat with the door of the chandlery open, her feet near the embers of the fire that had been used to heat the wax, and the cold air cooling her after a day spent over the hot vats. The frame above the vat had rows of leather thongs stretched across its breadth, and from each thong hung half a dozen drip-candles, tied by their wicks, still drying.

"He's ready," Ocyrhoe announced as they entered. "All that's left is the climb down the mountain. I'll take him tonight. He was very good in the tunnel."

Rixenda looked at the two of them for a long moment. "I have spoken to Matheus. You will not take him," she said, gently, a grandmother trying not to disappoint a toddler.

Ocyrhoe frowned. "Why not?" she asked.

"There has been a ray of light dazzling this courtyard for several hours," said Rixenda. "I was in here working and even I could see it. Do you know what it was, Ocyrhoe?" The girl shook her head. "It was you."

"Oh," said Ocyrhoe, looking surprised. She smiled, slightly quizzical. "Thank you."

"It is not a compliment," said Rixenda. She glanced briefly but pointedly at Ferenc and again he felt himself redden. "And I am sorry to shame you both, but I must end this before it begins. You are a young woman in the presence of a young man, and..."

"No, no, no," said Ocyrhoe lightly, waving her hand at Rixenda. "I'm sure it looks like that, but I promise you, if you knew our history—"

"...and you are flooded with delight," Rixenda continued over the interruption. "It is streaming out of you like water over a dam. This fortress, this sanctuary, is no place for such a thing. We must all focus our attention on prayer and purity. Your young friend here means well, I am sure, but you and he will prevent each other from finding God."

Ocyrhoe bit her lip and turned to Ferenc to roll her eyes. "That God fellow," she whispered, "is forever complicating things. First in Rome, and now here."

"I do not wish to displease someone so important to my friend," Ferenc said to Rixenda. "Out of regard for you personally, not for your religion's belief, I will remove myself. For now," he added to placate Ocyrhoe, seeing her frown. "Certainly I understand that a young man and a young woman should not go gallivanting out on a moonlit night alone together."

"It's not 'gallivanting'," said Ocyrhoe under her breath.

"Where a troubadour might surprise them," Ferenc said.

Both women looked at him in confusion.

What he had felt—when Ocyrhoe had mentioned the troubadour earlier—was jealousy. He was jealous that his sweet friend referred to some man whom he didn't know as dashing. The revelation was embarrassing but woke him up. And so he chose to obey Rixenda's wishes, because he was afraid she might be right.

"I happen to know they need an extra man on guard duty at the watchtower tonight," said Rixenda. "Let Peire-Roger know you are available."

"Oh, for pity's sake," Ocyrhoe grumbled.

"I'll go and speak to him," said Ferenc. "I assume he's in the donjon." Rixenda nodded. Ferenc squeezed Ocyrhoe's hand affectionately, smiled at her—suddenly feeling depressingly mature—and left the cozy warmth of the chandlery for the breezy courtyard.

He'd forgotten to ask Ocyrhoe about the cup. She had probably disposed of it in a river bank or sold it somewhere, or even given it away. It was not important; he was only passing curious. He made a mental note to ask her tomorrow.

Of more urgent interest was how to get an extra woolen wrap for duty out on the watchtower.

◆ ◆ ◆

On the eastern edge of the camp, as the sun set, Dietrich and Hugue looked over the nine Gascony recruits. They were called the best mountain-climbers of their region, and they were all armed with knives and daggers; swords were too cumbersome for what they were about to attempt. A doleful-looking shepherd, whose son was even now scrambling home with a sizable bag of French gold, stood nearly lachrymose before them.

"This fellow knows the way up the eastern side," Dietrich explained briskly to the Gascons. "The cloud cover should make it possible to get up past where they would normally see you. And then what, fellow?"

The shepherd swallowed and looked at all of them. He had been glad enough to take the gold, but now that it was safely removed toward his farmstead, he seemed to be having second thoughts. "We will move sideways along the southern flank and then up around the eastern end of the pog, which is narrow and steep," he said. "The watchtower will have no reason to expect us from that direction. At night there are only five men posted. If you can surprise the watch, it should be easy to take the tower."

Dietrich opened his mouth to issue orders to the climbers, but was stopped by a gesture from the leader of the army, who wanted to do it himself.

"And once we have taken the tower," said Hugue de Arcis, "we will set up a siege-machine and destroy the fortress walls." This had been Dietrich's idea, and he was irritated to be upstaged by this commanding lout. "You, my sons," continued Hugue expansively, "are about to shift the tide of this battle. God shall watch over you all. May dawn bring us good news."

CHAPTER 20:

ECCO-LA

His Holiness the Pope was up late after celebrating the feast of St. Alexander of Jerusalem. Normally he would have retired for the night and renewed his work in the morning, but he was agitated by several missives that had arrived before supper, from the eastern borders of Frederick's realm. These were political diamonds—written proof that the citizenry, having lost faith in their emperor, was turning to the Church for assistance. These notes he could wave in front of Frederick's squint-eyed face when they finally met in person, as evidence that the Emperor must put himself on better footing with the Church lest the Church allow the Empire to give itself, spontaneously and wholeheartedly, to the Church.

On the other hand, these notes were direct requests for assistance, and if he did not give any, then he was just as bad as Frederick. He told the cleric to summon his captain-at-arms for an audience the next morning just after mass. Then he made a mental calculation of how many papal troops he could afford to send east, as he needed so many of them in Lombardy to keep Frederick in check.

The situation was agitating enough that despite a bellyful of good food and even better wine he could not relax. He kept the oil-lamps burning in his office and announced to his steward, Aelius, who looked as if he would rather be asleep, that if any messengers arrived with late-night dispatches, he would receive them.

"There is one message just arrived, from the Pyrenees," Aelius said, almost reluctantly, and handed him the scroll. Innocent broke off the seal and unrolled it. He summoned the chandler to hold the candelabrum closer.

"Greetings to Your Holiness from Dietrich von Grüningen at Montségur, on this cold day of memorial to St. Gemellus." Innocent was not much concerned with the situation in the Occitan. It was a relatively minor land-grab by the King of France, which he would eventually have to rein in. "Your Holiness, a startling story has been circling the army camp, which I believe is worthy of note, although His Eminence the Archbishop of Narbonne is trying to suppress it. According to this story, one of the most stalwart local soldiers has defected to the Cathar cause after a supposed angel appeared to him in a nearby farmhouse and ordered him to protect the heretics. This remarkable story has been taken very seriously by many of the men, to the point that Hugue de Arcis is concerned about further desertions. I cannot but wonder if it is a coincidence that it has happened so immediately after the covert arrival in camp of a knight of the heretical Shield-Brethren. I will keep my eyes and ears open, my step light, and my mouth shut, but I wished to alert you to this development as soon as possible as I do not believe the archbishop will choose to tell you of it. I believe it deserves scrutiny. It might occur again. Please advise me on a further path of action." He yawned and decided to set the letter aside for the morning; Dietrich took himself and all his activities very seriously, but Innocent had the Mongol horde to deal with. And the Emperor. And other matters. However, he continued to read.

"Let me add something peculiar about this story. Vidal of Foix's pageboy was outside the building in which the angel appeared and chose to remain silent regarding all that he saw until I used some of your gold—usefully, I hope—for details. While the boy cannot account for the appearance or disappearance of the so-called angel, he told me that he saw her with his own eyes and that she appeared to be a young woman, small in stature, dressed in very simple homespun and a local style of boot that is good for climbing these mountains. Her hair was long, dark, and uncovered, and in her left hand she carried a fine metal cup that seemed somehow to reflect more light than was being shone upon it."

Innocent looked up abruptly from the note. "*It's her!*" he barked at Aelius, who gave him the look of a devoted, confused lapdog. Innocent wished someone else present understood the significance of this. He almost wished Frederick was in the room just so he could wave the message at him and gloat, "I've found her! Before you could!"

Instead, he forced a mask of calm across his face. "I require my spymaster," he said to Aelius, who in turn relayed the message to an ostiarius, who left the room through the half-hidden door behind the silk tapestry. "The rest of you are dismissed," he said, trying to sound indulgent and not overeager. "You may sleep through morning mass to account for this unusually late night. I will see you at morning Council. Thank you."

In a moment he was alone in the small marble room, his heart racing. He had found the cup, and better yet, it had been revealed to him by one of his own men, who—best of all—had no inkling of its significance, and therefore would not try to meddle with it.

As he sat completely alone—such a rare gift—in the room, waiting for Rufus, the heavy truth of the matter hit him like a missile: There was nobody in all the Vatican he could trust to go and get it. He dare not even send a message to Dietrich lest the message itself fall into the wrong hands.

I must go myself. I will have to take the cup from her with my own hands. And nobody can know that I have done so.

Which meant nobody here at the Lateran Palace, or indeed all of Rome, could know that he was going to Montségur. And nobody in Montségur—except Dietrich—could know he had arrived.

The girl with the cup was at Montségur.

Did Frederick know? Had Frederick, for some perverse reason, *sent* her there?

"Aelius," he called out to his steward, who had almost disappeared down the hall that would lead eventually to the dormitories. Aelius turned around and rushed back to him. He was devoted, was Aelius, even if he was not particularly bright.

"I must make a clandestine trip to Salerno on urgent business. Nobody can know that I am going. People must believe that I am going to Apulia instead. Arrange transport. I will travel with a brace of bodyguards and one servant, but nobody is to know where I am. Report that I am in Apulia, and write to Apulia to tell them to pretend I am there."

Aelius blinked in confusion.

"If you cannot do this, I will find somebody else worthy of the office," Innocent said sharply. "This is very urgent. The future and security of the Church depend upon swift action and absolute secrecy. There are forces abroad, with dangerous powers. I must bring them to heel."

Now Aelius's eyes opened wide. "If people ask why you are in Apulia, what should they hear?"

Innocent did not hesitate—nor, to his own mind, did he lie. "I must get away from the bustle of the Vatican so that I may determine the nature of the next crusade." He gave Aelius a confiding look. "It is a crusade that will change the world forever."

CHAPTER 21:

AT THE ROC de la TOR

Even the watchtower was lit by beeswax candles. Ferenc, leaning against the wall (the stools all being taken), pulled the wool cloak tighter around his shoulders and rubbed the cold tip of his nose with his cold fingers. He watched the three men-at-arms playing cards by candlelight. He had nothing to bet with, but Frederick had taught him this game, and he guessed he could beat any of them. "I am surprised your sect allows gambling," he said.

"The Perfecti do not gamble, of course," said chubby, leather-clad Milos, who was captain of the night watch. Ferenc envied him his gloves. "Luckily for us, we are far from perfect. Well, maybe not lucky for you, Otz, eh? Not your night." He laid down his four cards, chuckled smugly, and took a coin from Otz's side of the table. Otz, naturally long-faced, sighed as if he had expected nothing else. He reminded Ferenc of a poet Frederick had sent away from court for excessive melancholia.

The third man, Savis, was handsome and well dressed, his dark hair dramatic above pale skin and dark eyes. Ferenc wondered—in passing—if he was a troubadour. "You're new, boy, so perhaps nobody has explained this to you," he said. "Most of us aren't even Cathars. Everyone is pretending this is some kind of religious war.

It isn't. My land was taken by the French—I should be lording it over a manse, not crammed into a freezing, bizarre little hellhole, standing guard over the empty, dull blackness of night. Why they need six of us in here tonight is beyond me."

"Full moon, isn't it?" said Otz. "Easier for the enemy to get around."

"Who is going to attempt to climb an unclimbable cliff in the middle of the night?"

As the other two grunted agreement, Ferenc said, "Myself, I am happy to help as asked. My master and I want to prove we're worthy of—"

"What brought you here?" Otz asked. "Given you're not Credents?"

"I heard it was to take away that eccentric, Percival," said jowly Milos.

"I am squire to Raphael of Acre," said Ferenc diplomatically. "It isn't fit that I speak on my master's behalf."

"I saw you with Ocyrhoe today," said Savis in a leering tone. "Never seen that girl light up so, and you seemed pretty buoyant yourself. Whyever you came, seems to me that's what might keep you here."

"Ocyrhoe?" chortled Milos. "That little bean? With all the lovely women here to fawn over—"

"As long as the Bishop doesn't notice," laughed Savis. To Ferenc, confidingly: "Otz here got himself into hot water last month, writing love letters to sickly little Esclarmonde de Perelha."

Otz reddened. "They were intended as expressions of courtly regard," he said, fussing with the pin that fastened his cloak.

"Bullshit. You wanted to get up her skirt," said Savis gaily. "Myself, I'm not impervious to the charms of her buxom sister."

"Meaning Peire-Roger's wife," said Savis, a scandalized aside to Ferenc.

"It's Amelie for me," declared Milos. "And let me tell you, it's not unreciprocated."

The other two men chortled. "Careful the Bishop or Rixenda don't find out!" Otz cried. "Let me tell you: the humiliation!"

"I thought they would throw you out of the fortress for that, my friend," Savis said in an admiring yet vicious tone.

Ferenc frowned uncomfortably. "This is supposed to be a religious sanctuary. Everyone is chaste."

All three made dismissive faces, chuckling.

"Ocyrhoe, eh?" said Milos. Ferenc immediately blushed so hard his whole head felt warmer, making the rest of him shiver.

"She's a friend," he said, staring at the deck of cards in the center of the table.

Savis rolled his eyes. "I hope that's all she is, or we need to teach you something about appreciation of the feminine form."

"There's nothing wrong with her form," Ferenc shot back hotly.

"She's got no meat on her, boy," said Milos. "You should only put your meat where you're going to get some meat in return."

Ferenc pushed himself away from the wall so abruptly he almost stumbled forward. "That is no way to speak of any woman and especially no way to talk about a friend of mine." A sound caught his attention, and he turned his head instinctively toward the window.

The other three were hooting with laughter. "Now don't get defensive, fellow," Milos began. Ferenc silenced him with a sharp gesture.

"Somebody is here," he said in an urgent whisper. "Just outside the window."

Milos made a dismissive face. "We're a whole floor up! There's nothing but air outside the window," he said.

Ferenc shook his head worriedly and pointed toward the nearest of the four small windows. Downstairs, Nicholas rested alone beside the barred door; above, on the roof, Pons peered into the darkness of the mountaintop in search of lights moving toward them from the army camp. Otz, with a curious grimace, put down his cards, got to his feet, and started toward the window where Ferenc was pointing. As he approached, there was abrupt confusion in the candlelit room.

A small man in dark tunic and leggings erupted through the window straight at Otz, as if he had been shoved by a giant. He entered with knife held out before him, and sank his blade deep into Otz's shoulder before his feet touched the ground. Otz shrieked in pain and surprise and shoved the stranger off him with his good arm, but the man fell to the floor and bounced back up again, the edge of the knife blade making a flashing arc toward Otz's neck. In the dim light, Ferenc saw Otz's terror as the blade landed; Otz made a thick, strangling sound as he watched his own blood spray into the face of his attacker. The man threw him disdainfully to the wooden floor without bothering to watch him die.

Two other men sprang into the room from two other windows, one with a dagger between his teeth, the other with his knife in stabbing position. They set themselves on Milos and Savis; Ferenc, standing closer to the wall, avoided immediate attention. But he knew what Otz's killer was up to now: Ferenc scrambled to follow him down the ladder before he could unbolt the door. Three men through three upper windows. Each must have been at the top of a human ladder at least three men high. That meant there were six marauders out in the dark, waiting to be let in once the door was unbarred.

"Nicholas!" Ferenc screamed down the hatch, and threw himself onto the man scrambling down the stairs. His weight shoved the man off the steep rises. They landed in a loud heap on the raised wooden floor, the invader losing his knife and reaching frantically for purchase somewhere, which gave Ferenc the advantage of grabbing at his limbs.

Nicholas, a lanky fellow with bad skin, was startled out of an illicit nap. He shouted with disoriented alarm, leapt away from the flailing men, and looked in astonishment up the stairway. Ferenc landed on top of the invader. "Up there," Ferenc shouted, trying to use the weight of his own elbows to keep the intruder's elbows pinned to the ground. "He killed Otz. Help Milos and Savis!"

"Killed Otz?" Nicholas echoed haplessly.

"Or help me," Ferenc suggested with a grunt.

The man brought his forearms up, grabbed hold of Ferenc's woolen tunic at the collar, and with a growl of effort flipped Ferenc so that they now lay on their sides, still face to face. Ferenc's arm was trapped under his own body, freeing the invader's arm. The other man grabbed Ferenc by the hair and pulled the young hunter's head back, then reached for a second blade at his belt. Ferenc couldn't see this move directly, but understood what was about to happen. He brought his knee up and kicked the man's hand hard to keep it from reaching his belt, and then, lightning-fast, reached for the same spot himself, snatching away the dagger and shoving the point of it straight into the man's lower jaw and throat. The man's eyes rolled and he made a tormented noise, his jaw pinned shut by the hilt of the dagger. Ferenc felt a rush of adrenaline and dread, and pushed himself away from the dying man, rolling away over the floor then scrambling to his feet, gasping for breath. He ignored the man squirming like an unearthed worm near him and looked for Nicholas. Ferenc was alone in this room, which meant Nicholas had gone upstairs to join the fight. Above he heard scuffling but no shouting, no sound of metal against metal. The absolute surprise of the attack had succeeded. He wondered if Pons was still up on the roof, or if they had already found him. There was no way for him to get down.

As Ferenc stood wondering what to do there was a loud, communal grunt at the three downstairs windows, and suddenly three more men appeared. These did not spring into the room as the previous ones had; they were hoisting themselves up from the ground. It cost them. Ferenc was holding the enemy's dagger, but in his own belt he had a long knife; he dropped the stabbing weapon in favor of the slicing one, rushed toward the closest window, and with one sharp horizontal move, slit the throat of one man who was pulling himself through the window.

Shaking violently, Ferenc leapt toward the next window; the attacker in that one, seeing what had happened to his comrade, dropped out of sight back outside with a curse; the third, directly across from the first one, shouted at whoever was outside supporting him, scrambled into the room and rolled as he landed on the floor, coming up quickly with dagger in one hand and knife in the other, both held curled in close to him, ready to strike as soon as Ferenc moved in.

Ferenc saw this in time, wheeled back, and held his knife out defensively before him, wishing he had not dropped the dagger, even though his knife was longer than the stranger's. The stranger's urgent goal was not to kill Ferenc, however; it was to unbolt the door. As Ferenc realized this and tried to get between him and the entrance, the man slashed out in Ferenc's direction and the youth jumped back; the attacker had a clear route to the door.

Ferenc tried to hear if there were still sounds of struggle above, but his own breath and pounding pulse, and the pounding on the door from outside, made it hard for him to hear anything upstairs. The man reached the door, stuck his dagger in his belt, and began to open the bolt one-handed, his knife-arm still held warningly in Ferenc's direction. Ferenc ran at him with a shout, aiming his long knife for the man's outstretched bicep, but as he came in close, the man released the door briefly, and walloped Ferenc on the side of the head with a round-house punch that toppled the Hungarian to his knees just before his knife would have hit home. Dazed and gasping, he somersaulted backward to relative safety.

The man turned back to the door and unbolted it. Four large soldiers came in—the three who had been at the bottom of the human ladders, and the soldier who had ducked out of the window to avoid Ferenc's knife. Without a glance around the ground-floor room, they swarmed up the steep staircase. Only the man who had let them in knew Ferenc was down here and still alive.

He turned, and closed the door behind him. "Little shit," he said in perfect Latin. "You killed my Gascon brothers. You die."

"Oh, you are from *Gascony*," Ferenc said, panting more than he needed to. He raised his head a little and then, as if that hurt too much, moaned a little and lowered it gingerly. "That explains much. I thought you were French, but at least the French fight like men, not like stray cats."

The man's eyes flashed in the candlelight. He threw himself toward Ferenc. Ferenc lay limp as if unable even to defend himself. When the man's knife came whipping down, Ferenc suddenly unfurled his arm and slashed the approaching blade out of the way, then from his curled position kicked the aggressor in the kneecap as hard as he could. The man snarled and leapt back; Ferenc jumped up and attacked him as if he would climb up on top of him; the man staggered backwards, and they both fell to the floor, Ferenc on top. This time he did not hesitate; he held the man's head to the floor, chin pushed up, and cut his throat. He jumped up and back, trying bootlessly to avoid the blood, and then, breathing so hard he was sobbing, he ran back to the foot of the steps. There was no sound of struggle from above.

From where he stood he could see out of the door easily. There was a rough guffaw upstairs and a moment later a lanky, limp body came hurling from above, flashed past Ferenc, and fell through the winter night until it landed so far down the steep slope Ferenc could hardly hear the thud—he knew Nicholas's corpse had landed mostly because of the cries of glee from the top of the tower. A moment later, more grunted effort from the voices above, and Pons' heavy frame dove limp and headfirst past his vision. If Milos or Savis were still alive, they would be making noise; he had only met them this evening but both were noisemakers, he was sure.

He was the only survivor, and the Gascons upstairs did not know that he lived—or that he had killed another of their mates. With a prayer to Saint Emeric and Nagy Asszony, he opened the door and sprinted up the slope toward the fortress.

CHAPTER 22:

INFINITA PECUNIA

Ferenc had never been told the code word for entrance, and the guard at the fortress gate had never met him. The shocking news he cried out in distress was greeted by Ferrer, at the gate, with stupefied silence, but the upset brought the sleep-doped Peire-Roger and a cluster of knights. Raphael and Vera were among them. They recognized Ferenc's voice.

"Let him in," Raphael ordered. "That's my squire. Your own Ocyrhoe can vouch for him."

"Ocyrhoe sleeps down in the Good Ones' village," said the porter.

"Open the gate," Peire-Roger growled.

The gate opened just enough for Ferenc, blood smeared into his hair and across his face and tunic, to push his way through. He was so out of breath from his sprint up the slope that he collapsed as he entered the safety of the compound. "The watchtower's been taken," he said thickly. "Everyone's dead."

Amidst the shocked protests, Peire-Roger took a step closer and stood menacingly over him. "How came you to be the sole survivor?" he demanded. "Newcomer that you are, are we to believe that is mere coincidence?"

"He is my squire," Raphael said sternly. "Percival can tell you I am…"

"The tower was barred from the inside. Is it not possible he somehow admitted the French?"

"They were Gascon climbers," Ferenc said hoarsely. "They made human ladders to get in through the upper windows. I killed two, but there are seven living." He looked up at all of them. "As God is my judge, I did what I could."

"Of course you did," Raphael said gruffly. He reached out a hand to help Ferenc up. "They don't know I survived," said Ferenc. "I killed the ones who saw me."

Raphael turned instantly to Peire-Roger. "A counterattack. Immediately. While we have the benefit of surprise."

Peire-Roger looked flummoxed. "We don't know enough."

"We know there are seven of them, and two dead, and Ferenc can tell us how they're armed."

"They may be the vanguard for an entire host!"

"Going up the slope? In the dark?" Ferrer the porter said. "I'm amazed there were a handful of them capable of it."

Peire-Roger glared briefly at him.

"If you're too drunk to organize a sortie, I will do it," said Raphael. It was not an offer; it was a declaration.

"The village first," Ferenc said. "We have to get all the Good Ones up here into the courtyard."

"They're safe enough down there," said Peire-Roger. "The French would have to take the barbican to get a bead on them."

"Warn them, at least," Ferenc insisted, thinking chiefly of Ocyrhoe.

Peire-Roger grimaced. "You're right." He turned to Vera. "Wake Phillipa and her women. Tell them to dress and come down with us. Men mustn't go into the women's village."

"Do you really think that matters now?" Raphael demanded.

"Proper conduct matters more to the Good Ones than do their own lives," Peire-Roger assured him. "Sometimes it is a nuisance."

"No need to wake them. I can do it myself," said Vera. "I'm better armed than they are, anyway."

"Let's go," said Ferenc urgently to Raphael. "The three of us are enough."

Raphael glanced at Peire-Roger, who nodded urgently. "Thank you. I'll spread the word in here."

"And gather men for an immediate sortie," Raphael amended.

"I think it is ill-advised to rush into such danger."

"It's far more ill-advised to wait," Raphael countered. "If you don't send men, Vera and I will take Ferenc and Percival." He gestured for Ferrer to open the gate.

Vera grabbed a torch from a brazier by the gate and stared down the porter. "We'll need two torches," she said to Ferenc; after a blink, he grabbed the other one from the other side of the gate. Raphael followed behind them with his knife drawn. They hurried grimly out of the gate and down the path toward the north-facing stone huts. On the other side of the wall, they heard Peire-Roger's growling voice bellowing orders to the garrison.

"Good work, Ferenc. I am glad you're safe," Raphael said from the darkness behind him.

"Thank you, sir," said Ferenc, miserable.

"Don't call me sir, Ferenc," Raphael said wearily.

At the low, stone wall delineating the village, Vera moved straight off into the darkness to wake the Goodwomen; Ferenc gestured to Raphael with the torch, and they took the path down the steps to the village of the Goodmen. Already Vera's voice was calling out a warning into the frigid, moonlit night.

"Wake yourselves," Raphael hollered. He slammed his fist on the nearest wooden door; Ferenc moved past him to the next one and hammered his fist there.

"Awake! The watchtower is taken! Come up into the fortress, until we know the risk to you here!"

Raphael passed by him to go to the next hut; there were sounds of doors opening, and dozens of voices began to respond to them in the darkness. None of these voices sounded either sleepy or alarmed; Ferenc supposed they had all been awake praying. He wondered if and when the Good Ones ever slept. Men were responding to the news and sharing it, but Ferenc and Raphael sounded almost panicked compared to the tone with which the Goodmen communicated this new crisis to their neighbors.

The second door he approached opened as he pulled his hand back in preparation to knock on it. Standing in the doorway was an imposing figure dressed not as a Goodman but as a soldier. The light from the torch shown warmly on Percival's calm face, and Ferenc signaled with the light to get Raphael's attention. Raphael saw who it was and ran to join them at the doorway.

"Well then," said Raphael. "Here we are, trapped in someone else's story. Put on your maille. We're taking back the watchtower."

◆ ◆ ◆

Fewer than half of the Good Ones responded to the alarm, and even these seemed to file up the night slope mostly to put the self-appointed heralds at ease. The rest thanked them for their message and returned calmly to their huts. Ferenc watched from the back of the line as the Good Ones trudged up the slope with a remarkable absence of fear. Every third or fourth one carried a torch that smelled of burning olive oil. In their long, black robes they resembled a dour funeral procession. He looked for the small figure in paler tunic but could not find her in the procession.

Inside, the fortress was modulated chaos. Children and women were alarmed, some wailing for the death of a loved one in the tower; the men-at-arms were grimly arming themselves and streaming up the stairs to line the wall-walk. The Good Ones were somber but calm, offering quiet, muffled words of comfort that were mostly ignored. Ferenc pushed through the press of people, ran up the wooden steps, and entered the donjon. Here was a smaller, warmer version of the same cacophony—most people had moved outside, but there was still grieving and grimness enough within. In a corner was a huddle of men, Peire-Roger sitting tallest among them with his back to the wall. He held a wooden cup with steaming liquid in it. Raphael stood next to him. Percival was there, as well as old Raimon de Perelha. Rixenda was the only woman in the gathering, but as he approached, Ferenc saw Vera stalking away from the group with a resigned, glowering look.

"Aren't we going to attack the attackers?" Ferenc asked.

Vera rolled her eyes with a dour expression. "Peire-Roger says something else must happen first. If your hands are cold, warm them over Raphael's ears—there is hot steam coming out of them."

In the shadows, Ferenc saw Ocyrhoe, hiding in plain sight, listening in on the conference with bright, concerned eyes. He took a step to head toward her, but Raphael called out for him.

"We will need additional troops now, troops attacking the French army down on the ground," Peire-Roger was saying as Ferenc sat beside Percival.

"If we do not take the tower back *now*, while we can," Raphael said between gritted teeth, "then no amount of additional troops will make any difference."

"This is my fortress," Peire-Roger said sharply. "You have been here one day and half of two nights. We are grateful to have you, but you know nothing of our—"

"I know the value of the watchtower and the level ground beside it," Raphael interrupted. "I saw it from the battlements—there's enough flat land there for them to use as a staging area, and tonight, this *instant*, is the only opportunity to prevent them."

"You are an excellent tactician, sir," Peire-Roger said, his teeth now gritted like Raphael's. "But I'm a strategist, and commander of this fortress, and if you argue with me once again, you will be reprimanded."

Ferenc watched Raphael, with tremendous effort, suppress his anger. "You were talking about additional troops," he said, in such a low, flat, disgusted voice it sounded almost as if he were about to vomit.

"The Count of Toulouse has promised..." old Raimon began.

Peire-Roger spat on the floor. "That man has been promising us the same thing for six months and we've yet to see a single soldier. We need to hire mercenary troops."

"That is disgraceful," said old Raimon. "In all of the years of the Albigensian crusade, nobody ever had to resort to hiring mercenaries!"

"Those glorious old days, if you perversely wish to think of them that way, are over," his son-in-law retorted. "There are very few lords left who have not caved in to the French king's power. We are not the force we once were. Even if most of that army down there has no stomach for attacking us, neither have they the nerve to turn on their overlord and ambush his troops. They will attack because they must. We have to defend ourselves. There are those who will be sympathetic to our cause, but they will not fight for free."

An unhappy pause.

"Forgive me for being uncouth," Raphael said sourly. "But how do you intend to pay them?"

The expressions on the faces of the local men briefly relaxed.

"That is one thing we need not worry over," said Peire-Roger. "The Cathar treasury is huge, and most of it is hidden in this fortress or in small caves just below the walls."

"But the Good Ones beshrew the material world," said Percival. "How came they to be wealthy?"

"We have been fugitives from the Roman Church for decades now," said Bishop Marti. "Fugitives need gold in hand to survive. We are very grateful that our Credents understand this and make donations to us. Sometimes when we ask directly, sometimes in their wills. Also most of us, *sir knight*, have had professions at which we work and earn our keep." Percival looked slightly chastised by his tone. "We keep the money for emergencies, and even we ourselves do not know where most of it is. We turn it over to Credents, who bury it somewhere secret, so that if we are caught and tortured for information we cannot betray our common body."

Ferenc had a few cynical thoughts about this, and was sure that if Vera were here, she would not only share them but speak them aloud. "How do you know the Credents do not run off with the money?" he asked, forcing his voice to stay uninflected with sarcasm.

"We have faith," said Marti simply. "Over the span of decades, we have never been betrayed. When we need money, it is provided to us. But what we will need for a mercenary army cannot be gathered quickly from around the countryside. We will need to take every coin and object of worth from Montségur and spirit it beyond the reaches of the army immediately, so that we can buy help. We have been saving it for a crisis. This is the crisis."

Peire-Roger gave Raphael a superior look. "That is what takes precedence," he said. "Getting the treasure out before they think to scout for it."

"Some of us can fight while the rest of you collect the treasure," Raphael said.

Peire-Roger's stormy, dark eyes blazed a warning. "I told you not to challenge me. If your attack fails, we risk drawing attention to those carrying the treasure away. You will not speak another word of an attack tonight or I'll have you thrown into the cistern." He turned his attention back to the group. "I will order all of them to bring their valuables to the center of the courtyard, and those who know where the money is in the cave, to bring it up now. The nights are long and there are hours yet before dawn. If we hurry we can send a party out before daybreak."

"Agreed," said Marti and old Raimon.

Ferenc heard a faint rustle in the darkness where Ocyrhoe had been listening in. He glanced over; she was gone.

The gathering stood to disperse, as Peire-Roger peremptorily assigned each person a section of the courtyard or donjon to speak to. Ferenc was sent up to the southern wall-walk, with instructions to stand in for each soldier as they went to collect their own contributions.

As he rushed through the single room of the donjon, he glanced about carefully, but Ocyrhoe, he already knew, was not in here. He pushed open the door and ran his eyes over the bustle in the torchlit yard, but she was nowhere to be seen.

Ignoring a vague sense of unease, he pushed through the crowd and mounted the nearer set of wooden steps. He explained Peire-Roger's order to the first soldier. He expected some kind of balking or resentment, but the fellow nodded with understanding and then sprinted down the steps as if nothing could make him more eager than to part with his modest worldly wealth. *There is something to this place,* Ferenc thought. He could never be a believer in such a peculiar creed, but the mutual care and respect within this community of fugitives was touching.

◆ ◆ ◆

Ocryhoe practically slid down the frozen slope to the Good Ones' village wall, her pulse loud in her head. She was ashamed of the feeling of panic but it was more potent than the feeling of shame.

She ran into the yard and then into Rixenda's tiny hut, throwing herself onto her own bedroll, which she had abandoned not an hour before when word had come of the tower. Her hands frantically reached under the lumpy pillow for the cup. It was warm in her hands—enough to heat them without losing its own heat. She took a deep breath and let it out in a sigh.

She heard Rixenda enter.

"I thought you might have come back down here," the older woman said. Ocyrhoe sat up very straight, but did not look over at her. "Perhaps the time has come for you to use the cup for something useful," Rixenda said gently. "Perhaps this is a blessing for you."

"I can't," Ocryhoe said. "Please, Rixenda, please don't make me give it away. I can't. I know we need the valuables, I understand that, but I need to keep it."

"It's pure silver," said Rixenda. "It would secure the services of a knight at least."

"I can't let it go," she said. "I wish I could explain why. It isn't safe to let it out into the world."

"But it's safe to keep it here?"

"I can't explain it, but yes, it is. It cannot come to mischief here."

Rixenda made a disapproving noise. It was very much unlike her, and Ocyrhoe cringed. "The material world is nothing but mischief," the Goodwoman said. "I do not see why one cup should be more mischievous than anything else. I know you do not enjoy possession of it."

"Please trust my judgment. Do you remember the effect it had upon your nephew?"

"That was his own imagination getting the better of him in the aftermath of your throwing yourself through a window."

"No, it wasn't," Ocyrhoe assured her. "I'm telling you it was the cup. But it isn't always beneficent that way. I'm begging you not to tell anyone about it, lest they take it from me by force."

"Nobody is going to force anyone into anything," said Rixenda, clipped. "The most force they would use would be to try to shame you from holding something back from the common good."

"It is not for the common good for the cup to leave here," Ocyrhoe said firmly. "Nor for anyone else to know about it."

Rixenda spread her hands in resignation. "I will not gainsay you. But I will rejoice if you change your mind on this. And the Credents may yet come through here seeking objects."

"Why would they look here?" Ocyrhoe said. "Among the Perfecti? None of you own anything. Why would anyone bother looking through your huts?"

"We use objects in the process of living," Rixenda pointed out. "We are not attached to them, so we do not think of them as having value, but sometimes they do—brooches to keep cloaks closed, or objects from our trades, like gold and diamonds that are ground into medicines. Someone is likely to sweep through to see if we've been careless. Or corrupt. Or fearful. Somebody might be hoarding something, in fear of worse catastrophe to come, and might secretly disagree with the bishop that now is the time to yield all up."

"I'll hide it," said Ocyrhoe.

◆ ◆ ◆

Children self-importantly held up oil-drenched torches, flooding the courtyard with light. Most of the community gathered around two mounds in the middle of the courtyard, the children and some of the servants outright gawking at the wealth. Two large satchels sat agape, waiting for the coins, plate, jewelry, and other valuable objects. Most of it, Percival saw, was actual money. He looked for a cup in the valuable tumble of objects but could not find one.

When he'd questioned Vidal a week or so earlier, Vidal had been unequivocal—there had been a chalice. It had been brandished by a smallish, female angel. Never mind that the Good Ones held no truck with angels.

That night, Percival's dreams had been full of Ocyrhoe. She was not dressed in her usual rags, however, but in radiant garments. She had held out her hand, offering him something he could not make out because it emanated such intense, blue-white light that the object itself was invisible. This was the clearest dream he had had since childhood.

Now, a woolen wrap clutched around his shoulders, he perused the pile very carefully. He could not walk right up to it and sift through it, but he managed to scrutinize it fairly thoroughly. There were more coins by far than he'd ever seen amassed anywhere, ever, in his life. In addition, there was no small amount of jewelry—necklaces, chains, brooches, rings, hair-pins, belt buckles—and small decorative statues, and silver and gold plate. When Percival thought of great mounds of valuables, his inner eye instinctively saw religious images, icons, and paraphernalia, but there was none of that here.

Directly across from him he saw Ocyrhoe standing with the youth, Ferenc, still covered with blood and seemingly shaken by his own survival. They were surveying the treasure as intensely as he was—as intensely as *everyone* was, except the Good Ones.

✦ ✦ ✦

"I was surprised Raphael put the emperor's money into the pile," said Ocyrhoe. "He does not believe you should even be here."

"He understands there is a need for help, although he disagrees with what kind. But the sooner help arrives, the sooner he can quit this place with a clean conscience," said Ferenc.

They watched, shivering together in the moon-bright, torchlit night, as the two satchels were bundled up. Matheus and Peire Bonnet had been charged with getting the treasury down the mountain to a secret spot; they were working with a few other Credents to create packs that would distribute the weight safely across their shoulders, so that each could carry half the weight without hurting themselves.

"If they can hire mercenaries, what do you think it will accomplish?" asked Ferenc. He rubbed his hands together for warmth, wishing he had not lost his gloves.

"I think they want the newcomers to attack the army down there on its own level, create a new front, and then have to divert resources away from the siege," said Ocyrhoe. "Also, I bet if the invading army is distressed too far—in this weather, after so many months, when most of them never cared much for this assignment in the first place—there are likely to be many turncoats against the French."

Ferenc considered this. "So it is not just an act of desperation."

"No, in some ways it may bring a happier conclusion than simply fending off the French in the hopes they will give up and wander back to France. That's why Peire-Roger rated it more urgent than retaking the watchtower. This way, the French may actually have to retreat, or even surrender. Then the local lords might get their lands back." She spoke matter-of-factly, with a weary pragmatism extraordinarily unlike the child he had met two years ago in Rome.

"What will you do when it's all over?" he asked, and then felt awkward for having asked.

Ocyrhoe gave him a secretive smile. "Why do you want to know?"

He shrugged uncomfortably. "Just curious. We will head back to Frederick's…"

"I will go with you!" she said abruptly.

"…with Percival," he finished.

"Oh," she said, frowning. "Perhaps not, then."

"Why? What's wrong with Percival?"

She avoided his look. "He is a bit peculiar," she said. "I'm not at ease around him."

"Peculiar how?" asked Ferenc. "Raphael loves him dearly, but has said he worries his fancies will lead him to ruin."

She shrugged and began to fidget with her lock of knotted hair. "Just an odd one, that's all. Nothing in particular."

"Such an odd one that you would give up going back to Frederick's court with me, just to avoid him."

"Oh," she said, twisting the tress around her finger like a little girl. "Hmm. I would have to think about that."

A pause.

"Raphael says Percival suffers from hallucinations."

A pause.

"Perhaps," said Ocyrhoe.

A pause.

"Not unlike Father Rodrigo," added Ferenc quietly. He understood her fear of madmen; the last one they'd both known had very nearly murdered her.

A pause. Ocyrhoe nodded.

"That is the heart of it," she said.

"He's not like that. Raphael would not have agreed to this if he thought Percival was harmful."

"Rodrigo wasn't *harmful* either," said Ocyrhoe unhappily. "Things change. We thought the French army was not terribly *harmful* until last night." She gestured toward the two heavy piles of valuables and coins before them. "Now look at this. Once they take this away, there will be nothing left here. If there is a new emergency, they will have no resources left to attend to it."

"They have good fighters," said Ferenc.

She shook her head. "How do you know they're any good? You saw five good fighters killed in a few moments. Besides, these men are outnumbered one to a hundred," she said. "They are not good enough to kill one hundred enemies each. This money—I hate to think it, I never valued money in my life—this is their best protection, and they are about to entrust it all to strangers."

"In exchange for an *army*," Ferenc pointed out. Ocyrhoe made a noncommittal gesture and blew into her cupped hands to warm them. "Ocyrhoe, you are fretting about them as if they were children. They have been dealing with persecution since before we were born."

Ocyrhoe shook her head, but not in disagreement; it was more an expression of helplessness. "This has been my home, these people have been family, I've felt protected. Do you know how desperately I needed that?"

"I can imagine," Ferenc said carefully.

"So of course I am worried. It is a selfish worry." She gestured across the circle of gawkers, toward Percival. He was moving deosil around the circle, nearing them. "When I avoid his strangeness, that is also a selfish worry."

"If you come back with us to Frederick's, I promise to protect you from him," Ferenc said indulgently, trying to lighten the mood.

Percival was a quarter of the way around the torchlit circle, his eyes on the people around him to avoid walking into someone. Then he raised his head and stared straight at Ocyrhoe with a queer expression in the uneven light, almost beseeching. Ferenc shivered.

"All right then," said Ocyrhoe, her look trapped in Percival's. "Protect me. Starting now."

◆ ◆ ◆

Percival approached them, wishing he did not have to interrupt. They seemed so content in each other's presence, even while their faces puckered with concern at what they witnessed. But he had to ask her. He had to know.

He caught her eye and kept it as he circled around toward them. Ferenc moved in front of her, not quite hiding her, but shielding; Percival regretted making her unhappy, but this was much more important than mere human comfort. Besides, if she really understood, she would know she had nothing to fear from him. He wanted her help to do the Virgin's bidding.

Soon he was standing before them. "Good morning," he said. It was almost morning; beyond the torches and lamps, the depth of night was flattening to dawning grey.

"Good morning," they both replied, guardedly.

"Ocyrhoe, my sister, may I speak alone with you a moment?"

They glanced at each other, then both looked back at him. "Ocyrhoe has no secrets from me," said Ferenc. "You may speak to her in my company."

"Is this true?" Percival asked her in a confiding tone suggesting he believed it was not true.

"Yes. What is it?" Ocyrhoe asked brusquely, folding her skinny arms across her skinny torso and shivering in the chill dawn air. It was that time of day when exhaustion filled everyone's pores.

"I have been having visions," Percival began gently.

"I have heard about your visions," Ocyrhoe said shortly, staring at the ground and moving a limestone pebble about with the toe of her boot.

"I have been having them for a long time now. They seem to have brought me here, but for what reason, I cannot say. I thought it was to help protect these people, but they are now in need of far more protection than I can ever give them. So I think it is something else and I am trying to determine what it is."

"I wish you luck with that," she said, fidgeting. She turned away from him, toward Ferenc. On reflex Percival reached toward her shoulder to turn her back, but as he did so, two things happened: Ferenc's hand went to his knife hilt, and Peire Bonnet approached them, with an open, smiling face. "Brother Percival, Peire-Roger has asked you to do us the honor of accompanying my brother and myself down the mountain with the treasure."

"Gladly," Percival said immediately. "Of course." He had released his grip on Ocyrhoe's shoulder; glancing toward her, he saw her hurry to Ferenc, who took her hand comfortingly as they met.

"We will meet at sundown at the gate," said Matheus. "Thank you."

"Who else is going?" asked Percival.

"I volunteered," said Vera, showing up from nowhere behind him. "Peire-Roger was having none of that."

"I am sorry he has insulted you," said Percival. "I will happily tell him that your presence is a better surety of these men's safety than even my own."

"I already volunteered you for that service," Vera said. "He is not interested in hearing what you have to say for me."

Percival smiled at her and rested a hand on her shoulder. "I prophesy that he will come in time to value you as the warrior you are."

CHAPTER 23:
TREBUCHET

"*Thank you, my son,*" read the letter from His Holiness, which Dietrich held close to the flickering flame, "*for alerting us to the possible presence of such insidious heretics within the ranks of our otherwise devout and Catholic troops. We are grateful for the presence of such wise and rational counsel as yours is, that will keep us informed of any suspicious developments. There is of course no need to alarm His Eminence Pierre Amelii nor any of the secular leaders of the army of this danger. Keep eyes alert and lips closed, but keep ink and parchment at hand to write to us if the need arises.*"

It was not the dramatic call to action that Dietrich had hoped for, but there was satisfaction still in knowing His Holiness relied on him—and would allow him to destroy the Shield-Brethren should the opportunity arise. It made up, somewhat, for the cold shoulders he was still treated to here, in the stark army tent at the foot of Montségur.

The Gascon climbers had been *his* idea. *He* had found the old shepherd. The sudden surge in progress owed a tremendous amount to him, but Hugue and the archbishop refused to acknowledge that. He did not mind so much that they did not admit it publicly—he was used to stealth, preferred it in fact—but they would not admit it even *to him*, and that rankled.

He was ignored as he watched the French troops enact another idea of his: disassembling the enormous, counterweighted trebuchet that had been so ineffective at the foot of the mountain. With the watchtower under their control, it would be safe now—if still disturbingly treacherous—to carry the timber around the mountain and use pulleys to haul it up the slope scaled by the Gascon climbers. Here it could be safely reassembled on the relatively level ground near the watchtower.

Hugue had reluctantly acknowledged that the mountaintop itself might provide ammunition, that projectiles could be mined and shaped right out of the limestone. As could the bigger challenge: the ton of counterweight required to sling the rocks.

"But it will take time to set up workshops to accomplish that," he griped.

"More time than it will take to starve out the Cathars, when half the countryside is feeding them?" asked Dietrich.

"And the accuracy from such a distance—"

"Trebuchets are built on wheels, my lord," Dietrich said.

"That is chiefly to assist in the efficacy of their action."

"But a wheeled object can be moved."

Hugue frowned at him as if Dietrich were a simpleton. "Wheel it where? It will be resting on the only level ground of the entire slope."

Dietrich's eyes glittered. "You wheel it *up the slope*. And take the barbican."

Hugue's eyes bulged wide. Dietrich felt a moment of satisfaction at having impressed the army leader—until the army leader burst out guffawing. "Push that unwieldy thing up a rocky slope on wheels the size of my boot? That's absurd! What have you been drinking?"

Nothing Dietrich said would sway him. The most Hugue would contemplate was the trebuchet hurling rocks from the distance of the watchtower. As of just after dawn, French and Gascon crossbow-men had already crowded into the tower, and were now shooting relentlessly up the slope at the wall-walks of Montségur, to prevent the heretics' archers from shooting at the minions given the grim task of hauling half a ton of lumber, hardware, and mining equipment up the pog.

A trebuchet, in essence, used a lever to exaggerate the work of an enormous slingshot. A triangular frame on a wheeled platform supported a long beam—attached asymmetrically on a pin—that see-sawed on the top of the frame. The shorter segment of the beam was ended with an enormous weight, a ton or more; this side was winched up and held up by a system of pulleys and pins. The longer, unweighted segment of the beam tilted nearly to the ground. Attached to the end of it was a long slingshot—the longer, the better—that lay on the ground. Resting in the sling was a rock or boulder.

When the counterweight was released, it pulled its end of the beam hard and fast toward the ground—and so the other end of the beam jerked upward, raising the sling with a centripetal force that whipped the sling up and overhead and sent the stone soaring. This particular trebuchet supposedly had been designed by Bishop Durand of Albi. Dietrich found it odd, and somewhat distasteful, that a man of the church would seek credit for an instrument of warfare. But he found it even more distasteful that anyone would claim to have designed what was entirely generic in form; not one particular element of it seemed to have been re-envisioned.

✦ ✦ ✦

"Rixenda told us not to work together," Ferenc said.

Ocyrhoe made a dismissive gesture. "That was before the tower fell. Now it's not safe to be out here but in pairs, and none of the women will scout with me. So I have to scout with a fellow, and better it be you than one of them, who would feel they were doing something wrong."

He liked her logic.

The Perfecti who had abandoned the village in the dead of night had already decided to return to it, but Ocyrhoe did not rejoin Rixenda in her hut. She had left the cup there, in part because she was afraid of it now, and while she was not willing to let it go unchaperoned out into the world, neither did she want to be around it overmuch. She especially did not want to have to explain its presence here to Ferenc, who would probably think she had lost her wits for keeping it.

It was wonderful to have Ferenc here—a friend, somebody from her life before, somebody near her own age who treated her like a confidante and not a peculiar outsider. It was calming to have his features, familiar and yet strange, in view.

Not that she saw him much the day after the tower was taken. Once the treasure had been secreted down the mountain, he was dismissed to get some sleep, as he would be spending the rest of the day up on the wall with the knights and men-at-arms shooting at the watchtower.

By mid-morning, French arrows from the tower were flying right over the battlements into the courtyard. The women and children were ordered to stay indoors, but Ocyrhoe could not possibly have stayed cooped up in the donjon all that day. There was an air of sorrowful domesticity to all the ladies and children in there, made worse by those grieving the death of the slain soldiers. There had never been so many deaths together on the pog. Some part of her felt vaguely guilty for not grieving more.

Without asking leave from Rixenda, Ocyrhoe slipped nervously out the door and into the courtyard, straining her neck to look over the top of the eastern wall. The arrows were terrifying—the sound of them more than anything. Some went right over the entire courtyard and landed on the slopes outside the western gate. That gate was opened, briefly, for the first time since the siege began soldiers rushed out to collect the arrows and bring them back in for Montségur's own arsenal.

"It must be tonight," she heard Raphael say fiercely. She glanced over to see Raphael and Peire-Roger standing close together near her, behind the armory. "Already we've lost the advantage. Last night there were seven men, who thought we weren't aware of them. Now there's a whole army."

"They won't be camping up here," said Peire-Roger. "They will keep a contingent in the watchtower of course, but it would be death to spend the night exposed on the pog. No matter how many men they have up here now, when the sunlight falls, they will go back down to the encampment."

"Leaving an unknown number of soldiers in the tower," said Raphael. "So you'll need to let me take as many of your knights as I see fit."

Peire-Roger gave him a strange look. "I thought you would wait for the return of Percival."

"I'd want that if we had the time. We don't. Vera and I will go, but I need some of your men. It's what they're here for," he added, with forced patience, as Peire-Roger hesitated. "And I'll take Ferenc. Let him sleep today so he's prepared for it. I've never fought beside him but he more than proved himself last night."

Ocyrhoe made a small noise of protest before she even realized it; both men turned sharply toward her. "Hasn't Ferenc done enough already?" she said. "He's not a soldier."

"He's my squire," Raphael said, but she thought she heard a note of hesitation. "And I would not send him on a suicide mission. Neither him nor Vera. Nor anybody else," he said in a meaningful tone.

"I do not begrudge you soldiers," said Peire-Roger quickly. "But I wonder at the wisdom…"

"I have fought—on both sides of the wall—during sieges at Córdoba and Damietta," interrupted Raphael, "and do not mistake my tone as insulting to your status here, but I know exactly what we need to do."

The commander of Montségur stared at Raphael for a moment, then nodded brusquely. "My men are yours."

✦ ✦ ✦

At dusk, Ocyrhoe was sent out to scout the area around the tower and estimate how many French were there on watch. Ferenc insisted on going with her. She did not need anyone to go with her, but because it was Ferenc she didn't argue. Outside the gate, they squatted low and crawled to the southern extreme of the wind-blown mountaintop. They moved slowly, in almost perfect silence, down the incline toward the eastern cliff.

From the sound as Ferenc and Ocyrhoe approached, the garrison guards were enjoying themselves a bit too much for men on duty. Cocksure there would be no immediate counterstrike, they were drinking freely and had lit the tower brightly with tallow-fueled torches. Ocyrhoe was struck by the stink of the tallow, something she hadn't smelled in years.

Their night vision was ruined by the torches, but the torches themselves shed light enough to reveal much. Farther to the east, just at the cliff's edge, was a work-station of some sort. Ocyrhoe guessed the French were setting up a pulley system, from which they could haul up supplies. There was no buildable timber on the pog, but lumber could be hauled up and there was plenty of scrub for fueling fires. The crusaders had done more than secure the watchtower: They had won themselves a staging station for more attacks.

Ferenc nudged her and nodded toward the tower. There were four armed men atop it, well-lit by a bonfire on a makeshift brazier in the center of the roof. Each had a bow in one hand and a cup of wine in the other, and none of them seemed aware what easy marks they were, silhouetted in the firelight. There was off-key singing from within, some debauched madrigal comparing a Cathar to a cat's backside.

"The windows are too narrow to see much, but I'm listening to voices," Ferenc whispered. "I count maybe six, plus the men on the roof."

"Let's say a dozen total to be cautious," Ocyrhoe whispered back.

They worked their way carefully back uphill over the frozen terrain, to the fortress gate, noting in the moonlight the best passage for a group of armed soldiers. Inside, they reported to Raphael and Peire-Roger. Raphael considered their news briefly, then asked Peire-Roger for his best three archers and someone exceptional at hand-to-hand. Rixenda's nephew, Vidal, who was in the courtyard, heard this and volunteered his grappling skills. When the assigned party was armed and girded, they all circled by torchlight in the courtyard. Raphael explained the fight plan.

Ocyrhoe would come with the party but stay at a distance, so that she could get word to Peire-Roger to send more men as soon as it was safe.

The nine of them moved out of the gate and carefully edged along the south side of the mountaintop, retracing Ferenc and Ocyrhoe's route under the rising moon. They moved slowly and paused at irregular intervals to avoid the sound of their arms and weapons giving them away, although the wind was blowing from the north, carrying what few sounds they made off the mountainside.

When they drew even with the tower, Raphael placed a hand on Ferenc's arm, signaling him to remain there: he would take aim at the south-facing archer on the tower. He also gestured to Ocyrhoe that she was close enough now and should wait with Ferenc until she knew the outcome of the sortie.

The remaining seven moved on, cautiously, to the extreme eastern edge of the pog. Raphael tapped one of the Montségur archers, who stayed there to take aim at the eastern-facing roof guard. Inside, the shadows of tipsy men moved across the windows. Their singing was extremely out of tune.

The rest of the sortie party moved widdershins around the tower, to the north face of the mountain. This was most treacherous, as the tower was sited only a few yards from the northeast cliff face. The footing was slick and icy, and there was little vegetation to either hide behind or grab on to for stability. Raphael noticed, gratefully, that the wind had suddenly died. That seemed extraordinary, given their altitude and exposure.

They positioned a third archer on the north side; Raphael remained with him. Vera and Vidal moved carefully closer to either side of the watchtower door, and the final archer continued his way around the tower until he stood to the west of it on the nearly level ground that the French intended to use as a staging area. He had not approached in a way that drew attention, but this man alone stood where the French would expect an attack. Raphael, crouched with the northern archer, watched the final bowman get into position. Then he stood to his full height briefly, waved both arms, and crouched again; the eastern archer, seeing him, waved in response, so that Ferenc could see him from the southern side. As Raphael had instructed them, all four bowmen nocked their arrows, found their targets, and began a silent, slow count to three.

Four arrows zinged into the cold night within a few heartbeats of each other, and all four guards atop the tower, as in a grotesque dance, staggered, bellowing, as the arrows pierced the thin leather armor of the local, conscripted soldiers. The north-facing guard fell gurgling off the roof and landed hard on the frozen limestone below, almost right beside the door, where Vera looked at him dispassionately and Vidal glowered. Two of the other roof guards stumbled backward into the fire brazier, shrieked, and scrambled trying to get out of it; the fourth man stumbled blindly seeking the safety of the stairwell.

The response from within was immediate and expected. One soldier raced from the upper floor up to the roof, where Ferenc dispatched him at once. One fool stuck his head out the upper western window, where Raphael's western archer struck him. The door opened abruptly, and two armed men appeared in it, staring wildly around. Vidal grabbed the first one and yanked him out onto the frozen ground, throwing himself on top of him and pulling out his knife to slice the man's throat. Vera's axe split the second soldier's skull while he was still in the doorway; she shoved his dying body out the door, onto the fallen guard from the roof, and then shifted her axe to her left hand, drew her sword with her right, and rushed into the tower. Raphael drew his sword and followed close on her heels, slapping Vidal's shoulder as he passed him. Vidal's man wasn't moving, but Vidal kept stabbing him. Perhaps it was guilt that made him so ferocious, Raphael thought, or fear—until recently, Vidal himself might have been one of the crusading soldiers garrisoned here tonight.

Inside, the ground floor was abandoned, stinking of wine, and well lit; Raphael heard scuffling above as he entered, and strange shadows played across the walls as the upstairs torches were chucked out the windows. Now upstairs would be lit only by the light coming up from the stairwell—lighting whomever was ascending, keeping the French defenders safe in darkness. Raphael had anticipated all of this.

He and Vera glanced at each other and nodded briefly. Raphael grabbed a torch from the brazier closest to the door with his left hand. They were about to head up the stairs as a unit, backs together, torch foremost, but as they began a blood-streaked Vidal came rushing through the door, pushed past them, and instantly ran up the stairs, turning in a circle as he did so to try to see all the way around while moving. He had the energy of a berserker.

Raphael grunted with frustration, and signaled. Back to back he and Vera moved up the stairs into the darkness. Vidal shrieked from above, and Raphael's heart sank for a moment, but then he realized Vidal was shouting "Three!"

One for each of them. They could handle that. Vidal had already engaged one guard, in the darkness behind the stairwell; the other two were hovering over the opening in the floor, waiting for them. Vera swung her axe in a wide, controlled arc above their heads as they mounted the stairs, and both waiting men leapt back.

Once off the stairs, Raphael felt Vera move away from him toward one of the guards. He turned to thrust the torch in that direction, but a large, roundish object came at him too fast to see clearly. It hit the torch at an angle that torqued his wrist and also doused the flame with a loud, complaining hiss. It was a heavy, woolen cape that had been soaked in water; he flung it down the stairwell, keeping hold of the torch as a smoking club. In the darkness he heard Vera's axe clash loudly against something metal. The cry of pain that followed was a man's.

A second cry, more strangled, came from Vidal's corner, and Vidal's voice jubilantly called out as Raphael heard a body slump to the floor. Another sword clanged hard against Raphael's own in the shadows and then disengaged. He sensed his opponent lunging toward him, which likely meant a dagger. If he leaped back out of reach, he'd stumble down the stairwell; instead he raised his leg to kick his opponent off balance before the man could follow through on his thrust.

But the lunge had been a feint; Raphael's boot found nobody to kick, and his own momentum sent him stumbling further into the room. Briefly disoriented about the location of his opponent, he dropped the smoking torch and pulled out his knife. He turned quickly, both sword and knife held out before him.

Vera grunted in the darkness to his left. Vidal's victim was still rasping painfully, and Vidal was chortling with a sadistic satisfaction.

Raphael stopped moving and focused on sounds. The other man had also stopped. Blindly, Raphael thrust out with his sword, moving his left-hand blade protectively under his right armpit. Nothing. He spun ninety degrees and tried again. Nothing. The only sounds were Vera pummeling her man, and Vidal enjoying his victim's death throes. It was as if the third man had vanished out a window.

Then he heard a soft sound right against the wall, about the level of his head: the Frenchman was climbing up the stairwell to the roof. *Let him*, Raphael thought; *one of the archers will get him.*

There was a loud crack, and Vera's man, with an offended grunt, fell to his knees.

"That's it!" Vidal crowed. "We got them all! And not a casualty among us!"

A booted foot came flying out of the darkness and kicked Raphael viciously right in the groin. He lost his grip on both weapons, doubling over in pain. As he landed on his knees, he heard the metallic rasp of a sword being freed from its sheath. A heavy weight fell on him, and everything went blank.

CHAPTER 24:

OCYHROE DEFLECTS

The giraffe was tame enough to eat from Frederick's hand, unless the lion was also in the building; then it was too skittish to trust anyone, even its handler. Everyone counseled him against bringing the lion along in the menagerie, but he would not consider parting with it. It looked magnificent and exotic; it symbolized a special majesty but in truth, it was old and tired and spent most of its time asleep. Had there been other lions about it would not even appear to be magnificent and exotic.

"It's like me in that way," he explained to the giraffe, offering it a leafy branch to nibble on. "I only seem magnificent and exotic because there are no other handsome geniuses to compare me to. Léna, I said that just so you could mock me," he continued as if to the giraffe. As quietly as Léna walked, he could smell the perfume he personally dabbed onto her robes each morning.

A moment of silence, and then from the darkness of the partitioned room, her voice: "Your Majesty, my sisters have brought me some news I believe you will want to hear."

"Has the Pope conveniently died?"

"It is not about the Pope."

"Have the Mongols stopped pecking at my eastern frontier?"

"It is not about the Mongols."

"Has that awful German minnesinger been flayed for subjecting us to that awful German poem?"

"Montségur," she said, with tension in her voice. "It is about Montségur. The Tor, their watchtower, has been taken, and a siege machine is being built just outside the barbican. I am almost certain our sundry friends are all still up there."

"I know Raphael," said Frederick. "If there is imminent danger, he won't leave innocent people unprotected."

"There are other knights there. About a hundred men-at-arms."

Frederick laughed briefly, harshly. "Against an army of ten thousand? They're doomed. Can you get a message back up there through the Binders? Tell Raphael I order him to come back immediately. And bring Ferenc. Nobody else is as good with the horses and hawks as Ferenc is. And I will not lose the best knight and one of the only real friends I've ever had to a doomed attempt to protect a heretical cult. What an utterly absurd demise that would be for him. I'll not have it."

He turned away from the giraffe, following Léna's voice to the chamber nearest the door. She looked even more solemn than usual. He suspected she was worried about Ocyrhoe, even if she would not say so.

"I'll write to Count Raimondo of Toulouse," said Frederick, "and tell him I am sending reinforcements. I can send three thousand. To protect the Credents, get them out safely, even if we can't protect the Good Ones themselves."

"And will you send reinforcements?" Léna asked. "Or are you claiming you will just so Raphael will hear about it, and believe that because you are replacing him a thousand times over, it's morally acceptable for him to quit the place?"

"Well that's obviously the only reason to send anyone," said Frederick. "Why should I care about heretics stupid enough to trap themselves in a stone box in the sky? They're not even my subjects."

"So you are not sending men?"

Frederick shrugged. "I'll send them as soon as I can collect them. That might take awhile. Given that Count Raimondo is pledged to *attack* the place I'd be sending men to *defend*, he might not *want* me to follow through with my offer. It would put him in a terribly awkward position, if he used my men to do the precise opposite of what I sent them there for. But I'm sure he'll appreciate my good intention. Shall I wake a monk to write the letter, or would you take it down for me? I do like a woman who knows her way around a quill."

◆ ◆ ◆

Once he was awake enough to pay attention, nobody could explain to Raphael's satisfaction what had happened. There had been two French soldiers hiding in the darkened room, Vera said. One of them had been the bugler, crouching behind the upturned table, and in the commotion he had snuck up to the roof, where he threw himself onto his back, trumpet to his lips, and blew an alarm that could be heard a mile in every direction. It did not matter that Vidal chased him up there and hacked his heart out moments later; the alarm had been sounded, and the French would start pushing up the hillside in greater numbers than the sortie party could possibly hold off.

The second man had been holding himself from a brazier imbedded in the rock wall near the ceiling; his comrade's deliberate retreat had led Raphael close enough for him to get a good kick in; after the kick, he jumped directly at Raphael, and as soon as he landed, he'd pounded him with his fists, knocking him instantly unconscious, and then kept pummeling until Vera took his head off with her axe.

He had cracked ribs, internal injuries, and his bruised face was too swollen for him to see from either eye. The worst damage, Vera reported, was a badly broken leg.

"The worst damage," Raphael corrected her, "was the bugler sounding the alarm. They've taken back the tower, haven't they." He spoke without inflection; it was a statement, not a question.

Vera nodded, then said, "Yes," when she remembered he could not see her.

Raphael had lain in a twilight state for nearly a week, his leg set by the best among the Perfect healers. Percival returned before the others who had spirited away the treasure; he and Vera sat with their injured comrade in the rare moments they were not on the battlements or sleeping. Old Bishop Marti had some skill with healing, and pacifist though he was, he was used to treating fallen soldiers. Groundsel was the herb of choice for wounds caused by iron, but Vera knew Raphael carried with him tinctures from the east that also helped with the fever that was more of a danger to him than the physical wound.

Eventually the Levantine had come back to wakefulness; he dressed himself properly, and when the swelling on his face subsided enough for him to see he insisted on hobbling gingerly around within the keep, on crutches Ferenc fashioned for him. For several days he could not manage to get up the single step to the door, and he found it maddening to be shut in with the women and children all day. He could guess what was happening outside the fortress walls as clearly as any of the others could see it from the battlements.

Down the slope, the French grew greatly industrious, hauling lumber and hardware up the eastern cliff, and starting to mine the mountaintop for limestone.

❖ ❖ ❖

The very night of Raphael's injury, Peire-Roger had sent an urgent plea to one the Credent barons still in residence, and within three days a constructor of siege-machines, Bertran de Bacalaira of Capdenac, had arrived from Castèlnòu d'Arri, having broken through the French lines at night. A sturdily built, self-important man, he'd immediately turned the courtyard into chaos. He instructed a number of the wooden buildings be disassembled, both to provide lumber to build a trebuchet for Montségur itself, and to allow room for it to maneuver.

Ocyrhoe did not like him: clearly he considered himself, prematurely, the hero of Montségur, for having answered the summons for help. A Credent himself, he had grandly announced he wanted no monetary reward, just the satisfaction of helping his beloved Good Ones. Within an hour, however, it had seemed to Ocyrhoe that he wanted in payment was obsequious gratitude. He wanted to be omnipotent within the fortress walls. That would not, she was certain, sit well with Peire-Roger—nor even with the blacksmith, who had immediately gotten into a furious argument with Bacalaira about saving the smithy, at least, from disassembly. She herself wondered about the wisdom of a trebuchet; once Ferenc explained to her how it worked, she asked him the most obvious question, which did not seem to have occurred to Bacalaira: where would their ammunition come from? They had no means to mine the mountain. They had nothing to use as a counterweight. It seemed an implausible undertaking. Almost as implausible as what the French were doing.

❖ ❖ ❖

Every sunset, Ferenc and Ocyrhoe would bundle up in white-and-dun wool clothing, sneak out the gate, and move undetected across the north face of the wintry mountain to check on the enemy. The snow was glaringly white where it remained, but much of it had blown away.

Once the lumber, ropes, and hardware had been brought up, the frame of the French trebuchet had been reassembled within days. It was enormous, three times the height of a man. Makeshift workshops had also been built; villeins and soldiers started mining limestone around the summit through the snow, and within the workshops, others were shaping raw blocks into round projectiles; they were stored carefully in piles outside and ranged from what looked about the weight of a large dog up to what looked about the weight of a large man. Other blocks were being shaped and pressed together to be contained within a massive iron net: the counterweight. The mining of the counterweight seemed to be very slow going. In contrast, within the walls of Montségur, that had turned out to be the easiest aspect of the much smaller trebuchet: the men had simply begun to disassemble the interior walls separating the Goodmen's village from the Goodwomen's, and the stones were loaded into a large cage the smith had forged. The cage used up the last of his iron, and the forging used up the last of his charcoal. Bacalaira then demanded the smithy be taken apart, on the grounds that without iron or charcoal it was just an empty building—sited in the best possible place to put the trebuchet.

But even with an assembled trebuchet, they had no ammunition. Unless they were perfectly round and smooth, the balls would swing wide of their intended targets. They had no way to shape the projectiles.

Meanwhile, the French men were working around the clock, miserable in the cold. Other men protected them with metal canopies of overlapping shields. No matter how good a Montségur archer's aim, there were no vulnerable targets.

One evening, when Ferenc and Ocyrhoe went on their sunset reconnaissance, the counterweight on the French trebuchet suddenly seemed much larger. Days of mining and trimming stone had created the misleading impression that everything was moving very slowly—but now suddenly, the fruit of the Frenchmen's labor was before them.

"That's terrifying," said Ferenc, calmly. "The weight of that? Think how hard those stones will be coming at us."

"But it's from such a distance," Ocyrhoe said nervously. "They're shooting uphill across the length of a mountain ridge!"

"At first they will be," Ferenc agreed. "But Raphael says they are going to move that monster a few yards every day."

Ocyrhoe shook her head, incredulous. "Look at that thing, Ferenc. It will topple over the moment it hits a frozen tuft of grass."

"Raphael—"

"He isn't *always* right, Ferenc. Anyhow, the days are so short now, and they can't shoot at night. They have no way to aim."

"You don't aim something like that," said Ferenc of the machine. "If every rock is the same weight and shape, and you throw it with the same force from the same angle, it will get flung to about the same spot every time, whether you're looking at the target or not." Seeing her startled face, he smiled and said, "Algebra, geometry, and physics. Frederick taught me."

"Are...is that true?" asked unschooled Ocyrhoe. "That sounds like a magician's formula."

"It's magic in the sense that it always works," said Ferenc, warm with the pleasure of amazing her. He had stopped resisting the chemistry that was obvious to everyone but her. "Unless there's some outstanding variable, like a gale blowing or some object interrupting the rock's movement. Like a hawk, or a giraffe."

"A what?"

"I'll show you when we're back at Frederick's court. You would not believe me if I described it to you. An animal taller than the trebuchet. Similarly built, come to think of it."

Ocyrhoe was horrified, but not about the giraffe. "But that means they can bombard us without stop."

"And I am sure they will. It would take a miracle to save the fortress now."

"There are no such things as miracles," scoffed Ocyrhoe. "Who knows that better than the two of us? There are only disasters that madmen think are miracles."

She paused wondering if that had been a tactical error. The last thing she wanted was to start a conversation that could lead to the cup. It was embarrassing, here with Ferenc, to think of how perversely attached to the cup she was. It was nothing but a cup, as Rixenda had said. She decided that as soon as they were off duty, she would give it to Rixenda and rid herself of it.

"I would consider a disaster falling upon our enemies to be a miracle," Ferenc was saying. "Whatever happened to the cup? That could be very useful now."

Ocyrhoe's sudden nervousness masqueraded as contempt. "How?"

"You saw what it did to the masses of Rome. If we had it, we could use it to hypnotize the crusading army and make them all forswear their allegiance to the French king. We could send them home and end this."

"Only Rodrigo could do that," said Ocyrhoe, trying to disregard the dizzy feeling that came from being untruthful to him. "Rodrigo's dead. Because of the accursed cup."

"We don't *know* it was only Rodrigo."

"Who else had that power? When anyone else held it, it was only a cup."

"What did you do with it, Ocyrhoe?" he asked bluntly.

She lowered her gaze quickly, knowing she couldn't look him in the eye without being honest. She was ashamed to still be keeping it. Yes, she would definitely give it to Rixenda.

"Gave it to an old lady in need, who sold it," she said as offhandedly as possible. She was *going* to do that, so it wasn't *too* much of a lie.

"You were that certain it had no power of its own?"

"He was a madman, Ferenc."

"He was a madman who turned the heads of thousands. Because of the cup."

She swallowed uncomfortably. "Frederick understood. It was the alchemy of man and cup together. He sent me to separate them, and with your help I did. Now the cup is as inert as the man." She crossed herself.

A pause. "Well, it's a shame," said Ferenc. "I bet it could be used to upset the enemy camp. It could have done that already, and then Raphael would never have been wounded."

"It *is* a shame," said Ocyrhoe, suddenly desperate to get away from his company. "Come, it's too dark to see anything else. Let's head back and report." The top layer of snow was very dry here and creaked under her feet like stiff leather.

She parted ways with him after they reported to Peire-Roger. She moved by feel in the dim of the rising moon, and went down into the Good Ones' village, sliding on the trampled ice of earlier, damper snowfall. The cup was still hidden in her hard little bed in Rixenda's hut. She had not touched it since Ferenc's wonderful appearance. The metal was warm to her touch in the freezing night. She held it against her, and its warmth radiated through her entire body.

She would give it to Rixenda. Rixenda and the others here were somehow impervious to its properties—perhaps their beliefs inured them to any kind of material wonder. Rixenda was up in the fortress making the last batch of candles before the chandlery was disassembled to accommodate Bacalaira's trebuchet. Ocyrhoe would give her the cup when she came down to pray or sleep.

No, that was no good—as long as it was on the mountaintop she would feel fidgety about it. She had to get rid of it.

Ocyrhoe had brought her heaviest wool blanket up to the donjon, where she was sleeping now, but the lighter coverlet was still here in the hut. She picked it up, shook it to remove the loose bits of straw clinging to it, and draped it around her shoulders, over her mantle. Having sheltered the cup, it was itself warmer than it should have been. She stepped back outside, the starlight suddenly bright to her after the total darkness of the hut. She walked through the Goodwomen's village, down the brief flight of stairs, through the Goodmen's village, to the wall that faced north. The wall was to a height just above her head, but it was not smoothly finished—there were such large protrusions that, even one-handed, she could make her way up to the top. She gazed over the dark abyss of the foothills and the plains. In her imagination she could see the city of Toulouse from here, though it was more than twenty miles distant.

She would throw the cup into the abyss of air. Here. Now. It would fall clattering down the northern slope and be lost in the tangle of bushes below. Whatever strange power it had would be lost. It only responded to her because she had known Rodrigo, had nearly been killed by him—somehow the cup must be picking up some strange remnant of his influence on her, finding his ghost on her skin and responding to that. If the cup was claimed by somebody else, somebody who had never known Rodrigo, it would remain inert. This theory made perfect sense to her.

She took a deep, quivering breath and raised her arm, cup clenched in her hand. The tension in her chest as she began to hurl her arm forward almost choked her.

No. She swung her arm all the way around, back down to her side, still clenching the cup. It was not her attachment that kept her from throwing it. It was the fear that perhaps she was wrong and that the cup did have some freakish power, no matter who held it...and if it were down the slope it would most likely be found by one of the enemy. They might do terrible things with it.

She was stuck with it.

If only she could *use* it.

She climbed down the wall, walked back up through both levels of the Good Ones' village, and stopped against the fortress wall, facing east to the thick sliver of rising moon. She took off her mantle and placed it on the snow, then sat on it, the thin blanket draped around her shoulders, the cup in her hands. It glowed slightly, lighting her tunic-skirt and leggings, her slim hands loosely draped around it, wonderfully warmed by its touch.

Ferenc's idea was not a bad one. She could go down to the army camp—become again the chalice-wielding Angel of Conversion—and find the local soldiers at some convening point, perhaps at mess. She could exhort them all to turn their backs on the French and go back to their ploughs and forges and vineyards, and rebuild Occitania.

If she did this, she would probably be killed immediately. It was a noble way to die, but then the cup would fall into enemy hands and could be used against Montségur as readily as if she'd given it to them for that purpose.

She was stuck with it.

If only she could use it.

A sound up the slope, to her right, caught her attention. A person approaching. A man, but no maille. She could not see him clearly enough in the darkness, but suddenly she was afraid that it was Ferenc, and he would see the cup. She tucked it behind her, hidden between her body and the thin wool wrap.

The person came nearer, sliding on the black ice. Paused. He had sensed her, but also could not identify her. "Hello," said a baritone voice. Even his *voice* was handsome.

"God's evening to you, Percival," she said. A good thing, then, that she had hidden the chalice.

"Ocyrhoe," he said, in a voice more thoughtful than she wanted it to be. "Perhaps you are why sleep has eluded me."

"What?" she said nervously.

"I have been plagued by bad dreams lately. My visions are tormenting me for not attempting harder to find their source. I have nightmares."

"I suspect we all have nightmares, sir, given that we are under attack by an army a hundred times our size whilst freezing to death."

"These are a different sort of nightmare," said the knight. "But have I interrupted you at prayer?"

She almost said yes, but didn't. "I am just sitting here and thinking," she said. "Wishing I could do something really useful."

"We all wish that," he said. "May I sit with you a moment? I think it is no coincidence that I've stumbled upon you here. There's something I must speak with you about."

Oh, no, thought Ocyrhoe. "Of course," she said. "Although I was thinking of retiring soon."

"I will be direct then," said Percival. "And the conversation may be short." A pause. "As you know, I see things. Visions."

"Yes," said Ocyrhoe. "They brought you here. We have already had this discussion."

He glanced around in the darkness as if he'd heard something. "It's warm here," he said. "Right here, just in this spot. How interesting. Since I could not find any material reason to have been summoned here, I thought perhaps it was to defend the place. But my presence here has had no effect at all on the safety of the people."

"We've already had this discussion," Ocyrhoe said, jaw clenched. Was his wit diseased or was he trying to irritate her?

"In fact, they are in much greater danger now than when I first arrived."

"That is not your fault," said Ocyrhoe.

"I know. That's not the point." A pause. She did not ask him what the point was, so he continued on his own. "There must be some other purpose to my being here. The visions are so strong now; every night they fill my mind. They leave me so exhausted sometimes it is hard to concentrate on my duties. Usually they take the form of swirling light, but lately there has been a more concrete image. It looks like a chalice."

"Oh," said Ocyrhoe, feeling faint. He really did not remember that they had already had this conversation. That was disturbing.

"I heard from Vidal that the angel that he saw when he was converted to the cause was a young woman with a cup."

"Maybe that's why you're having visions of a chalice. Maybe his story put that idea into your head," said Ocyrhoe quickly. "I know when I hear stories that affect me deeply, the things that affect me almost always make their way into my dreams."

"That's possible," said Percival, but he sounded dubious. "I rather think that I was drawn here in order to meet the angel with the cup."

"Rixenda can assure you that I'm not an angel," said Ocyrhoe sardonically.

"I know there is something special about you, Ocyrhoe," he said gently. "I sense you have a secret, and I hope you will not keep it from me if you come to believe that I am its intended recipient. That's all."

A pause. If she told him something—something *else*—then that might throw him off the scent.

"I do have a secret," she said. "Do you know who the Binders are?"

He smiled. "I thought you might be one."

"I'm a renegade Binder," she said. "I'm not trustworthy."

She could see him smile in the darkness. "Really? That must be an interesting story."

"Not at all. But it's the secret that you sense I'm carrying. You see? It has nothing to do with you." *Go away, go away, go away,* she thought.

She would happily have given up the cup now to almost anyone but Percival. He was the only man she'd met since Father Rodrigo's death who had that glimmer of otherworldliness that reminded her of the priest. He was a good man, she felt that instinctively, but he was unbalanced by this quest of his. Just as

Rodrigo had been. Men like that should not have access to objects of a questionable nature. He was repeating a conversation they had had a few days earlier, with no apparent memory of having had it. That was something madmen did. Madmen and schemers, and Percival was not a schemer.

"I think you have a cup, and that it is of great power, and that I am its intended bearer," he said. "There. I have said it as clearly as I could."

"And now I have heard you. And I am telling you, I do not have such an object, and if I did, I would not yield it up just because you ask me for it."

"And now I have heard you, but I do not believe you."

"Well, as I said, I am not trustworthy," she said. She wished she could stand up and leave without drawing attention to the cup. It was behind her, between her clothing and her cloak, warming her; if she reached with her left hand around her right-hand side, under the cloak, she could grasp it, but in pulling it out she would expose it to Percival. "If you do not mind, I would like to be left in peace now to meditate and pray a bit."

"How does a Binder pray?" asked Percival.

"Not at all like a renegade does," said Ocyrhoe. "That also is a secret that I carry. I will willingly divulge it to you, but later, not now."

"Well enough, God's evening to you then," he said, suddenly very ordinary and agreeable. He made the slightest bow in her direction—not mockingly, but genuinely, like a knight from a romantic poem taking leave of a lady. Then he pointed at her. "You have potent meditations, my friend. The snow has melted in a circle all around you." She looked down. Yes, she was now sitting on her mantle in the mud. Percival walked slowly back up the slope in the moonlight.

She waited until he had actually re-entered the fortress, fearful that the light from the cup would draw his eye back down the slope toward her. Then she grabbed the cup, holding it against her chest, scrambled to her feet, and scuttled down the slope, through the gate, and back into Rixenda's cottage. She shoved the cup into the straw of her bed and covered it with the thin wool blanket she'd had around her shoulders. Then just to be safe, she doubled the blanket and put her thin pillow over the whole thing.

CHAPTER 25:
FATHER SINIBALDO

Dietrich was in his tent with his fellow Livonians, huddled around a lamp-lit camp table. Between his shift and his tunic, one end resting on his upper lap and the rest leaning against his stomach, was a flat, fire-warmed piece of limestone. His men had similar warmers. They had just eaten. They were used to the swill that passed as food here, more than the local soldiers were, and so they were experiencing a level of contentment shared by nobody else in the army.

Except possibly Hugue de Arcis and the Archbishop of Narbonne, and those elite members of the French corps, all of whom had taken over the comfortable village with its tight, little houses. They had long depleted the stores of grain and dried fruits, but the two crusading leaders and their men also had money and manpower to scout for food, which the rest of the army would never even know about. Dietrich and his brothers should have been part of that elite insider group. He did not mind the hardships—in fact he felt a measure of superiority that he and his men were comfortable in a setting that would probably reduce the frail, overprivileged archbishop and bloated seneschal to shivering tears. But on principle it still rankled that his position as the Pope's agent was completely disregarded.

Outside, the camp was settling down to sleep. Only a few dozen men remained up on the pog overnight, just enough to load and spring the trebuchet, and to man the watchtower. But the camp was quieter now that there was productive and often exhaustive work to be done. Even the local soldiers were excited at the prospect of bursting open the gate of the untouchable fortress of Montségur. Their perception of feudal duty shifted gracefully from odious to titillating. They slept well, very well, at night.

So the camp was quiet. This meant that any outside noise was disproportionately loud. Like the grumbling and the footsteps that were coming down the slushy avenue. There was no particular reason to think the footsteps would stop at their tent, and yet somehow Dietrich knew they would.

A scout opened the flap without asking permission, and stuck his head in. He was wearing Hugue's colors. "A party has come to the village looking for you," he said gruffly. "Nobody we know. Will you receive 'em?"

No doubt more of his Livonian brothers, but why they would need to seek him out here…unless something nefarious was happening farther north. "Let them come," he said.

"Tell your friends not to come loitering at the general's camp," the fellow said blandly, as he gestured the newcomers into the tent.

A tall, cloaked figure, his hood shadowing his face, entered first, with three stocky men behind him. They were all dressed in the muted, generic dress of winter travelers. The three companions, from their stance, were clearly soldiers, but Dietrich did not recognize their faces. The taller figure did not hold himself like a fighter.

"Thank you," Dietrich said tersely to the Frenchman, who left without further comment. He looked at the newcomers. "Welcome to the Livonian brotherhood," he said carefully. "Whom do we have the honor of receiving?"

"I require a word alone with the Heermeister," said the hooded figure. "Tell the others to leave."

Dietrich exchanged looks with his men. "May I ask the need for secrecy? These are my brothers, ultimately. I will not keep them from my counsel."

"Determine that when you have heard my news. I bring a message from Rome and it is for your ears only."

Dietrich nodded to the other knights. "Excuse us, brothers. This is a fine time for you to pay your final evening respects to the latrines."

The other knights, accustomed to Dietrich, filed out without comment.

The tall man reached up with two long-fingered, elegant hands, and pulled back his hood to reveal a hawklike face. Dietrich recognized the man at once. He immediately went down on one knee. "Your Holiness! What are you doing here?"

"The angel. With the cup."

That made no sense. "What about it, Your Holiness?"

"It's why I am here," said Innocent severely. He unpinned his cloak and let it slide off his shoulders, stepping away from it as one of his bodyguards caught it and draped it ceremoniously over his arm. Beneath the cloak, Innocent was dressed as a priest.

"You will call me Father Sinibaldo during my stay here," he informed Dietrich. "Nobody is to know me unless I choose to reveal myself to them."

"Yes Your H...Father. May I ask why the story of the girl with the cup has brought the Father to Montségur?"

"I do not have time to tell the story twice. Come with me while I explain to the archbishop."

"Your...Father...you will have a hard time gaining access to His Eminence if you are merely a priest."

"Do you think so?" asked Pope Innocent loftily. "Come and watch. You stay here," he said to his three guards. Then he turned and without ceremony let himself out of the tent.

Dietrich hurried to follow after him in the cold dark alley between tents. "Will he not recognize you, Father?" he asked.

"I do not know that we have ever met in person, and if we did it was years ago, before I was even a cardinal," said Innocent, walking briskly through the slush. "I am confident he will not know me."

"How did...how did you get here?" Dietrich demanded, astounded by this development. His Holiness's stride was so long and brisk, Dietrich was almost jogging to keep up with him.

"The same way most people do. It took longer than it should have, because we had to avoid areas where I might be recognized. I do not care for the hardships of a common priest. The insults to my person since I left the Lateran Palace are appalling, worse than my captivity in the Septizodium, and would have been even worse if I were a layman. You must live a demeaning life indeed, Dietrich, if you are satisfied with living in a tent."

"I am not satisfied," Dietrich said quickly, gruffly. "But I am duty-bound to His Holiness to maintain a presence here, and this is the only way to do it."

"Not when I've finished with them," Innocent muttered, and turned a muddy corner in the tent-avenue so that he entered the village. A Carcassonne guard stood at the berm, but Sinibaldo disregarded him so entirely the man seemed to have been gagged—he opened his mouth to speak but no sound came out, only the vapor of his breath; he reached an arm to restrain the priest but seemed frozen in place. Sinibaldo di Fieschi kept walking. Having only been here an hour, and having passed through the army camp only once, he had already memorized its layout. Without hesitating he walked straight to the cottage that housed the Archbishop of Narbonne.

He rapped hard on the door, then pushed it open without waiting. It was well lit within, although the torches were smoking and making a stench. The last time Dietrich had been in here, everything had been lit by candlelight. They had run out of candles by now.

Without waiting for a response, Innocent entered. Immediately, as Dietrich watched from the threshold, he was surrounded by four of the bishop's guard, all with knives drawn and held threateningly toward him. Innocent made a dismissive gesture and walked past them; they watched him in astonishment as he approached the archbishop, who sat on a chair (a real chair, with a back and a cushion, something unheard of in the army tents) examining papers on a lap desk.

Dietrich stepped into the house. Both more tentative and more obviously martial than the first intruder, he was accosted by the guards. He quickly held up his empty hands to show he meant no harm, and he did not attempt to move in beyond the doorframe. He could not take his eyes away from Father Sinibaldo. Even from the back, dressed in simple priest's vestments, the man had a majestic energy of entitlement that made it impossible to resist him.

Archbishop Pierre Amelii looked up in astonishment, his jaw dropping slack and his eyes widening enough to show the whites around the pupils.

"Do not be alarmed. I am a friend. I have been sent from Rome," Father Sinibaldo said briskly. "Put down your work and hear my message. Dietrich, close the door."

The archbishop blinked, and Father Sinibaldo impatiently lifted the desk off Pierre Amelii's lap, turned on his heel and handed it to one of the guards as if that was the purpose of the guard's lurking presence. The guard, not expecting this, reflexively sheathed his knife so that he could receive the burden. Sinibaldo immediately turned back to His Eminence and continued without interruption. "Where is Count Raimondo of Toulouse? I have looked all around the camp and see no evidence of his presence. Is he not supposed to be among those fighting these heretics? What do you suppose can account for his absence?"

"I have excommunicated him," said the archbishop, with a concerted display of self-importance, trying to overcome his startlement at being confronted so confidently by a mere priest.

"Well the Pope hasn't," said Father Sinibaldo. "Get his arse here from Toulouse and force him to help us. Meanwhile, if we cannot defeat these heretics, we must at least defame them, and immediately, so that they cease to have such a romantic hold on the minds and hearts of the people of Occitania. You do see the necessity of that, do you not?" He gave the archbishop a blistering look.

"Yes, but...no, but...well, yes, it would be ideal, but it is highly unlikely that could happen given the depth of the history between—" he stammered.

"As you know," Father Sinibaldo continued, as if the archbishop had not spoken, "it is His Holiness's desire to promote the sacrament of Holy Communion." The briefest pause, and then, with a soupcon of condescending concern, "You did know that, didn't you? You are all paying attention to the Mother Church out here in the hinterlands, are you not?"

Pierre of Amelii was flabbergasted. His face was red with anger, but the stranger's intensity and directness seemed to rob him of the will to confront him. "Yes, of course," he said hotly. "Of course we are aware of His Holiness's desire to promote the sacrament of Holy Communion."

"Excellent! Do you know why he wishes it?"

"I do not see how that—"

"So you don't know why. I shall tell you. It's one of the reasons he required me to come to you. Listen, so that if you are ever in the presence of His Holiness and you are questioned, you can answer with confidence. First, the ritual of communion is in itself a spiritually potent ceremony. To eat the body and blood of Christ is an act of dazzling and transformative ritual."

"Yes of course," said the archbishop, relieved he could finally comment on a matter with confidence.

"But more than that," continued Father Sinibaldo, "it is an excellent way of differentiating the Roman Church from the Eastern Church and all the heretical masses. The more ubiquitous and central the sacrament becomes in our mass, the more it helps us to notice those who avoid partaking of it. Promoting the sacrament of Holy Communion helps us to know, to shepherd, and to control our flocks. You'll agree that is an excellent thing?"

He had the archbishop pinned to his chair with his gaze alone. "I do," the archbishop said, as if giving way under torture, as if all he wanted was to be released from Father Sinibaldo's intense, relentless attention.

"I am glad you agree with His Holiness on that. The question then becomes a matter of how best to promote the sacrament. Do you know the poems about the quest for the Holy Grail?"

Again, bug-eyed confusion overwhelmed the old man's face. "What does that have to do with—"

"Surely here in the Languedoc all those stories are familiar to you, no?"

This time when Father Sinibaldo paused, it was with the energy of a man actually wanting to hear a response. After a troubled moment, Peter of Amelii gave him one.

"Of course we are familiar with the troubadour works. But what has that to do with the Church? These are heathenish tales of romance and fancy, and some versions of them flirt uncomfortably with pagan elements."

"You say they are heathenish?" said Father Sinibaldo, like a boxer about to challenge an opponent to a fight. "The Holy Father says it is all a matter of presentation."

"What does that mean, my son?" asked the archbishop, struggling to remind himself that he was the superior here.

"If those stories are told in the proper way, from the right perspective and with the right details, they will enhance the prestige of the sacrament of communion. The masses are all enamored with the image of a special chalice that has magical powers because of the fairy world or some such nonsense. If we can coax the masses to associate that chalice with the one priests use in church, we will suddenly have a revivification of interest in observing holy communion. Every grail in every church can be associated with the Holy Grail of the troubadours. Isn't that clever? Take a moment, think about it."

"Er...yes, I do not need a moment, I can see what you are saying, the only question is how to coax people to associate the troubadours' grail with a mass chalice."

"Are troubadours the only ones allowed to tell stories?" demanded the priest. "We, the Church, tell the stories, we promote the poems, and our apparent regard for them will make them seem innately tied to Christian ritual. There is very little work involved."

"It's a very interesting idea," said Pierre Amelii, looking exhausted but trying to seem lively. "I would be honored to discuss this idea in greater detail with His Holiness when the time is right, but first we must attend to this crusade ahead of us."

"Do not assume the two are not connected, Your Eminence," said Father Sinibaldo.

The archbishop seemed to physically get smaller. "How rash of me," he said, sounding enervated.

"Wouldn't it be a wonderful thing if I told you that there really is such a grail?"

For a moment the bishop looked terrified, then confused. "You mean...do you mean the chalice in the troubadour's poem, or the original cup that Our Lord used at the Last Supper?"

"What does it matter? I am simply saying there is a magical grail."

The Archbishop of Narbonne pursed his lips together worriedly. He began to speak, then stopped himself, looked so confused that he appeared nearly to be in pain, and then ventured, "Well the poems aren't Christian. There's nothing to suggest that the knights are seeking the cup from Christ's hand, so if you're saying that the chalice in the poem really exists, then pardon my slow-wittedness, but I don't see why that should be of any interest to the Church."

Father Sinibaldo grimaced a moment. Dietrich wished he knew what was going on behind those cold, grey eyes.

"No of course not," he said. Dietrich instinctively felt that His Holiness made a snap decision. "I am referring to the cup of Christ from the last supper."

"You are saying that it really exists?" And here the archbishop's aging, tired face suddenly began to beam with hope.

"Yes, and more than that, I am informing you that these heretics have taken possession of it and wish to keep it from the world."

His Eminence collapsed against the back of his chair. "What?" he demanded breathlessly.

"They do not want it for themselves, clearly, for they do not practice the sacrament, and worldly things have no meaning to them. They have stolen a treasure of the Church and are using it for their own dark purposes."

"How do you know this? You must tell me how you know this!" said the bishop.

"I have seen it in Rome. I know its power. That's why His Holiness chose me to pursue it here. I know how it got from there to here. I know it is up there."

"Yes!" said Pierre of Amelii. "Yes, my son, you're right! And they are using the power of the grail for perverse gain to their own heresies—they used it to seduce one of our most stalwart local soldiers to defect to them!"

The priest calmed immediately. "Now," said Innocent, "do you understand how important it is that we do the right thing?

We need that cup more than we need the death of a few hundred heretics. I," and here he paused for dramatic effect, "*I* need that cup, my son. Do you understand?"

He looked directly at the archbishop and suddenly the archbishop cringed with elated awe as he understood. "Your Holiness!" he cried, pushing himself out of the chair and kneeling on his long, knobby, aging legs before the Bishop of Rome. "Forgive me for not recognizing you at once!" With a collective baritone cry of shock, every man in the room knelt likewise.

Innocent held out his hand so the Bishop could kiss his ring.

"You are a good shepherd, my son," he said.

"Your Holiness!" said Pierre of Amelii again, and began to stagger to his feet. His cleric on instinct also rose and moved closer to him, to give him an arm to lean on. "Your Holiness, why have you not come in all your glory as—"

"No, no," said Pope Innocent, clicking his tongue. "My presence here would cause an uproar, so I must stay in the shadows. Everyone in this room must swear an oath to me and to you that they will say nothing of my presence. However, my men and I—by which of course I mean the esteemed Dietrich and the rest of the Livonian order," he paused a moment, and Dietrich enjoyed the surprise and awe on the faces of the men who had been snubbing him for months. "We require decent housing, out of the morass of the general camp. I am sure one of the houses in the village can be cleared for us, without much fuss being made about the reason."

"Of course," said the Archbishop of Narbonne, trying not to wince.

His Holiness smiled. "Excellent. Then all that remains is for you to find a way to make sure the commanders know that the safe return of that cup to the Church is the most urgent thing to happen here."

CHAPTER 26:

ON ST. AGNES' DAY

The next morning, Raphael declared himself fully restored and ready for duty, despite the crutches. He hauled himself out to the frosty courtyard to examine the siege machine everybody had been talking about since he recovered consciousness.

When he exited the keep at sun-up, Vera and Ferenc beside him, most of the population of the fortress was taking their morning walk before the French began their daily shower of arrows. This was a ritual that allowed the hall to air out, allowed everyone to get a little exercise, and kept the courtyard empty of civilians for most of the day. It was the closest the fortress ever came to joyful, with some two dozen children running around the frozen ground, ducking behind sheds to hide from each other while throwing snowballs from the diminishing piles against the walls. Off-duty soldiers would roughhouse with the boys and even the girls; it was as if every morning, for an hour, there was a village festival.

Raphael noticed all of this as he slowly headed across the altered landscape of the yard, mindful of the slick stone and snow, toward the gangly-looking trebuchet. Bacalaira and Peire-Roger were standing beside it, looking up at it. Since Bacalaira had presented himself the day before, quite pompously, to Raphael at board, the knight felt no need for greetings now. "So this is the catapult I've heard so much about," he said.

"It is not a *catapult*," sniffed Bertran de Bacalaira. "It is a *trebuchet*."

"It's just a piece of furniture if you have no ammunition for it," Raphael said.

"I was just learning about that unfortunate detail," said Peire-Roger, glowering.

Bacalaira hissed impatiently. "I am engineer, not a supplier. Do you expect your candle-maker to light your candles for you? It never *occurred* to me that on a hilltop made of limestone you would not have found yourselves some decent projectiles. It would not have occurred to *anyone* in my position."

There was a shout of alarm from the wall-walk: the French trebuchet was launching its first stone.

This inaugural projectile was small and did not make it as far as the wall. But hearing the sound of it hissing through the air was unnerving; hearing it land safely away from the walls brought no comfort. Immediately the festive air evaporated; the children started bleating, and with the women they hurried back into the rank hall with its fetid air.

"We must evacuate the village," Peire-Roger said urgently. "Really evacuate it this time—they have no choice now."

"Yes," said Raphael. "We have at least a quarter of an hour before they send another stone. It will take that long for them to winch their counterweight and get safely out of the way. If you act quickly, you can get everyone to safety before the next attack."

"And then nobody is to leave the fortress walls again, except under cover of darkness for emergencies." Peire-Roger ran toward the keep to summon men.

Bacalaira continued to stare at his useless machine. Vera and Ferenc, after a glance at Raphael, both followed Peire-Roger.

Raphael turned to Bacalaira. "Once the French have offered us a few more projectiles, we'll send you out the fortress gate to collect them."

❖ ❖ ❖

The evacuation of the village took little effort; the Good Ones had almost nothing to bring with them but their bedrolls. When the fortress gate closed behind the last of the Perfecti, Peire-Roger announced loudly to the courtyard, "It is now safe nowhere beyond these walls."

Ocyrhoe had been in the pantry-shed helping to stack the bags of flour delivered from the last shipment of food. She did not realize what was happening until she exited the tent and heard Peire-Roger finish his declaration.

"Nobody is to go out this gate unless it is for military or scouting purposes, with my express permission." A wave of alarm washed over her. She would never get leave to sneak down on her own. And the cup was still in Rixenda's hut down in the village.

For the rest of the day, in addition to the sporadic spate of arrows, bombardment from the trebuchet was not frequent, but it was regular. Twice or thrice an hour there was a new roar of rock tearing the air, a new thud too close to their gate. One did hit the wall, which made an entirely new and dreadful sound; there was a round of surprised yelps from within the donjon.

Most of the rocks hit the same location near the barbican, so that the men on the walls saw an indentation growing in the mountain's rocky summit, a pocked circle the width of a man and a hand's span deep.

"That is what they are going to do to the walls eventually," Raphael warned Peire-Roger late in the day. For at least an hour there had been no more bombardments. The two men stood together looking east out the peek-hole in the gate, shivering even in extra layers of wool wraps.

"If that's the farthest they can throw their stones, let them make a crater twenty times that size," said Peire Roger. "It will not harm us."

"They are going to push it up the mountain," Raphael warned.

Peire-Roger laughed and shook his head. "However frequently you are proving to be right, this particular idea of yours is simply foolish."

"They are working on it even now. That's why they've stopped the bombardments. Look," said Raphael gravely, and pointed down the mountain.

The trebuchet of the French, rickety as it looked from here, and treacherously slick as the mountainside must have been, was wobbling with infinitesimal slowness up the slope. With the counterweight attached it to it, it weighed well over a ton, and it was being pushed up an uneven, icy slope on tiny wheels. There was a lot of shouting and cursing, and more tipping than forward movement on the part of the trebuchet itself.

Peire-Roger gaped a moment as he realized that the French were, in fact, attempting the impossible. He left the peek-hole and ran up the stone staircase to the battlements to get a better look. Then, somewhat forced, he laughed again. "But they will never get it up the slope," he called down to Raphael. "Not at that rate."

"Exactly at that rate," Raphael countered. "They only need to advance it by a few yards a day, and eventually it will make its way close enough to hit our walls, and then it will sling those boulders directly into the courtyard. Eventually, it will reach the barbican, where there is level ground to rest it safely. It will destroy this fortress if we do not destroy it first."

"How best to do that?" asked the Lord of Montségur.

"It's made of wood, so burn it down. I'd say forge some fire-arrows," Raphael said tiredly. "But I understand you destroyed your smithy for the sake of building that useless siege machine."

✦ ✦ ✦

Peire-Roger was loathe to let them leave the fortress for their evening scouting sortie. After many admonitions and warnings from him, and an unasked-for grim blessing from the bishop, Ocyrhoe and Ferenc geared up and slipped out while the sun hovered above the western walls of Montségur, casting deep shadows that camouflaged their exit. A dozen soldiers went out with them—the bombardments had stopped because the French appeared still to be moving the trebuchet. As Ocyrhoe and Ferenc moved toward the northern face, the soldiers rushed toward the barbican to collect the heavy, round projectiles the French had sent their way and bring them back into the fortress. Raphael's ironic comment was applied: their only ammunition was the very rocks the French had hurled at them.

Wrapped up against the permanent, chill winds of the mountaintop, Ferenc and Ocyrhoe edged their way eastward along the northern lip of the summit to see how things had changed in the French camp with the successful first day of bombardment.

A French captain at the trebuchet called out; a heartbeat passed in which nothing seemed to happen. Then with a cacophony of sounds the counterweight tumbled heavily toward earth, and the sling-arm whirled up and whipped a rock toward the fortress. It tore through the air and smashed against the limestone wall near the donjon. Ocyrhoe shuddered.

"I thought they had stopped for the night," she said.

She felt the warm vapor of Ferenc's breath against her cheek. It made her feel protected. He pointed to a man walking with deliberate slowness up the slope. A long-legged man with shield and weapons, he moved too quietly, and recovered too smoothly from a slip on the icy snow, to be wearing maille beneath his surcoat. He veered into the shadow of the barbican in the fading sunset. The barbican was full of archers but not one arrow flew from the loops toward him: he was using the twilight to create a blindspot.

The man reached the barbican, held a moment, and then began to walk away just as slowly. Meanwhile, the mass of workers at the trebuchet continued their grunt work, a pack of them laboring together to hoist the massive counterweight back up to its starting height, while one of their mates, clambering up the side of the machine, struggled to cinch the thick, iron pin that would hold the counterweight in place until the next attack.

The walker returned to the trebuchet before the machine was ready to propel again. He reported to the captain as several other men moved around to listen. By now the light had faded completely and Ocyrhoe could make out no other details. The moon was already high in the sky, waxing close to full; they might be able to make out something once their eyes had adjusted to moonlight.

"You see what's happening," said Ferenc, as if assuming it was clear to her.

"No," she admitted.

"They will try to take the barbican. That man was sent to establish timing. To see if a force of men can travel there between trebuchet shots. They don't want to shoot at their own men, but they don't want to stop shooting. Once it's dark the moon would give away their movements to the archers in the tower, but the night will be clouding over soon and if they move slowly enough, they now believe they will be able to get all the way up to the tower without being noticed by the archers inside. They can get there, take shelter, and prepare to fight, while the trebuchet works as a decoy."

Ocyrhoe slowly took a breath as this registered. Her fist tightened and she smacked the fat of it on the freezing rock. "Whoresons! Why don't they just leave us alone! What have we done to them?"

"You consider yourself one of the Cathars?" asked Ferenc.

"Don't call them that; it's disrespectful," said Ocryhoe. "It doesn't matter what I call myself or even what I believe—this is my home, these people have protected me, and this siege, it's...it is so..." she grimaced with frustration. "It accomplishes nothing! Those French bastards want victory for its own sake! They gain nothing. *Nothing.* There are two hundred Good Ones here, but there are hundreds more out in the world. Killing these accomplishes nothing in the bigger picture. This is an absolutely useless outpost. Taking it accomplishes nothing. It's pure tyranny on their part. There is no *reason* for any of it."

"Shhssh, Ocyrhoe," Ferenc said, wrapping his arm around her and squeezing her a little. "I agree with you, but your anger also accomplishes nothing. We have to tell Peire-Roger."

"And to think he almost didn't let us come out tonight," harrumphed Ocyrhoe, wanting to stay angry at someone, anyone.

They snuck back toward the fortress, where they signaled a man on the wall. Ferrer let them in at once.

The courtyard was already torchlit. Soldiers were loading the smallest of the collected round rocks into the Montségur trebuchet's sling, which Raphael and Vera were staring at it with disapproval. The courtyard ground was so uneven that Bacalaira was having a devil of a time keeping the machine balanced as the counterweight was winched up. Peire-Roger, dressed as usual elegantly in black, with thick furs pulled around himself, was standing beside Bacalaira as if his glowering presence could somehow frighten the trebuchet into functioning. Percival, Ocyrhoe was sure, was off somewhere praying or meditating or speaking in tongues. Everywhere shivering pages and squires stood with torches that threw strange lights and shadows across the courtyard.

"It is much smaller than the French trebuchet," Raphael was saying to a displeased Peire-Roger. "Using it now is a waste of ammunition. It cannot throw as far—it will accomplish nothing until the French are perilously close." Peire-Roger gave Bacalaira an accusing look, as if he had deliberately handicapped them.

Ferenc led Ocyrhoe straight to Raphael. "The French are planning to take the barbican," he said.

Peire-Roger ceased glowering at the trebuchet-maker and spun on his heel to face the young hunter.

"When?" he demanded.

"I think tonight," said Ferenc. "The evening bombardments are intended as a distraction."

"Tell us what you know," Raphael said. He gave Vera a look that Ocyrhoe guessed meant she was to find Percival. She hoped Percival was a good enough knight to put aside his mystical musings in the face of an emergency. She'd seen him do nothing at all so far to suggest he was any good at fighting, but there had been little chance for any of them to prove themselves here in this crowded corner in the sky.

Peire-Roger smacked young Artal on the shoulder and with a few muttered words sent him to collect men. Work on the trebuchet stopped. The counterweight was carefully lowered back to earth. Ocyrhoe was cold and wanted to go inside but Peire-Roger ordered her and Ferenc to stay and report. Ferenc, sensing her dismay, placed his large hands heavily on her shoulders and asked if it would be possible to have hot wine brought to them. Like the moment when his breath had warmed her cheek out on the mountain ridge, this filled her with an unfamiliar sense of contentment despite their situation.

The wine arrived before all of Peire-Roger's requested men did, so she was in a better mood by the time Ferenc began his report. "The moon is just past full, and they know we will be watching over the walls and from the arrow loops of the barbican," he said. "But they expect we will be watching only the trebuchet, nothing closer. There will be clouds coming in by midnight, very thick and very sudden. If I know that, then they must have local mountain men who know that too."

"How do you know it?" asked Peire-Roger.

Ferenc shrugged. "How do you know when it is going to snow instead of rain? I feel it. I am a child of the fields and woods and mountains. Not these mountains, but the cloud-gods of all the mountains know each other."

There was a silence after this remarkably pagan declaration. Ocyrhoe pursed her lips to repress a smile.

"That is poetic, my friend," Raphael said carefully, into the silence. "I for one would be grateful for a more scientific explanation, as I am sure the knowledge that you draw upon could instruct us all."

"I was not being poetic," said Ferenc, almost impatiently. "The French are using this time until midnight to prepare in the moonlight. After that, it will be too dark for anyone to see anything clearly. Until midnight is the time that you have."

The men looked at one another. There were a score here in the courtyard, perhaps thirty. "Gear up," said Peire-Roger loudly. He was clearly uneasy about having to actually strategize a battle plan after months of nothing but defensive moves, but he rose to the occasion.

"I suggest—" began Raphael, but Peire-Roger, blustery, spoke over him to the group.

"We'll wait until we hear them approach the barbican. The men on the walls and in the barbican itself will not let on that we expect them. We allow them to get close, believing we are not expecting them. Then, on my signal, the archers will shoot, and once the archers have engaged them we will rush out the gate and fight them on the ground."

"You will 'rush'?" echoed Raphael doubtfully. "There is a *very* narrow ridge connecting our walls and the barbican."

"Yes, but the barbican itself is on a big stretch of level ground—"

"How does that help you?" demanded Raphael, clutching his crutch-handle to contain his impatience. "You have to *get* there first. The French who escape our archers will be waiting for you. They'll dispatch you as you are coming out along the ridge."

"They will be too distracted by the archers," Peire-Roger retorted. "They probably will not even notice our approach, and they certainly won't be prepared to respond."

"You are sending men to their deaths," warned Raphael.

Peire-Roger gave him a warning look. "You have already been told not to challenge my authority." He turned his back on Raphael as if to push his way through his men toward the gate.

"How will your archers avoid shooting you?" demanded Raphael. "In the dark?"

The fortress commander stopped and turned sharply. He glared at the Levantine. "They're good archers," he said.

Raphael began to retort, then caught himself and took a breath. "Would it not, perhaps, be wise to first see what the archers alone can do?" he counseled.

"There are not many of them in the barbican. I have men in here who are very good on the ground," said Peire-Roger. "If we start to shoot too soon—or if we only shoot, without engaging more directly—the French will back off, regroup, and think up some other plan we might not discover in time. At this moment, we have the element of surprise. That is our strongest weapon and I want to make use of it."

From Raphael's expression he clearly disagreed with how best to make use of a "surprise," but he grimly stopped debating.

◆ ◆ ◆

Hours later, it occurred to Ocyrhoe that she had been unofficially excused, and that she could probably have snuck into the donjon for warmth, if not sleep. But she felt safe next to Ferenc, and Ferenc was going out with the armed men. She had no fighting skills of any sort, much less any protective gear, but she could not bring herself to go inside while he was there in the courtyard. They remained by Raphael, who kept impatiently tapping the bottoms of his crutch onto the frozen ground. Ocyrhoe liked and trusted Raphael for reasons she could not have put into words, despite his ties to creepy Percival.

"Percival and Vera never came back," Ferenc said.

"Mmm," said Raphael, noncommittal and yet, Ocyrhoe thought, privately pleased. "Why don't you *find* them?"

Ferenc nodded, flashed Ocyrhoe a strange little smile, and darted into the crowd of soldiers. Then she understood: Percival and Vera were in the barbican. They had gone to join the archers already there. Ferenc—somehow—was joining them. And Peire-Roger was aware of none of this.

"I suppose Vera's not on kitchen duty," she said to Raphael.

His dark eyes, in the torchlight, slid slowly in her direction. "An accurate supposition," he said quietly, approvingly.

"But—" It felt presumptuous to question him. "There are already archers in the barbican," she whispered. "Why do they need three more?"

"Because," replied Raphael, also in a whisper, "if the Lord of Montségur gives foolish orders, there will be three archers not obeying him. That man is no tactician. *And* no strategist. That this place still stands defiant is a testament to the site itself, not to the lord of it."

"I wish I were a fighter," she said. "I feel so useless."

"Go into the donjon with the rest of the women and children," he said, dismissively but not unkindly. "You will hear word soon enough how this has gone. There is no danger to you there, at least not tonight. The worst that will happen is that they take the barbican, but they would not also make a play for the fortress itself in one evening."

That possibility had not even entered Ocyrhoe's head until he said it, and now she knew she would not be able to cease contemplating it. When Raphael turned his attention back toward the gate, she slipped away into the darkness, not toward the donjon but away from it.

The men were all in maille, heavily armed, and waiting just inside the gate. Their collective breath in the frigid night air formed a wispy, pulsating cloud in the torchlight. Ocyrhoe wanted to climb up to the wall and look out with the archers. It was claustrophobic here, between the solid corps of soldiers and the awkward tangle of the skeletal trebuchet. It made her nervous to think of Ferenc in the barbican, with who knows how many French soldiers about to attack.

Reaching the south side of the yard, she found a wooden ladder to the wall-walk. There was one stone stairway built into the wall near the gate, but elsewhere wooden ladders allowed easily mobility on and off the walls. She quickly climbed it and found herself between two archers, both standing motionless and breathing nervously, staring into the moonlight.

At Peire-Roger's orders, all the torches in the courtyard were completely doused, leaving Montségur in total darkness.

CHAPTER 27:

THE BATTLE FOR THE BARBICAN

For what seemed forever, nothing happened. The French were clearly waiting for the cloud cover to roll in, so that they could move forward under cover of darkness. Peire-Roger wanted his men to hold until the French were close enough to engage them in hand-to-hand combat. To Ocyrhoe's reckoning, as Raphael had said, this was inviting danger. It was surely foolish to lay an inviting trap for an enemy that outnumbered you by a factor of one hundred. Surely better just to keep the enemy away.

After a very long time—so long the bells rang twice in the occupied village below—there was movement. The clouds had rolled in quickly and completely covered the moon, as Ferenc had said would happen; the darkness was not absolute but it was dark enough to be confusing. The archers in the barbican lit a candle in a westward-facing loop; archers on the walls passed the message on by tossing pebbles down to the men at the gate. The great gate swung open; the hinges had been greased, and it was silent.

Ocyrhoe listened to the men of Montségur file quickly across the long, narrow spit of land that led to the barbican. They could jog only two abreast, and their armor and weapons clanked enough that the approaching French, who were still a ways down the slope, must have heard them. Before the French could respond—and also, conspicuously, before Peire-Roger signaled—there was a zinging sound above and then shrieks from down the slope. The Montségur archers had begun their deadly work.

Ocyrhoe could see almost nothing, but knew there were about two dozen men from Montségur. However many French there were to start with, lights down the slope meant backup troops at the watchtower.

A French commander suddenly shouted an order to charge. There was a horribly loud rasping sound as a mass of swords were unsheathed on both sides. The Montségur defenders circled the barbican, swords and axes drawn, and waited as the French began to rush them.

Suddenly from the barbican fiery branches of collected scrub-timber seemed somehow to explode out of the arrow loops onto the frozen ground below. There was precious little for the fire to feed on besides the branches themselves, but the muddied snow was too frozen to damp the fire, and there was flame enough to light what would become the battleground. The tactic was clear: any Frenchman who tried to rush the barbican, or the Montségur soldiers on the ground near it, would either have to expose themselves in this firelit area or else detour so far around it as to risk walking off the edge of the mountaintop. The body of French attackers, collectively, paused. This was not what Peire-Roger had wanted, but it was safer for the fortress.

Suddenly there was a much more intense eruption of arrows from the barbican, and the men on the walls of Montségur cheered and followed suit. Arrows in a lethal rain headed straight toward the French, and few of the crusaders even reached the level land by the tower. Now Peire-Roger cried out an order, arm raised with sword held high, and his score of followers rushed toward the barbican to engage with the French who had escaped his archers.

◆ ◆ ◆

All men on the battlements had hurried to the eastern wall and were crowded on it, shooting. Ocyrhoe crept up behind them, knelt down to watch between their greaves. Everyone she recognized—Peire-Roger, Artal, the Bonnet brothers—she saw in silhouette, with the burning branches scattered on the ground behind them.

Peire-Roger was nearly at the door to the barbican, but a large Frenchman appeared from around the curve of the building and intercepted him, sword out, with a vicious cut aimed at his neck. Unused to watching combat, Ocryhoe squealed despite herself. Peire-Roger seemed to sense the blow as it came at him, and raised his shield defensively, so that the attacker's sword glanced off the center of it and the man staggered slightly back. But Peire-Roger staggered back himself, his chest unprotected, and another Frenchman behind the first came at him with an axe raised high. Ocyrhoe gasped and clenched her fists so hard she hurt her fingers.

"Get out of here," an archer towering above her hissed angrily over his shoulder as he reached for his quiver. "You're a distraction, making noise like that."

Ocyrhoe could not move. She stared in horror while the second soldier's axe sliced through the air toward the leader of Montségur.

Suddenly the door of the barbican burst open and a ferocious form erupted from it, axe in right hand, knife in left, both blades moving in a frenzy, slashing so fast it was hard to believe the wielder saw what he was doing—no, what *she* was doing. This was Vera, Shield-Maiden, shield slung over her back now and doubly armed. In a heartbeat she had disarmed the man about to fell Peire-Roger, then sank the axe into his neck and pushed his corpse away from her with one booted foot.

Ocyrhoe screamed in amazement. The archer snarled at her, without looking back, "Get the hell out of here, girl. You are a danger to us with that screaming! I'll *kick* you off if you don't go down *now*!"

Breathing hard, Ocyrhoe retreated to the ladder and nearly fell down it in her haste. But she did not stop at the bottom. She ran toward the gate; all of the men had rushed out to the small field, but the gate stood open, with Ferrer and a few other men guarding it.

"Let me out there," she said, willing her voice and her arms not to tremble. "I have a message for his lordship from the bishop." She sounded confident enough, and the supposed sender was portentous enough, that Ferrer did not challenge her.

She ran halfway along the narrow strip of mountain-ridge, almost slipped off it on an icy patch, and stopped herself. If the French had broken through their ranks, she'd have been first in line for death. But it was clear the French would get nowhere close to her; already Peire-Roger's men were in command of the field. In the few brief moments it had taken her to get outside the walls, Vera had dispatched two more crusaders, and was now fighting knife-to-knife with a burly third. Percival had exited the barbican, too; she could see his shape silhouetted by the dying fires of the branches, tall and broad-shouldered as he was; he fought with nothing but a sword against a corpulent but nimble enemy.

A torch was lit in the barbican, and then another, and then another. She saw a few figures dash out, but then the door was bolted behind them. On the wall-walk of Montségur she heard another cheer: The barbican was securely bolted. The French had already failed in their plan; the only sensible course for them now was to retreat and regroup far down the slope of the mountaintop in soupy darkness. There would be no more bloodshed tonight.

Or so Ocyrhoe thought. As she watched, she saw Percival attempt to slice his adversary across the middle, only to have his blow repelled by thick maille under the man's tunic. "Hugue, you whoreson!" Peire-Roger's voice cried out furiously over the din, and his figure, somehow darker than all the others, marched resolutely toward the two men. Ocyrhoe took a sharp breath: Percival was fighting with the enemy general, the man who had kept the siege going despite months of getting nowhere. With a wave of fury and loyalty, Ocyrhoe wanted to kill Hugue, too.

Percival immediately dropped back from his engagement with Hugue, his sword held protectively in front of him, and then kicked Hugue hard in the hip to make him stagger toward Peire-Roger. Percival again moved his sword to a more offensive position but made no move to attack the man. To Ocyrhoe it looked as if he were offering to be a backup while Peire-Roger attacked his nemesis.

She wanted to get closer to see. She knew this terrain well enough to navigate almost without vision, but it made her nervous to attempt it in the frozen dark.

She considered her options. She could move forward beyond this narrow ridge, and stand directly on the field of battle. Or she could lower herself carefully down the slope and climb laterally, spiderlike, below the top of the ridge until she was just below the field. Then she could raise herself high enough to get a ground-level view. She would be unnoticed and safe. Unnoticed, that is, unless somebody threw their enemy off the side of the mountain where she was. But so far all the fallen were lying on the field.

✦ ✦ ✦

Peire-Roger saw Percival make way for him. His blood heated when he'd recognized Hugue de Arcis: that bloated, arrogant toady of the French king, the spiritual heir of the accursed Simon de Montfort, the most hated man in Occitania, the most hated man in Peire-Roger's life. His presence at this moment showed how cocky the French had been of victory tonight: he would only be here if he genuinely believed he was about to receive

Peire-Roger's capitulation. With a surge of fury and gleeful disgust, Peire-Roger raised his sword and swung hard at Hugue's broad shoulder. But the lord of Carcassonne saw this coming; he stepped in toward the blow and met it with his own heavy blade so intensely that both men were repelled away from each other. Peire-Roger recovered the quicker and swung around toward Hugue while he was still recovering. But Hugue unexpectedly crouched, and the shift in his hulking center of gravity spun him back around toward Peire-Roger more quickly than the lord of Montségur had expected. Hugue held his sword upward and slightly forward and began to rise, the tip of the sword headed straight for Peire-Roger's throat.

Out of the blackness, a broad axe fell hard between them, smashing Hugue's sword out of the way. The heavy man fell sideways from the intensity of the blow. The axe-wielder disappeared into the darkness just as Peire-Roger registered, with amazement, that it was a woman.

As Peire-Roger stepped in for an easy strike at the back of Hugue's neck, Hugue thrust his blade over his left shoulder to protect himself and connected to Peire-Roger's blade, shoving it aside. It gave Hugue the chance to heave himself up to stand, but as he faced Peire-Roger again the leader of Montségur was already striking, this time a low swing aimed at Hugue's legs.

Hugue took one firm step back, then suddenly stepped forward again and mirrored Peire-Roger's attack. Peire-Roger, still striking out furiously, leapt back away from danger and stumbled as the ground beneath his heels crumbled away. He had lost his sense of place in his fury; he was about to tumble backward toward the precipice of the mountain ridge, and Hugue was about to push him over it.

Two things happened then, swiftly, but to Peire-Roger they seemed to take forever. First, he felt his knife being pulled out of his belt, and a moment later saw it in the dim, as a child's hand, holding the hilt, sliced at Hugue's face. It made contact near the Frenchman's chin—a superficial wound, but enough to distract; blood spurted and Hugue, shouting, staggered backward.

A blink later, somebody else grabbed Peire-Roger by the front of the tunic and pulled him forward, down onto the frozen ground, before his own lost balance could propel him backwards off the mountain. Peire-Roger landed hard on top of whoever was pulling him to safety. Winded, he managed to sit up and saw in the flickering unsteady light that his two saviors were the strange young duo of Ferenc, who had pulled him forward, and Ocyrhoe, who held his knife and was staring at its bloody blade with wide, alarmed eyes at what she had just done.

"It's over, milord," Ferenc said. Peire-Roger, stunned, got up and then offered his hand to Ferenc to help him stand. Fighting had warmed him, but now his wet hands stung with cold. "Look—they're in retreat. We have the barbican, and we didn't lose a single man."

Peire-Roger took a moment to register this. "You were in the tower," he said, realizing. "You were the first archer. You minimized the number who attacked us."

"Percival and Vera shot with me," Ferenc said. "Your men obeyed you and waited to shoot until it was folly not to. If you are angry that your initial plan was not implemented, the fault is ours, not theirs."

Peire-Roger ran his sleeve across his sweaty face to collect himself. "I think you may have saved us," he said. "'Twas hubris on my part to think we could take on an endless stream of Frenchmen and win." He looked around. His men—and only his men—remained standing on the bloody ground around the barbican tower. Inside, the tower was now well lit, and some of his soldiers were inside staring out toward him. He hailed them silently, and they gave a whooping cry of triumph in response.

"Well done, lads," he shouted out. "No more of this sneaky French nonsense." He smiled briefly at Ferenc and Ocyrhoe and then walked toward the barbican door.

Leaning against it was Vera, calmly wiping blood off her axe with a ragged piece of leather she had cut from the uniform of a dead French soldier. Percival stood beside her, looking levelly at Peire-Roger.

"Vera saved your life twice tonight," he informed the lord of Montségur.

Peire-Roger looked at Vera. She continued to wipe the blade clean, with only the briefest glance in his direction.

"You're relieved of kitchen duty," he said.

CHAPTER 28:

APRÈS-SIEGE

An hour later they were all inside, where the defending heroes were saluted and cheered and given hot wine. The Good Ones, led by Bishop Marti, went upstairs to the donjon to give relieved prayers of thanks for their deliverance. But the Credents all stayed below to celebrate with Peire-Roger, who almost instantly got drunk.

The community was too tired and wearied by anxiety for song or dance, but there was animated talking, storytelling, and children play-acting their innocent imaginings of what had happened outside the wall. The wives of those who'd been in combat wove themselves around their heroes, the unwed soldiers covertly eyed the unwed ladies, who covertly eyed them back, and Ferenc and Ocyrhoe sat flushed and delighted beside each other on a table near Peire-Roger. He had put them on display for their role in saving him. Vera was not given as prominent a spot, but her services had been pointed out and described by the lord of Montségur, and then repeated not infrequently about the room by Raphael, who perhaps slightly embellished what he'd heard from Percival.

Ocyrhoe did not mind the attention as long as Ferenc was beside her. When his attention was turned elsewhere—if somebody across the room asked him a question about arrow fletchings, say, and he rose to move close enough to hear—she suddenly felt horribly exposed and wanted to tail him, hide up against his back. She did not like to be singled out, but a catlike contentment settled over her as long as Ferenc was beside her.

As the excitement was finally softening to sleepy pleasure, the door to the keep was suddenly thrown open. Matheus Bonnet—one of the brothers who had taken the treasure into hiding weeks earlier—stood blinking at them. "Milords," he called out. There was a moment of silence and then a moment of boisterous greeting. "Milords! I bring assistance from Isarn de Fanjeaux!" He stepped aside to reveal two soldiers—extremely well-kempt compared to the Montségur garrison, their tunics striped red and blue and looking almost new. Each carried a crossbow, and behind each stood a young squire dressed in similar livery.

The entire room erupted into applause; the newcomers looked almost sheepish to receive such an ovation.

"Ah, we don't need them," called out Peire-Roger, laughing. "We whipped the French's backsides all on our own tonight, with women and children doing some of the best work. But you're welcome all the same, gentlemen!"

Now the crossbowmen looked uncertainly at each other.

"Come and welcome," said Raphael above the din. "Never mind the clatter. We've had an eventful night. If you have news, his lordship is not quite too drunk to hear it, and the rest of us will take note well enough."

Ocyrhoe wriggled over to make room for the approaching figures. This meant that she was wriggling up against Ferenc. Ferenc did not wriggle. He stayed exactly where he was, so that she ended up almost on his lap. She wasn't sure why that pleased her so much, but she forced her attention to stay on Matheus.

"I bring four pieces of news," he said to Peire-Roger, who grinned at him drunkenly. Matheus blinked a moment, then removed his hat and continued to speak, delivering his speech to old Raimon de Perelha instead. "First, my brother and I have safely hidden the treasure in the Sabarthes Mountains, with Credents who know what it's intended for."

"Excellent," said both old lord and young at the same moment, but in very different voices.

"Second, my brother has made contact with the agents of Corbario, the Aragonese mercenary captain. He has agreed to a rendezvous in ten days' time at Usson. I have tallied the whole of our hidden treasure and will offer him that amount."

"The whole thing?" said Peire-Roger.

"Of course the whole thing," said his father-in-law sternly. "What is the use in saving it if we are obliterated?"

"All right, then, the whole thing," said Peire-Roger with sudden, offhand gallantry.

This led to some cheering at the table; the rest of the room grew quiet and everyone's attention, especially the men's, turned toward Matheus Bonnet. "Third, of course, these excellent crossbowmen from Isarn de Fanjeaux, who sends his regrets for not having more men available." Again the new arrivals were cheered and welcomed.

"Finally," said Matheus, raising his voice slightly, and trying to get Peire-Roger's gleefully inebriated attention. "I bring word from Count Raimondo of Toulouse."

This immediately focused Peire-Roger. "When is he sending men?" he demanded, bolting upright.

"He asks you—urges you—to hold out until spring. He is trying to put together an army without the French king or the Catholic Church realizing that he is doing so, and he needs time."

"It is only January," Peire-Roger fumed. "The equinox is two months distant."

"When he comes," Matheus pressed on, "he will bring not only his own men, but troops from Emperor Frederick."

Raphael startled violently at that. "What?" he demanded, setting down his cup of wine.

Matheus nodded. "Frederick has sent word to the Count that he will support him, and us."

"Oh for the love of all things holy," Raphael muttered under his breath. And then quietly to Percival, who was standing beside him, "That's it, we're leaving." Percival responded with a look of confusion. "I'll explain later," Raphael said in a longsuffering tone.

"The Emperor, eh?" said Peire-Roger. "What price does he exact for his help? We're not his people, and we don't want to be. We want to be our own people!"

Everyone cheered and toasted their agreement.

"I suspect it is a strategic move on his part," said Raphael diplomatically. "He wants to show some muscle against the French throne, which has gained a dramatic amount of land and power in the campaign against the Cathars. I assure you, he has no ambition to claim the Occitaine. He simply wants allies against France, and Fate has given him a wonderful opportunity to cultivate some." He smiled reassuringly, ignoring Percival's continued confused look.

"All right," said Peire-Roger indulgently. "Then we'll accept his help. To his Imperial Majesty's health!" he cried out, and downed the rest of the wine in his wooden cup.

Raphael glanced at Percival, then at Vera. With a nod of his head he gestured toward the hall door. They rose and followed him as he hobbled on his crutches. As Raphael passed by Ferenc, the young hunter tapped his arm with a questioning look. Raphael shook his head, glancing between Ocyrhoe and Ferenc and then almost—*almost*—smiling. Ocyrhoe was sure of it.

Once Raphael and the others had left the table, the newcomers moved in to fill their places, meaning Ocyrhoe no longer had to shift over to give them room. In fact, she and Ferenc were now smack up against each other, closer than any two other people in the room, and there was a considerable gap between her rear (planted on the planks of the table) and Peire-Roger's elbows (likewise). She supposed she should move away from Ferenc, but she did not want to.

She glanced up at him. He seemed to be avoiding her gaze, which was awkward since he clearly could not avoid her presence: she was snuggled up against his torso, the top of her shoulder pressing into the back of his upper arm, his arm itself resting forward, his hand on his lap. It felt wonderful, as if they had been carved out of the same piece of wood. But his refusal to meet her gaze made her chest constrict nervously. He raised his hand above his head, and she grimaced slightly, certain he was about to use the moment to move entirely, to shift away from her.

Instead he raised his arm completely, rocked slightly back, and then lowered it again—draping it around her shoulder. Without looking at her. As if it were something that happened all the time between them. She grinned hugely and despite herself, she giggled.

In the hubbub of the room, he could not hear the sound, but he could feel the vibration in her shoulders. "Don't do that," he said quietly into her ear. "We are already drawing too much attention to ourselves."

"*You're* the one who put your arm around *me*!" she retorted in a whisper, tilting her head toward him but keeping her eyes averted.

"Only because you were *burrowing* into my side for no good reason," he said.

"Very well, I shall unburrow," she said tartly, and began to shift away from him. He pulled her back, bumping her against himself, and smiled sheepishly.

"Stop that." He glanced around. "At least everyone here is fairly drunk. There is no privacy anywhere here, is there?"

"We could go down to the Good Ones' settlement," Ocyrhoe said, suddenly thrilled with nervous excitement. "The French are nursing their wounds, they won't be up to anything else tonight."

"The porter will not let us out."

"There is the chicken coop," Ocyrhoe suggested. Eggs were not part of the Good Ones' diet, but the cook always snuck them into the bread for the Credents. There were only about a dozen hens, and they hardly laid this time of year, but Peire-Roger had decided to maintain them through the winter.

Ferenc frowned thoughtfully. This keep was free from the stench he associated with a crowd of humans in an airless place, mostly because nobody living here ate meat. But it was still stuffy and unpleasant, while the coop had airholes. And privacy.

But he still hesitated; the idea of sneaking off to be alone with Ocyrhoe made him wobbly.

"I'll bring a blanket for the floor, so we don't have to sit on the chicken shit," Ocyrhoe offered, misunderstanding his hesitation.

"They only shit around the edges where the perches are," said Ferenc. "Let's just go." He leaned back, removed his arm, and then casually slid off the table to the floor. He began, unhurriedly, to walk through the sleepy, mumbling crowd toward the exit stairs. After a heartbeat or two, Ocyrhoe also slipped off the table and began to walk after him. Her heart was banging happily against her ribs. She knew why they were sneaking off, but she did not know what might happen when they got there. Both these facts delighted her.

Outside, the air was very still but very cold. She did not notice. The courtyard was still lit from earlier in the evening, although the torches were starting to sputter out. There were very few people about—a skeleton crew of men atop the walls, a porter at the gate. The strange knights—Raphael, Percival, and Vera—argued quietly near the trebuchet, their breath billowing in vapors into the darkness, their voices tiny in the thin, still, weak air. She hoped Ferenc would not be called over there.

The trio paused and watched them. Ferenc kept walking resolutely toward the chicken coop, near the gate. He did not look at them. Ocyrhoe pretended not to look at them, but in her excellent peripheral vision, she saw them glancing back and forth between her and the hunter, and then exchanging glances between themselves. It seemed to take forever before she had entered into the coop and shut it behind her. It was considerably warmer in here.

"Sit here," she heard Ferenc say from the level of her waist. He had already taken off his outer wrap and put it on the floor. The hens clucked a warning, sleepily, but sensed there was no danger here and ignored them.

She sat so that she was facing him. "No," he said. He moved around so that they were facing in the same direction, and put his arm around her again. "Let's start with this."

She grinned again. "Now is it safe to giggle?" she asked.

"As long as you do not disturb the chickens."

"You were a hero today," she said adoringly. "That's the second time in as many full moons that you've been a hero."

"You were a hero with me," he said.

"I wasn't in the barbican shooting Frenchmen," she said.

"You saved Peire-Roger's life."

"With you," said Ocyrhoe. "I like that we worked together against that whoreson Hugue de Arcis. We're a good team." She closed her eyes in the dark and beamed contentment.

"Yes," said Ferenc after a moment, sounding pleased. "Yes, we are. From the first moment we met. Someday, I would like us to be a good team under less interesting circumstances."

"Me too," Ocyrhoe said instantly. "Let's run away together from all this and see what happens if we go out into the world alone."

He pulled her closer and rested his cheek on the top of her head. The feel of it made each of them secretly dizzy. "I would like nothing better," he said. "But I cannot. I am in Frederick's service and now I am Raphael's squire. They deserve better than my sudden disappearance."

"Frederick doesn't," Ocyrhoe said, suddenly sharp. "He sent me out into the world alone—"

"I know, I know," Ferenc said soothingly, rocking her gently. "And you will never have to do that again. I give you my oath. You will never have to go anywhere alone."

"Because?" she prompted, hardly breathing.

"Because I will stay with you. Or you will stay with me. And I'll tell the emperor I said so. He'll allow it. He owes you that at least."

"Then there is nothing in the world that I'm afraid of."

"Good," he said, "That makes me happy. I want you to feel safe. With me." A small, nervous chuckle escaped him. "Maybe I have *always* wanted that, without knowing it."

"It wasn't time to know it before," she said, smiling. She pulled her head away and looked up toward his face in the dark. "Now it is time."

"Now it is time," he agreed, and gently brought his lips to hers.

❖❖❖

"Never mind what I said to Peire-Roger," Raphael insisted with barely contained impatience. "I know why Frederick is sending men. Or claiming to send men. He wants us to leave. He knows I won't leave if I think innocents are undefended. He wants me to think that help is coming so that I will be willing to leave here and come back to him. Let me tell you: I *am* willing to leave here."

"These people are under attack," Percival protested. "Most of the effective defense tonight was *us*. Without Vera and Ferenc, the French would have taken the barbican and Montségur would be leaderless. We are hugely useful here. It would be absolutely wrong for us to leave now."

"It is not our fight," Raphael said tightly between clenched teeth. "I agree with your sentiment but it is a specious argument. We are not meant to be here. Frederick sent me to get you, and then return to him. I am honor-bound to do that."

"Before anything, you are honor-bound to lend your sword to those in need of it," Percival retorted. Raphael suppressed a wince of acknowledgement.

"*Quiet*," Vera whispered sharply, and gestured toward the entrance to the donjon.

As they watched, the door opened and Ferenc, wrapped in an extra blanket, came out. He did not close the door behind him, and a moment later, petite Ocyrhoe exited as well. She closed the door and pulled the bolt, following him. All three of the older adults watched the two younger ones walk with nervous determination toward the chicken coop. Ferenc did a perfect job of not acknowledging their presence. Ocyrhoe pretended to, but Percival could see her eyes swerve toward them once.

They waited until the two had disappeared inside the coop.

"That's another reason not to stay," Percival said drily.

"It's not, really," Raphael said, softening. "Neither of them are breaking any vows. And she is not a Cathar. We can bring her back with us."

"I don't think she'll come," said Percival, and then pushed forward with his argument. "You know we cannot leave now. The three of us—perhaps the five of us—are vital to the survival of this place."

Raphael, clearly pained by the absence of a purely good choice, said, "I cannot travel for a few weeks, and I have put in a request for sulphur. Charcoal and hemp they have enough of. We make fire-arrows, or some improvised form of them, without the smithy to forge the proper heads. We burn the French trebuchet. When Matheus Bonnet heads out again to find Corbario the mercenary in Usson, we go with him."

"I won't," said Percival calmly. "I have already told you I'm staying here."

Raphael grimaced but did not argue; instead, he turned his attention to Vera. "We will hear for ourselves that an army is coming to help, and once we are satisfied with proof that the defenders have that security, we will leave Occitania behind us." A pause. "Agreed?"

A pause. "I think we should stay until the help actually arrives," said Vera.

"What?" Raphael said crossly.

"Percival is right. Until tonight, there was no way to judge how useful our particular skills are. It turns out they are very useful. Including yours, Raphael—you're the one that sent us ahead to the tower, and that gave us the advantage tonight. Peire-Roger is a strong fighter on the field, or at least brave, but the man has gotten blind drunk nearly every night we've been here, and his father-in-law is a gentle soul who has few days left before dementia sets in. They need us. I agree with Percival. We stay until there are satisfactory reinforcements."

"I stay until I have the grail," said Percival.

"*Don't*—" Raphael began warningly.

"And then I'll do what the grail tells me to do."

"The grail will tell you to sit down abruptly and cry out in pain, because I will take it and smash it over your head," Raphael said fiercely. Vera barked a laugh despite herself.

Percival was unperturbed. "That might be what it takes," he said, agreeably. "Perhaps I will have to be in a somewhat twilit state to really hear the message it is trying to send me."

"This conversation is over," Raphael growled, and used his crutches to lope in irritation back toward the keep entrance. He slipped once on icy ground, cursed under his breath, and slowed to a moderate pace. Vera, laughing without real malice, followed after him.

Alone in the courtyard, Percival glanced toward the chicken coop. If only he could will Ocyrhoe to admit she had the grail. She had her reasons, and he wanted to respect them.

But if she fell in love with Ferenc, maybe her priorities would shift a little.

Ferenc. Maybe Ferenc could help him get the grail. When there was a free moment, he would talk to Ferenc.

CHAPTER 29:

THE REVELATION OF THE CUP

Despite the French failure to take the barbican, the bombardment marked a dangerous turning point in the siege. The crusaders had developed a new fervor. Their collective identity had swung from failing besiegers to successful bombardiers. The mining and shaping of limestone projectiles happened even as the trebuchet was being loaded, sprung, and reloaded.

And moved, very slowly, up the slope.

By the next day, Raphael—without ever getting up onto the battlements to see for himself—had convinced the entire fortress that the trebuchet was being pushed up the side of the pog. Even the women and children took a turn up on the battlements to watch these attempts, in stupefied amazement. For the rest of the day, people could talk of nothing else. Peire-Roger declared to everyone, over the very thin bread and gruel that passed as dinner, that the French would defeat themselves, for obviously at some point the thing would either topple over or roll back down all the way to the watchtower. If nothing else, he claimed, the movement up the mountainside would take so long that the French would starve or freeze before they got too close—there were now several hundred Frenchman camping full time on the unprotected mountaintop.

His speech was bravado intended to calm an increasing terror. While there was something slightly farcical in the look of the trebuchet in motion, the reality of its approach was horrifying, especially now that all of them were penned in this extremely small, unhygienic, claustrophobic, unheated fortress, which since the start of the bombardment had fewer options for laying in supplies.

Meanwhile the bombardment never ceased. The rocks, about eighty a day, gradually got larger as their path of travel shortened. The French had mined and shaped so many before the bombardment even started that they had enough to last for weeks. The only benefit to this was that they themselves now had some ammunition, and Bacalaira very grandly slung a few projectiles toward the attackers. The rocks fell short by two-score paces.

"At least that means they're still quite far away," Percival pointed out.

The days slowly, slowly lengthened but the supplies got ever tighter. It was not safe to be on the mountaintop at all now, ever. There could be no scouting missions, and no supplies could be smuggled through the lines under cover of night, because the mountaintop was covered with crusaders. Even the entrance to their primary tunnel was endangered; all that remained for access to the outside world was the southern tunnel, a very narrow tributary into which only Ocyrhoe could fit. The tunnel-head was in the courtyard, beneath the southern wall. She went down every other day to check for messages, but in the bleakness of midwinter the Credents of the valleys had no food left to offer.

Except for when she was in the southern tunnel, Ferenc and Ocyrhoe were together almost every moment, waking and sleeping. Some spell seemed to have fallen over the fortress and not even the Good Ones—not even Rixenda or the Bishop—objected. They would sleep, full-clothed but nestled close, among the Credents on the first floor of the keep, and by day their tasks were varied, often arduous, but almost always together. Even when Ferenc was assigned to the wall, Ocyrhoe was put on runners' duty, to carry messages and bring fresh quivers of arrows.

Despite their miserable surroundings and the miserable weather, everything seemed to glow for Ocyrhoe. The relentless, harsh pounding of the catapulted boulders continued, several times each hour all night, less often during the day when the French would stop shooting to move it slowly up the slope; to her it was a background rumble. The snow, frost, sleet, and hail caused minor chills and all melted away, unremarkable, as long as Ferenc was in sight. Their lives were constantly in danger but she felt safe; they were freezing but she felt warm; they were hungry but she felt sated; they never had a moment of privacy but she felt wrapped in a cocoon alone with him.

There was hardly a moment in all that time even for another kiss, and yet they both knew—indeed, the whole fortress seemed to be in collusion with them—that they were now permanently bound together. Prone to thinking too much, she hardly thought at all—she was present, constantly, keeping vigil over the safety of the fortress but also her own happiness.

Eventually, the French trebuchet moved far enough up the slope that it began to sling rocks directly into the courtyard of the fortress. After a horrified reaction from the civilians, the defenders set up a simple warning system: A scout in the barbican kept a trained eye on the French trebuchet and sounded a shrill whistle when he saw the counterbalance start to drop. This gave anyone in the courtyard enough time to sprint to shelter either in the donjon or against the eastern wall. Since the trebuchet sent rocks flying to almost the same place each time (until it was repositioned, as happened once or twice a day), the courtyard traffic always diverted around the area of likeliest danger. The women and children spent almost the entire day cramped in the donjon, emerging en masse for air a few moments after each rock landed, or to relieve themselves, or to check on the well-being of a kinsman. The morning romps and snowball fights faded to memory.

Piere Bonnet had not returned yet, and now there would be no way to get him up the mountain. The store of food began, for the first time, to dwindle noticeably, as did their store of arrows and beeswax candles. And yet, with the foolish excitement of new love, all of this felt like a game to Ocyrhoe. Such giddiness as hers insisted that somehow, in the end, all would be well.

Best of all, Percival avoided her, although she knew he did not wish to. Something about Ferenc must have warned him off, for often she would catch a glimpse of him, on duty on the walls, or speaking with Raphael or Vera, and always his eyes would rest on her and follow her. But as long as she was with Ferenc, he never would approach her. *Good*, she thought, *repair your madness on your own*. She never thought about the cup—or rather, when she did, it was a passing thought and she knew now that when the time came to depart, she'd simply leave it behind with Rixenda. It had no hold on her now. Her fixation on it seemed ridiculous. A silly, adolescent obsession with an object in which she had invested far too much.

✦ ✦ ✦

It had snowed overnight, with perhaps a handspan collecting on the ground by morning. What was not shoveled to the sides was ground into the dirt of the courtyard within an hour. Raphael, Vera, and Percival were meeting outside with Peire-Roger and Bishop Marti, in part for privacy but largely for fresh air. Raphael, now using only a cane, was still stymied from action by circumstances and growing irritable. He had demanded this parley. Anxiously awaiting for weeks now the sulphur they needed to make fire arrows, they were debating the merits of asking the Count of Toulouse to supply it. The fresh snowfall meant that it would be easier for the French scouts to track Ocyrhoe if they sent her down the tunnel. But there were other issues to consider, too.

A boulder had just landed in the courtyard. As soldiers rolled it toward their own siege machine, the scouts in the barbican called out that the French were preparing the trebuchet for movement farther up the hill. At least that meant there would be no more boulders until some time after noon. The Montségur archers rained arrows down on the French crusaders' efforts, but with little effect; half of the Frenchmen on the mountainside were there only to protect the other half with shields held high, the edges overlapping.

Raphael saw Ferenc and Ocyrhoe across the yard, speaking to Rixenda. He stared into the back of Ferenc's head with such intensity the young man seemed to feel it and turned. Raphael gestured him toward the group with a single finger. On reflex, Ferenc reached out toward Ocyrhoe's shoulder as she continued to speak to Rixenda; Raphael shook his head once: *No.*

Ferenc paused. He whispered something to Ocyrhoe, then began to jog across the muddy snow to join them. Behind him, Rixenda watched him a moment; then her eyes strayed to Raphael and the group he stood with. For a heartbeat she stared hard at them, then gestured toward the donjon door. Ocyrhoe was already headed in that direction, and Rixenda walked slightly behind her, her eyes glancing back several times to watch Ferenc approach the group.

"Fine squire you are," Raphael said drily as the youth approached. "I do not think we've even spoken in a week."

Ferenc pursed his lips sheepishly. "My failing, sir," he said. "I'm sorry."

"Just don't get her pregnant, lad," said Peire-Roger cheerfully.

Ferenc turned crimson and gave Peire-Roger a mortified look. "Milord, you misjudge me," he protested, hardly able to speak over his embarrassment.

Peire-Roger laughed. "You mean I've overestimated you," he chortled.

"Underestimated, rather," said Raphael, putting a hand on Ferenc's shoulder. "Thank you for joining us. It's Ocyrhoe we are discussing, and I wanted you to be in on it."

Ferenc frowned protectively. "Why Ocyrhoe?" he said.

Raphael cleared his throat and drummed his gloved fingers across the top of his cane, staring at them.

"We will soon be in a position to destroy the trebuchet with fire-arrows," Peire-Roger said.

"And then we are leaving," said Raphael. "As soon as I can travel without being an encumbrance."

"Until then, we're staying here," said Vera.

"We will be leaving very soon," Raphael continued to his fingertips.

"There's some disagreement about when we're leaving," Vera said to Ferenc.

"But we *are* leaving," said Raphael.

"Not all of us," said Percival; at the same moment, Peire-Roger said "At some point" and Bishop Marti commented, "Later on."

"Very well," said Ferenc, uncertainly.

"But here's the thing," said Raphael, even more intently drumming his fingertips on the handle of the cane as he spoke. "They want Ocyrhoe to stay."

"We *need* Ocyrhoe to stay," Peire-Roger corrected hurriedly. "We are in trouble if she leaves with you."

"Why?" Ferenc asked.

"Nobody knows the tunnels like she does," Peire-Roger explained. "A couple of the men, perhaps—the Bonnet brothers, but of course Peire is gone and Matheus will be leaving again soon. A few others, but we need them in the garrison. She's the only one familiar with the tunnels and the transport and communication channels, whom we don't also need full-time somewhere else. And while we have access only to the southern tunnel, she's the only one who can get up and down at all."

"Does she know all this?" Ferenc asked.

"I'm sure she hasn't *thought* about it," said Peire-Roger. "But if she did, she'd realize it's true."

Ferenc bit his lip. "I see." Raphael, still staring at his gloved fingers on the cane handle, felt more than saw Ferenc look at him. "And you are telling me this because you assume I'll want to stay with her."

"Oh, I wish it were that simple, Ferenc," Raphael said with a sigh. "That is of course a concern, which you and I can discuss privately in a moment. First, however, Percival refuses to leave Montségur unless..." Without looking at his fellow knight, he pointed at him briefly and then resumed tapping his fingertips on the cane handle. "Why don't you explain yourself, Percival, since I cannot rationally describe something I find irrational."

"Of course," said Percival seriously, as if he had not just been insulted. He gave Ferenc a look of mesmerizing, solemn earnestness. "I was brought here by a vision."

"I know about all that," said Ferenc quickly.

"I am meant to have the grail. And I am sure she is the cup-bearer. I will not force it from her, but I must not leave her company until..."

"What exactly," Ferenc demanded in a suddenly tense voice, "is a grail?"

"It's a cup," said Percival. "A metal cup, I think it's silver, although sometimes in my visions it's gold. It's nothing special to look at but it contains tremendous powers."

Raphael watched a spectrum of emotions flash across Ferenc's face: confusion, surprise, distaste, impatience, irritation, and then dread. "What else did she tell you about the cup?" he demanded.

Surprised, Raphael exchanged glances with an astonished Vera and a delighted-looking Percival. "Well, that's the challenge," said Percival, with the relieved warmth of a man who had discovered an unexpected comrade. "She hasn't told me anything. She refuses to talk about it."

Ferenc squinted and blinked. "Then why is her name being mentioned in conjunction with it?"

"Because I know she has it," said Percival. "She *used* it. Everyone has heard the story, but in the story it was an angel—and I know, in my soul, I know that it was not an angel, but Ocyr—"

"*What story?*" Ferenc demanded, rigid, jaws clenched.

"There was an incident at a farm in the foothills," Raphael said, deciding that Percival's rendition would do nothing to calm Ferenc. "He mentioned it when we first arrived, but I don't think he mentioned the grail. Supposedly a female angel bearing a chalice appeared to a group of men, and prevented one of them—Vidal, in fact—from betraying the Cathars."

"I have spoken to Vidal," said Percival. He did not notice, as Raphael did, the increasing distress on Ferenc's face. "And I have no doubt that the supposed angel was Ocyrhoe, and that she caused him to have a change of heart, and saved the fortress, by whatever force is in the grail. She is the cup-bearer, but I believe—"

"You want the cup?" Ferenc spat. "Is that how mad you are?" His face darkened; his breathing was instantly ragged; his voice tightened as if someone were choking him. "You want that evil, poisonous cup that causes death and madness? How can you possibly think there is any good to come out of it?"

"I just told you the—" Percival began, looking slightly perplexed by Ferenc's outburst. The youth stormed on.

"And why the hell does Ocyrhoe still have that fucking thing?" he shouted, shaking his fists at the knight. "Why did she not tell me? Only madmen want that cup and only evil comes from it!" He shouted, a long, loud, almost wailing cry without words. Every person in the courtyard turned to stare at him. Raphael, concerned, reached out a calming hand, but he angrily snatched his arm out of reach and stepped away from the rest of the group. He looked around the courtyard. "*Ocyrhoe!*" he yelled. Nobody responded, except a few guards on the walls who called out crude jokes about his mistress going missing. Looking almost apoplectic, he turned back to Percival. "Where is she?" he demanded in a low, accusing growl.

"You're the one whose side she hasn't left for weeks now," Percival said. "I should be the one asking you that."

Ferenc shook his head as if he wanted to fling away this entire conversation. "You don't want that cup," he said. "And I don't want to believe the cup is here. It best not be. If it is, we're all in trouble." He turned and looked around the courtyard wildly. "Where could she be hiding it?" he muttered, then exclaimed, "Oh!"

He ran toward the gate, gesturing to a bemused Ferrer to open it. Ferrer didn't move. Raphael, Percival, Vera, and the Montségur leaders pursued him, Raphael using the cane to propel him with unsafe speed, and Bishop Marti struggling to keep up.

"Where are you going?" Raphael demanded sharply.

"To the Perfecti village," Ferenc shouted over his shoulder. "She must have hidden it there. If it were anywhere in the fortress I'd have known."

"You can't go to the village!" Peire-Roger shouted at Ferenc's back. The youth was nearly at the gate. "Do not leave the safety of these walls!"

Ferenc shoved Ferrer out of the way and began to unbolt the heavy, oiled gate. The older man stumbled to his knees; by the time he was able to get up, Ferenc was already out the gate.

"Stop him!" Bishop Marti yelled, uselessly. Ferrer grabbed the gate and pulled it closed, uncertain if he should bolt it with Ferenc now outside.

As Raphael, Vera, and Percival reached the gate, the door to the keep opened and Ocyrhoe stepped out. Raphael saw her. Ocyrhoe looked at them all; perhaps something in Percival's exuberant expression said more than it meant to, but suddenly she seemed to know exactly what had happened. Looking alarmed, she broke into a run.

"What?" she asked breathlessly as she approached.

"Something about a cup," Raphael said quietly. "Ferenc's running to the village looking for it."

Ocyrhoe looked as if she were about to burst into tears. "Oh, *shit*," she hissed and with stunning abruptness, pushed Ferrer out of the way, opened the gate, and ran out after Ferenc, ignoring Peire-Roger and Bishop Marti's urgent orders not to leave. Ferrer miserably pulled the gate closed.

"When will this be finished?" Raphael snapped at Percival.

"Brother, it almost is," Percival said. "It must be in the village. Ferenc is going to take it from her."

"And chuck it off the mountain, by his behavior," Raphael said. "At least I hope so."

"They are both unarmed," Vera said sharply. "And they've just run into no-man's land—perhaps it is even enemy territory now."

Raphael grimaced and glanced at Peire-Roger. "With your permission, commander?" he said grimly.

"All of us," Peire-Roger said. "Let's go."

Ferrer stepped away from the gate; Vera pushed it open, and they all rushed out. Outside the gate, the snow lay slick and frozen where no human foot had trampled it yet. Down the slope toward the abandoned Good Ones' village, Ocyrhoe and Ferenc were two small, colliding figures. Ocyrhoe was grabbing at Ferenc, who kept pushing her off as if she had a disease he was afraid he'd catch. She was sobbing by the time the two of them reached the gate to the village. On level ground again, they each righted themselves and ran out of sight.

At least the French took no interest in the little drama, their collective attention focused on the movement of their siege machinery.

Raphael glanced at his cane and was about to toss it aside when Percival stepped in front of him with a grin. "Allow me, brother," said the Frank, then bowed in toward Raphael, clasped his arm behind Raphael's back to bend his friend over his shoulder, and stood up again, the Levantine dangling over his shoulder like a child. "Thank God you're not in armor," said Percival. "Hold on." He half-slid, half-walked down the slope, grabbing at the stone wall for stability along the way. At the level entrance to the terrace, he set Raphael down and gestured that he would follow him. His face was shining.

"You can't be in here!" Ocyrhoe was shouting at Ferenc.

"Which is yours?" Ferenc shouted. "Where did you stay? Where are you keeping it?"

"You're not allowed to be here," Ocyrhoe insisted, teary. Despite herself she was standing in front of one particular hut. "It's disrespectful to the Goodwomen—"

"Disrespectful!" Ferenc barked with laughter, staring at her like a feral creature. "That was your home? That one?" He ran past her, pushing open the door to the shack and disappearing inside.

"No!" Ocyrhoe nearly screamed, and scrambled to follow him.

Raphael cursed and propelled himself toward the small building, entering a moment after her.

"Where is it?" Ferenc shouted. The space was very small—a tiny table with two stools beside it and two small bowls on it; an unlit lantern; two abandoned bedrolls on the floor; a simple altar. "Where? Where, Ocyrhoe? Why do you still have it?" He pushed past the table, knocking the bowls to the packed-earth floor; he reached for the closer bedroll and grabbed the coverlet and cushion, throwing them into the corner.

"Stop! Ferenc! Stop this outrage!" Ocyrhoe shouted desperately. She grabbed for his shoulders, but he pushed her aside so hard that she fell against the wall; he lifted the entire bedroll and shook it, then threw it aside, too; the wooden pallet that it rested on he grabbed and shook as if expecting something to fall out.

"Where is it?" he snarled again at Ocyrhoe, who kept crying, "Stop this!" as she reached out for him. He smacked her hand every time it came near him. He tore apart the second bed with equal intensity. He found nothing.

"Where the hell is it?" he shouted at her.

"Ferenc, calm down," Raphael said sharply from the doorway. He peered in without entering.

"Do you know what she has? Do you know what she's *done?*" Ferenc retorted, looking almost crazed.

"I haven't done anything!" Ocyrhoe shouted at him from behind. He turned suddenly and in two long, angry strides was standing over her; she shrank from him but he grabbed her wrist and dragged her back over to the door.

"Tell him," he ordered furiously, through clenched jaws. "Tell him everything. Tell all of them. Explain to that demented man why he must never have the cup."

"Let go of her," Raphael said sharply. "Ferenc, contain yourself." In his peripheral vision, he saw Vera, Percival, and Peire-Roger approaching the door. The elderly Bishop Marti must have opted against braving the icy slope.

"Ocyrhoe has something to explain to you," Ferenc said. Still grabbing her by the wrist, he righted one of the overturned stools and then firmly pushed her down to sit on it. "Go ahead. Explain."

"Hold a moment," Raphael said, silently cursing everyone with visions and all objects related to them. "We'll only make her tell it once." He gestured for the others to enter the tiny hut.

It was very crowded in here with six people. Ocyrhoe sat on the stool, with Ferenc hovering over her; Peire-Roger rested his butt against the table; the other stool remained overturned while Raphael, Vera, and Percival stood listening.

"Tell them about the cup," Ferenc said.

"Let go of her," Raphael insisted.

Ferenc released her. "*Tell them about the cup,*" he repeated.

Ocyrhoe looked around at all the faces, frightened. "There is a cup that our friend the priest has possession of, which seemed to have magical powers. But he was a madman."

"He tried to kill her for the cup," Ferenc said. "Frederick ordered her to get the cup away from him because it gave him dreadful powers, and when she tried to take it, he nearly killed her. That is why I killed him, because he was about to kill her. Over the cup." Looking at Ocyrhoe: "Why have you kept it all this time? Why didn't you get rid of it?"

"She was holding it for me," said Percival suddenly, his face luminous with certainty. "It is meant for me. Please, trust me. I have been driven to you by forces I do not understand, to free you from what I know must be a burden to you."

"You're as mad as Rodrigo was," Ocyrhoe said shakily. "You should not be in possession of it."

Percival smiled calmly at her. "Do I seem to you a madman?"

"Neither did he!" Ocyrhoe shouted.

Ferenc seemed suddenly to deflate. He took a step away from Ocyrhoe. His expression softened. "Father Rodrigo was very ill for a long time," said Ferenc. "I knew him, Ocyrhoe, in a way you never could have. He had lost his mind. He had moments of lucidity—seductive moments, he was so convincing—but he really was mad. His madness seemed to—" he broke off, confused, and said specifically to Vera and Raphael, "I do not believe in what I am about to say, and yet I know it's true." Then to the whole room, "His madness seemed to express itself *into* the cup, like milk or venom from a living creature. And then the cup became something else. I thought when it was severed from him, and surely when he was dead, it would just go back to being a cup."

"It didn't," said Ocyrhoe, adding sardonically, "It must be waiting for the next madman to fuel it." With a surly look at Percival, "And that's you, I suppose."

"I am not mad," Percival said pleasantly.

"I just fought beside him in battle," Ferenc said wearily. "He is not deranged as Rodrigo was."

"But he is a little *touched*," said Vera. "So there might be something to the idea that he's a better owner for the cup than are you." This, to Ocyrhoe. "Just give it to him so we can move on and address the real issues at hand."

"Nobody *owns* it," Ocyrhoe replied. She turned to Percival. "It's true, I feel that I am a steward waiting for directions to do something with it, but I don't know what, and I don't know why it should be *you* just because you happen to have shown up here."

Percival smiled at her, handsome and serene, and luminous again with spiritual certainty. "Let me describe to you just one vision, my most recent," he suggested. "If it resonates with you at all, let that be evidence the grail is meant for me."

"And if it doesn't?" Ocyrhoe demanded instantly.

"Then you hold onto it," Percival said. "Until some opportunity presents itself for me to earn your trust." He righted the other stool and sat across from Ocyrhoe at the table. Peire-Roger, who looked so mystified that he almost appeared bored, stood up away from the table and leaned back against a wall, watching them.

Percival held his hands out palm up on the table, an offering to Ocyrhoe to clasp hands. She did not move.

"Very well," Percival said after a moment. "It is a wonderful thing that you are so protective of it."

"No, it's not," said Ferenc.

"Shut up," Raphael said. "Stop interfering."

Percival looked at Ocyrhoe for a moment, smiling gently. "The grail," he began, "as it appears to me in visions, with increasing clarity, is a drinking cup made of silver, I think. There is some decoration on a band around the middle. Sometimes there is a rosy glow that comes out of the center of it. Enough to light your way in darkness." Ocyrhoe blinked, sat up taller, and grew very still.

"Yes," she said quietly.

"Not everybody sees the glow. Some people just see a cup. Even if you shine the light in a dark room, so that you can see what it lights up, other people see nothing but darkness." Ocyrhoe glanced at Peire-Roger. She nodded. "It is warm in winter and cool in summer," Percival continued, "but not always."

"Yes," she said, looking down, almost in a whisper.

Percival continued peacefully, gentle and monklike in his certainty, "There is a kind of wondrous alchemy that occurs when it is in the presence of a small piece of wood, a living piece of wood, a tiny sprig that appears to be just on the verge of blooming into leaf."

"*What?*" Raphael and Vera said at the same moment.

"Oh my God," said Ferenc, remembering the sprig Frederick— no, *Léna*—had ordered him to pinch from Raphael's clothes.

Ocyrhoe shook her head. "That is not familiar. I don't know anything about that."

The three who did know exchanged concerned glances. Raphael felt as if the top of his head were coming off. "Tell us more about the sprig, Percival," he said.

Percival peaceably shrugged. "I do not know much about it. It's only appeared recently—since you arrived, Raphael, now that I think of it. It's inert when I see it. It is waiting for something. It is waiting to turn into something, and the grail is waiting to receive something." Seeing the look of stunned dismay on his friend's face, Percival gently prodded, "Why, Raphael? Do you know something about a sprig?"

Raphael stared at him, mouth slack. "Feronantus," he said, naming the last elder of their order. "Feronantus is no more."

"You told me that, when you first arrived here," Percival said gently.

"Before he died..." he shook his head. "But this is mad."

"Raphael received a thing like you are describing," Vera said brusquely. "Without any explanation worth the name. Then the Emperor sent for him and told him to come here and get you, but he had Ferenc steal the sprig before we left, as surety that we'd come back."

"It wasn't Frederick doing any of those things," Ferenc argued. "It was Léna."

"I'm so confused," said Peire-Roger. "Who is Léna? Who is Frederick?"

"Emperor Frederick," said Raphael. "And we have no time to waste on confusion. We do not have the time for this mystical *nonsense.*"

"How can you say it's nonsense when it's real?" Percival asked. "I had a vision about a grail and a sprig. Lo and behold: there *is* a grail, and there *is* a sprig."

"There's a cup and there's a piece of wood, and we don't know what any of it means," countered Raphael. "The only path to clarity takes us back to Frederick's court. We are going there immediately. Take the cup or don't, that is your choice, but we cannot stay here."

"It's not my choice," said Percival. He looked at Ocyrhoe. "It's yours."

Ocyrhoe looked plaintive. "What you have said is interesting," she said. "But I am waiting to receive a sign that is meaningful to me, myself, not to just hear about someone else's sign."

Immediately Ferenc went back into a paroxysm of rage. "How can you say that there is anything meaningful about this fucking cup? I admit it's powerful, in ways I do not understand, but the power is random, it's senseless, it's nonsense, there is no *purpose* to it, no *meaning.*"

Ocyrhoe suddenly burst into tears. "It has a purpose. I just need to find it!" she cried. "How can you possibly understand what I have been through and what the cup has meant? You went back to Frederick, you were *taken in*—I was ripped away from everything I'd ever known, banished from my own life!" She turned on him, stood up, and despite her small size suddenly seemed almost to tower over him. "Don't tell me there was no *reason* for that! Don't tell me it was all for nonsense! You are telling me my *life* is nonsense!"

"Of course it's not," Ferenc said, chastened.

But she continued to shout over him, her anger pulling her up to tiptoes as she barked, "The only sustaining force I've had in all that time is the cup itself. I would never have survived without it. I had nothing. Do you understand that? Nothing, nobody, nowhere. No friends, no tribe, no city, no sister-binders, no vocation, no training. Nothing. Just the cup." To the room at large, gesturing at Percival, she said, "How can anyone possibly expect me to just give it away to some madman who obviously is going to be just fine whether he has it or not?" Turning more directly to Percival. "You don't need it. You might *want* it, but you don't *need* it. You are not *bereft of everything* without it. Here are your friends and there is your sword and the God-almighty *Emperor Frederick* wants you at his *court*. Perhaps you have an avocation as a visionary madman, but you have a fine and noble life without *indulging* in that *compulsion*."

"I agree with her there," said Raphael, then wished he hadn't as she collapsed back onto the stool, sobbing into her hands.

Ferenc immediately bent over her and gently rested his hands on her shaking shoulders. She shrugged him off.

"Ocyrhoe," he said gently.

"Leave me alone, Ferenc," she sobbed. "Just shut up and leave me alone, you have no idea—"

"I didn't, you're right. I do now." He carefully put his hands back on her shoulders. She did not shrug them off this time. He softly kissed the top of her head. "You had nothing, but that is no longer true. Now you have me. You don't need the cup. You have me." He knelt on one knee to be beside her, and pressed her head against his shoulder. "You have been tested by the gods. I do not know why, but you have been found good and strong and worthy," he said. He cradled her and rocked gently; she collapsed against him, sobbing with the abandon of a baby about to fall asleep. "You were cast out but now it is time to return to your people. I am your people. I will try to keep you warm in winter and cool in summer, and I will try, very hard, to shine a glimmer of light for you when it is dark."

Raphael, touched, pursed his lips and glanced at Vera. Vera was pursing her lips and glancing at him. He almost reached out his hand for her but stopped himself.

There was a long moment when nobody spoke, and Ocyrhoe's sobs subsided.

Raphael cleared his throat. "Well," he said. "Where does that leave us?"

Ocyrhoe interlaced her fingers with Ferenc's, and sat upright. In a nasal-stuffed voice, sniffing, she said, "Percival can have the cup."

Everyone in the hut relaxed; there was a palpable feeling of release in the air.

"Only one thing," she said. "I don't know where it is."

CHAPTER 30:

AN END

"What?" said Vera, sharply. "I was so hysterical because I thought that Ferenc was about to find it...but then it wasn't here. Last I saw it, it was in my bedroll here. I could not get down here when the village was evacuated to claim it." She groaned. "Perhaps Rixenda brought it up into the fort during the evacuation and hid it, although that seems very unlikely—she never approved of my attachment to it."

"If she does have it, presumably she will give it back to you," said Raphael.

"I think so," said Ocyrhoe. "Although now..." she hesitated. It still was not an easy thing to say. "I suppose she should give it to Percival. If she has it."

"I think it must come to me from you," said Percival. "I don't know if there should be some sort of ritual transfer, but I think it should leave your hands by your choice, not because somebody else snuck it away. And I wish to receive it with your blessing." His face was shining; he was suffused with bliss now that he knew he would finally receive the thing.

"Let's go back up to the fortress," said Raphael. "Ocyrhoe will take the cup back from Rixenda, assuming Rixenda has it."

"What if Rixenda doesn't have it?" asked Percival.

"If she doesn't have it, she may know where it is, and if she doesn't know where it is, you'll have to ask your visions," said Raphael. "They seem to be getting pretty specific. But if Rixenda does have it, Ocyrhoe will give the cup to Percival, and if the two of you think you need some kind of ritual, work it out between yourselves."

"Perhaps we should..." Percival began.

"I'm not finished," said Raphael. "Once you've transferred stewardship or whatever you're calling it, Percival comes with Vera and me back to Frederick's, immediately."

"How will you get out of here?" asked Peire-Roger.

"We'll risk the main tunnel. The three of us can do it. Or we'll fight out way down the side. That's not my main concern. Ferenc, I would like you to come with us, but it sounds like you've just promised not to. I suspect that if Frederick was told he had to choose between his squire and whatever the hell it is he gets if Percival and the cup show up, he'd probably choose the latter."

"He's not choosing," Ferenc said coldly. "Léna is. She won't miss me if I do not return." He rested his hand on Ocyrhoe's shoulder; Ocyrhoe reached her hand up to rest on his. "Wherever Ocyrhoe goes, I go with her."

"She has to stay here," Peire-Roger said, suddenly involved in the discussion. "Until this is over. We need her. She is our only means of communicating with the outside world."

Ferenc squeezed Ocyrhoe's shoulder and she looked up at him. "This won't go on forever," she said quietly to him. "I'm not a Credent, but I certainly owe more to these people than I do to Frederick."

Ferenc nodded with calm agreement. "So, remain here until it's over, and then back to Frederick? Or if he has no use for us, then wherever?"

"Wherever is a fine destination," said Ocyrhoe, with a wan smile.

"All right," said Ferenc, looking up at the rest of them. "Milord, you have her, and myself as well, for whatever good that is, until you've no more need of us. Sir," he said to Raphael, "I hope you will forgive me for abandoning…"

"Of course," said Raphael impatiently, embarrassed by the drama of the moment. "Just please encourage them to transfer the thing quickly so we can get out of here. Milord, I'm sorry we cannot stay, but there are multitudes coming to support you from the ground."

"I understand," said Peire-Roger gruffly. "Let's get back up to the fort. I'm violating my own orders being here, and so are all of you. Besides, it's colder than a witch's teat in this place. If I lived in one of these huts I'd hate the material world, too. No wonder they don't eat meat—their bellies would too be cold and sluggish to digest it."

Vera assisted Raphael up the icy slope. Back in the courtyard, she went in search of Rixenda while Raphael finally indulged Percival in talking about ritual procedure to Ocyrhoe. As they stood beside the chicken coop, Ocyrhoe looped her arms around Ferenc and pressed herself to him under his arm for warmth. He squeezed her protectively, and kissed the top of her head. *Life is miraculously strange*, he thought.

"I want to be a part of whatever happens," he said. "To me this isn't just about that damned cup; it's about Ocyrhoe." He looked down at her. "If it were up to me, I'd grab it from you and throw it far away and he'd have to go retrieve it."

"I don't think that is how it should happen," said Percival seriously. Ferenc repressed an urge to chortle.

"Let me keep it overnight," said Ocyrhoe. "I have hardly thought of it, but perhaps I should have a final moment with it before I hand it over so that I really feel the magnitude of what I'm doing."

Raphael made a dubious sound.

"Sir, whatever it is, it is powerful," Ferenc assured him. "I do not understand it, and I do not like it, but I do *not* dismiss it. I saw a *mob* in Rome..." he trailed off, choosing not to remember those days of havoc. "Whatever they want to do is fine with me as long as Ocryhoe releases it. I want to be there to see that actually happening."

"Of course," said Ocyrhoe lightly, squeezing him. "Stay with me from the moment Rixenda hands it back to me."

"Assuming Rixenda has it," said Percival. "This is all dependent on her knowing where it is."

"I might need to spit on it when I see it again," Ferenc said almost under his breath. He felt Ocyrhoe, under his arm, huff quietly and was not sure if this was annoyance or amusement. He looked around the glare of the muddy-snowy courtyard. Men were working on the trebuchet, and guards were on the wall-walk, but otherwise it was empty. There was a strange moment of calm, almost of peace.

"I wonder where Vera has got to," said Raphael.

"She was going to find Rixenda for me. Let's see if she's in the donjon," said Ocyrhoe. She squeezed Ferenc briefly, then released her grip and began to walk toward the steps to the keep. As her foot fell upon the muddy snow, as she completed the first step away from him, Ferenc heard the siren from the barbican that warned of an incoming trebuchet rock. It was fainter than usual, as if there was a blockage in the whistle. Nobody else in the courtyard seemed to hear it: The usual collective tensing was absent, and absent also was the collective glance to the east before running for shelter. Ocyrhoe continued to walk as if completely unaware of it. Raphael began to follow her, also indifferent to the warning call.

Ferenc opened his mouth to speak, but stopped because he heard the whoosh of the incoming rock. Compared to the damaged whistle, it sounded loud to him.

But only to him. Ocyrhoe and Raphael continued across the courtyard. Out of his peripheral vision, Ferenc saw the stone. Its trajectory was a hair's-breadth north of where the trebuchet had been shooting all morning. Ocyrhoe and Raphael were walking directly into its path.

"Ocyrhoe!" Ferenc shouted. Everything slowed as he ran toward them across the slush; it was as if his body were encased in honey, or running upstream in a river; he could not move fast enough. With a feeling of dread he realized even calling out her name had taken too long, or perhaps he had not really called it at all, or perhaps he had but the sound was trapped in whatever held him back and was taking too long to reach her.

At the same moment, as he approached too slowly, he saw both Raphael and Ocyrhoe startle slightly, then turn together and look up to their right. He wanted to shout at them not to do that, to keep moving forward, to get the hell out of the way, but he could not even draw breath to make the sound. He begged Nagy Asszony, the Great Mother, to break the invisible chains that prevented his rushing, to put wings on his feet so he could reach them in time and drag them to safety.

The Great Mother heard him; suddenly, with a strength he had never known inside himself, he felt propelled by some greater force across the yard and reached an arm out toward each one to push them out of the way.

"*Run!*" he heard his own voice thundering around the courtyard and inside his own head. He saw with relief and gratitude that they both stumbled from his shoving them, stumbled far enough toward the steps that surely they would be out of the stone's path. Still everything moved in slow motion—their looks of shock, Ocyrhoe opening her mouth, he thought, to thank him, but instead, a look of horror on her face and a scream that sounded very far away. He saw her reach her hands up toward her head. Raphael opened his mouth, a look of furious urgency on his face. Why were they upset when he had just saved them from the missile?

"You're safe!" Ferenc said. There was a deafening roar, he tasted metal, and then everything went black.

CHAPTER 31:

GRIEF

The first hour was confusion, too much confusion to think or feel. She was aware that Raphael, grimacing from the pain in his leg, had grabbed her and turned her forcibly away from Ferenc's body. She heard him shout, she heard people approach, she felt other hands and arms reach out to her, pick her up, help her to walk, take her indoors. Somebody gave her something hot to drink, somebody wrapped her in a blanket, somebody even gave her a pillow. Whether it was all the same somebody or a collection of persons she had no idea. She kept waiting for somebody to tell her how badly Ferenc was injured, or at least for somebody to mention it in hushed tones where she might overhear it. Nobody was talking about him. There was nothing to talk about.

She closed her eyes and tried to force her body to relax. Cutting out the light helped. In the darkness the brew she had been given seemed warmer.

There was a horrible thud and everything around her shook. A wave of worried voices washed over her and then faded away. She opened her eyes properly and looked around. Women and children were running to the far side of the hall. She understood at once that the thud had been the French trebuchet, that the stones were now being slung at the walls of the donjon as well as into the yard. She had finished drinking whatever was in the cup. Now she remembered: the drink had come from Raphael and the cushion had come from Rixenda. She could not remember the rest.

Rixenda was sitting beside her against the eastern wall. She made a small, clucking sound when she caught Ocyrhoe's eye, and moments later, Raphael was beside her on the other side. She was glad of Percival's absence. Vera's too, she realized. Raphael was the gentlest of these strange intruders.

"How are you?" he said. His voice was very heavy.

"That depends," she heard herself say. Her voice was also heavy; it sounded strange in her own ears. "Tell me."

"He felt nothing," Raphael said gently. "It was instant."

She dropped the empty cup and fell over against Rixenda. There was a throbbing in her stomach and her ears. "I want to see him," she said.

"No," Raphael said, too quickly. She grimaced, then nodded.

"He saved us," she said dully. Raphael nodded. "I don't want to have been saved if he's not here. There doesn't seem any point in it."

"You should eat something. I think you missed breakfast and you have certainly missed dinner. There's been so much today."

"No thank you," she said. "Let's just…what do we…I don't know." She pressed the heels of her hands against her eyes. "What happens now?" she asked.

"The bishop and Peire-Roger will determine what to do with his…with him. There is no way to bury him or cremate him."

"I think she needs another draught," urged Rixenda, slowly edging Ocyrhoe back to sitting upright. "Put her out entirely, let her sleep."

"Can we go back and do it again, and hear the whistle ourselves this time?" asked Ocyhroe.

Rixenda put her hand over Ocyrhoe's; the aged thumb stroked the youthful one. "The whistle didn't sound. It split, and the guard on the barbican was trying to squeeze it, hold it together."

"Ferenc's hearing was unusually acute," said Raphael. Ocyrhoe nodded. "If it hadn't been, that would be you or me, or both of us, on the ground."

Ocyrhoe looked at him wearily. She was about to talk, and then realized she lacked the energy completely.

Dimly she was aware that the rest of the keep was full of people, but they were now filing out of the building and into the courtyard. It was safe out there, briefly, in the moments following a trebuchet attack, while the enemy was repositioning the counterweight.

But among the figures leaving, one moved toward them. Ocyrhoe sighed with resignation. "Hello," she said to Vera.

"I'm sorry," said Vera gently. Ocyrhoe had actually been expecting Vera to criticize her for even having feelings. "He was a good man. He was my friend, and I do not have many friends."

"Yes," said Ocyrhoe, not knowing what else to say.

"But we must continue," said Vera. Turning to Rixenda: "Do you have the cup?"

Ocyrhoe groaned a little; Rixenda rubbed the girl's knuckles with her thumb. "I do not have it with me," she said. "But yes, I took it from the cabin and I know where it is."

"Why did you take it?" Ocyrhoe asked, hardly caring.

"Common sense," said Rixenda, with a shrug. "We were evacuating the village and I knew would you not be able to come for it."

"But you didn't approve of my attachment to it."

Rixenda's warm face made her words sound kinder than they really were. "It's still worth money if it's sold, so leaving it behind would make no sense. I did not bring it for your sake."

"But you won't keep it from her, will you?" asked Vera. "Percival still will not leave until you've given it to him," she said to Ocyrhoe. "He sent me to speak to you. He felt his presence here would be unwelcome."

Ocyrhoe's weariness was so great she wished that she could faint. "He cannot have it now," she said.

A pause.

"You're not serious," said Raphael.

"I was willing to give up what the cup offered me because I would have Ferenc to fill that void. And now I don't. I have nothing but the cup. Percival has *everything* he needs in his life—*except* the cup. Let him have Frederick's court and his Shield-Brethren and his training. His prestige, his community, his skills, his living. He has so much, he will survive the absence of a cup. I'm done talking now, it's time to sleep." She closed her eyes and leaned her head back against the cold, uneven stone wall.

"If you came with us to Frederick's..." Raphael began.

"I can't do that. I'm needed here."

"If you came to us afterwards."

"Would you be at Frederick's then? Would I not be returning to Léna's lair? Would I not become a piece of flotsam in the general currents of the world? Where is there a place for me?"

"Léna could complete your Binder training," Raphael suggested.

Ocyrhoe made a disgusted sound. "One outlaw Binder teaching another outlaw Binder. That's not training."

Vera frowned and opened her mouth to rebuke the girl, but Raphael stopped her with a gesture. "This is not the time. Let her rest. We'll discuss it tonight, or tomorrow. Nothing is going to change between Montségur and the French in that time."

Vera turned to Rixenda. "We could cut through this Gordian Knot if you would just give us the cup."

Ocyrhoe gave her a look but was too enervated to protest.

"It is not mine to give," said Rixenda, putting a comforting arm around Ocyrhoe. "All of us here are beholden to this young woman. I will not betray her trust."

"Besides which, it is in your interest for us to stay here, so why would you give us the one thing that anchors Percival, and therefore us, to this place?" Vera added sardonically.

Rixenda shook her head peaceably. "Peire-Roger might do that. I would not. I will give it to Ocyrhoe when she desires it. At this moment, she desires nothing more than sleep."

CHAPTER 32:

A TEMPORARY TRUCE

Nobody dared to question the archbishop's authority, but "Father Sinibaldo" and the Livonian knights—who somehow knew each other—had been given one of the village houses, turning a score of Narbonnese soldiers out into a tent. Now, in the common room of the house, Father Sinibaldo sat with His Eminence and Dietrich.

"I require the chalice more than I require the death of heretics," said Sinibaldo.

"Your Holiness," began the bishop.

"Stop that. Even in private. Break the habit. I am a priest. Speak to me as a priest, Your Eminence."

"Yes, Father."

"You mean, of course, *yes, my son.*"

"Yes, my son. If that is the Holy Father's—dictum, of course it is my wish to honor it. However, you must remember this is the French king's crusade as least as much as ours. He wants all the lords of Occitania to yield to him. On His Majesty's behalf, Hugue de Arcis will not agree to any plan that does not include the absolute surrender of the Cathars and their supporters."

Father Sinibaldo grimaced. "His Majesty claims he is acting on behalf of the Pope. If the Pope has plans that deviate from His

Majesty's, *His Majesty* is the one who needs to change plans. I will make that very clear when I am back in Rome. Meanwhile, let us consider the current plan. Dietrich, make your point."

"We want the Shield-Brethren knight. There is no proof of it, but the timing of his arrival and the sudden appearance of the Grail might be more than coincidence. We take him as our political hostage and question him, and during such time as we have him, the trebuchet stops. He yields the grail, or helps lead us to it, in exchange for the entire population of the fortress being freed to safety."

"Why would he do that?" asked Archbishop Pierre.

"Because he is a *knight*," said Dietrich, more sharply than he should have. "Given the opportunity to save a community of people with whom he has aligned, he will do it, even if it requires a deep sacrifice on his part."

"But Dietrich, what if you're mistaken and he knows nothing about the cup?" asked Father Sinibaldo.

"Then we resume bombardments," said Dietrich, with a shrug. "Return to things as they were. The trebuchet is almost at their barbican, and once we take the barbican—which we will—they're doomed. We certainly have *lost* nothing in this attempt."

◆ ◆ ◆

The trebuchet—now alarmingly close to the barbican—had been still for the day. The counterweight was at its resting position on the ground, visible to the barbican guards, who bemusedly assured the fortress population they were in no present danger. The archers had not shot a single arrow all day.

Then came the message for a request to parley. Peire-Roger looked confused when Artal ran in from the walls with the news.

"They have a white flag and everything," the youth said, wide-eyed. "There is one knight and a few men-at-arms. He asks to speak with you, milord, in private."

The only private, indoor space remaining was the chicken coop, which would not do. Peire-Roger instructed that the upstairs chapel be respectfully cleared of all meditating Good Ones, and told the guard at the keep door that nobody was to be allowed upstairs with weapons. He called his own entourage around him and went up the rickety wooden stairs to await the enemy. Torches were lit, but they were running low now even on the oils, and they had to conserve. It was colder up here than in the hall below.

They did not have to wait long. Soon a thin-faced knight entered with three followers, all unarmed. The knight wore a surcoat with a cross and a sword emblazoned on his left shoulder, and he carried himself with an air of slightly piqued arrogance.

Behind the visitors, to Peire-Roger's surprise and irritation, appeared Raphael, fully armed and limping—it was the first time he had taken stairs without using his cane for support. Raphael ignored Peire-Roger's scowl and came around to stand behind Peire-Roger as if a member of his entourage.

"Welcome," the Lord of Montségur said brusquely.

"Thank you for receiving me, milord," said the visitor loftily.

"I am Peire-Roger of Mirepoix. This is Raphael of Acre." He tried to sound as if he had been expecting, even desiring, Raphael's presence.

"Dietrich von Grüningen," said the visitor, gesturing to himself, and bowed.

"Sit," said Peire-Roger, gesturing vaguely to the stools scattered about the empty prayer-hall. He chose the nearest one, and Dietrich the one across from him. Raphael placed a stool close beside Peire-Roger, his eyes never leaving Dietrich. "So," he said briskly, as he sat, "you are a knight of the Livonian order. I myself am of the *Ordo Militum Vindicis Intactae*. I hope our orders' history does not account for your presence here today."

"Not at all, my friend. I assure you, I am here only as a spokesman for the leaders of the army," said Dietrich. "Although it is a happy coincidence to find you at this meeting."

"Why?" asked Peire-Roger, before Raphael had a chance. "What do you want?"

"Well, not to put too fine a point on it, his lordship wants *you*," Dietrich said to Raphael. "There was a rumor of a Shield-Brethren knight in residence in the fortress, and his lordship wishes to speak with you. If you will surrender yourself as a temporary hostage, we promise a cessation of all hostilities as long as you are in our care."

There was a long pause.

"Why me?" asked Raphael. To Peire-Roger he said, in a casual aside despite Dietrich's proximity, "The Livonian order has a dark history, and they are ill-disposed toward my brothers, so the likelihood that this as straightforward as it seems is infinitesimal." To Dietrich: "Nevertheless, in the interest of the general welfare, I am willing to entertain your request. But explain, please."

Dietrich shrugged. "It is not for me to say. They wish to question you about a matter unrelated to the heresy."

"So why do the heretics benefit from it?" Peire-Roger demanded.

Again, Dietrich shrugged. "Someone in authority must have assessed that a knight would unstintingly use his own situation for the betterment of others, when possible."

Peire-Roger gave Raphael a skeptical look. Raphael smiled in response, an expression sporting a sort of noble sheepishness. "That's true," he said. "I'd rather not entrust myself to a Livonian, but I'll certainly meet with Hugue de Arcis if that will spare everyone here from the trebuchet awhile."

"And how do we know you are not just taking him to murder him?" demanded Peire-Roger.

"I offer myself in his stead," said Dietrich. "I will stay here as your hostage, and my companions will lead Raphael down the mountain. When they have finished their negotiations, he and I will swap places again. Perhaps something will come of it that may end hostilities altogether." He smiled graciously. "Myself, I do not know the details of these matters. I am merely the messenger."

"Let me do it, milord," said Raphael. "Even if there is treachery afoot I can protect myself."

"There will be no need of it, I assure you."

"Strange that Hugue did not send his own men up to fetch you," said Peire-Roger.

"These *are* Hugue's men," Dietrich lied cheerfully, referring to his own sword-brothers. Unlike him they were not in ceremonial attire; their surcoats were a neutral white, showing no allegiance. "I cannot account for why they sent me in particular, but I am sure they will explain that if you accept the offer. They might be unaware of our history, and perhaps chose me because of my distinguished service record."

Raphael and Peire-Roger exchanged looks. "I'll do it," Raphael insisted.

Peire-Roger looked between the two knights, his face gradually darkening, the sneer that was a permanent element of his expression deepening with disgust. "Absolutely not," he said. "I will not compromise with these villains. For *decades* they have destroyed our land and our families. If they are trying to parley now, it's because they are on the verge of giving up and so are desperate."

"We are hardly desperate, milord," Dietrich countered with a syrupy arrogance. "As you must be aware, we are within days of taking the barbican."

"You are also within days of running out of food. I have sources; I know what conditions are like in your camp. Your bravado does not fool me. Go back down to your lord, you *vermin*, and tell him we have nothing to discuss. We are in our own home; we have easy, constant access to food and weapons, by channels your general cannot find or replicate. All of the men working your trebuchet out there resemble undernourished peasants." Raphael was impressed by how fluidly Peire-Roger lied. Save for what Ocyrhoe could carry on her back, they no longer had access to outside supplies at all. "We are in far better shape than you, and I am not interested in listening to parleys."

"Milord, it's not a parley," insisted Raphael quietly, his eyes still examining Dietrich's face; Dietrich sensed this but kept his focus on Peire-Roger. "They want to interrogate me for some reason. I believe him that it is not related to the siege. And yet it might yield collateral benefit."

"While you are in this fortress, you are my knight, and I won't spare you," said Peire-Roger irritably. To Dietrich he said, "Tell your lord if he wants to come up here to interview Raphael in person, I'll allow a day of truce for that, but I will determine when. Do you understand? Take that back to your lord Hugue the Arsehole of Arcis."

Dietrich's face darkened. "That language is uncalled for, milord."

"This siege is uncalled for," Peire-Roger shot back. "The entire Albigensian Crusade was uncalled for, and even when it was called off, it continued—to this day. You are no longer welcome here. Depart."

◆ ◆ ◆

"I should have said I was from the archbishop," mused Dietrich a few hours later. "The very *mention* of Hugue's name was a mistake. There is such ferocious hatred within the secular ranks between the local men and the French occupiers. I regret how badly I erred in that."

"But neither could you have said you were from me," said the archbishop. "They would never have allowed a religious leader to interrogate somebody during a religious persecution. Hugue does not even know we used his name."

A long pause.

"Perhaps we tell him," Father Sinibaldo said at last.

❖ ❖ ❖

The crusaders' trebuchet was now so close that there was sporadic fighting on the mountaintop between the two sides daily. Mostly it was archers, and mostly this was a waste of arrows, so Peire-Roger discouraged the soldiers on watch in the barbican from indulging in it. "The French have set up such a well-constructed shield, and we are so outnumbered, we are like flies trying to puncture the hide of a bull," he grumbled.

The trebuchet was now actually too close to fling anything at the barbican, but the French had shortened the sling length and were bombarding the walls of the donjon with increasingly enormous stones, the weight of a man, that came with greater rapidity, day and night, shuddering the entire building and terrifying everyone within. The garrison had to kneel on the battlements and shoot between the crenellations at the French archers on the ground—who in turn shot at them whenever they caught a glimpse of movement on the battlements.

Worse, the French archers were close enough now that they could shoot over the walls of Montségur and rain down arrows randomly within the courtyard all the time. Peire-Roger announced it was no longer safe for anyone to go outside without an urgent reason. The door was kept open to allow air in and out of the keep, but it was dark and increasingly fetid inside. The population of the fortress grew more solemn and more silent. Ocyrhoe, for all her grieving, at least had the benefit of keeping busy. She spent most of her waking hours up and down the small southern tunnel. With the dwindling help of soldiers and farmers from the countryside, she continued bringing up a very limited supply of food, fuel, and the makings of good arrows. They were still awaiting sulphur to make fire-arrows; it might be weeks before that arrived. Given the tunnel's narrowness and occasional sliding inclines, she could never carry more than what would fit into a small backpack. It was the starving time of year anyhow, a fact the priests cleverly masked as spiritually nourishing, making a virtue of necessity. The falling-off of food worried all but surprised none.

Ocyrhoe found farmers, peasants, and deserters from the French army who could help her bring things partway up the tunnels to the narrow, claustrophobic, final measure. Then she herself, painstakingly and slowly, over hours, would move whatever material was incoming—hardtack, arrowheads, fletchings. These would be collected at the courtyard tunnel mouth and carried to wherever it was needed. Ocyrhoe's face and clothes grew brown from grime and the detritus of the supplies she carried. The glow of the love-drunk maiden was utterly extinguished. She lived for nothing but to do her work. She worked herself ragged, almost never sleeping and rarely eating.

The French trebuchet had moved so close to the barbican that the fortress's own hurled boulders were now useless, flying harmlessly over the heads of the enemy and landing halfway down the ridge, where the French no longer were. French scouts endlessly patrolled the rest of the mountaintop, seeking the secret to the tunnel entrances in the snow, but the trebuchet was too static to hit any moving target. It became a large, useless piece of furniture, fast splintering with arrows.

◆ ◆ ◆

There had been a thaw and then another cold snap, so the snow had turned to ice and, with a second thawing, almost everything turned to mud. The day came, the last week of February, when the French archers took control of the ground near the barbican, and the guard could not safely move in or out of the tower. The same dozen men remained trapped inside for days, exhausted, hungry, and running out of arrows. Under cover of night, the fastest of the young Montségur soldiers sprinted across the narrow, limestone ridge, carrying food and arrows on their backs. A few archers joined them, but truthfully the archers already in the barbican were the best in Montségur; strategically, it did not make sense to move them. The barbican was no fouler, colder, or more crowded than the keep, so Peire-Roger determined that most archers should remain in the barbican.

While Rixenda was crossing the courtyard after bringing the guards a basket of warmed hardtack, a blunted arrow was shot into the fortress from the barbican with a piece of vellum rolled around the shaft. It wobbled crazily in the air, and when it landed near Rixenda she could see why: it had no feathers to stabilize it. She brought it into the keep, where Peire-Roger glumly held court on a stool near the fire.

Written on the vellum was a distress message: Something had gone wrong with the glue holding the fletching to the shafts of the arrows; the barbican fletcher had adjusted the formula, and the glue should work now, but thousands of feathers had been rendered useless in the process, and they needed new ones immediately.

Ocyrhoe, who had become ubiquitous, hovering always in the background wherever Peire-Roger was, immediately offered to take more feathers over.

"We'll wait until nightfall," said Peire-Roger.

"I don't think they have until nightfall," said Ocyrhoe. "I'll take them now."

"You'll be peppered with arrows before you get halfway across the ridge," argued his lordship.

Ocyrhoe shook her head. Her grief and weariness gave her the gravity of a much older woman, although her unkempt state made her look like the Roman street urchin of old. "There's a tunnel entrance I can take that will get me outside onto the mountaintop. It will be a bit of a hustle to the barbican entrance, but the French won't be looking for me. I can get there safely. If I draw too much attention getting in, I'll simply stay in the tower until nightfall. Then the mud will freeze, so it will be easier to run back."

Rixenda muttered with worried disapproval. But an hour later another featherless arrow wobbled through the air into the courtyard, with a message that now implored immediate assistance. Peire-Roger accepted Ocyrhoe's offer, and she scuttled out of the gate, a pack of goose feathers (all from the left side of the geese) on her back.

She was right: None of the French noticed her skittering across the mountaintop. Her presence was not marked until she was safely inside the tower.

But peering out through the arrow-loops the barbican soldiers saw the French archers muttering together and then rearranging their formation. At least a dozen put arrow to string and aimed at the barbican door, waiting for it to open again. Ocyrhoe announced she would stay there until dark, when she should be able to cross back safely; the waning moon was full enough but there was heavy cloud cover, and the only French archers who remained out here after sunset were those guarding the trebuchet. She curled up in a corner of the barbican and fell asleep.

At nightfall she awoke on instinct, barely rested. The captain of the barbican listened to a report of the French action, then gave her leave to race back to the fortress.

Ocyrhoe stepped outside and shivered in the endless breeze that brushed the mountaintop. As if she were appreciating somebody else's capabilities, not her own, she noticed how acute her hearing was, how quick to respond to noises her body was, how attuned to all possible dangers she was. She took no pleasure in these abilities.

She did not want to be the person crossing the chasm back to the fortress; she wanted to be the person who fell off the ridge, to remove herself from the miserable life she was caught in. With no Ferenc. And soon, nothing at all. She could not keep the cup; clinging to it was humiliating. If her life's purpose was to hold on to one object whose existence was troublesome to her…no. She would tell Rixenda—who still held it—to give it to the knight, and that would be the end of it. That would remove the only bond that kept her tethered to this earth.

She could not share her thoughts, for the others would be appalled and call her sick and keep her under watch; being under watch was the last thing in the world she wanted now. She wanted to be left alone. That was the attraction of the work in the tunnels. It was hours and hours every day that nobody could try to penetrate her focus.

Unfreighted by cargo, she sprinted along the ridge and her top speed got her across the limestone span in less than the time it took her heart to beat a dozen times. As she approached the fortress, she cried out to Ferrer on the other side of the gate; her cry caught the attention of a French archer, and a moment later an arrow whizzed by her arm; then another by the other arm, then one very close to her ear. As she reached the gate and felt it push open toward her, she heard the swish of another arrow and suddenly her left arm grew very hot and heavy, and she knew she had received a superficial hit.

"Damn you!" she screamed, and burst out sobbing. Not because she had been wounded—but because she had been *merely* wounded. She decided she would stop running right now, and turn to face the archers, and let them have her. Let it be over. *I am done*, she thought, and felt a great weight lift from her.

But her body, to her rage, disregarded her decision. It continued to rush toward the gate, and as she watched, her good arm raised itself—even as she furiously forbade it to—and her hand prepared to beat down on the gate in case the porter had not heard her. No risk of that—the gate on its oiled hinges began to open outward just enough for her to slip in.

I am not going inside, she silently instructed her body. *I am staying here and letting them take me.* She shouted this silently as her legs carried her in through the opening, and she heard the gate lumber closed behind her. Suddenly she found her voice, heard it swearing fiercely in the cold night air.

Softer than her anger, other people appeared, reacting to her bleeding arm; voices called out Raphael and Rixenda's names, and a few moments later, she stopped cursing, and crumpled over in pain.

✦ ✦ ✦

Ocyrhoe was returning from the southern tunnel in search of news—and tallow to burn for warmth and light. The Good Ones were disgusted with the idea, but with the chandlery dismantled to make room for the now-useless trebuchet, they were down to the crisis-reserve of beeswax candles and were nearly out of oils.

Vera, Percival, and Raphael approached her at the door. She stared at them from hurt, dark eyes, her lips pursed, and brushed past them to the corner of the hall. The Bonnet brothers' surrogate was waiting with an open codex, to receive her news. They watched her return the covered lantern and shrug the thick woolen cloak from off her narrow shoulders. Beneath it, the backpack bulged with something. She glanced almost disdainfully back over her shoulder at Raphael and Percival as they approached.

There was, they heard her tell the scribe, no further word of any troops arriving—not from Corbario the Aragonese mercenary, not from the Count of Toulouse, not from Emperor Frederick.

She paused. Without excusing herself form the scribe, she turned to face them as if waiting for something.

"Frederick is not really sending men," Raphael muttered. The trio preferred to speak privately on the steps of the doorway, the only spot in the keep that was not overrun with Credents. The air there was chilly but much fresher than anywhere else indoor, and they could immediately see developments outside. But he wanted Ocyrhoe to be a part of this discussion and he understood from her defiant stance she would not leave the warmth of the keep. "He only sent word so that we would hear and think it was safe to leave. He wants us back as soon as possible."

"If our young friend here would give me the grail, then I'd be willing to leave," said Percival.

"Would you really?" snapped Vera, who had stood in her usual taciturn silence until now. "Hypocrites, both of you. You would leave these people before help arrives? What part of your precious prophecy does that fulfill, oh sacred vision-master? And you," turning sharply to Raphael, "A renegade witch-spy is puppeteering a man to whom you owe no fealty. That takes precedence for you over besieged innocents whom you are in the midst of? Beside whom you have fought? Is this the code of the Shield-Brethren?" She looked furious and disgusted. She stood up. "I do not think *our young friend* will give you the grail anyway, but if she tries to, I will intercept it and keep it out of your reach. Shame upon you both."

Ocyrhoe gave her a teary smile. "Thank you, sister," she said. "You will be glad to know I have one more piece of news." Turning back to the scribe, she shrugged off the backpack and offered it to him very carefully. "Please add to the inventory that we now have sulphur. To make fire-arrows."

CHAPTER 33:

INFORMING HUGUE

Hugue de Arcis, his cheek still bandaged from the urchin's knife-strike, scowled from the doorway, his broad frame filling it almost entirely. "I am not accustomed to being *summoned*," he said sharply. The Archbishop of Narbonne gave him a bland look.

"Not even by the king?" he asked.

"His Majesty is not here," Hugue retorted.

"Not even by the Pope?"

"His Holiness is not here, either. And I am beginning to consider you a very inadequate proxy for him."

"That's a coincidence," said the archbishop tersely. "I am beginning to consider you an inadequate proxy for His Majesty. But at least I have had the decency to yield my position to my superior."

Hugue frowned. "You've summoned the Pope?" he said mockingly.

"He did not *summon* me," said Father Sinibaldo severely. "I came by my own judgment. Your king is a fool not to have done the same by now. Clearly his investment in this project lags behind mine."

Hugue stared in confusion at the stranger. He was dressed like a regular priest but held himself with an air of importance that made him almost shine compared to the rest of the gathering in this small, airless room. "Are you...you are not..."

"You will refer to me as Father Sinibaldo," said the man sharply. "Do you understand?"

Hugue, realizing he had been gaping, closed his mouth. "Sinibaldo? *di Fieschi*?" he huffed.

The priest stared back at him without moving for a long moment, then very slowly nodded.

"Your Holiness—" Hugue breathed, and knelt, head bowed.

"Stand," His Holiness said sharply. "Nobody outside this room is to know that I am here. I am glad you keep up with affairs of the church," he said in a regular voice. "That makes you a good Christian soldier. As I am sure you will demonstrate to me by playing the endgame of this siege the way the Church requires it."

"We will kill all the heretics who don't repent," said Hugue uncertainly, "If that is what you mean." He fidgeted nervously with the bandage.

"You will do more than that," Father Sinibaldo informed him. Hugue felt mesmerized by his gaze; he would have been terrified to refuse this man anything, lest he strike out suddenly like a poisonous snake and disable him. "You will support whatever conditions of surrender I dictate."

"Don't ask us to kill civilians, Father. The ones called Credents, who have not taken heretical vows, we won't hurt them. Most of the population in this area are Credents, it's why we haven't been able to cut Montségur off. I have never wanted to hurt them. Many of them are children and women. I would like to spare them, if Your Holiness—"

"Father Sinibaldo," said His Holiness sharply.

"If His Holiness would allow it, we wish to atone for the sins of the crusaders who came before us and spare the innocent."

"Indeed you shall," said Sinibaldo. "You'll do more than that, in fact. All of them but the unrepentant Good Ones will be released without punishment once we have taken the fortress."

"Isn't that what I just said?" said Hugue.

"Everyone," Sinibaldo repeated emphatically.

"Do you mean the lords? We can spare the lords, even that fucking drunk whoreson Peire-Roger, if you will pardon my language, Father."

"I do not just mean the lords. You will spare *everyone*. Including the soldiers. Knights, men-at-arms, all of them. Even if there is among them one you recognize for having killed your men. There will be a total pardon. Only the Perfecti will be put to death, and any of them who repent, even at the last moment, will be spared."

Hugue grimaced and rubbed the side of his face with one gloved hand. "That's irregular, Father," he said. "And of course there are men, on both sides, who have already fallen in combat, and there'll be more before this ends."

"But we will offer terms of peace that promise no more violence." Father Sinibaldo spoke in a voice of great composure, suddenly the Bishop of Rome, the all-powerful but all-compassionate spokesman of Christ. "For any Christian. We must astonish them, through charity, into wanting to embrace the true Church."

Hugue sighed with relief. He'd been afraid His Holiness would demand something that would trod upon the toes and plans of the French king. This assignment, although it would disgruntle many of his soldiers, would cause no trouble between himself and King Louis. "Easily accomplished, Father, I will make it clear when we approach a surrender on their part."

"And there is just one other thing," said Father Sinibaldo shrewdly. "All of the former landowners up there, who lost their fiefdoms when they fled for safety, will have all of their lands restored to them."

"Pardon me?" said Hugue after a momentary pause.

"And that will be true going back a generation," continued Sinibaldo firmly. "Any lord whose father was rendered landless by Simon de Montfort or the crusaders, as well as any disenfranchised lord himself—all of them will have their estates restored."

Hugue stared at him for a moment, horrified. "That's impossible. Those lands are settled now. They have been awarded to Frenchmen by the French crown."

"My apologies to the French crown, but my charity outranks Louis' greed in this arena."

The Lord of Carcassonne was confounded. "If anyone, even His Majesty, tried to take those lands away now, we'd be in a bloodbath that would make the Albigensian Crusade seem tame. You cannot do that, Father. You cannot unmake a map any sooner than you can unplough a field."

Father Sinibaldo scowled.

"He has a point," said the archbishop. "If you would limit your terms to the lords who lost their lands recently by retreating to Montségur."

"Even then," protested Hugue, "the French lords who were given those estates were not told, *Here, steward these until the Occitanian lords return to the bosom of Christ.* They were told, *Here's land, complete with farms and vineyards and serfs. You have earned it.* And they have, by fighting on behalf of the true Church." His voice constricted somewhat. "I am such a man myself. Would you remove me from Carcassonne and replace me with some lord I am about to defeat? What element of canon law allows for that?"

"There is no lord of Carcassonne up there waiting to replace you," said Sinibaldo impatiently. "The direct family line was massacred, quite spectacularly, by Simon. The closest thing to an heir,

Raimon Trencavel, rescinded his claim voluntarily when you were given Carcassonne in '40. Your estates are not threatened by this."

Hugue relaxed a little. "That helps me," he said. "But it will not help a number of my captains. Peire-Roger has rights to Mirepoix, an estate in which one of my lieutenants is currently ensconced. His children are growing up there."

"They can grow up somewhere else," said Pope Innocent. "That is not my concern. I require these terms for a peaceable surrender that will publicly lure the heretics back to the Mother Church. A military victory here is meritless if there is not a spiritual victory that goes with it. 'And the greatest of these is charity.'"

Hugue looked disgusted. "You would reward those whoresons for all the trouble they have caused," he grunted only half under his breath, his fingers brushing his bandaged jaw.

"I would *forgive* them," Father Sinibaldo said, his voice steelier than ever. "It is the *Christian* thing to do. I would forgive them for the trouble they have caused, and I would *embrace* them for returning to us. Unlike my overeager predecessors, I shall set an example that will encourage heretics to abandon the devil, not just seek more subtle ways to dance with him. Decades of threats, massacres, and torture have not worn down the Cathars' fervor one jot. I will be remembered as the Pope who defeated the Cathars. This is the way to defeat them."

Hugue had broken out in a sweat. "I hope His Holiness is willing to break the news of this to His Majesty directly. As well as to the French army. It will be hard enough to follow this directive without also being reviled for heralding it."

"Such details can be worked out later," said Father Sinibaldo breezily.

Hugue blinked. "Is this not imminent?" he said. "I thought you would be sending someone up the mountainside at once with a white flag."

"There is a more pressing matter to be determined first," said Innocent.

Hugue frowned and held his hands out helplessly. "We are in the middle of a siege in winter. What could be more pressing than determining how to proceed with it?"

"We're looking for something," said the priest cryptically. To the archbishop and the Livonian soldier, Dietrich von Grüningen, he asked, "More thoughts?"

Dietrich cleared his throat. "I still believe the Shield-Brethren up there have some connection to the grail."

"We've already tried that," said Father Sinibaldo impatiently.

"We went about it the wrong way. We used the Lord of Carcassonne's name, and it inflamed Peire-Roger against us."

"You did what?" said the Lord of Carcassonne.

Dietrich was happy to ignore him. "If Peire-Roger won't give us the knight as a hostage, is it possible we could get a message up to the knight in private? We thought it was a tactical advantage to intertwine two separate missions—the grail, and taking the fortress—but perhaps we should, in fact, keep them separate."

"The what?" asked Hugue.

"I don't think a Shield-Brethren knight would indulge in such intrigue," said Father Sinibaldo. "But if we were to try it, do we know his name?"

"He was introduced to me as Raphael."

Hugue sat up. "What, the fellow with the rose on his tunic? The tall, good-looking fellow?"

Dietrich hesitated. "The knight I met was swarthy, looked Levantine. Wasn't tall. He had a limp."

"There was a knight came through here months ago."

"That's right," said the archbishop, with vicious agreement. "You let him slip through your fingers."

Hugue ignored him, staring intensely at the Holy Father. "His name was Percival. If your man here met someone else, then there are two of them—at least—up there."

Father Sinibaldo stared at him sharply. "*Percival?*" The tone was somewhere between an accusation and a dare.

Hugue nodded.

The priest's eyes darted angrily at Dietrich. "Did you know that?"

Dietrich looked flustered to suddenly be the one under scrutiny. "I think Hugue mentioned it when I attempted to get information."

"You're German," said Father Sinibaldo irritably. "You are an *educated, German knight.*" He spat out each word distinctly. "How could you not know the story of Parzifal?"

Dietrich grimaced dismissively. "That was written decades before this fellow was even born. If there ever were a real Parzival, he'd be long dead by now."

"Of course there was never a real Percival, and clearly it's not this fellow's real name," Sinibaldo pressed, still irritable. "It is a code. He is *advertising* his connection to the grail to anyone who would be in the know. You should have been among that number, Dietrich."

"Excuse me, Father, but I heard the name once, in passing, before I knew anything about the grail," said Dietrich irritably.

"What are you *talking* about?" Hugue cried, increasingly alarmed.

"It's not your matter," said the Holy Father shortly.

"Excuse me, *Father*, but I disagree," said Hugue. "You are asking me to go against the express directives of my own king, apparently as a cover for some other intrigue you're not telling me about."

"I have the power to do that," said His Holiness.

"With all due respect, not on the battlefield," Hugue shot back. "Not on *my* battlefield."

"There is no battlefield here," said Dietrich with contempt. "That's the problem. It's a war with no battles."

Hugues reddened with anger. "But it *is* a war, and *I* am the general."

"It is a *religious* war, and *I* am the *Pope*," said His Holiness in a furious staccato.

"But I am not allowed to tell anyone that you're the Pope," Hugue retorted in the same style. "If you are going to impose outrageous terms that favor the vanquished over the victors, I need some explanation, some rationale, some believable excuse to give my men. I am the only one in this room who does not know of what you speak. Do not tell me it is not my matter!"

"I will explain it," said His Holiness, "as soon as you have won."

CHAPTER 34:

BACK TO THE BARBICAN

The preparations for the fire arrows were grim and frustrating; it was not safe in the courtyard, so the soldiers, their men-at-arms, and squires pressed against the eastern wall to work.

Given their limited resources, making the fire-arrows was particularly tricky. A proper fire-tipped arrow had a special arrowhead with a small, bulbous cage just behind the point, into which could be stuffed both hemp and the sulfur-and-charcoal mixture to be lighted before shooting. They could not make these arrowheads with the smithy disassembled. There was no time to try to collect them from the outside world. So they would have to be inventive, but an arrow that flew with fire was no easy thing to conjure.

Rags saturated in the flammable mixture would be tied to each shaft just behind the head. But the wooden shafts would burn through if the fire worked quickly, and a slow-burning flame was easily extinguished by the rush of the arrow's flight. Also, the weight of this addition to the front of arrow limited its range and altered the angle at which it had to be shot. In the field, the archers would have to contend with all these variables.

Crouching against the eastern wall for safety, the squires and servants boiled up the flammable mixture, creating a terrible stench in the courtyard. The wind from the northeast and the smoke away from the French on the mountaintop, but the smoke was obvious and it was likely the army camp—on the southwestern flank of the mountain—would recognize the smell.

Once the mixture was ready, rags were soaked in it, and then these had to be tied onto hundreds of arrows. This was also was done along the eastern wall, by men and boys fighting off frostbite and nausea at the stench.

As the shadows grew longer and the air colder, Raphael and Percival conferred with the men who would control the fire on the field, to help improvise braziers that could be moved quickly without danger of spilling the fuel or being extinguished by the wind.

The attack would be by night—the moon was past full, but in the cold, clear, winter air it shone bright enough for the French to easily discern what the Montségurians were up to. The raiding party would have to get out of the gate and across the narrow ridge for forty strides until the ridge widened to the flat area on which the barbican was built. About fifty men—archers, guards, and assistants—would have to make that trek before alerting the French guarding the trebuchet. The barbican largely blocked the French view of the gate, which was a blessing, but still there would be very little time to get around the barbican and start their work. The trebuchet had moved so far up the slope it was almost level with the barbican.

Vera took Ocyrhoe as her squire. The raiding party slept fitfully, sitting huddled together in the chapel, until the watch woke them all when it was so late it was nearly early. They had been waiting for the moon to slope down toward the western horizon so that the dim moonlight would be at their backs, throwing their shadows over the enemies' ground, lighting the enemy for them. There would be a brief period of total darkness, and then the sun would rise upon the smoking ruins of the French siege machine.

Surely this would all be over soon. They were running very low on supplies, but the troops below were running out of both food and spirit, and the desertion rate was surely rising. The last thing the crusaders had to their advantage was the siege machine; with that destroyed, it was hoped, they would give up and go home.

The raiding troop collected behind the gate, in formation for a quick crossing: six archers moving two abreast, followed by two assistants carrying between them a bucket or brassiere with a well-banked coal fire in it, then four more assistants following with shields and more materials. Six such units would hurry out to the barbican, huddling together so that the tower's bulk shielded them from the French guards at the trebuchet.

On a signal from Peire-Roger, the archers would move into attack formation: three groups moving to either side around the barbican in a phalanx, with one unit of six archers and their aides in front, the other two units flanking them from behind. Raphael, still limping slightly, was in the front unit on the left with Vera; Peire-Roger and Percival were both among the right-hand leaders. The primary goal was to sink as much fire into the wooden trebuchet as possible, but taking down the French guard along with it was also urgent. If they could move close enough to the trebuchet, the buckets of burning fuel used to the light the arrows would be dumped onto the trebuchet directly.

Crowded with others behind the barbican, Ocyrhoe shivered in her layers of thin wool and watched the moon in the southwestern sky, sinking toward its diurnal rest. Her bandaged arm was still sore, but she could use it without difficulty now. She would serve Vera well and fearlessly, for she did not care if she died tonight, so nothing would make her hesitate. She was not at all sure where dead souls went, but certainly wherever Ferenc's was, she'd go there, too, and hellish as it might be she would be spending it in a friend's embrace, which was more than this world offered her.

Peire Roger made a raised-arm gesture that was picked up and imitated by the archers, and immediately the six groups moved around the tower. There was no need to go closer to the trebuchet; the arrows could easily hit it.

In the darkness, almost wordlessly, each unit hurriedly prepared itself. First, three guards set up large shields to protect everyone else; behind these, squires and other assistants, like Ocyrhoe, settled the fire-pots and dipped one arrow at a time into the burning coals. As Ocyrhoe did this, grateful for the warmth of the flame, she sensed and heard, more than saw, Vera beside her, string her bow, gauge the distance to the siege machine, and then hold out her hand. Ocyrhoe handed her an arrow. Before the fire could burn through the shaft, Vera fitted it onto her string, pulled the arrow back with an admirable appearance of ease, and released it twanging up into the darkness. She sent it high on a trajectory to counterbalance the extra weight of the burning fuel; it made a fantastic whooshing sound as it flew into the air, but Ocyrhoe was disappointed to watch it sputter and go dark while still high up.

"The fire needs to take more—hurry," Vera said. Ocyrhoe immediately dipped the next arrow into the fire, then held it up to Vera. Vera took it, examined it, fitted it to the bowstring, and hesitated a moment, wanting to make sure the tuft of sulphur-muddied hemp at the front was indeed alight. Satisfied, she drew back the bow and shot. She and Ocyrhoe watched the arrow as it quietly soared into the air, then plummeted suddenly to the ground halfway to the trebuchet.

Vera swore. "Shaft burned through because I waited too long. Must find the golden mean." Ocyrhoe handed her the next arrow, already prepared. Vera again fitted it to the bowstring.

As Vera pulled back, Ocyrhoe glanced around the night to see how others were faring. With three dozen archers, arrows were loosed about every heartbeat, but it was hardly a rain of fire; only a handful of arrows had struck the trebuchet and of them, only two had remained lit enough to even singe the wood.

Worse, the French guard had been alerted to their presence by the sound of the arrows striking, and now could see very easily where the attacks were coming from. There was shouting and a vague, grey bustle of movement around the trebuchet.

"Second!" shouted Peire-Roger. This was the signal to start shooting directly at the French, who obligingly appeared before the trebuchet to gauge the size of the attacking force.

Ocyrhoe watched Vera unhesitatingly lower the angle of her shot, so that she was aiming almost dead straight, over the level top of the shield in front of her. She aimed carefully—something she had not had to do when she was trying to hit a large target—and released. Ocyrhoe despite herself watched the fire-arrow as it flashed across the darkness. Its fire flared brightly as it flew, invigorated rather than imperiled by the rushing air. With a decisive *thunk*, it landed in the midriff of a French sergeant at the foot of the trebuchet; he fell screaming to the ground, trying desperately to pull the arrow out of his body. Ocryhoe felt sickened and turned her head away, even as she was automatically plunging the next arrow into the flames for Vera.

She lit half a dozen more arrows. It was hard to tell in the dim light if they were accomplishing anything; the French were scurrying around their prize machinery now, hundreds of them it seemed, little insects, moving ladders with impressive speed and precision as figures scrambled up, pulled out arrows, damped out fires, and began to douse the machine with handfuls of grimy snow to prevent any fire from taking hold.

Then with alarming speed the French organized a counterattack. Suddenly glinting in the moonlight were hundreds of shields, protecting every Frenchman. The French were far more accustomed to moving effectively behind the protection of overlapping shields; they did it all day long, every day, while the men of Montségur had had to simply squat along the crenellated battlements.

Shields up, the French archers began to shoot at the Cathar forces in far greater number. There were at least a hundred of them, and Ocyrhoe saw torch-toting boys scrambling down the slope toward the watchtower, where dozens more waited in reserve for emergencies like this. And no doubt a runner was also headed straight down to alert the camp. There might be a thousand French up here by morning, and meanwhile they had done no damage to the trebuchet.

"He will tell us to retreat," Vera said in an irritated voice, assessing the situation even more quickly than Ocyrhoe had.

Instead, however, Peire-Roger yelled out "Three!" which nobody had been expecting, not even Vera. She frowned in startlement and turned to stare into the darkness from the direction his voice had come.

"What is three?" Ocyrhoe asked, overwhelmed. She was no stranger to street-fights and had survived her share of danger, but she had never been in the middle of an organized battle like this before. It alarmed her that she found it slightly thrilling.

"He wants us to attack," said Vera. "Hand to hand. Swords and knives." She put one tip of her bow on the ground and leaned her weight into the curve to slacken the string. "The rear units will cover us with bows."

"You're going over there?" Ocyrhoe said, suddenly terrified.

Vera unstrung her bow. "Of course," she said and handed the bow to Ocyrhoe. "Take this. If he cries out *four*, you and the other squires carry the braziers across and dump them up against the trebuchet."

"But we're *losing*," said Ocyrhoe. "Why are there plans for moving forward when we should be retreating? There is no possible way you will open up a clear path for us to bring the fire." She felt dizzy. Maybe she actually did care about staying alive.

Vera frowned at her. "We're not losing," she said. "We are restrategizing."

"How many of you are there?" Ocyrhoe demanded. "How many of them?"

Vera pulled her knife from her belt with her left hand, and with her right she drew her sword from its scabbard. "If you look at the numbers, then we are clearly on the defensive," she said. "And the best defense is a good offense. If we don't do this, they will absolutely take the barbican. If that happens we are done for."

Ocyrhoe felt sudden panic and tried to digest this news. They had been just moments from the start of victory; how could such a reversal happen without any warning or fanfare?

Vera, indifferent to the girl's befuddlement, was glancing around in the darkness, assessing things Ocyrhoe could not begin to guess at. "They are about to drop the shields for us," she informed Ocyrhoe, who could not imagine how Vera knew this. "So we can rush forward. Once that happens you'll be totally exposed. Move back around the barbican for safety, but stay light on your toes. If Peire-Roger gives the signal, come in with the brazier straight to the trebuchet. Do not bother to look for me. Only look for me if you hear me call your name in particular, which is not likely to happen."

There was an ominous, metallic sound, and Ocyrhoe glanced toward it. She watched as men-at-arms who had been holding up actual shields, edges overlapped to protect the archers, separated and melted elegantly back behind the first group of archers, one of them sliding between Vera and Ocyrhoe, his shield raised high above his head.

"Not the way to do it," Vera informed Ocryhoe with a disapproving snort, cocking her head toward him. "All goodness go with you, sister." She pivoted from where she was standing and ran into the darkness toward the French.

Ocyrhoe watched her for the briefest moment, slack-jawed. Then she realized the shield-bearers were already reconstituting their protective wall of iron in front of the two remaining archery units, behind her. She ran for the barbican wall.

The next half-hour was chaos and confusion, and Ocyrhoe did not conduct herself the way she thought she would. She had been relatively fearless with Ferenc beside her, even though she valued her life; here, without valuing it, she was too frightened to put it on the line. She listened for Peire-Roger to sound the call, hoping he would not do it and then feeling wracked with guilt for such a wish, for it meant that the Montségur defenders were not prospering. The sounds of battle were all around her, so loud she felt them as much as heard them. Bodies thudding against each other, bodies being thrown to the ground, blade striking blade, and shield smashing against shield. Through it all, Ocyrhoe cowered against the barbican, hating herself for cowering, and watched the violence escalate around her. They were losing. Montségur was losing; the hand-to-hand combat was moving inexorably toward the fortress. She was on the fortress side of the barbican tower but suddenly she saw dueling soldiers snarled together in mortal combat. In most cases the French were winning, pushing the fortress defenders backward to the gates of Montségur. As Ocyrhoe watched, the slaughter and chaos expanded, bloated, around the barbican until she was in danger of being engulfed by it.

"Retreat!" cried a voice. "Retreat!" It was Peire-Roger, and still overwhelmed with shame, Ocyrhoe welcomed it. In the quickly narrowing corridor between the fighting that had moved around from either side, she ran. She dodged men she recognized even in their armor—Percival, Peire-Roger himself, all of them fighting for their lives against men whose names and homelands would be forever unknown to them. She approached Raphael struggling with a Frenchman; they had both dropped their swords and grabbed each other around the shoulders as if hugging or trying to throw each other in a wrestling move. Her eye stayed on them as she drew even with them. As Raphael took the Frenchman's balance, hurtling him to the ground, he disappeared completely. With a floating feeling in her stomach, Ocyrhoe realized Raphael had just thrown his enemy off the frozen, cliff-sharp side of the ridge. Even as she had that thought, Raphael was reaching to pick up both his sword and the Frenchman's. "Ocyrhoe!" he shouted sternly over the din. It brought her up short. Raphael hurled the short French sword toward her so that it flipped hilt-over-tip and sliced into the frozen ground near her. "Take it," he ordered, then threw himself back into the fracas by the barbican.

Ocyrhoe yanked hard at the sword. It resisted her. She marveled at what Raphael had just done, with such seeming ease: On a mountaintop made almost entirely of limestone, he had flung the sword with such precision that, in the darkness, he had landed it on a small spot of actual soil, barely visible even in the daylight, with enough force to sink into the frozen ground.

She tugged again and dislodged it. Heavy, stomping footfalls sounded behind her; others were retreating onto the ridge. With a surge of thrilled terror she tore along the narrow ridge, raising the hilt of the sword to pound the gate, but Ferrer opened it before she could, and the force of her intended knock threw her to her knees inside the courtyard walls.

For hours more, chaos continued. She scrambled up the cold stone stairs to the wall-walk, where the garrison guards were shooting as fast and as accurately as they could into the pressing crowd. It was an armed melee, and Ocyrhoe was grateful it was getting darker with the moon-set, for there must have been blood everywhere. It was staining what snow had not been trod away in all the scuffles, but surely there was more she could not even sense in this darkness. In the dim she saw soldiers being flung to their deaths down the sides of the ridge, and many more falling to the sword near the barbican.

As Montségur men were able to retreat safely across the ridge, Ferrer allowed them back in. Several times they were pursued by

French swordsmen who forced their way through the gate as well, but these came in small numbers and were immediately felled by Montségur men just inside the walls.

Peire-Roger, who was among these men, ordered the others to hack up the dead Frenchmen and hurl their body parts over the parapet at their compatriots. Ocyrhoe scrambled to another part of the wall, closer to the keep, to get far away from that grisly undertaking.

Suddenly the soldier next to Ocyrhoe cried out in shocked pain and grabbed at his chest. He had been struck by an arrow, but in the instant before he crashed off the wall to the courtyard floor Ocyrhoe saw that the arrow had entered his body straight on, as if from the same height. She immediately understood what that meant: the barbican had been taken. Now French archers were atop of the tower, shooting straight over the treacherous ridge directly at the garrison guard. The barbican was better defended than the wall-walk; the French soldiers had an advantage. Everywhere.

With the Montségur defenders in retreat, the French pulled back, flocking into the barbican and lighting it with torches, celebrating their conquest. As the clanging and clashes of weapons diminished to be replaced by the groans of dying men, the gate of the fortress opened wider than it had been, and Ocyrhoe saw a dreadful sight below her: at least a dozen men too wounded to walk, being trundled between comrades back across the ridge to the safety of the fortress.

No, there is no safety for them here, she corrected herself. *These walls cannot hold death out now.*

The French, despite their hallowing bellows of triumph from the barbican, ceased shooting or chasing after them, allowing the tattered remnants of the Montségur force to return unmolested to the fortress.

The wounded were carried straight through the courtyard and up into the keep. Ocyrhoe looked for the nearest wooden ladder and hurried down it, then chased after the grim procession to see who was in it.

Inside the keep, she expected to see the dying laid out on the trestle tables or at least on the floor, but instead they were being carried right up the second set of stairs to the chapel above. The women, children, and old men huddled together and softly sobbed the names of their dear ones. Ocyrhoe glanced around the hall; there were no Good Ones here. They must have gone upstairs too. Suddenly realizing what was happening, she followed up the stairs.

Ocyrhoe stepped inside and watched in the torchlight. The dozens and dozens of Good Ones were clustered together on the far side of the chapel, all in black, faces calm, watching. The soldiers laid their fallen colleagues gently on the floor, sometimes resting a hand on a shoulder or planting a kiss on a forehead. Then the men who had carried the dying filed out of the room, past Ocyrhoe, back down the stairs to the hall. The Goodmen moved to surround the prone soldiers.

Ocyrhoe stayed where she was. Rixenda and the other Goodwomen began to move around the edges of the chapel, but Rixenda, seeing her, cut straight across toward her. "You cannot stay here, child," she said as gently as she could. "The Goodmen are about to give the consolamentum. It is a sacred ritual and unless you are here to partake of it yourself you must not stay."

Ocyrhoe blinked. "They are all taking the vows of the Good Ones right before."

"Yes, right before they pass on," said Rixenda gently. "They have done good work in this life protecting us, holding back from their final vows so that they could be in the world in a way that we are not. They have earned the right to go to God and escape the endless cycle of being reborn into the cruel world. They all wanted this. And now they will receive it. Go, Ocyrhoe, and comfort those trapped still in this hellish life. It is our job to prepare those who are about to escape it."

Ocyrhoe pursed her lips together and closed her eyes to keep tears from spilling out. Rixenda kissed her on the forehead, then gently turned her around to face the stairs. Ocyrhoe began to descend them. Behind her, she knew, Rixenda knelt beside her nephew, Vidal, whose wounds had left in him not an hour of life.

✦ ✦ ✦

The fortress slept fitfully, only the weary, scant garrison alert. Raphael, Vera and Percival slept in a clutch in the corner of the keep, having muttered between themselves about the best plans for the next day. Only the treacherous ridge, some few dozen strides long, now protected Montségur from guaranteed defeat. Would the French attack the fortress with such a narrow easement? When only two soldiers abreast could approach the walls? Yes, argued Vera; no, said Percival. Raphael was unconvinced of either, and Peire-Roger kept himself aloof, huddled in a corner with his wife's father, Raimon de Perelha. The two lords of Montségur wore miserable expressions.

"They are discussing a surrender," said Raphael, watching them across the rows and clumps of sleeping forms.

"Of course they're not," said Vera. "They will go down fighting before they surrender. If they give in, it is the end of Occitania. The French will never leave."

"We're in a stronger position than we realize," Percival said. "It would be madness on the French's part to attack the fortress. We're in a stalemate, no different than before but uncomfortably closer to our gate, that's all. Things will stay like this until we freeze them out and they go home, or until the reinforcements arrive, attack the outskirts of the army, and draw Hugue de Arcis's attention back down the mountain in self-defense. In the bigger picture, this setback changes nothing."

"They've taken the barbican," argued Raphael. "That changes everything. They can shoot directly into the courtyard now, not blindly but with intention. Ocyrhoe can no longer get to the entrance of the southern tunnel."

"We can protect her with shields," said Percival. "Everything but the trebuchet is made of stone, so even if they shoot with fire-arrows, there's nothing for them to burn or…"

His words were interrupted by a cry of alarm from outside, together with a tremendously loud crack that made the whole keep shake. Instantly, the three of them were up, blankets thrown off, hands on sword hilts. Around them sleepers woke and cried out in alarm, mothers grabbed children close to them, and people huddled together.

The trio of warriors raced through the clutches of bodies, heading directly for the door. Raphael saw other soldiers and knights also grabbing for their weapons and following after.

In the frigid dawn light, the garrison soldiers were on their knees behind the crenellations of the wall-walk, trying to move back and forth quickly without exposing themselves. Some were shooting at the barbican, from which a sideways rain of arrows erupted. Others of the Montségur guard were shooting almost straight down over the wall at the French soldiers directly on the other side. The French were pressing their advantage; they were risking the ridge to gain the fortress. In three places, the tops of wooden ladders appeared over the walls; the nearest guards, lacking leverage, were hard put to push them off.

Worst of all, the smash against the donjon wall had been a stone hurled from the trebuchet. While giving the denizens of Montségur a moment to breathe and collect their wounded, the French had been shortening the sling of the trebuchet so that it could hurl rocks against the fortress once again.

One Montségur soldier, desperate to dislodge the nearest ladder, stood to give himself the leverage to shove the ladder away from the wall. "Don't!" shouted Raphael, looking up from the porthouse. "Down!" Even as he spoke the words, an arrow from the barbican shredded the air and lodged itself high in the man's right ribcage. He had been propelling his weight forward over the ramparts; once hit, he lost the balance and ability to right himself and toppled over the wall onto the waiting blades of the French soldiers below.

A second soldier, not seeing what happened to his comrade in the panicked dawn confusion, stood to dislodge the ladder that rose by him; before Raphael could even speak, an arrow from the barbican took him down, too.

"Do not stand upright!" Raphael hollered up at all of them. "Let them keep the ladders up. Only one can climb at a time; let them, and then spear them or behead them as they reach you. Stay low and safe behind the wall!" He had no idea if any of them could hear him.

Behind him, he heard Percival explaining in low, urgent tones to Peire-Roger what Raphael had just said. Peire-Roger, his bull's voice louder than anyone else, repeated Raphael's orders in a bellow. Instantly a sense of order overtook the courtyard.

What had been the French advantage—the vulnerability of the Montségur forces stuck on the wall-walk—turned to their disadvantage. Hunched down behind the low wall, the soldiers simply waited for the French to appear at the top of the ladders and easily dispatched each as he came.

Within an hour it was clear there would be no conquest this way. But the French had thousands of expendable, local troops, so they continued this tactic, to encumber as many of the Montségur soldiers as they could. Meanwhile, the French archers in the barbican now lacked visible targets—the Montségurians were crouching out of view—but this did not stop them from sending lethal flocks of arrows into the courtyard. Only flush against the eastern wall was there any safety from these; the most dangerous stretch in the fortress was now the stone's-throw sprint between the donjon door and the safety of the eastern wall. Peire-Roger ordered seven men-at-arms to set up a canopy of wooden boards along this path to allow messengers and soldiers some safety as they moved in and out of the donjon. Two men were wounded in the course of attempting this; Raphael attended to them, but one of them had been struck in the ear by an arrow and had only a few moments of life left in him. Percival carried him up to the Good Ones in the chapel to receive the consolamentum.

"These hypocrites," said Vera with disgust, under her breath. They were standing at the bottom of the stairs waiting for Percival to return. "These Perfect Ones. They call themselves pacifists and yet they're content to let good soldiers die defending them."

"The soldiers are not only defending the Good Ones," Raphael corrected her. "They are also protecting the civilians who have come here seeking refuge."

Vera huffed. "They are only forced to seek refuge here because of their sense of obligation to the Good Ones! If the Good Ones left, the rest of them would not be in danger."

"Yes, they would," said Raphael patiently. "The religious elements of this fight are only a thin patina over the French king's desire to control the region. He'd be attacking regardless."

"But he wouldn't have the backing of the archbishop," Vera retorted quickly. "The archbishop's only excuse for being here is that this is a religious issue. Take away the religious aspect and he'd have to pack up and go back to Narbonne. Along with all the troops who are here out of obligation to him. That must be a good third of the army."

Raphael considered this. "That's true. If you know of any way to get the Good Ones out of Montségur, tell Peire-Roger and Bishop Marti."

"They don't really need to leave," said Vera smartly. "The French only must *think* they've left."

Raphael nodded. "Work on that," he suggested. "Meanwhile, let's try not to be sacked."

For most of the day, the predictable unpredictability was wearying. There was nothing any of them could do but take their turn, in hour-long stretches, of waiting along the wall-walk for the French soldiers to stubbornly make their way up the ladders for quick dispatching. The courtyard was littered revoltingly with French heads, and carpeted in arrows, the majority bouncing off the limestone rocks to lie flat on the ground, fletches and tips bundled up together. Not knowing whether or not they were killing anyone within—but encountering no resistance—the French continued to shoot into the courtyard as the morning stretched to midday and then to late afternoon. Meanwhile, the soldiers on the wall-walk continued to dispatch the French as each man topped the ladders. The squires had the sickening job of carrying the heads up the ladders and hurling them back to the French. There was a strange monotony to the danger.

Worst of all, the boulders continued to slam against the side of the keep, with the deadly precision Raphael had feared from the beginning. The damage was not visible from where they were, but if they continued unabated like that even for a few days, so frequently and at such close range, they would bring the wall down.

In the late afternoon, as Vera, Percival, and Raphael each descended from their turn on the walls, Peire-Roger summoned them to meet at the porthouse. "Come with me out there to fight them off," he proposed. "If we are a well-armed, well-protected corps, we can push them back to the barbican and find a way to keep them back."

Raphael looked at him wearily. "And what will that accomplish," he asked, "when they can continue to sling projectiles that will tear the donjon wall down within days?"

"We can't not fight," Vera upbraided the Levantine. And to Peire-Roger: "Of course we'll go with you."

◆ ◆ ◆

Late that night, Ocyhroe sat wide-eyed listening to Vera describe the battle outside the gate. A good part of her amazement was at how steadily Vera spoke, even as Raphael was cleaning, splinting, and bandaging a wound on Vera's calf that looked to Ocyrhoe as if surely it would cost her her leg.

In short, the defenders had successfully repelled the French attackers, in large part by shoving many of them off the ridge. The Montségur contingent was very small, but the French could only come at them in small groups. The archers in the barbican soon realized their arrows would find no purchase against the heavily armored defenders, and so Hugue de Arcis had ordered his men to focus on the trebuchet attacks. There were some vicious skirmishes outside the walls—Vera had been wounded in the last of these—but by far the worst danger came from the wall being hacked away with each successful catapulted boulder. From out on the ridge they could look back at the fortress, and the damage to the donjon wall was alarming.

As darkness came, the French fell back completely. Peire-Roger had ordered the door to the barbican destroyed and sent his own troops swarming up into it. With the door off, it could not be secured, and after two hours of fierce fighting it was a no-man's land. But the French were repelled from the walls and the ridge, and so despite the thundering attacks on the donjon wall, the news that reached the ears of those inside was positive: The most dangerous attack had come and gone, and they had all survived it. Surely the French would pack up soon and go home to the Isle de France and their accursed king.

Those who knew better gathered in a corner of the chapel that night. Most of the wounded had died by now, making the place largely a morgue. Several were still in their final throes of suffering. These were all attended to by the Goodwomen, including Rixenda. Vidal had already passed. Ocyrhoe took his death very hard, knowing herself responsible for his having come here in the first place.

Ocyrhoe had been summoned to the leadership council. She assumed it would be a strategic discussion to determine how best to bring in new supplies. She was the last to arrive, however, and the discussion had begun without her. It was not going as she had assumed it would.

Raphael shook his head. "We have been in battle beside you," said Raphael to Peire-Roger, "and we have failed to protect you from the enemy. It would be appalling of us to leave you before we know the terms, and that the women and children at least are safe."

Ocyrhoe cringed. In her cowardice she'd wanted nothing but a cessation to hostilities, but were they talking of surrendering?

At that moment, a boulder was hurled against the wall, hitting precisely the same location that it always had, near the ceiling of the downstairs hall. Only this time, it was different.

The rock broke through the wall. Two things happened at once beyond the usual shudder of masonry: People downstairs screamed in fear, and the floor on which they stood—the ceiling of the room below—trembled as it never had before and fell away beneath them a good hand-span from where they sat. The Goodwomen gasped in shock, and the men still on the floor groaned. The penetrated wall had dislodged a broad, wooden beam supporting the floor—but only one beam, so that now, when things settled, the floor tilted slightly to the east as if in a heeling ship.

"Go and calm them," Peire-Roger said to one of his men-at-arms, and all three of them went downstairs. He turned back to the group. "Anyone hurt?"

"My leg could have done without the jolt," said Vera, who was white-faced from pain she would never fully admit to.

"Well, that is it, then," said Bishop Marti in a voice of defeat. "If any of us wondered if we were surrendering too soon, we know we aren't."

"They know it, too," said Raphael, trying to offer comfort. "There will be no more stones tonight. They can see their handiwork. They know the effect it will have."

"Well then," said Peire-Roger grimly. "We surrender at dawn." He turned to Raphael. "I do think it is in your interest to be gone before then."

"We're going nowhere until we are sure we can be of no further service to you," said Raphael. "Were Frederick on his deathbed and sending giant eagles to carry us to him, we would not leave a people so in need of help."

The Lord of Montségur smiled grimly. "A generous and noble statement, and it is not lost on us. But this is over now. The three of you cannot make a difference as to what happens next. And I know you have pressing reasons to quit this place."

"We will not leave you," Percival insisted.

"Ocyrhoe can get you safely away from here," said Peire-Roger. At this, Percival turned pleading eyes upon her.

"I will take them when they're ready to go," she said. And added, heavily, but knowing it was the right thing to say: "And I'll give then what they need." Looking directly at Percival. "Whatever they need. If they believe they absolutely need it."

Percival smiled at her. She almost thought he teared up. "You are a goodwoman," he said quietly.

CHAPTER 35:

SURRENDER

The next morning, as the sun rose on a blood-smeared, frozen mountaintop, Peire-Roger dressed in the only other robes he had in the fortress, which were marginally cleaner and crisper than what he had been wearing since the siege began in May. He ordered the fortress's one trumpet to be sounded. At the gate to the fortress, he kissed his wife and children, embraced his father-in-law, and warmly thanked for their faithful assistance the assembled lords, knights, and men-at-arms who could still stand. The captain of the garrison guard somberly handed him a large, white banner. With his unarmed trio of guards behind him, he left through the gate as Ferrer opened it and raised the banner high to be seen by those in the French encampment at the trebuchet.

Ocyrhoe was on the wall-walk, watching with an uncomfortable mix of emotions. A heavyset man in opulent military dress, whom she assumed must be the widely loathed Hugue de Arcis, stepped forward, likewise with bodyguards, and received him in the no-man's land near the barbican doorway. They saluted each other with fists to chests, and then Peire-Roger lowered the white banner and handed it to Hugue. Within the courtyard Credents were weeping openly. The Good Ones were grim but silent.

After a few moments of quiet conversation, too soft for Ocyrhoe to hear, Peire-Roger's three men saluted him, saluted the enemy leader, then turned on their heels and marched back toward the fortress.

Ocyrhoe scrambled back down the ladder so she could hear their report: Peire-Roger was being taken down to the army camp to discuss terms. The fat man had not, in fact, been Hugue de Arcis; Hugue de Arcis had not been back up on the mountain since the first battle for the barbican. That seemed to Ocyrhoe a shameful way to lead an army.

❖ ❖ ❖

They waited for anxious hours. Ocyrhoe wrapped extra blankets around herself and went up onto the wall-walk to look down the southwestern slope toward the army camp. Smoke rose complacently from the chimneys of the village houses. Their bellicose leader was down there, chastened, begging for their lives. Or perhaps not. Perhaps he was making a deal with the French that would protect his own affairs while destroying the lives of everyone else up here?

Terrible what fear can do, she chastised herself. *He is a difficult man but he is not dishonorable.*

Outside the walls to the east, hundreds of French soldiers on the mountain were relaxing as much as one can in frigid weather without shelter. They looked tired, and relieved. They did not exude any triumphal joy. This siege had been good for nobody; the end of it improved nobody's lot. Except for King Louis of France, who had never come near it.

Feeling she was being stared at, she turned and saw Percival in the middle of the courtyard, trying not to be obvious about staring at her. *Oh, for the sake of the gods*, she thought with some exasperation. She gestured him to join her on the wall-walk. After a hesitation, he crossed to the nearest wooden ladder, climbed it, and then strolled along the battlement to join her.

"Are you wondering when you'll get the cup?" she asked, sardonically.

"Among many other things," he said peaceably. "Assuming this surrender goes decently."

"I have been catechized in local history, and I assure you there has never been a 'decent surrender' in the history of Occitanian persecution," said Ocyrhoe crossly. "Peire-Roger has just gone to his death. They will spare him long enough to make him watch every person in this fortress burned at the stake, and then they'll torture him. And then they'll kill him. You need only look at history, at the record of Simon de Montfort, to see how this will all play out."

"Perhaps this time they will be merciful."

She made a disgusted sound. "Why this time would they be more merciful than they've ever been before? What is different about this time?"

"Well," said Percival. "To begin with, there's the grail."

She froze. Blinked. "We don't really understand that thing," she said. "Are you suggesting we try to use it to ensure mercy? It certainly has never done that before."

"It has never been with *me* before," said Percival. There was a pleading quality in his voice...no, not pleading. Intense yearning overlaid with desperation.

"You think if I give it to you now, something magical will happen and we'll all be spared?" she asked, trying not to sound sardonic.

"It is possible. If you do *not* give it to me now, then certainly nothing will change from how it has been."

She grimaced, pulled the blanket tighter around herself, considered this. "Very well," she said. "I should rid myself of it in any case. It, and this life I've been living, everything. I am so young to be starting from scratch a third time in my life, but that's the lot that has fallen to me. You know, the worst part was not that he died," she said suddenly, pushing back a rush of emotion. "It's that he stays dead. So intractably. In a world where everything changes, that one element alone stays constant."

Percival, at a loss for words, put an arm around her shoulders in a stiff hug. She found the good intention coupled with the clumsy execution somehow endearing.

"You don't have to do that," Ocyrhoe said. "Rixenda is still holding it. She is helping with the dying upstairs yet, but when she's had a chance to recover from her labors, I will retrieve it from her and then give it to you."

His squeeze around her shoulders tightened. "Bless you, my friend." He released her and tensed. "They're returning," he said, pointing down the slope.

Because the hostilities were over and the fortress no longer being defended, the returning party was walking up the primary venue between village and fortress: the main switch-back path going up the western side of the pog. It had not been used since last May when the siege began. The trip up the pog could easily be accomplished in the time it took to walk a mile. "They're coming!" Percival called down to people in the courtyard.

Ocyrhoe looked harder. She could see Peire-Roger among the small party of men. He walked with his usual gait, arms swinging to either side of his body. That meant his hands were not bound. He was entirely free. Her heart leaped a little: perhaps this time, it would be different from all that had come before.

"They're on their way!" Ocyrhoe shouted and ran toward the ladder to help spread the news. "Peire-Roger is unharmed!"

By the time the French party reached the top of the mountain, the hall had been prepared to receive them. In a reversal of the last half-year, the civilians would now be banished to the courtyard, while within the hall the victors would meet with the

Bishop, Rixenda, and the highest-ranking knights and lords to give the terms of surrender. The women and children had spent the day tidying themselves in the wan hope of being so sweet-faced it would soften the punishment to come. There would be punishment, they all knew that. Nobody could resist the French king and the Archbishop of Narbonne for so long, so fiercely, with so many opportunities to concede, without being punished for such pertinacity.

Ocyrhoe saw Vera go into the hall and decided that meant she should be allowed in, too. Perhaps part of the surrender terms would include revealing all the secret tunnels, and that would be her duty. She decided she would not reveal everything. Just enough for appeasement. Her sudden anger and disgust at the men climbing the mountain surprised her. She took all of this personally, although these were not really her people and it was not really her fight. For two years she had had the chance to join their spiritual journey and had never once felt drawn to do so. But she loved them, appreciated their humanity, and was grateful to have been taken in by them. A fierce, protective instinct fired her, and her impotence now to act on it infuriated her. But she could at least keep an eye on what was happening to them.

So she walked into the hall with a casual insolence, and nobody within questioned her right to be there. The smallest trestle table had been set up in the middle of the room. The room was lit, surprisingly, with beeswax candles—the very final stash that Peire-Roger must have been holding back, for the end. It grieved her. She'd helped to make those candles, and it was an ignoble moment they'd be lighting.

Bishop Marti and old Raimon de Perelha, the two official representatives of the fortress's inhabitants, sat beside each other on one side of the table. Gathered around and behind them were all the other lords, spilling over to the two ends of the table. Raphael and Vera sat among the cluster of men to one side of the

Bishop, Percival to the other side. Ocyrhoe began to move toward Percival, then thought better of it and planted herself between Vera and Raphael. She could claim to be Vera's squire if anybody questioned her.

As she settled onto the bench, the door of the keep opened and the solemn procession entered. Besides Peire-Roger and a dozen armed guards, there was the knight, Dietrich von Grüningen, who had come before as a messenger, with a few young men who seemed to be acting as his squires; there was also a large man with leathery skin who was clearly an army general. He bore a facial scar that matched the blow she'd struck against Peire-Roger's attacker at the first battle of the barbican. Had she slashed the face of Hugue de Arcis? Finally, there was a tall, old man in archbishop's raiment. These last two had with them several of their own men; the archbishop had a priest in tow.

With very little introduction, these men all sat across from Raimon and Marti. Peire-Roger remained standing on the one side of the table where nobody was sitting. He looked tired and somewhat astonished.

"We have surrendered," he said to both sides of the table. "The crusaders have accepted our surrender and given us terms, and I have accepted them. It is now my burden to inform you what they are, that you may share this knowledge with the rest of the fortress."

"Give us the worst of it," said Marti quietly.

Peire-Roger looked pained. "The worst, of course, is that any Good Ones who refuse to renounce their oaths will be burned as heretics once the fortress has been emptied."

"They have the option of renouncing their oaths?" Raimon said in amazement.

"Yes," said Peire-Roger, glancing at the archbishop as if he still needed affirmation of this startling detail. "Up until the very last moment, any one of the Good Ones may renounce their faith—"

"Heresy," corrected the archbishop with a sniff.

"May renounce their heresy and with a small penance return to the arms of the mother church, with no further harm."

Marti's eyes opened wide. "This is a trick," he said. "The Church has never once taken such a position on our faith."

"We are tired of the decades of blood and iron," said His Eminence of Narbonne. "We wish only to welcome back repentant children into our bosom."

"Furthermore," said Peire-Roger quickly, as if anxious to get all the news out so that he could leave and grieve in the dark, "the Credents, all those here who have not taken the consolamentum oath, are to be released without penalty at all."

"*What?*" said every Montségur resident at the table.

"No punishment at all," Peire-Roger said. "They must report to the Inquisitors what they know of the heresy and promise their faith to the archbishop, and they will be allowed to leave here entirely unharmed, with all their property and family intact."

There was a stunned silence.

"That is *extraordinary*," said Raimon de Perelha.

"As His Eminence said," said Hugue de Arcis, "we want to end this. We realize that continued bloodshed will never do it. We want to beat swords into ploughshares before the Occitan is permanently destroyed. These are our lands too, now, and we do not seek a Pyrrhic victory."

"But many of us are soldiers," said one of the lords. "We have killed your soldiers. We have injured your people and taken up arms against the French king."

"And we forgive you for it," said Hugue. His tone implied this was not something he was pleased to offer; somebody higher up than he had insisted upon it, and he was being dutiful.

"And finally," Peire-Roger pushed on, "the other...oddity of this surrender is a fortnight's truce to precede the turnover. For two weeks, nobody is to leave the fortress, under any circumstances. We will not be attacked. We will be left in perfect peace."

"Why?" demanded Marti. "Why not just finish this, as you claim you wish to do?"

"We wish to give you Perfect Heretics the chance to see the error of your ways," said the archbishop coldly. "It is our dearest hope that given time to reflect you will realize how foolish it is to throw your lives away. We want to give our fallen children every possible chance to rise up and carry on. In the heat of this moment, it is easy for you to remain defiant. With days to rest and contemplate and see the hope of salvation in your Credents' eyes, perhaps you will choose to render up your heresy and join us again."

"They don't want martyrs," Raphael said quietly. "In the long view, for them, it's sensible."

A long pause.

"And that is it?" said Marti, disbelievingly. "That is the whole cause for a two-week truce?"

"It is," said the archbishop. "During the truce, Lord Hugue of Carcassonne will take political hostages to ensure your good behavior in the fortress."

"That is the least peculiar thing yet said about these arrangements," said Raimon. "I assume the hostages have been determined."

"Yes," said Peire Roger grimly. "Father, you are to go with Hugue."

"No surprise," said old Raimon with contented resignation. "I am surprised only not to be slaughtered instantly."

"No slaughter, no slaughter," Hugue insisted, as Peire-Roger continued to name the hostages: "Your son Jordan, my kinsman Arnaud-Roger, the bishop Marti's brother Raimon..." He asked Hugue, "Was there anybody else?"

"We discussed the knight."

"He is a stranger here," said Peire-Roger in a tone suggesting an earlier argument. "He has no value as a hostage, as his presence among you will vouchsafe the good behavior of none of us."

"We name the terms," said Hugue gruffly. "And we want him. His name—"

There was a sharp cough, and Hugue stopped suddenly. He glanced over toward the archbishop. The hooded priest sitting beside the archbishop leaned slightly forward and whispered in the archbishop's ear. His Eminence's eyes scanned the cluster of Montségurians as the priest settled back into the shadows, away from the table. Ocyrhoe could barely see the man, but something about him was unsettlingly familiar. The shape of the nose, which she could just make out under his hood, reminded her of Cardinal Fieschi from Rome. Also the way he held himself, and how he leaned forward. Of course it couldn't be Fieschi, but even a reminder of him caused a flutter of anxiety in her stomach. Which was instantly worsened when she realized the archbishop was staring straight at her.

"That one," he said, pointing at her. "She's the final hostage we want."

Ocryhoe's eyes snapped back to the priest. He was looking at her from the protection of his hood, leaning slightly back as her gaze hit him, as if to make sure she could not see him well. *It was Cardinal Fieschi.* He had tracked her to Montségur!

Because he wanted the cup.

"Why do you want Ocyrhoe?" Raphael asked, putting a protective hand on her shoulder. "She is hardly more than a girl, and she is not even a Credent. Taking a female hostage is most unorthodox."

"*We* determine the terms," Hugue reminded smugly. "The girl will come with us. She will not be hurt, and at the end of two weeks she will be released with all the others."

Raphael squeezed her shoulder and released it. As he lowered his hand, she grabbed it and pulled it down between the two of them on the bench.

Raphael was a traveler and knew many unexpected things. Perhaps he'd know the Binders' sign-language? Vera, after all, had recognized the knots in her hair. The lords began to discuss the logistics of bringing the hostages down to the village. As they spoke, she began to tap out the letters of Fieschi's name against the inside of Raphael's wrist. After a moment he glanced subtly at her and then away, with a very focused expression, as listening to something. Did he understand? He obviously guessed the danger, and clearly that the priest had some involvement—but did Raphael recognize him?

He shook his head very slightly, once, and closed his free hand around her signing fingers. *Wait*, he mouthed, without looking at her. She put her other hand over his and squeezed it hard, pressing her nails into his flesh, to make him understand that this was urgent.

Around them, everyone began to stand; the conference was over. The hostages in the room were being moved toward the door. Peire-Roger went out to find his wife and deliver the dread news to her.

As one of Hugue's bodyguards moved toward Ocyrhoe, Raphael took her firmly by the arm and pulled her away.

"She's to come with us," said the man gruffly.

"Am I not allowed a private farewell to my own daughter?" Raphael said fiercely. "If this is intended to be a civilized process, allow me that at least."

The man held both hands up in concession and took a step back.

Raphael turned to face Ocyrhoe directly, forearms aligned, grasping her behind the elbows. He brought his face so close to hers, her eyes could hardly focus to meet his. "Tell me," he whispered.

"The priest," she said. "He told the archbishop to ask for me. He's not a priest. He's a cardinal. In disguise. He's from Rome, and his name is Cardinal Fieschi. He wants the—" She stopped because his grip on her elbows tightened so intensely that it hurt her. He had suddenly gone rigid.

He drew his face back slightly so she could see his expression. The color had drained from his face. "Are you absolutely certain of that?" he asked, in a slow, intense voice.

She nodded. "He's why I fled from Rome. He wants the cup."

"Mother of God in Heaven," said Raphael. She had never seen him look so spooked. Out of her peripheral vision she saw Fieschi scolding the guard who was supposed to bring her along. Of course, Fieschi knew she was an orphan and therefore realized this was no father–daughter farewell. As the guard crossed back to them with an irritated expression, Raphael whispered to her hurriedly, "Fieschi's not a cardinal anymore."

"They defrocked him?" she asked hopefully.

"No," said Raphael, "they made him Pope."

CHAPTER 36:

THE CONSEQUENCES

When the hostages had gone, and French guards were stationed outside the fortress wall, Bishop Marti summoned all the Good Ones to the chapel to tell them the terms, while Peire-Roger summoned the Credents into the hall below, likewise to explain to them.

The only three people in the fortress not at one of these gatherings were the three visitors, who were on the battlements staring down toward the village.

"So," said Raphael. And then there was a long pause.

"If the Pope wants the grail, there must be something to it," said Percival.

"If *this* pope wants the grail, there must be something *suspicious* to it," said Raphael.

"Frederick wanted Percival..." Vera began

"No, Léna wanted Percival," Raphael corrected her. "Ferenc was always very clear that Léna was the driving force behind our coming to collect him. And she knew Ocyrhoe was here, with the cup."

"All of which reveals a struggle between church and emperor for the grail," said Percival. "Even if it is the woman behind the throne and not the emperor. The grail is significant, and I have been led to it by something greater than any of us."

He looked expectantly at Raphael, as did Vera. After a moment the Levantine said grudgingly, "It is possible you are not mistaken about that."

Percival allowed himself a satisfied smile.

"So now what?" demanded Vera.

"Either," said Raphael, "we take the cup from Rixenda and get the hell out of here before Fieschi can get his hands on it, or we wait two weeks until Ocyrhoe's released, and take her with us."

"We should rescue her from him," said Percival.

"No, we shouldn't," Vera scolded him. "Releasing a hostage breaks the terms of the truce and endangers everyone in Montségur."

"Leaving breaks the truce," said Percival. "So I suppose that means we're staying."

Vera ground her teeth. "Sitting here and *stewing* for a *fortnight*. That could be the final straw that sends us round the bend."

"It's an opportunity to practice a new and subtler kind of fortitude," said Raphael grimly. "I think that is the course we must take. Fieschi can't get the cup from Ocyrhoe because she doesn't have it. We have to wait to see what Fieschi does when he realizes that."

"If we could find the cup now, I might be able to help these people somehow," said Percival.

"That's a terrible idea," said Raphael. "Assuming it does indeed have some kind of mystical power that somehow requires your proximity to it. We don't know what that is. We have no way to control it. It is not necessarily benign. It is some wild energy of unknown provenance, trapped in a material object. This is not the time, especially with His Holiness lurking about in secret trying to get his hands on it. Frankly, Percival," Raphael continued, "your obsession with getting your hands on it smacks somewhat of a thirst for power."

Percival looked stung. "No, it's nothing like that. Quite the contrary. I want to be of service. I want to be *used by* the cup."

"Not here. Not yet," said Raphael with finality.

The door to the keep opened. The civilian population of the fortress began to emerge into the cool, clean air, many of them openly sobbing. A few moments later the Good Ones began to file out as well, looking solemn but calm. As the trio watched, the Credents and the Good Ones sought each other out and embraced, the Good Ones comforting the Credents. After a few moments, the Perfecti, in a group, moved toward the eastern gate and exited.

"Going back to their village to collect their possessions," guessed Vera. "What few they have."

"Let us just speak to Rixenda about the cup," said Raphael. "Now that we know it's wanted by His Holiness, we cannot allow what I'd originally hoped, that it would conveniently get lost in the shuffle of life here."

The sun had not moved discernibly in the sky when the Good Ones returned. As Vera predicted, they carried with them handfuls of ordinary objects wrapped in blankets and cloaks.

But all three of them were unprepared for what happened next: the Good Ones stopped in the middle of the courtyard, each claiming a small area. They spread their blankets and coats on the grimy ground and laid their personal possessions on them as if they were displaying wares at a primitive market. There were very few things: mostly metal crosses, or images of doves; clay statues, paintings on vellum. There were jars of oil, packets of pepper and others of salt, a few bolts of cloth, a few cakes of beeswax. Raphael saw a few pairs of boots, a couple of purses, a felt hat. Once the Good Ones had settled themselves with these objects, the Credents—who had until then clustered around the edges of the yard—moved in toward them. They circulated among them, settling on the blanket or wrap of a relative or someone to whom they had been especially close. Gentle conversation, a murmuring like lazy bees, filled the courtyard.

"There's Rixenda," said Raphael.

He climbed down the ladder, the other two behind him. Rixenda, on the edge of the "market," glanced up as if expecting them.

"Greetings, dear ones," she said. "Sit with me."

They did. On Rixenda's blanket were very few items. A cup was not among them. There was a wooden mug, however, which she offered to Raphael. "In here, I mixed tinctures and infusions," she said. "They brought health and comfort to many. You, I have learned in your time here, are likewise a sometime healer. I would be very pleased if you would take this cup and allow it to continue its useful purpose in the years to come."

Raphael received it from her. "I am honored by the gift," he said. "But why do you not keep it yourself?" Even as he asked, he knew and dreaded the answer.

"For I am bound to heaven in two weeks," she said comfortably. "As are we all. We know our loved ones will grieve for us, and to diminish their heart-heaviness we are divesting ourselves of our very final material goods now, so that our kin need not determine how to dispose of them when we are gone."

"You're giving up without a fight," Vera said, the disapproval not quite hidden.

"There has been fighting enough," said Rixenda. "It has not solved anything." She smiled at Raphael. "You want to know about the cup."

"I do."

"It's safe. Do you require it?"

Percival and Raphael exchanged looks. Raphael shifted his weight back on his heels, leaving Percival to answer.

"Soon," said the taller knight with some difficulty. "Very soon. But not yet."

"That shows some discipline, brother Percival," Rixenda said approvingly.

"But lady, will you really do this?" Raphael asked. "If you will just forswear it, you may continue to live."

She shrugged. "There is no better way to die than in defense of your beliefs," she said. "We die defiant, every one of us. We need not have a weapon in our hands to do so."

"But you are *throwing away* your life," said Percival, dismayed.

"To renounce my faith, when I have invested so much in it? *That* would be throwing away my life," Rixenda said. "And to die someday pretending to be Catholic, losing the opportunity to find my way to the true heaven—that would be throwing away my life *and* my death."

❖ ❖ ❖

Her hands were loosely bound with hemp rope, and the guard who had pulled her away from Raphael held the stray end of the rope. Sinibaldo Fieschi walked right behind her. The priest said nothing to the urchin for the entire, miserable trip down the mountainside.

Ocryhoe's mind was racing as she tried to make sense of the news Raphael had given her. Fieschi had been enthroned as the Bishop of Rome? When had that happened? And if he was supposed to be overseeing Christendom, what was he doing hiding out as a mere priest on a frigid mountainside weeks away from Rome? She shivered, trying to ignore the obvious answer: He had come for her, or for the cup, or both. He had gone into hiding and risked his own well-being. He had entrusted the task to no other, not even one of Senator Orsini's men, not even to another cardinal. He had come himself. For her.

And now he had her.

Thank God, thank gods, thank goddesses, she did not have the cup with her. But he would torture her to try to get it. She did not think she would be very strong in the face of torture. Perhaps he would be clumsy at the torture and kill her accidentally. Then it would be over. Let Percival's visions tell him what to do with it next.

They arrived at the village, now an army camp despite her many lively memories of it as a bustling little hub of civil life and commerce. Ocyrhoe was marched off away from the other hostages, remaining with the archbishop's party all the way into the village green. Then Sinibaldo nodded curtly to His Eminence and went into a cottage on the nearer side of the green. Ocyrhoe's guard tugged at her rope, and with a sinking feeling she followed after.

They entered the main room of the cottage. It was in good form despite having been abandoned by its owners more than half a year ago. Over the tamped-dirt floor, tapestries had been laid down as rugs, leaving a wide space in the middle for the firepit. The walls were also hung with tapestries—where did they get all these tapestries in the middle of an army camp?

Without a word, Sinibaldo di Fieschi crossed the small room to the backless chair that was against the wall, sat in it, threw back his hood, and stared at her.

"Sit," he said, pointing to a stool. The guard picked her up and placed her standing just in front of the stool, then jabbed his knee into the back of hers. She collapsed onto the stool.

"I would have sat," she snapped up at him. "There was no need for that."

"Leave us," said the priest. His eyes roamed the room briefly. "Everyone," he said. "Absolutely everyone. She has no power to hurt me. Leave the building empty and wait outside." Then he settled his gaze on Ocyrhoe, who stared back defiantly, until they were entirely alone.

"Where is it?" he demanded as the door closed.

"I hear congratulations are in order," she said. "Bishop of Rome! Who would have thought it?"

He put his elbows on his thighs and leaned forward. "Where. Is. It."

"I don't have it."

"Who is Percival, really?"

She should have been expecting that, but wasn't. The alarm showed in her face. Then she made herself laugh. "That's a question I am not sure even Percival can answer," she said.

"I mean what is his real name."

"Percival," she said. "What else should it be?"

"His name is not really Percival," said His Holiness impatiently.

"Then you now more about him than I do. I only know him as Percival. His closest friends call him Percival. He wants to endear himself to me, so you'd think he'd tell me secrets if he had them. Why do you want Percival?"

"If you don't have the cup, he does."

She shook her head. "He doesn't."

"Then who has it?"

She forced her muscles to relax enough to pull off a shrug. "Someone else, apparently," she said.

"Tell me who."

"Why?" she asked, willing a tone of boredom into her voice.

"Because I will kill you if you don't," he said.

She gave him a droll look, ignoring how furiously her heart was beating. *Imagine Ferenc is watching you,* she thought. *Impress him. Delight him.* "If you kill me, you will never find out where it is."

"I'll make you wish you were dead."

"Too late. I already wish it."

"I am threatening to torture you."

"Yes, I got that. It won't help much. I really don't know where it is."

"Why are you so bent on keeping it from me?"

"Why are you so bent on getting it?" she shot back.

Father Sinibaldo began to answer, thought better of it, then sat back against the wall, considering. "If I tell you why I want it, will you tell me where it is?"

"I just told you, I don't know where it is. But I might be willing to help you find it, if I know why you want it." That was truthful enough. After years of her life being dominated by the cup, she felt entitled to understand why people made a fuss about it.

He crossed his arms and considered her for a long moment. "You are a Binder who did not complete your training."

She nodded.

"If you had done, there are things you would know that you do not know. Things that might explain my interest. So, I will tell you a few things. As much as you would know had you matured into a proper Binder."

Ocyrhoe bit back a laugh at the irony of being instructed in her Binder duties by the man who'd interrupted her instruction in the first place. "Go on, then," she said, astonished at her own impudent tone.

"There are forces in the world that oppose order," said Fieschi carefully. "And there are forces that struggle to maintain order. It is my humble duty, sitting as I do in St. Peter's chair, to lead the battle to preserve order."

"Oh, *that* kind of order," Ocyrhoe sniffed.

He ignored her tone. "Many subtle things happen below the ken of most men. There are ancient grudges and animosities that predate even Our Lord's appearance. And likewise there are alliances. And there are certain *energies* that assist in maintaining those alliances. Those energies are often embodied in objects. Or people. Or the coming together of an object with a person."

"As with Father Rodrigo and the cup."

"Yes," he said. "You know yourself how erratic and uncontrolled such energy is. It must be claimed, it must be *harnessed*, by those who have the training to do so."

"My Binder training would have taught me how to harness it?" she asked.

"No. But it would have taught you how to recognize those capable of harnessing it. It would have taught you how to assist them."

"And you think just because you manipulated a group of moronic, hypocritical cardinals into voting for you, that makes you qualified to harness this so-called energy?"

Fieshi's face darkened but he did not rise to the bait. "No, in fact," he said. "But perhaps Percival is qualified. And so it is in my interest, as the shepherd of the church, to ensure a good alliance between Percival and myself."

"So that you can coerce him into doing what want?"

"I can still torture you, you know," he warned her. "I am being very generous with my time and arcane knowledge. You do not deserve it, but I am being civil to you. Do not test me. What the grail can do, *specifically*, is beyond my present certainty. It needs a handler, so to speak. I thought you were a handler, but if you were, you would have done something with it by now—beyond merely convincing one soldier to desert the French army." Seeing her expression, he nodded. "Yes, that's how I knew to find you here. But if you were an agent of the grail, you would have done far more by now. Percival, I think, is an agent."

When Ocyrhoe realized she was nodding without meaning to, she stopped herself. She would not say it aloud, but he was right, of course.

"Rodrigo was such an agent," she said.

"That is why I wanted him," said Sinibaldo Fieschi. "If Frederick were wiser and saw as deeply into things as he likes people to believe he does, he would have recognized Rodrigo's usefulness and held on to him instead of sending him off into the wilds. So Frederick himself does not really understand the significance of these matters."

But Léna does, thought Ocyrhoe.

"But Léna does," he said.

"You've seen her more recently than I have," said Ocyrhoe. "She abandoned me to the wilderness. I have no truck with her."

"Perhaps, perhaps not," he said. "But she certainly keeps company with Frederick. And Frederick has friends within the Shield-Brethren. Whose membership includes Percival."

She shrugged. "So what is your point? Léna wants the grail? Then why did she send me into the wilderness when I was in possession of it?"

"She wanted you to meet up with Percival so that she could regain the grail once Percival was attached to it," concluded Pope Innocent. "It's more useful to her that way."

"She wants it for Frederick?"

"For the good of all of Christendom, I hope not," said His Holiness.

CHAPTER 37:

A CHALLENGE

For days the three of them watched, impotently, as the Good Ones doled out their meager, quotidian possessions—shawls, the occasional stylus or table knife, blank parchment for writing prayers—prayed with the Credents, and meditated before the simple images of Jesus upstairs in the chapel, while around them wounded men lay dying.

Raphael had grimly made his peace with the Good Ones' attitude. Vera and Percival could not. Vera simply fumed to herself, disgusted by the fatalism that everyone—even the soldiers of Montségur—cloaked themselves in so comfortably.

Percival was far more agitated, nerves almost fraying as he tried to reconcile himself to waiting for the cup. Each passing day, as the snow melted and the days lengthened, he sought out a different Good One to debate. There was no reason to die, he argued; there were plenty of other Cathar outposts around the countryside and in other countries—in the shadow of Emperor Frederick's court in Cremona, even. Surely the Good Ones here should be left in peace to join their brethren elsewhere, as long as it was not in the French king's realm.

"Surely as long as they promise not to allow their spiritual beliefs to be exploited by secular powers again," he said finally to Peire-Roger. The lord of Montségur looked at him wearily, insulted.

"Is that what you perceive I have done here? I have exploited the spiritual beliefs of others to my own political advantage?" He gestured with weary irritation around the keep. "What advantage is there in this? I used to be lord of an actual castle, with a mansion to live in, and gardens and vineyards and fountains and featherbeds. There are other Occitanian lords who still have those things, because they would not risk losing them in order to protect their own people. For years now I have been trying to keep my father-in-law's desperate outpost as a functioning refuge for the persecuted minority of my people. I don't even believe in what they believe—do you know that? My father took the consolamentum on his deathbed, but I myself am no Credent. I think they're mad to believe what they do. In the world we live in now, to be pacifists? In a land as beautiful and plentiful as ours, to claim that the material world is pure evil, and that we who love the smell of lavender or the taste of good wine are indulging in the devil's work? It's nonsense. Every bit of it is nonsense. And yet," he concluded fiercely, "the people who believe this nonsense are *my people*. I am their lord and I'm responsible for them."

Percival was startled by the clear-eyed vigor of a man who had for months seemed composed mostly of blunder and booze.

"Then would you not save them, if you could?" he asked.

Peire-Roger looked deeply insulted. "I just spent the past eight months trying to save them. I failed."

"I have a notion," said Percival. "If you will allow me to pursue it, I believe it will save the Good Ones from unnecessary martyrdom."

✦ ✦ ✦

Innocent did not torture her. In fact, he offered her a chilly sort of kindness. He kept her tethered in a corner of the house where he was residing, and she was watched ceaselessly by Dietrich's men, but she was nesting on a featherbed and given warm, new stockings, a newly sewn, long tunic of heavy silk, and a warm, new mantle. For a brief span in the morning and again in the evening, she was allowed out into the cool, March air—always tethered—for exercise. It crushed her spirit to see the beautiful little village converted to a military camp. The paddock for the horses was now a training ring for knights; by design or coincidence, her daily walks took her by here when the German knight, Dietrich, was fighting somebody each day. She became familiar with his style. Somehow the way he executed his moves fit his personality—angry, arrogant, cold. Although she had seen them all in battle, she could not imagine any of her new acquaintances—except perhaps Vera—engaging in such exercise by choice. She was not sure what kind of duelist Raphael would make; considered, cautious, and particular, most likely. But Percival? That she could not conceive at all, although she had seen him in the skirmishes outside the barbican, but always in passing, briefly. In her imagination he was more visionary monk than warrior.

The rest of the time she remained tied loosely to the corner of the room. Her wounded arm was cared for, the bandage changed each day until it was no longer necessary. Sinibaldo offered her potions to numb the discomfort; she refused these. He offered her his own rations of wine; these too she refused, accepting only water and asking for bread.

He deprived her of food, though. After a few days she wore a dreamy, docile look. Then he made his move.

He sent all of his men from the cottage, and placed a low stool near her corner. In his priest's robes, he gazed at her as she lay quietly on the featherbed. His hawklike stare was gentler than usual. "Here we are, little one. You and I."

She looked at the wall.

"Do you know why I really asked for you instead of Percival?"

She did not acknowledge him.

"Ocyrhoe." She did not respond. He repeated her name three times, pausing between, without raising his voice, although the tone sharpened slightly. Finally her eyes turned to look at him. "Give me your oath you will help me get the grail. Bind yourself to me as Léna has bound herself to Frederick, and I will override every rule of army rationing that you may fill your belly as often as you like."

A long pause. Finally Ocyrhoe said, "Léna has broken the rules of the sisterhood in her allegiance to Frederick."

He gave her a knowing look. "You are already estranged from the sisterhood. Why not align yourself with the most powerful man alive, who will value your assistance beyond rubies?"

Another pause.

"I'm hungry," she said quietly. "Feed me first, and when I am clearheaded we'll discuss it."

After more than a week she was in a twilight stupor for want of nourishment, but no more willing to compromise. He had gruel brought to her and then, a few days later, bread and dried meat. Accustomed to the diet of the Cathars, she would not eat the meat.

She was not sure how she passed the time each day, but somehow each day passed. He gave her several days to regain some strength with food. Then he sent his entourage away again and spoke to her as if to an intimate friend. He explained, earnestly but calmly, his mission to preserve the order of the world against the hubris of the Mongols, the Emperor, the Infidels, the heresy of the Eastern Church. He spoke of the nobility of serving a cause greater than oneself.

"You and I together, with the cup," he said. "Perhaps as you mature you could learn to control it. We could steer the fate of the world."

She regarded him a moment. She stuck her lower lip out thoughtfully, then nodded. "Yes," she agreed. "Perhaps we could."

She saw the gleam in his eye, saw him repress the urge to smile triumphantly.

"Shall we?" he said softly. "Not many homeless orphans get that chance."

Ocyrhoe smiled very slightly and gave him a knowing look.

Then she spat in his face.

Sinibaldo di Fieschi was impassive as he rose and walked out of the cottage. A moment later, Dietrich entered, grimacing. Without a word he grabbed a tattered, woolen sleeping roll from the opposite corner and chucked it so hard at Ocyrhoe it almost knocked her over.

"Stand up," he said.

She did.

He leaned down and grabbed the featherbed she had been sleeping in. "Stupid girl," he said, disgusted. "Refusing him. Stupid little witch-spy."

He pushed her down onto the tattered bedroll, dropped the featherbed on the far side of the room, and left her alone in the cottage. That evening she was given back her ragged clothes from Montségur. Sinibaldo di Fieschi did not speak to her again.

Surely the two weeks was almost up. She would be released then, and she would collect the grail from Rixenda and get far away from here before Sinibaldo di Fieschi could get his hands on her. She agreed that Percival might be an agent for the grail, but that only made her doubt the wisdom of his having it. He certainly would not work with Sinibaldo Fieschi, but with whom *would* he work? She did not trust his judgment.

She thought perhaps twelve days had passed, but she was not sure. His Holiness, still dressed as a priest, was in the hut, eating dinner with Dietrich and the other Livonian knights. The smell of the meat sickened her stomach; she had accepted only bread dipped in olive oil.

There was a quick rap on the door; one of Dietrich's men unbolted it to reveal Hugue de Arcis and His Eminence the Archbishop of Narbonne standing at the threshold. Their retainers were clustered behind them, an ensemble too large to fit into the room.

"Just the two of you," said Innocent, without pausing in his eating. Hugue and the archbishop had given up pretending they were in charge when in Innocent's presence; his casual air of mastery made each of them seem foolish when they attempted to behave as if he were subservient to them.

The two men stepped into the room, furs and wools clutched about them as if it were still deep winter. Dietrich and the other knights stopped eating.

"We have received an interesting proposal from the fortress," said Hugue.

"It is not interesting, Your Holiness," corrected the archbishop. "It is absurd. It should be dismissed out of hand."

"His Holiness has requested that we confer with him before taking action of any sort," said Hugue to Pierre Amelii. "If he agrees with Your Eminence that it should be dismissed, of course it will be. But it involves the knight he once had an interest in, and that, I think, is not nothing."

Innocent put his knife down on the trencher and stopped chewing for a moment to ask. "Percival?" he asked.

Hugue nodded, and waved a scroll. "He has proposed to myself and the archbishop that the Perfecti be allowed to go free provided they leave Occitania forever and never return, and never attempt to stir up trouble for His Majesty."

"That does not address the matter of their heresy," argued the archbishop. "That would not contain the heresy; it would *spread* it."

"There's only about a hundred, two hundred, of them up there," said Hugue, relishing the opportunity to speak in a patronizing tone to a man who had treated him like an inferior for months now. "How much damage can they do? There are already hundreds more like them throughout Christendom." He returned his attention to Innocent. "If there is a way to end this debacle without making martyrs of anyone, I am in favor of it. Burning beloved members of a society is a terrible way to bring that society to heel. If we can offer amnesty to all of them, to every living soul up there, I tell you, after decades of slaughter, we will be worshipped for our mercy. The armed rebels will lose their right to call us butchers. True peace might come, and I can rest easy in my bed as I have never done since His Majesty made me lord of Carcassonne. I think we should accept his offer."

"Offer?" said Innocent. "What is he offering us?"

"He does not expect to simply reverse our position on the Perfecti. He acknowledges that such clemency must be earned. He offers to earn it on their behalf."

Innocent sat up very straight. Even Ocyrhoe, wrapped in a ratty blanket in the corner, sat up straight.

"How does he propose to do that?" asked Innocent.

"In the standard, primitive way that men of his background make such offers," said the archbishop with disgust.

"It is grandiose and symbolic, but sincere," Hugue spoke over him. "He says he will duel with any man in my army. If he wins, the Perfecti go free. If he loses, things keep as they are."

"I will do that!" Dietrich said hungrily, almost before Hugue had finished the statement.

Fieschi's heightened alertness relaxed. "Calm yourself, Dietrich. That is not enough," he said to Hugue. "We require more for this to be acceptable."

"The entire premise is unacceptable," the archbishop nearly bellowed. "To allow the heretic leaders to go free makes a mockery of this entire crusade."

"As I told you when I arrived," said Innocent sternly, "this crusade is not the most important thing at stake here. It is a pond, while I am trying to navigate an ocean. Do you understand?" He turned to Hugue. "Send back word that we will accept this offer as long as it is amended to include the grail. Whoever wins the duel wins possession of the grail."

"He will never agree to that," said Ocyrhoe from the corner, in a voice of almost amused disgust.

Innocent ignored her. "Send that message and sign it with both your signets." He looked warningly at the archbishop.

"He can't agree to it," said Ocyrhoe, a little nervous now. "The cup is not in his possession. It's not his to offer up."

"Who has it?" Innocent asked.

Ocyrhoe immediately lowered her eyes to the earthen floor and folded her hands on her lap. She pulled the blanket tighter round her narrow shoulders and set her jaw.

"Ocyrhoe," said His Holiness. "If you have friends among the Perfecti whom you would see survive, assist me now. Possession of the cup is a condition of the duel. Without the duel, your Cathar friends will be burned at the stake in two days' time. If there is a duel, they might be saved. Given that, you should *want* this duel to proceed."

"That's true," said Ocyrhoe, unhappily.

"By extension, that means you must want the cup to be on the table, as it were. You are claiming that's not possible. Tell us how to make it possible. Is somebody up there holding it in reserve, in secret, for you?"

Ocyrhoe blinked in surprise before she could control herself.

"I thought as much," said Innocent. "So with our response to this challenge you must also send word to that individual, telling them to release the cup."

Ocyrhoe bit her lower lip and glanced down into her lap again. Why was she fated never to escape responsibility for what happened to that infuriating piece of metal? It had been such a relief these past few weeks for it to rest in limbo with Rixenda.

Watching in the camp over the past few days, she knew already that Dietrich von Grüningen would be the chosen champion of the French army. He unarmed every opponent regardless of their weapon. In a duel between Percival and Dietrich, she had no idea who would survive. Putting the cup in Pope Innocent's grasp was an alarming prospect, but if she risked it Rixenda and the others might be spared a gruesome, pointless death.

"I will send such a message willingly," she said. "But Percival will never agree to the terms."

The response was drafted, a messenger was sent up the mountain, and Innocent resumed dining.

Ocyrhoe curled up in the corner and slept. Her dreams were troubled. In them, Raphael, Rixenda, and everybody else— Peire-Roger, Vera, even Ferenc, even Léna, even kindly Father Somercotes, who had died in Rome at the hands of Cardinal Fieschi; even Father Rodrigo—*everyone* interpreted her message to mean that she had joined forces with Sinibaldo Fieschi, Pope Innocent IV. That she was conspiring with him for his possession of the cup.

◆ ◆ ◆

In the dim of the keep, Peire-Roger pushed the message across the trestle table toward Raphael and Vera. At Raphael's request, Percival had not been told yet that an answer had arrived. Seeing the answer, he was very glad he'd issued the request. "This is quite a remarkable bit of scribbling," Peire-Roger said. "It requires not only my cooperation but Rixenda's."

"I will not cooperate," said Rixenda, her broad, motherly face looking pained.

"You have often said the cup is Ocyrhoe's, and that Ocyrhoe has the right to determine its fate," argued Raphael. "Ocyrhoe is formally offering it to the winner of the duel. Why would you hesitate to honor that?"

"The whole point of Percival's proposed duel is that we are to be preserved by his murdering another man," said Bishop Marti sharply. "That goes against our principles."

"He will be saving your lives," said Vera rebukingly.

"At a price too high for us to accept," said Rixenda. "Nobody further should suffer because of us, regardless of whose side they belong to. There has been too much suffering of innocents already."

Irritated, Vera tapped the piece of velum. "Your friend Ocyrhoe has said in writing, right here, that the cup should be brought out of hiding."

"That could be coerced," said Rixenda. "She has so deftly kept the thing a secret for years. Why should she suddenly agree to place it in plain sight?"

"To save her friends' lives, of course," said Raphael, exasperated. "You show disrespect not only for her request but for her very nature if you do not acknowledge her instructions in this matter."

Rixenda pursed her lips and lowered her eyes.

"Do not be swayed by sentimentality," warned the bishop.

Rixenda shook her head. "As long as we are trapped on this plain, Your Eminence, there are few things holier than bonds of loving loyalty. Our visitors are correct in this: Ocyrhoe trusts me to honor her request, and I would be betraying her not to do so." Her wide, blue eyes looked up at Raphael from her weathered face. "By Ocyrhoe's request, the cup may go to the winner of this duel."

❖ ❖ ❖

Ocyrhoe was awakened from vague, troubled, afternoon dreams by a most peculiar sound: an excited chortle, coming from the door.

"The terms are accepted!" said Dietrich von Grüningen's voice. "I fight him tomorrow!"

Ocyrhoe assumed she was still sleeping, until she heard Cardinal Fieschi's voice reply, with equally unwonted glee, "God be praised! See that the little wretch is bathed and given back those nice clothes we had made for her."

She opened her eyes and looked into the middle of the room. Pope Innocent, beaming with an excitement she could never have imagined, was reading a message over Dietrich's broad shoulder in a shaft of sunlight that poured through the open door.

"If you kill him, you've lost your *agent*," she pointed out. "The cup is nothing without a madman to be possessed by it."

"We won't kill him," Innocent said.

Dietrich looked disappointed.

"Wound him," His Holiness instructed. "Very badly. Render him useless as a warrior forever. But do not take his life. Spare his life at the last moment, magnanimously, and claim the grail as your prize. Once we have the grail, we will have Percival. He will tag along behind it, wherever it goes and whoever goes with it. And if he doesn't, the cup will summon someone else."

Dietrich grimaced. "I hope Your Holiness realizes what a sacrifice you ask of me."

"Get over your petty rivalries, Dietrich," said the Pope, a gleam in his eyes. "You are about to become a Knight of the Grail. Peevishness does not become you." He slapped the German companionably on the shoulder, beaming with such pleasure Ocyrhoe almost did not recognize him. "Ha! But this is wonderful."

"The archbishop might not think so," Ocyrhoe commented drily from the corner.

"The archbishop," said the priest, "will not be told."

◆ ◆ ◆

The following day was mild for the time of year. The sky was a brilliant blue, the air unusually still on the mountaintop. The ground was soft and moist to the step, the limestone slick with damp. Ocyrhoe was given back the new clothes to wear. She was left alone to change, and then her hands were bound loosely before her and she was led out of the house into the square. Here, the other hostages were already standing, also with hands bound. They nodded solemnly to her, and she to them. She felt relief flooding over her to see them. This was, thank God, almost over.

Father Sinibaldo and two groups of knights joined them: the Livonians who lodged with Father Sinibaldo, and Hugue de Arcis and his men, wearing the colors of Carcassonne. They all began to walk the main pathway to the fortress, up the southwest flank of the mountain, past mounds of gorse and scrub. Ocyrhoe was glad to leave the hideously transformed village after so many days cooped up in one small corner of it.

A few hundred paces up was an expanse of relatively level ground, almost a small field, that bulged out of the side of the pog. During Ocyrhoe's confinement, the French had built a wooden pen here, with a broad, wooden stepladder straddling the southern side. The walls were too high to view what was within; she could see only the tops of stakes, dozens of them, placed in rows. As they walked past it, soldiers were hauling bundles of straw, twigs, and branches up the ladder, and dropping them below.

"Oh, God," she said aloud, realizing. She clapped her hand over her mouth to keep a sob from escaping.

"Yes," said Dietrich smugly. "That is where your heretic friends will find their way to hell tomorrow at dawn."

"Unless Percival wins the duel," Ocyrhoe said hurriedly. "Then you've built it for nothing. That's right, isn't it?" she said, turning plaintively toward the Holy Father. "In that case they've built it for nothing."

"They won't have built it for nothing," said Dietrich. "Those heretics are dying in the morning. His Holiness should have staked even more upon the outcome."

"I have staked enough," said Father Sinibaldo. "In a sense, I have staked everything."

CHAPTER 38:

OFFERING TERMS

Percival had been told by Raphael only that his challenge had been accepted. He'd spent the day before the duel sparring with any knight on the mountaintop able and willing.

The civilians and soldiers of the fortress were gathered in the courtyard awaiting the party from the French camp. With light blankets and mantles wrapped around them, most of the Credents clustered on the southern side of the courtyard, facing the donjon, for the ritual that was to come. The Good Ones, in contrast, were inside the keep, up in the chapel, meditating. That had clearly stated their disapproval of the duel.

"I won't kill him," Percival assured Peire-Roger. "I will disarm him without hurting him and demand his concession."

"It's still violence. Violence and coercion. They do not want their lives ransomed at so high a price."

Handsome Percival frowned with dismay. "A knight's destiny is only to protect the innocent, not to be appreciated by them for it."

A trumpet sounded. Ferrer opened the western gate. Into the courtyard stepped a small, grim group: Surrounded by guards were Hugue, his soldiers, and most of the hostages.

"Where is Ocyrhoe?" Raphael muttered unhappily.

After a moment, a second, smaller group entered the courtyard: the so-called priest, Dietrich von Grüningen, with his fellow Livonians and the Roman orphan girl.

Peire-Roger stood at attention across the center of the courtyard. His father-in-law and the other hostages stared back at him. The space separating them was no more than twenty strides across, but it reflected an unfathomable gulf.

"As you see," said Hugue, "Here are our hostages, well treated and well behaved. Tomorrow morning they will be returned to you, but for this hour you may have their presence. It seemed cruel to come up here to see you and not bring them along."

"More cruel to let us see them only and then be forced to part with them again," said Peire-Roger gruffly. "But thank you enough for it."

Percival felt sorry for Ocyrhoe, whom nobody was particularly emotional about seeing. Her downcast expression made it hard to sense her state of mind.

Percival stepped forward. "I am Percival of the *Ordo Militum Vindicis Intactae*, and with the blessing of Peire-Roger de Mirepoix of Montségur I have challenged you, Hugue de Arcis of Carcassonne, to a duel to the death for the sake of the lives of the Good Ones of Montségur."

Hugue stepped forward across from him. "I have accepted your challenge, and my champion, Dietrich von Grüningen of the Livonian Brothers of the Sword, shall fight on my behalf." Dietrich stepped forward beside Hugue.

"Recite the terms of the duel," Peire-Roger said over his shoulder. Raphael on cue stepped stoically into the no-man's-land between the two swordsmen.

"Sirs," said Raphael. "The terms of the duel are these. You will each fight with a longsword and a dagger. You will have no armor but a helm."

"I forgo the helm," said Percival. "But I do not begrudge my honored opponent to wear his."

Dietrich gave him a scornful look and said nothing.

Raphael pushed on, eager to conclude. "In the event of a win by Percival of the *Ordo Militum Vindicis Intactae* you will release all residents of Montségur to freedom, Good Ones included, provided they remove themselves permanently from lands held by His Majesty the King of France. In the event of a win by Dietrich von Grüningen of the Livonian Order, the Good Ones who do not forswear their religious beliefs today will be burned en masse at the foot of this mountain at dawn tomorrow, and the cup come to be called the grail will be relinquished by the people of Montségur to the French army, to be dispersed as Hugue de Arcis sees fit."

Percival whirled around to stare at him, alarm on his face. Raphael ignored him and continued to speak. "Once the duel has begun..."

"*What?*" said Percival in a shocked whisper.

"You heard him," growled Vera, who was close, through gritted teeth.

"But—"

She glared at him. "If you are killed, the damn cup is no use to you," she whispered fiercely. "The rest of us have no love for it."

Percival grimaced. It was the first time Ocyrhoe had ever seen him angry.

Raphael pushed on: "Once the fight has begun, there is to be no interruption nor assistance from anyone on either side. The fight will end when one of the combatants is dead, too wounded to move, or acknowledges defeat, which amounts to conceding their impending death. If there are any here who oppose these terms, speak now or hold your peace hereafter."

Percival wanted to object, but Raphael and Vera gave him warning expressions.

"Where is the cup?" demanded the priest. "It should be placed somewhere neutral, where it can be seen by all, so that there is no question of its whereabouts."

"Get Rixenda," Raphael said quietly to Vera. "If she'll come. She said she'd be here." As Vera jogged toward the keep, Raphael turned his attention to Father Sinibaldo. "Release your hostage in the meanwhile, good Father."

"The hostages are released tomorrow," he retorted. "When the fortress is emptied. You may have her then. It is an indulgence to her that we have brought her to witness this today."

Raphael gave Ocyrhoe a sympathetic grimace from across the yard. She lifted her shoulders and dropped them in return, enervated.

For a long moment, people waited, shifting their weight and stamping their feet against the cold. Finally Vera and Rixenda exited the donjon and came down the steps, arm in arm—an unusual gesture for either woman. They crossed the courtyard to the dueling circle, and Vera led Rixenda to a spot where the limestone of the mountain caused a natural bulge in the uneven courtyard floor. As the assembly watched, Rixenda opened her arms to reveal a small packet wrapped in undyed wool, standing in sharp contrast against the black of her robe.

She unwrapped the contents slowly. Eyes were riveted. Percival in particular was rapt. The final layer of wool came away in Rixenda's hand. Nestled against the dull wool was an equally dull silver cup with a broad band of fine but simple chasework at the rim. Ocyrhoe felt her heart leap, a mix of pleasure and dread, seeing it again for the first time in weeks. As if it were a friend she had abandoned somewhere, she had a visceral impulse to run to it and embrace it. Knowing Father Sinibaldo would stop her, she restrained herself and simply stared at it. As she watched, it began to glow with that same rosy light she was used to. She forced herself to look away from it and around at the assembly.

None of the Montségurians seemed to notice the glow. Neither did Vera, nor Hugue de Arcis. Raphael frowned a little, as if he noticed something strange but could not make out what it was. The Archbishop of Narbonne had a similar expression. Dietrich's eyes widened as she watched, however; His Holiness's gaze took on the hungry, scheming look she remembered too well from that horrific week in Rome.

And Percival. For the first time, Percival was setting eyes upon the grail that had called to him in its mysterious ways for years. His face glowed like a small child seeing a magician at work or an infant being reunited with its mother. In the purity of his expression, in the simple, golden joy that he exuded, Ocyrhoe felt herself dirty and unworthy of the cup. That she could ever have doubted it belonged to Percival was a gross error on her part. As if it sensed the presence of its intended, the cup's rosy glow increased until it was almost blinding to look at. The majority of people in the courtyard glanced at it indifferently and then away. They saw nothing. The map of their faith had nothing in its legend for such a thing.

CHAPTER 39:

THE FOOL'S GUARD

Percival stood ready, the tip of sword resting against the ground in front of him. To an untrained eye, he appeared unprepared to fight, but he suspected his opponent knew otherwise. Dietrich stood opposite, his hands wrapped around the hilt of his sword, the blade resting lightly against his right shoulder. Equally ready for combat.

They surveyed each other for a moment, each willing the other to make the first move. Each of them had his left leg slightly forward, inviting an attack from the other that both of them knew would be easy to deflect.

After a few moments of intense silence and scrutiny, Dietrich raised his sword from his shoulder and swung wide, a cut to the outside of Percival's left leg. Percival moved his sword-point down across his body to parry the blow. Both of these moves had been to test the other, to sense how quickly and assertively the other could move. Percival, to let Dietrich know he was adroit, suddenly pivoted his wrists, flipping his sword in a flourish; he tapped the opposite side of Dietrich's blade hard enough to slap the German's sword back toward his body. The Credents chuckled happily. Dietrich glared at him.

The two men moved their swords to guard positions in front of them and slowly began to circle around the space. Neither wanted the sun in his face, so they kept pivoting until they were standing on an east-west axis, the slanting winter sun lighting them from the side.

Dietrich returned to resting-on-the-shoulder guard. Percival held his sword overhead facing Dietrich, his gloved left hand holding the forte of the sword. For another long moment, neither moved.

Then Dietrich stepped in and swung as if to cut Percival's left shoulder; Percival, keeping his upraised left hand still as a fulcrum, lowered his hilt to block the blow—then realizing it was a feint, shifted his guard across his body to prevent Dietrich's actual cut to his right shoulder. As all the Livonian's weight came barreling at him, Percival steeled himself for a strong parry, planting his center of gravity so low he was almost squatting, and slammed his forte into Dietrich's crossguard until the two swords were hilt to hilt. To avoid toppling back, he pushed himself forward into Dietrich and began to run, shoving the German knight backwards. The small crowd behind Dietrich leapt out of the way, several of them slipping in the thawed mud.

Dietrich collected himself before he stumbled and began to retreat faster than Percival was coming at him. In the space created between the two of them, Percival tried his first attack, coming around in a midriff cut to the German's left. Dietrich leapt back out of danger. "Ha!" he snapped at Percival, his pride still wounded from Percival's earlier flourish.

The force of Percival's swing carried his blade all the way left, and Percival himself followed its momentum, bringing the sword over his body so that he could slice it down towards Dietrich's crown. Dietrich raised his own sword horizontally above his head, supporting the forte with his left hand. Percival's blow landed between Dietrich's two hands, and again the fortes of each sword slid so that the crossguards rammed against each other.

Dietrich, with his hands on either side of the locked crossguards, had leverage Percival lacked. He was in control now. Slowly, his helmeted face staring into Percival's bare one, he lowered his arms with deliberate slowness, pulling Percival's sword down, too, so that the weapons descended between their faces, the staring men inhaling each other's heavy breaths. Percival did not resist, saving his strength to see what Dietrich intended next.

Dietrich lowered the blades to throat level. Then chest. Percival, his hands couched together on his pommel, which was being pressed down against his sternum, gazed calmly into Dietrich's fevered stare, refusing to waste energy in this position. He knew Dietrich would not keep them here long.

The German took a huge breath, then squatted and began to press Percival backwards—not quickly, as Percival had done to Dietrich a moment earlier, but with an earthbound heaviness that would land Percival helplessly on his ass if he could not disconnect.

Percival jumped back and turned his own left shoulder, deliberately leaving his right flank vulnerable, encouraging Dietrich to strike. Dietrich used his forward momentum to swing at Percival's flank, but the Shield-Brethren knight continued to spin left in a complete circle; his parry smacked Dietrich's sword hard away, and Percival continued into a second spin, raising his sword. Dietrich staggered to recover from the parry; he followed the blade in the direction it had been struck and raised the blade high to intercept Percival's shoulder cut. The two swords clanged loudly together at head-height, fortes into crossguards.

Percival, seeing an opportunity for a bind, released his left hand off the pommel. He reached underneath Dietrich's right hand as he stepped in behind Dietrich and slammed his left palm down on the crossed hilts. With a push, he forced the crossed swords downward, with his on top. He saw Dietrich's elbow jerking quickly back towards his face, but before the German could hit him Percival drove his left knee into the back of Dietrich's right one, collapsing it to the ground. Dietrich stumbled forward, dropping his sword to catch himself from falling face-first, and Percival moved both his hands again to the pommel of his sword.

He was just behind and to the right of Dietrich. It would take a simple, upward swing to decapitate the German. In that fraction of a moment, which seemed to stretch forever, he realized that Dietrich knew this, too. So did everyone watching. For the length of a heartbeat every person in the courtyard prepared himself to witness death.

Percival was about to strike the blow when the images of Bishop Marti, Rixenda, and the other Good Ones flashed through his mind, and a wash of regret came over him.

He had to end this duel without a death.

He shifted the angle of his wrist so that the flat of the blade, not the edge, faced Dietrich's neck. He raised the tip of his sword a few degrees. And then, instead of slicing his opponent's head off, he smacked the side of Dietrich's helm as hard as he could, sending the Livonian dazed and sprawling upon his face in the half-frozen muck.

There was a gasp of surprise from the onlookers, who had started to flee the anticipated splattered gore. Then, for a moment, silence and stillness.

Dietrich groaned and moved slightly. Percival pointed his sword at him, so that when the Livonian finally dragged himself from prone to supine, he found himself staring at the tip of the sword.

"Do you yield?" Percival demanded.

Dietrich stared at the tip, then up at Percival, then again at the tip of sword, looking dazed.

"Do you yield?" Percival repeated.

Dietrich held up both hands. His face behind the helm was unreadable. Percival smiled broadly, lowered his blade, and acknowledged the gawkers. He triumphantly plunged the tip of his sword into the dirt, then held up his arms and turned. He saw the grail on its rocky outcrop, and gratitude coursed through him.

"By the blessing of the Holy Virgin," he declared. "The grail—"

"Percival, behind you!" Raphael shouted. Percival turned back toward his opponent.

Despite his dazed state, Dietrich was very strong; he had pushed himself up onto both knees, then both legs, and he now grabbed Percival's sword hilt with both hands, yanking the blade out of the ground. He swung it around in a powerful but unsteady arc, meaning to slice through Percival's unarmored neck. Were he not dizzy he might have succeeded, but instead he repeated the blow with which Percival had just felled him, smashing Percival's head hard with the flat of blade. The blow knocked Percival on his face, where he lay suddenly inert and silent as the crowd around them shouted with surprise.

Dietrich, wobbly, fell to his knees again and dropped the sword, steadying himself with his right hand. But he groped for and then grabbed his dagger out of his belt with his left hand, and rose again. As he launched himself at Percival in a low lunge, Raphael yelled angrily and leapt in to block him, trying to get control of the German's dagger-hand. He grabbed the outside of Dietrich's left hand with his own right hand; the flat of his left hand slid up Dietrich's inner arm to his elbow, chopping at the ligaments so that Dietrich's arm reflexively bent inward while his ring and pinkie fingers curled tight around the dagger. By continuing to lunge at Raphael, he was propelling his own throat toward his dagger.

On instinct, Raphael's hand controlled the direction the dagger pointed. Both men saw the moment coming too quickly to prevent it: Guided by Raphael's hand, Dietrich impaled himself through the throat on his own blade. Blood spurted from his neck across Raphael's face, into his mouth and eyes, warm and metallic.

They were very close together. Even with Dietrich's helm on, Raphael could read the German's face as he registered surprise, shock, fury, fear, and finally, resignation. He coughed blood, shuddered, and went limp in Raphael's arms.

Raphael grabbed Dietrich's shoulder and gently lowered the body backward, cradling it so that it would not fall against the ground too hard. When the corpse was resting face-up on the courtyard floor, Raphael released it and stood up. For a moment, he could not remember why he had just killed this man.

CHAPTER 40:

CROSS PURPOSES

Raphael knelt at once over Percival's still form and began gently to palpate his head and neck. Vera moved to kneel beside him. Peire-Roger glanced at them worriedly, then turned his attention to the muttering crowd.

"All shall go free!" he called to the assembled Credents. "All the Good Ones! Tell them so!"

Artal howled with delighted approval, broke away from the group, and ran toward the keep. Everyone cheered and turned to watch him as he ran, until a commotion distracted the collected attention.

The heavy main gate was yanked open without Ferrer's assistance; a dozen well-appointed guards flanked a furious Pierre Amelii, Archbishop of Narbonne, weighted down by all his ecclesial finery as he strode into the yard, gasping to collect his breath from the hurried climb.

"Cease this mischief!" his raspy voice called out. "There shall be no pardon for the wicked!" Artal ignored him and kept running. The archbishop took a moment to get his breath before pressing on, enraged, to inform all present, "An agent of His Holiness condoned the pardon of the arch-heretics, but the agent himself is merely a priest, and I outrank him. As the shepherd whose flock has been infected with these dangerous heresies, I declare that mortal combat such as this cannot save souls, and must not pretend to." He glanced about, saw the Pope, and gave him a challenging look, daring to see if he would reveal his identity in public. Father Sinibaldo ignored him.

"You should have laid down that decree before one of your men lost his life over it," said Raphael harshly, glancing up from Percival's unmoving form as he wiped Dietrich's blood from his own face. "You have no right to step in now and gainsay what has been earned."

"I would have, had I been here!" the archbishop roared. "I was tricked and distracted by some mischief-maker in the half-heathen ranks of this God-forsaken farce of an army. Some scoundrel, some secret sympathizer, led me on a chase through half the camp claiming that the Good Ones had come down of their own accord this morning to repent and receive penance from me. Of course I would have been here otherwise!"

Ocyrhoe pursed her lips, blushing from the impulse to speak. Many men in that camp could have pulled such a prank, purely out of spite, angry from having been obliged to spend their winter in this ridiculous siege. But Ocyrhoe knew who had actually done it, although until this moment she had not understood the purpose. The Bishop of Rome himself was the culprit. Knowing the archbishop would object, and knowing his objection would result in the fight's cancellation, His Holiness had made sure the archbishop would be otherwise engaged.

"But I have arrived now!" His Eminence was continuing to shriek. "I condemn this action, and the Church, as represented and symbolized *in me*, shall not abide by the decision of secular lords! I shall prevent it!"

"You and what army?" sneered Peire-Roger with a mocking gesture. "Your own general has agreed to abide by the terms of this duel."

Hugue de Arcis frowned. "My champion was just killed by someone other than his sanctioned opponent. To me that invalidates the duel in all its terms."

"Our brother, our *Heermeister*, has just fallen in a duel of honor," one of the Livonian knights argued to Hugue. "It would besmirch the depth of his sacrifice if the terms of the duel are not upheld. The Cathar Perfecti have won the right to live, and we are honor-bound to defend that right, however much we despise it."

"Excellent!" shouted Peire-Roger with fierce sarcasm, punching the air. "Go to it, fellows! Nothing will bring me greater joy than to see my vanquishing enemies vanquish themselves with internal squabbles! Shall we clear the yard that you may all exterminate each other?"

"Not only will the rest of the army destroy all of you," warned the archbishop, "but I will excommunicate you and all of your men if you make any effort to protect these spawn of Satan. The Perfecti burn tomorrow. I do not care what specious spectacles have been staged in the meantime."

"You can't do that!" Peire-Roger shouted angrily. "It was an authorized duel."

"It was not authorized by me," Pierre of Amelii shouted back, enraged. "I am the only person here with the authority to pardon them, and I do not!"

"Besides, it ceased to be authorized when a second knight stepped in," Hugue argued.

"But it did not, sir!" shouted one of his own lieutenants. "The duel was concluded before that happened. His life was already accounted forfeit!"

The huddled Credents in the yard had been growing increasingly agitated during this exchange, and now they began to shout back, agreeing to this argument. Raphael tried to speak to the archbishop but his voice did not carry over the growing hubbub.

The somber Livonian knights turned defensively to face the Narbonnese soldiers; every armed man put his right hand on the hilt of his sword, and suddenly it seemed the two groups would indeed come to blows. A few of the Credents fled for the safety of the keep. But the Montségur knights and soldiers flanked the Livonians—their enemies until moments ago—to face off against the archbishop's men. Peire Roger actually stood beside the Livonians, glaring at the men across from him. Hugue de Arcis looked with alarm between the two factions, as his own men turned to him.

The Montségurians, pushed beyond their limit by recent events, began to shout and threaten the archbishop's men. Raphael, looking away from Percival, realized that unlike the crusading soldiers—who wanted desperately to keep the peace, despite their disagreements—the men of Montségur were spoiling for a fight. They were the ones who most needed to be contained. Percival lay unconscious, but his breathing was regular and nothing in his neck felt out of place, although the muscles on one side were clenched. "Stay with him," he murmured to Vera. "I'll deal with this."

Seldom in Raphael's life had he faced such a maddening cacophony of cross-purposes–violence erupting among people who did not really disagree, transient alliances between mortal enemies. There was too much anger and disgruntlement roiling the courtyard. Peire-Roger did not care what Bishop Marti said; he was still so furious about what his people had been subjected to for so long, he would have bitten Hugue de Arcis's head off could he have gotten close enough. The Livonians, outraged by their leader's death but even more outraged that the purpose of it was belittled, glowered as if they were hoping someone, anyone, would give them the excuse to draw. The Credents who had remained in the courtyard were still the most dangerous men there; ignoring their own bishop's words, they were fixated in their wrath on the gainsaying archbishop, the French king's toady. Somebody would snap, and chaos would break out at any moment.

The only person Raphael could think of with the presence to quell the danger was the one man who was most loath to draw attention to himself: Father Sinibaldo Fieschi. Pope Innocent IV. Raphael began to walk toward him.

✦ ✦ ✦

Ocyrhoe had watched the entire duel with her hands still bound loosely before her. As Dietrich fell, the dismayed Livonian holding the rope forgot about her and let go her tether, but she could not actually release her wrists from bondage. As the disorder in the courtyard grew louder, she put all her attention into trying to untie the knot that kept her hands held tight together. It was awkward and obvious; she turned away from the Livonians and Father Sinibaldo to shield her attempts from view, but her efforts were abysmal; her fingers could barely curl tightly enough to even touch the knot, let alone untie it. She tried bringing it to her mouth, working the rough, hempen cord with one hand while pulling it in the other direction with her teeth. That loosened something but she could not make out what it was because it was too close to see. She released it from her teeth, but when she lowered her hands her fingers jerked involuntarily and retightened what she had just loosened. With a growl of frustration, she tried again.

She was operating by feel, not sight; she could not see what she was doing, and her gaze wandered aimlessly over her left shoulder, toward Father Sinibaldo. The Livonians had shifted their position to face off against the archbishop's soldiers, so Sinibaldo was standing alone.

Very close to the limestone bulge on which stood the grail.

Toward which His Holiness subtly took a sidewise step.

Desperately she looked around for Raphael or Vera, but they were kneeling by Percival, and she could not see them in the fray. She glanced over her right shoulder. The Narbonne soldiers were nearby her but if she backed up ten paces she would be closer to Hugue's bodyguards and the other hostages. She looked back over her left shoulder.

Father Sinibaldo took another step toward the cup. He was at most three paces away from it now, and nobody was paying any attention to him.

Ocyrhoe brought the rope back to her mouth and tugged desperately at a new bump in the knot. Something gave. Carefully, she crooked the little finger of her left hand into the opening she had created to hold the cord where it was, then released her bite from that and tried gently tugging on another curve in the knot. This tightened the cord over her pinkie; she stopped tugging.

Sinibaldo took a step closer to the grail.

Ocyrhoe tugged at another part of the knot. It resisted, then suddenly released, and even the loop over her pinkie grew more slack. She closed her lips over it and pulled some more. Something tightened in the knot, something loosened, and she released it to try another angle.

Sinibaldo took a step closer to the grail. He could have reached down and grabbed it.

Ocyrhoe sidled toward him as she continued to pull at the knot with her teeth and tongue. The coarse fibers splintered off and tickled the back of her mouth unpleasantly, making her eyes water. Her stare stayed bent on the holy father now, frantically trying to will the cup away from him. If she released the knot to shout out a warning, she'd never figure out how to get her mouth back to the particular place it was now, just about to release the knot.

Father Sinibaldo reached down slowly and picked up the cup. He slipped it into the folds of his robes, then released both hands so that he stood there looking innocuous. He had a small satchel tied under his arm, or a pocket sewn into a layer of his clothing—wherever he had put it, he had come prepared to snatch it away in case Dietrich did not prevail. He had orchestrated the post-duel tension, starting with the archbishop's late arrival.

With a desperate tug, Ocyrhoe finally released the knot, spat out the hemp fibers, and screamed, "*Raphael!*" as loud as she could, although she would never be heard above the fray. She ran at Fieschi, now about ten paces away from her.

As she ran, she saw Raphael approaching him briskly but respectfully. He noticed Raphael, but not her, and seemed also to respond to something Raphael was calling out to him. He held up both hands, fingers spread, and hollered.

"Soldiers and gentlemen!" Sinibaldo de Fieschi's voice echoed off the courtyard walls. "In the name of our Lord Jesus Christ, for whose sake all of us are assembled here today, remember we are met in peace here! Stand down! Lower your fists! Do not draw your weapons!"

Remarkably, everyone obeyed him instantly. His voice was not the loudest or the deepest or the most passionate that had called out today; indeed there was something thin and cold about it. But Sinibaldo Fieschi had a presence that drew attention like a magnet when he so desired.

The courtyard quieted, and Ocyrhoe paused a moment. Raphael was standing right next to His Holiness, and His Holiness was successfully restraining the tension; she was not impetuous enough to disregard that. Raphael would attend to the cup.

"Bless you, my children, for heeding me," said the priest, with an aura of confidence that even the archbishop lacked. "Let us remember we are here to end strife, not to reignite it. Let the religious leaders debate amongst themselves—if debate even exists—what is proper in the eyes of God. The rest of you must only respect the terms of the truce. Those of the fortress, remain here until morning; as for the hostages and soldiers of the camp, the spectacle is ended and it is time for us to return to the foot of the pog and attend to the funereal needs of our fallen champion. It is disrespectful to him for all of you to bicker mindlessly among yourselves while his slain body lies on the bloody ground. Offer your enemies the sign of peace. *Now.* Surely His Eminence the archbishop desires to see as much?" He gestured across the yard to Pierre Amelii.

The archbishop was thrown, but recovered quickly. "It is a decent priest who says as much," he declared loftily. "Turn to each other now with the sign of peace."

That would never happen, but the men at least muttered with a gloss of shame as their hands released sword hilts and they stepped away from each other, dissolving bonds intended for combat. As Ocyrhoe watched, Raphael thanked Sinibaldo, eyeing him meaningfully. Suddenly from the center of the yard came a groan and Vera's voice calling urgently "Raphael!" Raphael turned to hurry back to Percival.

He had not realized the cup was missing.

"Raphael!" Ocyrhoe shouted, running again. "The cup! He took the cup!"

Sinibaldo heard her voice and began to run from both Raphael and her toward the smaller gate on the eastern side of the courtyard, the one they had used through all the months of siege. There was no porter attending it, and on the other side was the entire mountainside.

Raphael looked confused, not sure where the voice came from, not hearing it clearly over the muttering of the courtyard, and mostly concerned with seeing to his wounded friend. Fieschi's long legs took him quickly toward the gate. Ocyrhoe shouted in alarmed frustration, prayed to Ferenc's memory for the speed and strength to overtake the priest, and ran as fast as she had ever run in her life.

Fieschi grabbed the bolt of the gate, pushed it open, and stepped out of the fortress onto the mountaintop.

CHAPTER 41:

RECKONINGS

Outside the gate, Ocyrhoe sprinted around in front of Father Sinibaldo and stared at him, wild-eyed and defiant. He drew up short, surprised by the fierceness of her look. She threw herself at him, grabbing at his torso to seek out the concealed cup. He was much taller than she was, and it was easy enough for him to grab her head with his hand and push her back by straightening his arm. But Ocyrhoe, like a feral, rabid creature, used his arm like a taut rope, climbing hand over hand back toward him to grab his torso again. She saw a small bulge on the left side of his chest—the cup must be in a pocket sewn into his mantle there. She tried to lunge for it, but he grabbed her by the hair with his right hand to push her away again. She clutched his wrist and hung from his outstretched arm, quickly raised both legs off the ground, and slammed the soles of her feet against the outside of his right knee.

The priest groaned and sank to the left, pulling her down with him as he still held her hair with his right hand. He used his left hand to try to break the force of the stumbling fall, then resettled his weight onto both knees. He grabbed the back of Ocyrhoe's head with his left hand now as well as his right, and smashed her head face-down against the ground.

Ocyrhoe screamed as the force of the push slammed her nose against the limestone. Stars exploded behind her eyes and a freezing-burning sensation erupted over her entire face. She could not see, she tasted blood. He pulled at her hair, lifting her head again, and she tensed for a second impact.

But instead the priest released her and began gingerly to rise. She saw his left foot tense and move back a little; she realized that in her bent-over position he was perfectly situated to kick her in the stomach. She tried to move away but the pain in her face disoriented her.

Miraculously, he did not kick her. He gave her a warning look, straightened his robes, and began to move away. *We're being watched*, she realized with relief.

She pushed herself gingerly upright, staring at him as he limped along the narrow ridge to the barbican. Obviously he did not want to go back into the courtyard. In the barbican—full of French soldiers half-drunk from a fortnight's truce—he could easily find a place to hide it, and then claim he had no idea where it had got to.

She stared at his limping form, enraged. She wiped her sleeve across her face and it came away sticky and wet with blood. Hardly noticing, Ocyrhoe screamed viciously and jumped to her feet. She threw herself at the priest from behind, leaping up at his back so that she landed with her legs wrapped around his ribs and her arms around his shoulders. He staggered and tried to push her off but she was frantically kinetic. Scrambling, she swung her right leg up so that her knee hooked over his right shoulder; she pressed the back of her heel hard against his chest, to anchor herself. Secure in that hold, she let go of both hands so that her slight torso dropped back and down, to smack, inverted, against Sinibaldo's back; her head bounced once against his lower back and then she twisted up and to the left, and with both hands reached under his left arm to try to find the cup.

Sinibaldo, stumbling along the narrow ridge under her shifting weight, lifted his bent left arm, preparing to shove it back and elbow her in the face.

She saw his elbow rise and reached up for it before it could begin its backward motion. Pulling herself upright with leverage from her right knee, she grabbed his left elbow with her right hand when the elbow was at its highest point, and then redirected the force of his thrust, forcing his elbow out and then up over his own head. His center of gravity completely thrown, he staggered almost right off the ridge. As he stumbled toward the barbican, Ocyrhoe kept pushing his arm up with her right hand, while with her left, she reached down and around his left side, into the folds of his robes. Her fingers brushed against warm metal; she pulled at it and felt the cup in her grip, the curve of it like an old friend's hand taking hers. The sensation of touching it sated something in her, like water sates dry ground.

Her fingertips quickly brushed across it, remembering the bumps and ridges of the chasework. Then with a cry, she hurled it as far away as she could, following the arc of its escape with her eyes. She saw it land and was grateful she had not just accidentally thrown it off the cliff—where they were themselves in danger of ending up.

Father Sinibaldo stumbled on toward the far end of the ridge, trying to reach the broader plain before he fell under her furious writhing. Before he could quite get to safety, however, he was buffeted hard by the back-and-forth weight shift of her throwing the cup out of reach. He bent awkwardly at different angles and clawed the air before him in wild directions trying to right himself; but he began to fall, and falling, he began to twist so that his weight would land on top of hers.

Ocyrhoe, feeling what was happening, glanced around and realized they would hit the ground at the very edge of the ridge. If she obeyed the instinctual urge to leap away from him as he fell, she would throw herself off the cliff. Instead, she ignored the nauseated feeling in her gut as his tall frame turned, pulling her beneath him as the ground seemed to rush up toward them. She gritted her teeth and stayed inert until the last possible moment—then grabbed his arm as if he were a heavy blanket she were trying to pull over herself. At the moment they should have landed on the ridge, instead they slipped down over the edge of it and Sinibaldo, in a panicked reaction, grappled for purchase above him on the ridge itself. His left hand found a rock, and his right some indentation in the frozen earth from an earlier scuffle. Both of these he grabbed for life and stopped himself from tumbling down the cliff face; in stopping his own fall he also stopped Ocyrhoe's. She was now in the better position mechanically; she propelled herself up off of him and back onto the ridge, then turned back to face him.

Had she an axe she could have chopped off both his hands and watched him fall helplessly to his death below on the hard steep slopes. He looked at her, a fear and an alarm in his eyes that until this moment had been unimaginable to her. It blazed new fury and a sense of power in her.

"Murderer," she hissed at him. "Thief. Scoundrel. Agent of Satan."

He could not answer; his energy and focus was all on keeping his precarious grip on the ridge. His feet flailed, trying to find purchase on the nearly vertical surface below.

She could have left him there, but the soldiers from the barbican had seen them now and were surely headed their way; once they saved him, he would be in charge again. He would hound her forever. She looked at his hands and considered shoving him off the edge, but that was dangerous: as soon as she'd pried his fingers loose, those same fingers could easily grab her and take her with him to a gruesome death, dashed on the rocks below. She must somehow dispatch him here, and quickly.

With an aggravated sound she reached for his shoulder and grabbed his mantle, throwing her weight backward to try to drag him back up onto horizontal ground.

Her effort helped a little, but confused him greatly. Again she leaned forward, grabbing for his shoulders, throwing her weight backward and inching him slightly higher onto the ridge.

Enough of his upper body was on level ground now that he could pull himself up. He kicked away from the cliff face and rolled to safety on the ridge.

In the brief moment that he lay supine before collecting himself to rise, Ocyrhoe threw herself on top of him, straddling his torso and diving for his face with her muddied, outstretched fingers.

Immediately Father Sinibaldo reached up to grab her around the throat; quicker than he was, she hunched her shoulders, darted underneath his arms, and threw her body flat onto his, scratching at his face, trying to find his eyes with her fingers while her teeth, bloodied from her close encounter with the ground, reached for his nose to bite it hard. He shouted and tried to push her off, but she leaned even harder against him. "Murderer!" she shouted in his ear and then champed her teeth down hard on the ear itself, flinging her head side to side to try to rip it from his head. He cried out in alarm again and brought both hands up to her face to try to force her jaw open. She clutched at his skull, grabbing a fistful of his thick, greying hair, scratching his scalp so fiercely in the process his head began to bleed. Desperately he released her head and tried to grab and shove at her, but she was a whirlwind, crazed and frantic.

Finally he got a grip on her shoulders and used brute force to fling her away. But the hand that held a clump of his hair stayed gripped at his scalp, and so his intended fling simply arced the rest of her body up and over to land beside him on the ground; her free left hand, the lightest and least anchored thing on her, flipped further over and smacked the earth right beside the rock he'd grabbed when they nearly went off the cliff. It was a small rock, and mostly loosened from his grappling it before. She grabbed it and reversed the arc of movement: she brought her left arm to her right, walloping him on the forehead with the rock.

Sinibaldo screamed and jerked briefly, dazed by the blow. She let go of his hair and scrambled to her feet, still holding the rock.

Ocyrhoe looked at the rock. She looked at his unprotected head. She looked back at the rock. And back at his head.

She fell to her knees on the damp ground and smashed the rock hard against the priest's temple. He groaned and writhed. "Whoreson murderer!" she shrieked, and bashed him again.

The frozen ground shuddered with the footsteps of French soldiers from the barbican. After one final shriek of rage, Ocyrhoe leapt up a moment before gloved hands could grab her and sprinted across the mountaintop toward the spot where she had seen the grail fall.

CHAPTER 42:

DEPARTURES

Raphael pushed through the gate and ran along the ridge toward the barbican. A crowd of French soldiers gathered around an inert figure on the ground; a few soldiers were running across the mountain crest as if searching for something.

"What's happened?" he demanded.

"The girl and the priest fought," said a Frenchman with a captain's crest. "The priest is wounded very badly and the girl has disappeared."

"What do you mean, disappeared?" Raphael demanded. "Look around, man. It's a mountaintop. There's no place for her to disappear to."

"Tunnels," said the French soldier brusquely. "She disappeared into a tunnel." He whistled loudly; his comrades bounding over the ridge stopped and looked back. He shook his head once and broadly gestured them to return. "If she's out of sight now, she's gone for good." He gave Raphael an appraising look. "Are you the Levantine heretic who knows how to heal? This priest needs your help."

❖❖❖

The archbishop had prevailed. Father Sinibaldo, who had advocated forgiving the Good Ones, lay unconscious in the village, tended to by Raphael; the Good Ones made no argument in their own defense; Percival had regained consciousness, suffering strained muscles and a vicious headache, but suffering far more from knowing he had won the right to save them, and suffering most of all from the grail's disappearance. All night, he ranged wildly over the mountaintop crying out Ocyrhoe's name, like a hound baying for its missing master.

Disgusted by them all, Vera spent her final night in Montségur alone. The Good Ones and the Credents crowded all together in the chapel and spent the night in prayer and hymns, with sobs and embraces and comforting gestures. Vera remained below, in the cold, unlit hall, the space strangely large and quiet after so many weeks of overcrowded tension.

This was her first night without compatriots in more years than she could remember. Percival would probably freeze to death outside, which he deserved. Raphael would almost certainly be taken by the Livonian knights, who sat vigil over Sinibaldo's bed. Vera had been appalled when Raphael agreed to tend the man. She was now certain that she would be leaving here alone.

It was cold down here, without the warmth of living bodies. She could have gone upstairs and joined them, if only for the heat, but she could not bring herself to do that. They were fatalists, all of them, even those who would live. Not only had not a single Good One contemplated renouncing his or her beliefs, but more than *two dozen* Credents, who had the right to walk out the gate tomorrow morning and resume their lives unscathed, had just this afternoon requested the consolamentum from Father Marti. They were committing suicide under the guise of religious defiance. Some of them were battle-hardened knights whom she had fought beside—Brasillac de Calavello, Arnaud Domenc, Pons Narbona. Percival's duel had failed to save a soul; in fact, it might have egged on some of those stupid fools to throw their lives away on a nameless, formless, useless principle.

Vera shifted on her cloak, drawing her extra blanket up around her ears. Not a sentimental woman, still she missed the company of the men she knew, Raphael especially. She did not trust solitude and could not relax alone; if there was nobody watching her back, it was impossible to lower her guard.

She heard the quiet footsteps before she could make out the person, but she recognized them, somehow, as Rixenda's.

"You are welcome to join us," said the older woman in her fragile voice, when she reached the bottom of the steps. "This is a lonely place to be tonight." She was carrying a lit candle-stump.

"I do not belong with you," said Vera. "I do not understand you."

"You do not understand dying for a cause that you believe in?"

"The cause is in no way furthered by your dying for it."

Rixenda pursed her lips and took a few steps closer. "If we do not die—if we are not martyred—then our cause is diminished. We do not go out in a blaze of martial glory, but still our actions tomorrow, our very deaths, keep our cause alive."

"Not only do I not understand your methods, I do not understand your cause," said Vera uncomfortably. "But I do not wish to debate with you. Surely on this, your last night on earth, you have better things to do."

"I've done them," said Rixenda peaceably, her wide-set blue eyes calm in the candlelight. "My only sorrow is not to say farewell to Ocyrhoe. Please, if you see her again, give her my love and give her this for me." She reached for the round clasp holding closed her mantle. It was undecorated, made of wood. She disengaged it from the mantle, held the mantle closed with one hand, and with the other offered the clasp to Vera.

"I am not likely to see her again," said Vera, taking it.

"Then keep it for yourself," said Rixenda. "From one chaste militant sister to another." She smiled.

Vera blinked. "Well," she said gruffly after a moment. "There is that, I suppose. I thank you."

A pause.

"Nearly dawn now," said Rixenda, and glanced up the dark stairs again. "If you do not wish to join us, I will go up myself, for a final meditation before we meet our maker."

"It's a horrible way to die," Vera blurted out. "There are few things I am fearful of but death by fire is one of them. It frightens me."

Rixenda nodded. "Me, too," she said. "But fear is no deterrent when faith is strong."

❖ ❖ ❖

By dawn, Sinibaldo was conscious but in terrible pain. He lay in the largest, warmest bed in the village, the small room warmed by fire-heated rocks. Grim-faced, Raphael gave the priest an infusion to numb the worst of it. It would be days before he would be able to sit up without being sick.

Raphael was morally, ethically, even spiritually obligated to preserve a life when it was asked of him as a healer. But now, perched on the edge of the bed, pushing back the bed curtains, as he watched Sinibaldo's waking, he resented his oath.

The priest's eyes finally focused on the man beside him. "You are…" he let it trail off, looking confused.

"Raphael of Acre, Your Holiness," said Raphael, dryly. "Of the order of the Shield-Brethren. Close friend of His Majesty Frederick Hohenstaufen. I saved your life."

"The more fool you," said His Holiness.

"I am headed back to Frederick's court," said Raphael, studying Innocent's face. "Waiting there for my return is a small sprig of some sort that seems to mean a great deal to the Binder, Léna. She is expecting that I will return there with the grail. And Percival."

He saw a look of alarmed anger, almost despair, flash across Sinibaldo's face. Raphael nodded. "Thank you for that enlightening response," the Levantine said miserably. "You need not speak. You've revealed enough already."

"You should have let me die," said His Holiness warningly. "You will regret not doing so."

"Probably," said Raphael, standing. "I already regret not doing so many things in this poor life of mine. But it is never too late to start afresh. And you've a scalp wound that may yet do us the favor of putrefying and killing you. In the meanwhile, forewarned is forearmed, and so now I am armed indeed." He nodded his head curtly to the Livonian knights around the bed, then turned and walked out of the hut.

He walked through the occupied village, then out of it, and headed up the snowy foothill slope to the pen that would, in less than an hour, be ablaze with souls ascending to their idea of heaven. He looked up the western face of the pog. The dour procession had begun.

Guards, Credents, Good Ones, more guards, all moving down the mountainside. Nobody, as of yesterday, had recanted; in fact a score of people who would otherwise go free had thrown their lot in with the Good Ones and asked to take those final vows that spelled their death this morning. They included old Raimon de Perelha's wife, Corba, and several other noblewomen; the local farmers Ferrer and Artal; several knights and their wives; men-at-arms; and even the two crossbowmen Isarn had sent recently as military assistance. They could have walked away as freely as the Shield-Brethren were about to, returning undiminished to lives of valor, adventure, and status. Instead, after two weeks of meditation, they and a dozen other warriors were choosing to be burned as heretics in defiance of France and Rome's viciousness.

Raphael could almost understand that. He knew that Vera never could.

He looked over at the pen that would be set alight. One lone figure, heavily armed, lurked by it. Vera. Of course she would not join in the procession. He was glad to see her. Percival had disappeared again, tormented by his need to find the grail, but Vera, at least, had not deserted Raphael.

He walked up the slope to her, the dry snow crunching under his feet like wood chips. She greeted him with a solemn smile.

"Mornings like this make me appreciate what it is to be among the like-minded," she said. She surprised him by giving him a brief but fiercely tight embrace. "Let's get out of here before this immolation starts. It rubs me so intensely the wrong way I don't trust myself to just stand here and let it happen."

He nodded sadly. "No need to stay. Although not sure where to go instead. We've lost the grail—and Percival—again."

She shook her head and pointed to the wall of the pen. "We have not lost Percival. Although perhaps Percival has lost himself."

The Frankish knight squatted by the ladder that would lead the Good Ones up over the palisade to their deaths. His knees were bent up and his elbows rested on them, but his outstretched hands hung limp.

"I've failed in everything," he said when they approached him. His voice was heavy and dull with self-loathing.

"I've not done much better," said Raphael. "But there is no escaping destiny."

❖ ❖ ❖

In the bleak light of a damp, March sunrise, they struck out toward Toulouse. The notorious Count never had sent reinforcements; in fact, upon receiving word that the fortress had surrendered, he never even sent a message to either side acknowledging the ending of hostilities. *What sort of leader was that?* wondered Raphael with disgust.

They walked in silence north and then a little east. The pog remained just back of their right shoulders. After they had traveled about half a mile, the smell of smoke reached them, with a distant, dull roar, punctuated by human screams. Less than half a mile after that, the smell turned bitterly to something else, and the screams faded, but the roaring sound remained the same. Little bits of grey ash, like dirty snow, speckled the air around them. Percival, without changing stride, began to weep.

They continued with heavy hearts and heavy feet, until they reached a spot that looked vaguely familiar to Raphael and Vera. They halted.

"This is where Ferenc told us to take shelter when we first arrived," said Vera. "Where the Montségur men came and collected us. And took our horses."

"It was a tunnel entrance," said Raphael, a flicker of hope igniting in his chest. He grabbed the frozen underbrush and with a high-kneed stomp cleared a spot that opened onto a limestone boulder, with a ridge of wet ice edging its northern face. "Wasn't the entrance around the back of this rock?" He took another labored, high-kneed step, ready to clear thick brush away with his own hands.

"You needn't do that. There's a path over to your left," said a female voice directly overhead.

He looked up. Standing on the top of the boulder was Ocyrhoe. Her face and sleeve were bloody, and her eyes were bloodshot. She had no mantle or blanket. She stood in her muddy tunic and leggings, the grail between her hands.

Raphael backed onto the road. "Ocyrhoe," he said.

"Raphael."

A pause.

"Are you going to join us?" Vera demanded, impatient.

Ocyrhoe shrugged and held out the chalice. "This kept me alive last night," she said. "The warmth of it. If I give it up, you better damn well at least offer me a blanket."

She disappeared behind the boulder and then in a moment emerged from the dormant gorse on the road ahead of them. She walked straight to Percival, who was staring at the cup as if it were floating magically in air.

"Kneel," she ordered.

Instantly he dropped to both knees.

"Hold out your hands," she said. Percival, his eyes never leaving the cup, obeyed her. Raphael took Vera's arm, and they both stepped back one pace.

Ocyrhoe held the grail up over her head and improvised an incantation. "In the name of all the lost and wandering children of the earth," she intoned. "For the sake of those yearning for safety and gentle days, I, Ocyrhoe, steward of this chalice, yield it up into the hands of Percival the Seeker, that he may use it in ways as yet untried to bring goodness and light into the world."

Slowly she lowered her arms until the grail rested a finger's breadth above Percival's outstretched hands.

"Do you accept this instrument of peace with the terms whereby I surrender it?"

Percival looked too awestruck to speak. "I do," he stammered. "But know that I am *its* instrument, not the other way around."

Ocyrhoe released the warm weight of the cup into his hands. Her eyes welled and she felt her throat constrict, but she willingly moved her hands away.

Her palms went immediately ice-cold.

Nothing discernable happened, but she felt lighter. And Percival, kneeling before her on the muddy snow, radiated the same light that the cup sometimes did. The rapt wonder of his face reminded her of something beautiful and holy she could not specifically identify.

She turned to Raphael and Vera, and bowed her head. "My duty is fulfilled," she said. "We must get to Frederick's court, so that Percival may fulfill his."

1244
May Day

1244

May '07

EPILOGUE:
THE BINDING

In the cool foothills of Südtirol stood a grove of enormous, ancient trees. Ocyrhoe was certain Ferenc could have identified them, but city girl that she was, she could not. The six of them had traveled here with the smallest entourage of armed guards Frederick deemed safe.

Percival had held the grail the entire journey—a rushed, uncomfortable journey on horseback from the sun-kissed plains near Cremona into these shadowy, high valleys from whence winter had just recently departed. Ocyrhoe wondered what it was like for him to be united at last with that which had summoned him so long.

And what it would be like to relinquish it, as he would have to do in just moments.

The meaning of the grail and the meaning of the sprig—what they were, and the nature of their power—these things she could not wrest from Léna. But as they traveled, Ocyrhoe awkwardly riding pillion behind her, the elder Binder had yielded a little insight into the ritual that was to come.

In the dappled center of the grove of trees, Raphael had dug a hole in the soft, black-brown earth, as broad and deep as a man's forearm. He and Percival—in clean and mended Shield-Brethren surcoats—faced each other, kneeling, across it. Percival held the grail received from Ocyrhoe, and Raphael held the sprig, the mysterious piece of living wood that had made a strange journey from a distant land. Ocyrhoe, Léna, and Vera crowded around the northern curve of the hole. Emperor Frederick stood across from the women.

"We gather here to stem the tides of darkness," said Léna solemnly. "We acknowledge that in so doing we must also stem the tides of light, sequestering their forces into abeyance until the time is ripe. For this we require a man of power, the Wonder of the World, whose authority is purely temporal and secular, who is not allied to any occult forces, either light or dark."

"Damn right," said Frederick. "So let's get this over with."

"We thank him," said Léna, in a rebuking voice, glaring at him briefly. "For without his assistance, these objects of power risk falling into the hands of an equally powerful man whose spiritual allegiances are very dark."

"Are you insinuating that Sinibaldo is as powerful as I am?" Frederick protested.

"With all respect, please shut up, Frederick," said Raphael under his breath.

Léna ignored the interchange. "Two potent objects have been brought into this world, and now they are to be bound together. They reflect that which is born of nature and that which is created by men. We unite them now, that they may secure the future of the world. They are presented by two Virgin Defenders, and the Virgin herself witnesses the offering," here she gestured to the women on either side of her, "in her incarnations as both warrior woman and mystic wild child."

She gestured to Percival. He brought the grail up to his face, reverentially pressed his lips against the side of it, and then handed it to Frederick. Frederick received it, looking bemused. "It's warm," he said. "And *glowing*."

None of them responded to this.

He lowered himself to his knees, reached into the hole, and set the chalice upright in the bottom. Beside him was the pile of dirt; with both bare hands he tossed dirt into the hole until the grail was covered and the cup full, almost to the top.

"This," the emperor said, gazing approvingly at the final handful, "is good dirt." He raised the fistful to his nose and breathed in the musty fragrance deeply. "How strange it is that we who claim to rule the earth so rarely chance to touch it." He tossed in this final handful.

Now Léna gestured to Raphael. He took the small sprig, without bothering to kiss it, and offered it to the emperor. Frederick received it and placed it gently in the now shallow hole. Handful by handful he tossed in the rest of the dirt. When it began to pile up over ground level, all six of them together tamped the loose earth down with their fists and knuckles.

"Do we not need to water it?" asked Percival, brushing the soil from his hands.

Léna shook her head. "It lies dormant for now. When the world wills it, the rain will come and penetrate the soil to wake it."

"And then?" asked Ocyrhoe.

"And then it grows."

"And then?" demanded Ocyrhoe again.

"It grows until long after all of us are gone. It becomes someone else's story."

"So what do we do now?" the orphan girl of Rome demanded.

"Whatever you wish to," said Léna gently. "You were born with a destined obligation. Now that you have met it, the rest of your years are yours, not Fate's, to shape."

Here Ends Siege Perilous:

The Fifth Volume of the Medieval Cycle of the Foreworld Saga

ACKNOWLEDGMENTS

Monica Sagasser for the sanity.

Moira Squier for the timely use of her coffee table.

Dr. Andrew M. Riggsby for the Latin.

John Robichau and Chris Roberts for the fight choreography, aided and abetted by information, observations, and queries from Angus Trim, Mark Teppo, Scott Barrow, and Billy Meleady.

Liz Darhansoff, for being unflappably Darhansoffian.

Mark Teppo—look, we survived the perilous siege!

ABOUT THE AUTHOR

E. D. deBirmingham studied comparative religion and theater at Harvard University and believes they are pretty much the same thing. She has written historical fiction and screenplays under various pseudonyms, much to the dismay of her mother, who wishes hers was a household name. She was one of the co-authors of the *Mongoliad* books. E.D. lives in rural Massachusetts with her husband and the world's best dog.

The Foreworld Saga continues
in these other great titles from 47North!

Novels
The Mongoliad: Book 1
The Mongoliad: Book 2
The Mongoliad: Book 3

Katabasis

Foreworld SideQuests
Sinner
Dreamer
The Lion in Chains
The Shield-Maiden
The Beast of Calatrava
Seer
The Book of Seven Hands
The Assassination of Orange
Hearts of Iron
Tyr's Hammer
Marshal vs the Assassins

Symposium (three-issue graphic serial)
The Dead God (three-issue graphic serial)

Find out more about the Foreworld Saga at foreworld.com.

Information about all of these titles and other forthcoming titles can also be found at http://foreworld.com/store.